Storm (
Singaj

Storm Over Singapore

Alfred Draper

PIATKUS

Copyright © 1986 by Alfred Draper

First published in Great Britain in 1986 by
Judy Piatkus (Publishers) Ltd of
5 Windmill Street, London W1

British Library Cataloguing in Publication Data

Draper, Alfred
    Storm Over Singapore.
    I. Title
    823'914[F]   PR6054.R28

    ISBN 0–86188–566–X

Phototypeset in 11/12 pt Linotron Times
Printed and bound in Great Britain at
The Bath Press, Avon

Chapter 1

Commander Crispin Paton woke in his darkened cabin feeling as if the dead weight of a granite headstone was resting against his naked chest. The heat was oppressive and his body was bathed in perspiration that the solitary fan did little to ease. Condensation streamed in silent rivulets down the cork-based insulation coating the bulk heads so that it resembled the steam room in a Turkish bath. A slight breeze, hot and humid, came through the wind scoops fitted to the two portholes, but they provided little relief for the ship was steaming at less than nine knots – the pace of the convoy's slowest ship – and the old trawler would need to travel a great deal faster for any appreciable amount of fresh air to be drawn into the fetid cabin. They were specially designed to prevent light seeping out yet able to draw in fresh air. They were effective as far as the light went but totally ineffective otherwise. *Grey Seal* just wasn't built for the tropics. Before being converted at the beginning of the war into an anti-submarine escort vessel she had worked in the mountainous icy seas off Iceland where heat was welcomed, not in the humid flat waters of the Far East. Even a hasty and none too efficient conversion to equip her for the tropics had done little to improve conditions aboard; the ventilating system barely worked and when it did the vents filled the cabins with coal dust from the bunkers which seemed to permeate everywhere.

He groped for the hand torch on the deck below his bunk and directed the beam onto his watch. Apart from the monotonous thump, thump, thump of the triple expansion engine and the incessant ping, ping, ping of the Asdic, a total silence

1

pervaded the ship. There were still twenty minutes to go before the middle watch ended and Sub-Lieutenant Carnac was relieved on the bridge by the First Lieutenant Brian Phelp. Paton himself wasn't expected to appear on the bridge until he took over the forenoon watch which would end with the noon sextant reading to fix the position of the ship. But there was no point in remaining in the claustrophobic cabin feeling more and more like a wrung-out dish cloth; he might just as well go onto the bridge and enjoy the sunrise. He swung his feet over the edge of the bunk and tossed aside the towel which draped his waist, the only clothing he wore to prevent the fan, directed straight against his torso, causing a stomach chill that would result in repeated trips to the heads.

He switched on a light and lowered the hinged lid of the cabinet which contained the small wash basin. Running his hand over his chin he decided that he couldn't get away without shaving. The brain-numbing heat made everything such an important decision. He doused himself with cold water from head to feet but the relief was only momentary and soon he was sweating again. He moved across the cabin to one of the chairs where Hall, the officers' steward, had laid out a clean pair of white shorts, white stockings and shirt, the epaulettes with the three gold bars denoting his rank carefully laced through the eyeholes in the shoulders. Within a short time they would be sweat-drenched and grimy, and he wondered who at the Admiralty in their wisdom had decided that white was an ideal colour for the tropics. It might be all right in a cruiser or battlewagon, but it was the most ridiculous colour for a ship like *Grey Seal* where dhobeying had to be done in a galvanised bucket with a bar of pusser's soap which hardly raised a lather and often resulted in agonising dhobey itch.

As he stepped out of his cabin onto the upper deck he drew lungfuls of air, then stood quietly until his eyes became adjusted to the dark. Overhead the sky was canopied by a myriad of brightly shining stars. It was, he reflected, Joyce's blue milk upset. All over the deck he could see the recumbent forms of sleeping sailors with just a blanket beneath them and a makeshift pillow under their heads. It was not a sight that appealed to him, but he turned a blind eye to it; he could not expect his men to sleep in the mess decks where they could die of heat exhaustion. He stepped gingerly over Jolson, the black Labrador, asleep at the foot of the bridge ladder and twitching from time to time in the raptures of some canine escapade. It was amazing how the ship's mascot adapted. In the Med he had commandeered a corner of the wheelhouse for his sleeping quarters, but as soon as the temperature had begun to soar he had moved to the foot of the bridge ladder where there was always a slight but welcome breeze.

Paton clambered onto the bridge where Carnac was bent low over the compass binnacle taking a puff from a cigarette. Old habits, he mused, died hard. Although they were not in hostile waters the Sub was still conscientious about not allowing the glow of his cigarette to be spotted. There was always the remote possibility of a German U-boat or surface raider operating so far from home.

"Morning, Sub. Everything quiet?"

Carnac said, "Quiet as a mess deck when volunteers are called for, Sir." The young subbie had a habit of making such remarks which he considered revealed a great maturity but in fact merely emphasised his youth.

Paton glanced at the compass rose to check the course, then poked his head through the canvas curtain of the navigation table to see the last estimated position. The Andamans with their penal colony were well astern to starboard, and the Nicobars a short haul away off the starboard bow. Far away to port lay Tenasserim and ahead the Straits of Malacca, the approach to their final destination, Singapore.

"You're an early riser, Sir," said Carnac.

"Not willingly, Terence. I just can't sleep in this heat. Reminds me of what I might have to endure when I shuffle off this mortal coil."

He moved over to the port bridge wing and swept the sea with his night glasses. He could just make out the dim shapes of the troopships and cargo vessels which comprised the convoy. "No panics during the night? No stray sheep?"

"No, they've all been as good as gold and kept station pretty well. Haven't even had to rollick anyone for showing lights."

Suddenly out of the darkness a voice called to the bridge,

"Starboard Oerlikon gun's crew closed up, Sir," followed almost immediately by a similar announcement from port. Seconds later the crew of the fo'c's'le twelve-pounder announced they were at their action station.

Paton knew that the men thought it was all a waste of time; they were unlikely to meet any enemy ships in an area of the world still at peace, but he insisted that the routine of closing up at action stations at dawn and dusk should be maintained. It was good for morale and a curb to any temptation to slackness which the hours of monotonous inactivity could so easily breed. Time hung heavily, and anything that kept them on their toes was to be encouraged.

Even in the pitch dark the phosphorescent glow of the bow waves could be clearly seen and it brought with it an atmosphere of total peace.

The faintest of pinkish hues began to tint the horizon to the east as the tip of a molten sun pimpled the surface of the sea. With breathtaking beauty a crimson orb began to rise skywards like a balloon on a thermal. In a matter of minutes a perfectly round ball of fire was poised on the surface of the ocean gradually revealing the outlines of the ships, all regrettably crayoning the sky with plumes of smoke from their funnels. The sea resembled molten lava.

Paton called to Chalkie White the signalman, a tall, gangling Bristolian who was squatting by the signal flag locker. "Bunts, send a message to the Commodore, make less smoke." He knew it was a waste of time because the merchant navy masters couldn't see the point in not making smoke. It wasn't as if they were in enemy waters; everybody knew there wasn't a hostile ship within thousands of miles. Most of them had sailed in Atlantic convoys and in the Med where the slightest breach of convoy regulations was inviting a tin fish, but now they were damned if they would be bullied by a three straight ringer who issued orders just to make life that little bit more unpleasant.

Well astern he could just make out *Heron*, and on the port and starboard wings of the convoy *Walrus* and *Porpoise*, the three other escort trawlers which comprised the group he commanded.

Committing the safety of a valuable convoy to the protection of the clumsy, poorly armed trawlers was a pretty firm indication that Whitehall was confident the war would not spread to the Far East. He hoped they were right, although he had inward doubts, for so far there had been few indications that the service chiefs and politicians were endowed with any great perception. He and most of his ship's company had narrowly survived a series of military débâcles, in Norway, Dunkirk, then Greece and Crete, and there was no indication so far that any lessons had been learned or that the crystal ball wasn't still blurred over. Perhaps, he thought, he was being unduly pessimistic. If there were any doubts about Japan remaining neutral security about the convoy would have been much stricter; as it was the news of its departure had been publicly announced over the radio and in the English printed Calcutta newspapers. Then it occurred to him that the publicity might have been deliberate in order to deter the Japanese from taking the plunge. After all, there was nothing more likely to put off a potential aggressor than a show of strength.

A mug of thick scalding cocoa was thrust into his hand. It amazed him how sailors clung so tenaciously to their habits. Hot ki at the start of a watch was a ritual that was not allowed to be affected by outside conditions. To have queried the need for a hot drink would only have resulted in a look of total incomprehension; it was tantamount to asking a matelot if he still wanted his rum issue instead of a mug of cooling lime juice. A daft observation. Lime juice was drunk because it was a regulation and because it had been introduced to combat scurvy. So they diligently drank it although they knew scurvy was a thing of the past. But rum was different. It was a hallowed right that was not open to questioning. You drank it even when you were sea sick and brought it straight up again, just as you did even if it flowed down the gullet like molten metal and burned your guts out.

As the sun rose higher the sea became as green as an empty wine bottle and just as smooth, without the slightest sign of a white crested wave. It was a signal for the dolphins to commence their frantic gambollings and breathtaking leaps that carried them high above the surface of the sea.

When Lieutenant Phelp RNR clumped onto the bridge to take over the watch, Paton kept discreetly in the background; he had the utmost confidence in his Number One and did not want to undermine his authority merely because he happened to be on the bridge. When the watch had been formally handed over he chatted for a few minutes, then decided to stroll around the upper deck, for by now the ship was bustling with activity. Seamen were hosing down the decks, checking equipment and depth charges, and the tension on the Oerlikon drums. Imperceptibly the ship's routine had altered as the weather became more tiresome and the men had discovered that the early morning was the best time for hard work. By midday the steel parts of the ship would be unbearable to the touch, and the deck in some places akin to walking on hot coals. He began his tour astern where two coal-grimed stokers, their eyes shining like pierhead minstrels, were dousing each other down with buckets of water hauled inboard at the end of a heaving line. He wondered how they managed to remain so buoyantly cheerful; the temperature in the engine room must be unbearable. Even the blast from the engine room ventilators scorched the skin as one passed. He felt he ought to descend into the flame-flickering inferno to share their torment for a short time, if only to let them know he was acutely aware of the ordeals they suffered, but he was saved from doing so by the emergence of Petty Officer Reynolds's head at the engine room hatch.

"I was just about to pay a courtesy call, Chief."

The cockney engineer pulled off his oil-grimed hat and wiped his balding head with a wad of cotton waste. "Dunno what you'd've been letting youself in for, Sir. Deckplates down there are so hot you could grill a pork chop on 'em. Bit 'ard on my lads, Sir. Can't stand more'an an hour without comin' topsides. Just as well we're only doing nine knots. Nice economic speed and they don't 'ave to shovel their 'arts out."

"No problems, Chief?"

"Not really, Sir. Poor old cow's feeling' the 'eat a bit just like the rest of us. Groaning and grunting like my old lady after she climbed onto the top deck of a bus."

Reynolds had been with *Grey Seal* since she was commissioned and Paton was resigned to the fact that he would always endow the massive engine with human qualities and always refer to it in a personal intimate manner. It amused Paton that he felt the need to treat the massive iron and steel machine like a delicate child so that the slightest rumble or grating of a gear was seen as a death rattle, while the gauges and meters were studied with the attentiveness of a doctor looking at a thermometer, fearing a minor malaise will develop into a mortal sickness. It was an idiosyncrasy that Paton welcomed, for it meant that it was the one part of the ship which he need not personally worry about.

Reynolds peered over the stern at the foaming wake, then up at the totally cloudless sky before spitting contemptuously into the water. "I was out on the old China Station when I was a lad, Sir, and I swore I'd rather jump ship than come back this way again."

"I gather you didn't like it, Chief?"

"That's putting it mild, Sir. Nothing but 'eat and filth and toffee-nosed whites who would make sailors go round tinkling a bell if they 'ad their way. They looked upon navy ships as prison 'ulks, something to be kep' out of sight. Apart from that, the conditions ain't no good for a engin'. Did I ever tell you about the time we was showing the flag in Shanghai, Sir?"

"Not this morning you haven't, Chief," said Paton with the slightest of smiles. He was saved from enduring the oft-repeated story by the sight of the roly-poly figure of the coxswain, Chief Petty Officer Tiger Read, leaning over the bulwark midships enjoying his first lung-seering cough of the day, as he choked over a hand-rolled tickler cigarette.

He set his cap straight on his greying hair as Paton approached and wiped his streaming eyes. "Don't know why I don't jag it in, Sir. Must have left bits of my lungs in every ocean." Like so many other old salts Read had "swallowed the hook" years ago, but had been called back from retirement at the time of Munich because there was such an acute shortage of experienced and senior petty officers. Paton had never ceased to be grateful to Their Lordships for the old sweat had turned out to be the backbone of the ship. He ruled the lower deck firmly but scrupulously fairly, so that the ship's company had come to see him as a father figure. Even his nickname which originally had been seen as an indication of his fearsome temperament, was now almost a term of endearment.

Together they surveyed the wallowing troopers and spoke

7

aloud their shared thoughts.

"If we think it's tough aboard, Sir, think of those bloody pongoes cooped below decks for most of the time. Breathing the smell of their own vomit hour after hour, and joining a long queue every time they visit the heads. Must be like an old slaver. Can't see the point in reserving the upper decks for officers only. Poor buggers will be near death when we eventually dock."

"Come off it, Coxs'n, they have their PT and gunnery practice. They aren't battened down all the time." Inwardly he shared the views of the coxswain, but felt it would be unwise to involve himself in a discussion about the privileges enjoyed by officers. Discipline and commonsense seldom went hand in hand in the services.

Read expertly flicked his matchstick-thick cigarette into the sea and said, "Remember that army brass hat in Calcutta, Sir? Sympathising with them for missing out on the war. Made it sound as if they hadn't been picked for a game of soccer."

Paton's mind went back to the quayside scene just prior to the troops embarking and the insensitive homily that the Lieutenant-General had delivered to the hot and thirsty troops. While he appreciated that they would much rather be at home defending their loved ones, their presence in Singapore would act as a deterrent against any aggressive intentions by the Japanese. "Remember," he had said, "we are masters of a vast Empire on which the sun never sets. It is our duty to make sure it never does."

That same evening just before the convoy sailed Paton had been invited aboard one of the troopers for a drink with some of the army officers and he had been appalled to hear how ill-equipped and poorly trained these defenders of the Empire were. The officers had confided to him that they had been issued with weapons they had never fired before, and they hoped to overcome this lamentable shortcoming by regular practice with Brens, Tommy-guns and mortars during the voyage. Even worse, none of the soldiers had been trained for jungle warfare.

As the two men chatted the staccato chatter of gunfire and the crump of mortars echoed across the water as the daily practice shoot commenced. Paton hoped the pundits

8

were right and that the Japs did stay out of the war, otherwise the young soldiers were going to be little more than cannon fodder. He imagined it was extremely difficult to whip up enthusiasm among men who had repeatedly been told they would never be called upon to use in earnest the new weapons they had been issued with.

On the port side Oerlikon, Leading Seaman Isaac Morris and his oppo Dusty Miller were discussing the pleasures that awaited them in Singapore.

"I nearly pissed myself laughing at that old codger telling the brown jobs how sorry he was they would miss the shot, shit and shells. If the old fart had been through what we have he would realise what a load of cock he was talking. No one in his right mind would prefer fighting to fucking. I've had my fill of one of them, and I intend to catch up on the other," said Morris.

Miller, a two-badge able seaman, retorted, "People who haven't had a belly full of action don't see it that way, Isaac. Those pongoes probably do feel hard done by. It's not till you've seen guts spilled all over the place like we have that you realise war isn't what it's cracked up to be. The pongoes can cry their bloody hearts out that they've ended up as armchair heroes, but I give three cheers."

Morris paused as he was applying more tension to one of the ammunition drums. "You know wack, old Tiger can be a real wet cloth. Hasn't a good word to say about the place we're going. When I asked him about the local talent he said he was put right off it when he discovered their slits ran sideways same as the streets. Personally I don't believe it. But he said it was just like their eyes."

Miller, who was always haunted by the spectre of his wife whose nagging voice thousands of miles of separating ocean could not silence, said, "Up or down or sideways, I'm leaving them well alone. Tiger says they have a sort of pox that is incurable and kills in record time. How would you explain that away? He said he knew one bloke whose weapon actually fell off when he sneezed."

"If Tiger hadn't joined the Andrew he would have been a Sunday School teacher. He just says those things to put you off. Thinks every matelot should stick to the five-fingered widow."

"You're a crude bastard at times, Isaac, and no mistake."
Miller secretly feared that Morris was aware that he masturbated to ease the agonising longing for his shrewish wife.

"I'm a realist, Dusty. Grimsby, where I was born and raised, is full of old navy men who've been out East and I don't know any who have trouble piddling."

Their conversation was brought to an abrupt halt by the shrill of the bosun's pipe and the shout, "Up spirits".

The ship's company, apart from the lookouts, helmsman and duty stokers, converged on the small deck space forward of the wheelhouse where Tiger Read was supervising the issue of the daily tot of rum invariably referred to as Nelson's blood.

Morris laced his tot with his lime juice and said, "Dusty tells me you've been putting the frighteners on him, Coxs'n." There was a slight note of uncertainty in his voice. "I told him you were leg pulling; you were, weren't you?"

"No laddie, I wasn't. And if you won't believe me jump into a rickshaw when you go ashore. You'll find yourself in Lavender Street in double quick time because that's where the rickshaw wallahs take you irrespective of where you ask to go. Now Lavender Street isn't as sweet smelling as its name suggests. It's the red light district. It's plastered with out-of-bounds signs for the reasons I've given. But you go there and tell me a fortnight later if I wasn't right."

Morris thought he caught the faintest suggestion of a wink passing from Tiger Read to the engineer, as fleeting as the shutter on an Aldis lamp, but he couldn't be sure, and it did nothing to quell the faint feeling of unease he experienced. You never could tell when Tiger was being serious or not. Sometimes he got the impression that the old chief took too much of a fatherly interest in the ship's company and tended to remove the gilt from the gingerbread in what he considered were their best interests.

"Everyone else I've spoken to says Singapore's a tropical paradise; palm trees, big eats and crates of ice cold beer."

"It is, laddie, but not for the likes of us. You have to be what they call a tuan to enjoy the luxuries. If you aren't then it's malaria, cholera, prickly heat and mildew. But don't let me depress you, lad."

"I know, Chief, I shouldn't't've joined."

It was the answer always invoked by a sailor when he knew he had lost an argument.

Night had descended with tropical suddenness and even the brilliance of the stars high above did nothing to brighten the view from the bridge. All that could be seen was the occasional glimmer of a blue stern light as one of the ships swung momentarily off course. The last dog was only half way through and Paton wished it was longer than just two hours, but that was the system the navy had introduced in order that officers should not always keep the same watch. He found it much more comfortable to be on the bridge than in his cabin, but when he was off duty with no ship's duties to attend to he had to retire to his cabin in order to maintain that necessary degree of aloofness his rank and position demanded. He would have liked nothing better than to sling a hammock somewhere topsides and just look at the stars. As he sat hunched on the small folding chair attached to the bridge bulkhead, he was joined by the first lieutenant.

"Mind if I join you for a few moments, Sir? Can't stand the heat of the wardroom. Doesn't seem to bother young Carnac though. He crashes his swede and he's snoring in no time."

"I could when I was his age. No doubt you were the same."

"There's been a lot of water under the bridge since then, Sir. I've almost forgotten I was ever a young man."

"We still are in years, Number One; it's just the war that's aged us. It's certainly wearied us. Let's hope it doesn't make us cynical and disillusioned as the last lot did."

They deliberately kept their voices low to prevent their conversation being overheard by any of the lookouts. It wasn't good for morale if officers were known to harbour doubts about the conduct or outcome of the war. Such moments of intimacy were rare in the closed confines of a small ship for they seldom had the opportunity to be together. One was either on watch while the other was sleeping, or they were busy with the hundred and one tasks so necessary for the running of a happy and efficient ship.

Although Phelp was married to Paton's sister Lesley and they were the closest of friends, they always maintained a

11

degree of formality in the presence of any of the ship's company. It was something that came easily to both of them for each had the highest regard for the other. Like so many friendships that had started with slightly veiled antagonism it had become all the stronger when respect had replaced mistrust. When Phelp had first joined *Grey Seal* he had done little to hide his dislike for RN straight ringers – "gentlemen pretending to be sailors" while he was "a sailor pretending to be a gentleman". Phelp had long since revised his opinion. Paton had proved to be both a thoroughly professional sailor and a man of infinite courage and concern for the well-being of his officers and crew; a man who had been trained from boyhood to lead. Phelp had also discovered that the style of rings a man wore out of his uniform did not matter a damn to his captain. It was what lay beneath the tunic that counted.

"Do you ever think of the future, Sir, that is if there is one? Will you stay on? You've had what they call a good war – whatever that may mean – and you could rise to the highest rank. A DSO and bar at your age is no mean achievement."

"I'll stay on, just as the lads below will go back to being bus drivers, carpenters or fishermen, like Morris, while Tiger will return to his little sub post office. It's the only job I know. There have been Patons in the Royal Navy from the time of Frobisher. What else could I do? Become a golf club secretary?"

Phelp who had served in the Merchant Navy and only been called up because he was in the RNR, said quietly, "I don't think I'll return to the sea, Sir. It'll never be the same again for me. Think I'll take a pub in some remote village and plaster the walls with pictures of ships, old pennants, steering wheels and marlin spikes. Might even sport an eye patch."

Phelp broke off to bellow down to the helmsman to pay attention – he was moving off course.

"When we've had a few months sunshine in Singapore you'll forget the unpleasantness of the past couple of years and begin to see things in a different light," said Paton. "You'll forget the sinking ships and the screaming men coated in oil. The old enthusiasm will return."

"So you really think that it won't flare up out here, the

Japs will stay on the sidelines?"

"I'm not really in a position to say. I can only go by what the experts say. If the Japs take us on they'll have the Yanks to contend with. They won't stay out. The Pacific is too important to them, otherwise they wouldn't be backing Chiang Kai-shek to the hilt. Anyway, where we're going is an impregnable fortress."

As he spoke he realised that he did not share the general optimism that had been nurtured over the years about the island fortress of Singapore, for he recalled a peacetime visit to his father's home by Captain Gus Agar vc who had been outspokenly doubtful about the invulnerability of the base. And he remembered him recalling how in 1938 a party of men from his cruiser *HMS Emerald* had captured Raffles while another from *Dorsetshire* had seized the vital Causeway connecting the island with the mainland. The impression Agar had given was that too much importance had been attached to the massive naval guns defending the island against a sea assault and little or no thought to the fact that an enemy might decide to attack from the mainland. Crispin recalled his father, then a rear-admiral but close to retirement, saying he would raise it with the First Sea Lord. He had not had the opportunity, nor in fact even thought of asking his father what the result had been. Now he never would for when the war started the admiral had been called out of retirement and made a Commodore of Convoys and been killed in one of the earliest Atlantic convoys.

Maybe Agar's words had been heeded and steps taken to remedy the faults to protect the island from an overland attack. It would not be long before he knew.

Chapter 2

Paton sat in his cabin refreshing his memory about Singapore
Island by reading the relevant Admiralty pilot. His eyes
skimmed over the words for he had read them so often in
the past few days that they were indelibly printed in his mind.
It was a diamond-shape island one degree north of the equa-
tor measuring some 26 miles across and 14 miles from north
to south. It was the world's major producer of rubber and
tin, with hardly any seasonal changes and a temperature that
seldom fell below the eighties. It had originally been a rat-
infested swamp, rife with malaria, cholera and dengi, until
the visionary Sir Stamford Raffles arrived and saw its potential as a trading post. It could provide a sheltered harbour
safe from pirates and a link between the Indian Ocean and
the South China Seas. It had been named Singa Pura, or
Lion City, after the beautiful animal that Sang Nila Utama,
a descendant of Alexander the Great, had observed when
he was washed ashore by a storm. Raffles had founded the
modern Singapore in 1819 when he had made an agreement
with the then owners, Sultan Hussain Mohammed Shah and
Temenggong Abdul-Rahman, to permit the East India Company to set up a trading post at the mouth of the Singapore
River. In 1824 a new treaty was signed which ceded in perpe-
tuity the entire island and those islands within ten miles to
the Company. In a short time it had grown into a thriving
commercial centre. The Chinese settled in the Teluk Ayer
Basin to the south of the river; Teochews came from Swatow,
Hokkiens from Fukien Province, Cantonese from Kwantung,
Hainanese from Hainan and the nomadic Hakkas. Vast
numbers of Indians, Hindus, Muslims, Gujeratis, Sindhis,

15

Sikhs, Bengalis and Tamils, were imported as labourers to construct the roads, bridges, monsoon drains and government buildings. In their wake came clerks, teachers, merchants and money-lenders. The population was further swelled by Arabs, Javanese, Ceylonese, Poyanese and Malays from the mainland.

The Europeans had soon established a thriving business community in White Singapore which was in stark contrast to the squalid native areas. Stately government buildings rose above the reclaimed swampland, the elegant St Andrew's Cathedral became the principal place of worship, while the ivory coloured Cathay Building held pride of place as the highest on the island ... Paton could not be bothered to read on. Words and statistics meant little; they did not convey the smell and sound of a place any more than a picture postcard could. Not that such information mattered at this stage; all he needed to concern himself with were the approaches to the harbour and any possible navigational hazards. The Cathay might be useful for a possible fix.

Grey Seal had now passed the narrowest part of the Straits of Malacca and from the open portholes Sumatra was clearly visible to starboard and Malaya to port. He replaced the book and reached up to the chart rack attached to the bulkhead and took down the chart detailing the approaches to Singapore. He was pleased to find that Carnac had diligently inked in all the corrections which had been included in the batch of "Admiralty Notices to Mariners" which had been picked up in Calcutta. It was a time-consuming chore that could so easily be put aside until forgotten, but it was vital to the safety of the ship; failure to mark in a new sandbank or wreck could result in disaster and a court of inquiry.

As he pored over the chart with dividers and parallel ruler there was a knock on the door, followed almost immediately by the appearance of Steward Hall with a tray neatly laid out with tea pot, cup and saucer, sugar bowl and tongs and some thinly sliced corned beef sandwiches on a spotless napkin. Hall – inevitably nicknamed Albert – had been a waiter in an exclusive West End restaurant in peacetime, and he took immense pride in his job of looking after the officers. The food, he admitted, was bloody awful, hardly fit for humans, but that was no reason for dishing it up in a sloppy

16

fashion, and he adopted the same attitude to a cup of tea.

Paton was grateful for the tea although he eyed the sandwiches with thinly concealed dismay, the bread had been weavil-ridden for days, and even the most careful sifting of the flour could not eradicate their presence, so that they looked like caraway seeds in the bread. But he picked one up and ate it with feigned relish. Hall, he knew, would take offence if he didn't and would begin to worry that there was something wrong with his captain.

"It'll be a real treat to be able to shop ashore and get some fresh meat and vegetables, Sir. An uninterrupted diet of tram smash, soya link bangers, dehydrated spuds and corned beef isn't good for anyone. It's not scurvy we have to worry about but malnutrition. How far off are we now, Sir?"

"If my calculations are correct we should catch our first sight of Sultan Shoal light very shortly. Depending on the congestion in the roads we should be alongside before dark. Otherwise we may have to anchor offshore for the night. We'll just have to wait and see."

Hall glanced around the cabin and said, "Better run a duster round it in that case, Sir. Better be all ship shape and Bristol fashion; never know who might pop aboard." Hall was a first-class steward, but he was a far from competent sailor, a fact he acknowledged and tried to remedy with naval phrases culled from the glossary in the *Admiralty Manual of Seamanship*.

Paton thought his cabin was as neat and tidy as it ever could be and he suspected that Hall wanted to make sure that he ate the sandwiches, whether through a concern for his well-being or sheer sadism, he wasn't at all sure.

On the bridge, Sub-Lieutenant Carnac was watching Jolson playing cat and mouse with a half-dead flying fish stranded on the deck. Around him lay the sun-shrivelled corpses of other fish which had skimmed over the bulwarks and been unable to take off again. But the Labrador ignored them; only those still capable of spasmodic jerks attracted him. Carnac thought that they did not at all resemble the attractive creatures he had only read about before. It was just one more example of disillusion with the tropics.

He brought his attention back to the business of conning

the ship, and called out to the two lookouts on the bridge wings, "Keep a sharp look out, the pair of you. We should be sighting the lighthouse soon."

On the deck below working parties were busy tidying up in readiness for entering harbour. Wheeling and swooping above the wake were scores of screeching gulls, anticipating a feast of gash, their sudden presence a clear indication of land.

Carnac called down to the wheelhouse, "Keep her steady, for God's sake. You following the lubber's line or something?"

At the wheel the helmsman mouthed a silent obscenity, but called back, "Sorry, Sir," realising that he had been in imminent danger of committing the cardinal sin of following the ship's head instead of the compass rose.

Two hours later the port lookout bellowed, "Lighthouse ahead. Fine on the port bow, Sir."

Carnac had already seen it through his binoculars but had kept silent. It relieved the monotony if the lookouts were led to believe that their vigilance had been rewarded. He called over to Chalkie White, "Nip below, Bunts, and tell the captain."

When Paton arrived on the bridge he said, "Tell the Coxs'n I want the hands well turned out for entering harbour. These waters may be renowned for pirates but we aren't going to arrive looking like them. Bunts, send a signal off to the other trawlers in the group that I expect the same of them." He knew there would be some initial grumbling at the idea of dressing in spotless whites, but he was determined to show that Harry Tate's navy, as the trawlers were often called by the big ship men, could look as pusser as anybody else when the occasion arose.

An hour later as the convoy steered through the marked channel of Selat Sinki, the sea around for as far as the eyes could see was covered with a motley assortment of craft ranging from high-sterned junks with massive unwieldly looking sails to small sampans that lay low in the water. They seemed totally unconcerned at the long convoy passing through them, seemingly content to let the huge ships get out of their way rather than take avoiding action. It was difficult enough coping with the mass of tiny coral islands without having to contend with hordes of people who had never heard of the rules of the road.

"White, signal the other trawlers to take up station in line astern of me. Distance of one cable." As the ten-inch Aldis clattered away Paton reflected that he would have liked his group to have been a little closer, but one cable was about as much as anyone could expect in such conditions. They would certainly have to keep their eyes glued to the Stewart's Distance Meeting to achieve even that.

He devoutly wished that he had been able to command the services of a pilot as the Commodore's ship had done for he had seen the pilot boat moor alongside and the ladder lowered to take him inboard. But if every ship arriving at Singapore was given a pilot the harbour authorities would need to enlist a couple of thousand more men.

"Better nip below, Sub, and change. Tell Number One I would like him on the bridge as soon as possible. I'll need both of you up here if I'm to avoid running down any of that lot." He then leaned over the voice pipe. "Wheelhouse, Captain now on the bridge. Tell the coxswain I want him to take the wheel."

As soon as the slight hump of Singapore and the small offshore islands came into view, seamen began to crowd the forecastle to get a better look, and an air of urgency and expectation surged through the ship as it always did when the final destination hove into view.

As the convoy approached the entrance to the Roads, the marine congestion became even worse. Huge cargo ships lay at anchor and dozens of laden-down tongkangs, with huge eyes painted on their prows so that they could see where they were going, were heading inshore with cargoes to land or heading out with rubber and tin to fill the hulls of the waiting merchantmen. Their squat, ugly hulls were festooned with ancient, treadless tyres as a protection against collision. Junks, their decks crowded with entire families and squawking chickens in wooden coops, sailed perilously close, while bumboats filled with gesticulating traders offering souvenirs came so near they were in danger of being swamped.

A perspiring Phelp craned over the compass binnacle taking fix after fix on the myriad of slow-moving ships and anxiously informing Paton if the bearing remained constant.

Paton cursed as he was forced to take evasive action to avoid collisions, but after a time he realised that the native seamen had been doing the same thing for countless years and had learned the art of survival. If the approaching ships gave no sign of giving way then they did. Even so it was a nightmare experience, and he was extremely proud of the way in which his group were maintaining station.

Carnac, his head bent low over the chart table, was busy checking on the various buoys that marked the channel that passed between Pulau Bekum and Sister's Island, then swung on a wide arc to leave Lazarus and Kusu Islands to port marking the final approach to The Roads and Keppel Harbour, and calling out to Paton as each fresh one approached.

The voice of one of the lookouts broke Paton's concentration. "ML approaching, Sir."

He looked fore'ard and saw a wooden-hulled motor launch, almost obscured by the plume of its bow wave heading towards *Grey Seal*. The bridge became visible as it reduced speed and executed a neat U-turn that brought it abeam of the trawler's bridge. An RNVR lieutenant in enviable spotless whites bellowed through a megaphone, "Permission to come aboard, Sir?"

Paton called back through his own megaphone, "Delighted to welcome you." He turned to Carnac, "See he's helped inboard, Sub, and make sure he doesn't ruin that uniform."

Huge fenders the size of bolsters were lowered over the side to cushion the impact as the ML bumped gently alongside and a couple of *Grey Seal*'s seamen helped the lieutenant to negotiate the gap between the two ships while Carnac saluted smartly as he jumped down onto the deck.

"I'll take you up on the bridge, Sir," said Carnac.

When he had introduced himself to Paton, the young lieutenant explained that the motor launch had been sent out to escort the trawlers into their berth at Keppel. "It's a bit like Epsom Downs on Derby Day. Can't move for ships bringing troops and reinforcements in while others are taking aboard tin and rubber. They're calling Singapore the dollar arsenal these days. Seems the Yanks can't get enough rubber and tin for their rearmament programme. Strange when you think that everyone ashore here is convinced the war won't come to Malaya. Still, the traders aren't objecting. The money they're pulling in is helping the Mother Country, as they quaintly put it. The way they squander money makes you wonder if there's any left to send home."

Paton wondered why it had been thought necessary to put an officer aboard when he could easily have been given instructions just to follow the ML, but he remained silent thinking that perhaps there was such a surfeit of manpower that jobs had to be found to keep people from becoming idle.

Dead ahead he could clearly see the towering bulk of the Cathay Building and the docks lined with giant cranes and warehouses; the massive kettle drums of the oil storage tanks, and the golden domes of the occasional mosque. Other white graceful buildings which he could not identify glinted in the sunlight like bleached bones. Already the scent of spices wafted seawards, and as the ship approached closer the heat seemed to intensify, as if an oven door had been opened.

The bosun's pipe trilled, followed by the shout, "Hands fall in for entering harbour", and the sailors not needed for more active duty began to form up on the forecastle and quarter deck, feet wide apart, shoulders squarely set.

"They've done us proud, Sir," commented Phelp.

"You'd better join them fore'ard, Number One. The sub can fall in with the quarter deck party. I can cope up here on my own now."

An hour later the escort trawlers had tied up in trots alongside one of the huge quays where everywhere was a scene of bustling activity as teams of coolies loaded and unloaded lighters. Somewhere in the distance the loud shrill voice of a muzzein calling in the faithful to prayer could be heard above the clamour of voices and the clank clank of cranes and winches.

The RNVR lieutenant saluted Paton and said, "I'll take my leave now, Sir. Nice to know you all arrived in one piece. I think you'll enjoy Singapore. That's if you have a taste for the high life. Not much else to do here but eat, drink and dance."

"My lads won't object to that, I can assure you. They've been on almost continuous active service since the war started."

The lieutenant paused as he was about to leave the bridge.

"Almost forgot, Sir. There's an open invitation from the coastal forces officers to join them in a drink at Raffles. Afraid it means togging up, but you'll have to get used to that here, Sir. Very formal and very pukka."

"That would be very nice. It's been a long haul."

"Fine, say about 5 o'clock, Sir."

Paton bent over the engine room voice pipe and called, "Finished with engines, Chief." Reynolds's disembodied voice floated back repeating the order and an uncanny peace invaded the ship as the triple expansion engine was allowed to rest for the first time since leaving India.

Just astern of *Grey Seal* the first of the troopers were being nudged alongside by tugs, her decks crammed with hundreds of soldiers waving to the handful of spectators who lined the quay to welcome them ashore. An army officer from Movement Control in immaculate KD was dashing up and down bellowing orders to a party of red caps who seemed to be totally deaf. It reminded him very much of the chaos he had witnessed in Calcutta where the embarkation had been marked by an absence of movement or control. Sweating dock labourers clad only in tattered shorts and grimy singlets were manhandling gangways into position fore and aft and midships of the troop ship. But an inordinately long time passed before the first khaki-clad soldiers began descending the rickety gangways on legs still wobbly after the long voyage. Their red faces under the enormous topis glistened with sweat as they struggled ashore laden down with enormous kit bags and their heavy great coats rolled round their necks like horse collars. The long, unattractive Bombay bloomers that almost covered their knee caps would have been the despair of any reputable Chinese tailor, and made them appear absurdly ungainly. Even so, the soldiers managed to burst into song as they felt solid earth beneath their feet for the first time since they set out from the UK.

The disembarkation was long and muddled with companies of men lining the quay in ranks of two abreast. In a short time voices rose in unison chanting, "Order, counter order, disorder", until an officer patrolled the ranks with warnings of dire consequences if the banter did not stop. Then realising that the men had grounds for complaining he gave them permission to lower their kit bags and use them as make-shift seats.

The long streams of khaki lava continued to file down the gangways and Paton decided it would be a long time before all their equipment was put ashore. He called out at the top of his voice, "Good luck", and a few upended thumbs indicated that his message had been heard. He descended the bridge ladder and went into the wardroom where Phelp and Carnac were squatting on their bunks which in the daytime could be converted into what resembled rather uncomfortable sofas.

"I know they say the sun should be over the yard arm before a man touches hard liquor, but I think we can make an exception today. We've earned it. I don't know about you two, but I fancy a long cold gin and lime." He pressed the bell button on the bulkhead and summoned Hall. "Do you think you could rustle up some ice, Steward?"

Hall removed the white cloth covering a bowl of ice cubes. "I thought that might be the order of the day, Sir. Managed to fill this before those gannets below grabbed the lot."

As they sipped the long drinks which brought beads of perspiration to their foreheads and necks and dark patches on the backs of their shirts, Paton said, "As soon as I've cleaned up I've got to report to the SNOA. Unless he's got some strong objection I see no reason why most of the ship's company shouldn't have shore leave. They'll need to stretch their legs. I'll tell the other trawler skippers to mount an armed guard on the quay to deter any pilferers. Apart from them, each ship need only have a quartermaster on duty."

A knuckle wrapped on the door and Morris, the ship's self-appointed postman, poked his head into the wardroom, "Permission to proceed ashore for any mail, Sir. Like to take Jolson if that's all right, Sir."

Paton nodded his assent and hoped it would not prove to be a wasted journey for the Admiralty had an aptitude for seeing that letters often went to the wrong destination. "But don't let the dog off his lead, killick. They eat them here, so I'm told."

"I'll see to that, Sir. But he needs to get away from the ship and cock his leg against something that isn't Admiralty property for a change."

23

Jolson almost tore Morris's arm out of its shoulder socket as he darted off to stake his territory on nearly every bollard that lined the huge docks. Then he forsook the bollards for the huge palm trees that dotted the pavements of the streets outside the dock area. "You're going to have your time cut out if you intend to christen every bloody tree in this place, Jolson. So keep a drop in your tank. There're a couple of million rubber trees you haven't seen yet."

Having convinced Tiger Read and then his captain of the desperate anxiety of the ship's company for news of home, Morris was in no hurry to collect the mail. He was determined to see as much of the legendary tropical paradise as possible, but as he had no idea of the topography of Singapore he walked aimlessly in whatever direction took his fancy.

Numerous large cars, many of them of American make with peak-capped syces behind the wheel and lolling white men in the rear, hooted as they hurried through streets jam packed with rickshaws and bicycles. Yellow taxis added to the cacophony. "Two kinds of pedestrians here, Jolson, the quick and the dead." He wondered how the skinny rickshaw wallahs managed to haul three or four people squashed into the small space behind the shafts. They did not look as if they had had a decent meal in days for their ribs were poking through the skin while their shoulder blades stuck out like the glued-on wings of a pantomime fairy, and the muscles on their necks stood out like taut steel hawsers. He had read somewhere that they seldom reached thirty, and that did not surprise him in the least. The policemen also sprouted wings with which to direct the traffic with deft shoulder turns. Occasionally he glanced up to read the name of a road or street, but they gave no idea of where he was and he simply followed where his feet led him.

He strolled along Collyer Quay which reeked of clove cigarettes, through Raffles Place and over a bridge crossing Singapore River where he paused to look down on the armada of junks, lighters and sampans which choked the waterway. They were so close together an agile man could have stepped from bank to bank without wetting his feet. There were beautifully laid out gardens ablaze with a harlequinade of colours, among which darted brightly hued birds he had never seen before.

24

In a short time he found himself surrounded by imposing white buildings built in the colonial style, with large windows and colonnades. One of Christ's flagships stood in silent majesty anchored in a lush lagoon of emerald grass. He read the signboard outside giving the times of services and discovered it was St Andrew's Cathedral. He walked on with the sea now in view and passed an elaborate looking edifice fringed by grass and shaded by fan-shaped palms and decided it was worthy of closer scrutiny because it reminded him of postcard pictures of stately French palaces he had seen in history books. An impressive looking turbanned doorman in a most magnificent uniform was standing below the tall columns marking the entrance, helping out the men and women who seemed to be arriving in processions as if for a formal reception. A sign stated that it was Raffles Hotel, and he wondered why so much fuss was made of a gentleman burglar, for so far he had seen the name several times near the harbour and in the streets. An even more ominous sign-post stated "Out of Bounds" to other ranks. That did not bother him in the least, for judging from the appearance of the doorman and the size of the cars and the splendid clothes of their occupants, it was the kind of place which demanded an arm and a leg just to get inside. As he stood watching more people alight, a woman with a wide hat and a long summer dress imperiously waved him away and gesticulated towards the sign. He was only too willing to oblige, and he continued his stroll along the padang passing the red-tiled Cricket Club with its carefully rolled squares, bowling greens and tennis courts. Again he spotted the ominous "Out of Bounds" sign and wondered if there were any places in Singapore where the lower deck was welcomed.

He turned left and kept walking for at least half an hour and the scene changed with the swiftness of a lantern slide. The graceful government buildings and business houses gave way to narrow squalid streets teeming with humanity. Dried fish carpeted the pavement, and the stench churned his stomach, and when he passed swarms of black flies rose into the air. Old Chinese women squatted on the pavement attending to each other's hair, or eating rice with chopsticks from bowls held close to their mouths, old men with round black hats and wispy beards sat playing Chinese chess with

25

expressionless wrinkled faces. Occasionally a lumbering bullock cart trundled through with a large tank at the rear disgorging water to settle the dust that rose in thick clouds. Above the food shops and stalls were shuttered rooms and pennants of washing semaphored from bamboo poles. The smell of noodles and the clatter of wooden clogs and the rapid click, click of the abacus filled the air. Letter writers printed indecipherable characters on rice paper for illiterate peasants anxious to send news to relatives at home. Condemned cells of bamboo were filled to overcrowding with chickens resigned to their fate, and huge wicker baskets piled high with live crabs blocked the pavement. Freshly landed turtles silently gasped for water, alongside caged mice and snails.

The food looked and smelled wonderful, although he had no idea what it was. Flattened ducks red as clay hung in neat rows, and hawkers pushed barrows that contained steaming vats of meat, barbequed pork, rice and fish. This, he told himself, is what he had travelled thousands of miles to see, not a load of nose-in-the-air whites who had never held a spanner unless it was to toss into the works of something.

He spotted two Scottish soldiers sitting at a small table with several plates in front of them piled high with food, and he went over to speak to them. "My ship's just arrived and I'm taking stock of this place. What part of the city is this?"

One of the soldiers sporting an Argyll bonnet said in a broad aggressive brogue, "This is your own original Chinatown, Jack. Best and cheapest food available in Singapore. Fill your boots for a couple of dollars."

"You been out East long?"

"More years than you've had hot dinners, laddie. We were the garrison regiment and had the run of the place till they decided in their wisdom the place needed reinforcements. Waste of time. The only action you'll see is in Change Alley when some chettiar shortchanges a soldier or the Argylls and Aussies have a punch-up."

"That doesn't worry me. I've seen enough action to see me through, Jock."

"Go on, swing the ruddy lamp, Jack. Bet you haven't heard

26

a shot fired outside a shooting gallery."

"Quite true, if you don't take into account the Northern Patrol, the Atlantic, the Med, Dunkirk and the cock-up in Greece and Crete."

"Pull the other leg, Jack, it's got bells on."

"I could prove it only I came ashore without my medals. Got them for running an evacuation service for the army." And with that riposte, Morris resumed his wandering. As soon as he got back aboard, he told himself, he would let the lads know about this wonderful place he had found. On their first spot of shore leave they really would get stuck into some big eats. Thinking of the ship reminded him of the purpose of his run ashore, and he set off at a determined pace towards the Post Office. He passed what was obviously the Indian Quarter which seemed to be populated by consumptives for the roads and pavements were stained with crimson globs which he took for blood. He saw hawk-nosed women with diamonds in their nostrils, and men with heavy turbans, and stalls piled high with papaya, mangoes, pineapples and starfruit, and sacks bursting with lentils of all sizes and colour. A mortabak man was whirling some sort of pastry around his head until it turned into wafer-thin plates which were tossed onto a crude grill. It was Calcutta without the filth, squalor and abject poverty. He would have liked to see more but he did not relish being relieved of his job as ship's postman which was one of the cushiest aboard as it enabled him to nip ashore and avoid some of the more unpleasant tasks Tiger Read was in the habit of dishing out.

But he could not resist pausing by a fortune teller's stall where a small, perky bird did all the work by selecting an envelope from a row above its perch. As he watched he felt his sleeve tugged and he looked down to see a small boy with gleaming white teeth holding out his hand. "Two cigarettes, Jack?"

Morris extracted two Players and handed them to the boy who tucked them into the waistband of his football shorts. "You like my sister? Very clean. All red inside like Queen Victoria."

Morris said, "You'd better scarper sharpish, kid, before you feel the weight of a size nine up your backside."

The boy continued to grin, immune to such threats which

27

had become part of his way of life. "Next time, jig jig, sailor."

Morris swung his boot, but the child was far too agile and skipped away to disappear into the crowd.

The heat was beginning to make itself felt and he tugged at Jolson and headed for the Post Office. There he was surprised to find a canvas bag awaiting collection, which judging from its contents contained a fair haul of long-awaited mail. "Looks like the Andrew got it right for once, Jolson," he murmured as he signed for it.

By now he was so hot and sticky that he decided to get a rickshaw back to the ship, and he wondered whether the driver could be fobbed off with sterling for it had not occurred to him that he might need Malayan dollars ashore. He strolled over to one where the driver was resting beneath the wheels and the wooden seat seeking some shade from the heat, and showed him half a crown. Like all sailors in a new country he believed that pidgin English was a universal language. "Very good. King's head on side. Made in England." The rickshaw wallah looked at it suspiciously and bit hard on it with reddened teeth and apparently found it acceptable for he tucked it away in his shorts and took up position between the shafts. Morris clambered aboard and patted the seat alongside him inviting Jolson to join him. As the driver set off at a loping trot, he leaned well forward remembering the advice that Tiger Read had tendered: "Never lean back in a rickshaw because as likely as not the boy will let go of the shafts and send you out backwards arse over head. Then he'll filch your money."

When he arrived back at the docks the soldiers were still lolling idly on the quay while huge nets were swinging ammunition and other equipment ashore. He felt a deep compassion for the brown jobs, but all he could think of saying as he passed was, "Serves you right. Shouldn't have taken the King's shilling." A two-fingered gesture indicated their feelings.

In the wheelhouse Tiger Read sorted through the mail. "Take these to the wardroom, Morris," he said, then called out the name of every hand who had received letters. He put his own carefully aside wanting to read them at leisure and in the privacy of the Petty Officers Mess which he shared with Reynolds.

As each man collected his letters he sought out a secluded spot on the upper deck where he could settle down and catch up on the news from home. It was the most treasured moment and one not to be shared with even your closest oppo, for there was always a slight feeling of trepidation as the envelopes were opened in case one contained bad news. Unwelcome news was always worse when you were thousands of miles away and in no position to influence events.

Reynolds took his own small batch onto the quarter deck where he sat on a coiled manilla, carefully sorting them out into date order before starting to read through them. Ruby his wife still lived in the neat terraced house in West Ham, stubbornly refusing all his appeals to move somewhere else for the Germans were still pounding the East End and the neighbouring docks. The younger kids he had no need to worry about for they had been evacuated to Bedfordshire. He read the letters as if they were one uninterrupted narrative, and he was amazed at her fortitude. Everyone, she wrote, was saying that Adolph had missed the bus and wouldn't invade now because the splendid boys in blue had not allowed him to gain air supremacy. Something *he* would never get because everyone was buying a Spitfire and handing in all their old aluminium saucepans and pots. There had been some lovely sing songs in the communal street shelter, but she never stayed the night, preferring to return to the Anderson in the garden. "I've a nice little primus there and can boil a kettle whenever I like. Like you, darling, I can't manage without my cuppa." Edith their eldest, married to an aircraftsman on barrage balloon duty, had not heeded her advice that this was no time to bring youngsters into the world and had got herself pregnant. "Still, it's kept me busy knitting, which does help pass the long shelter nights." Food, she went on, was becoming a problem, so was clothing, but everyone was mucking in and making the most of it. She was glad he was well away from it all because although he had never told her she suspected he had gone to distant climes where everyone was certain the war would never reach. The letters ended with the usual endearments and the double line of crosses. It always embarrassed him slightly that she wrote Swalk on the back of the envelopes; despite the many years they had been married she remained a girl at heart. Not that the sentiments upset him; it was just that he hated the ship's company seeing the youthful lover's message. Reynolds replaced the letters in their envelopes and went down to his cabin where he carefully put them in an oilskin folder alongside all the others he had received since the outbreak of war.

Tiger Read had just finished reading his own mail and he commented laconically, "Makes you ashamed being out here when they're 'aving such a tough time at 'ome."

"Business at the post office," he had read, "has dropped right off, no one seems to have any money to spare except those in munitions factories. They're coining it. Mrs Melrose at the end of the road passed peacefully in her sleep which was a merciful relief as she had been ill for a long time. The garden has been turned over to vegetables which is hard work but more rewarding than grass. Churchill is doing a grand job but it would be nice to see a little light at the end of the tunnel. Everyone is chokka at the way it's dragging on . . ." They were chatty, affectionate and consoling, which was all Tiger needed. He especially liked the little bits of naval slang she threw in. He supposed it made her feel that little bit closer.

Similar letters were being read throughout the ship.

Paton had several from his mother which hinted that the big house in Hampshire was proving too much for her and she would sell it but for the evacuees she had taken in and who made it a home from home. Not that it was a time to sell, for the market was very depressed, and in any case she would never make such a momentous decision without him being there. Carnac's father wrote of the difficulties of the business world and how little could be achieved without permits from one source or another. Phelp's letters from his wife Lesley were full of Wren gossip and long intimate passages expressing her love and longing for him.

They were in fact a microcosm of scores of thousands of letters being read by soldiers, sailors and airmen in every theatre of war. But they all served to preserve the invisible umbilical cord so vital when loved ones are separated.

Chalkie White's last letter from his wife, in a bundle that

had expressed undying love, confided that she could no longer maintain the pretence of loving him. She had met a chap in a reserved occupation who had shown her just what she had missed as the wife of a long serving sailor. He was free every night and didn't have to worry about where the next penny was coming from. She had fought against it, but now she knew there could never be anyone else. He knew how to treat a lady. She ended, "Sorry about this, Chalkie, but I'm sure you'll understand." He had not, and immediately confided his problem to Tiger Read who had promised to raise it with the captain at the first possible opportunity. "Maybe he can arrange some compassionate leave, Chalkie. I'll bring it up first thing after requestmen and defaulters in the morning."

"I don't want that Coxs'n. Maybe the old man can arrange for my parish priest to call round and have a chat with her. She's frightened to death of going to hell, and maybe he can put the fear of Christ up her. But I couldn't run out on the lads, not after all we've been through. I'm no rat, and this isn't a sinking ship."

Read had comforted him with a double tot from his hoard of bottled rum and counselled that the best thing he could do was take a run ashore and get as tight as a duck's arse. During his long years of service he had witnessed it too often to be surprised; even so, it hurt to see a good man wounded. Women could be incredibly cruel, long lovey-dovey letters could be followed by one with the shattering finality of a thrown plate. He could have said that time heals everything, for he knew it was true, but he refrained from saying so for in his experience no one believed it any more than he believed his own promise about compassionate leave. If that was granted to everyone whose wife did a moonlight with somebody else the ocean lanes would be filled with ships loaded to the gunwales with heartbroken servicemen. Sadly but truly they were the unrecorded casualties of war.

As Paton and the other officers changed into Red Sea Rig – white shirts with epaulettes and black trousers – the bosun's pipe summoned, "Hands going ashore to fall in for inspection".

"Nip out and run your eyes over them, Sub, and don't rush it. They've gone to a lot of trouble to look tiddly, so

31

show that it's appreciated."

Paton had returned aboard after reporting to the SNOA with the news that naturally shore leave could be granted to all watches. He had been slightly piqued by the indifference displayed by the shore staff who seemed to take it for granted that everyone went ashore at night as there was no valid reason for remaining aboard. If things were so darn safe, why in heaven's name were they sending so many troops out? He had also managed to obtain some Malayan dollars from the paymaster in order that the ship's company could enjoy themselves.

Tiger Read called the liberty men to attention as Carnac emerged onto the open deck. The tops of their white caps were newly blancoed, their shirts and shorts neatly pressed. He walked slowly along the line picking a fault here and there and muttering the occasional congratulatory remark. It was all part of a regular ritual for none of the men would risk being kept aboard for not being properly turned out.

"Are you going ashore, Cox'n?"

"The Chief and I thought we would show our faces at the petty officers' wet canteen, Sir. A few pints of Tiger will go down well. Might even take in a flick."

Carnac watched the liberty men tumble ashore like children released from school early. A string of rickshaws had assembled on the quay, informed by some telepathic communication that fresh fares had just arrived in harbour.

A Japanese photographer with a gold smile and dressed in a neat duck suit and sporting a Panama hat, snapped the sailors with their arms around each others' shoulders and informed them he would have the prints ready by the time they returned aboard.

Carnac watched the rickshaws pull away as if competing in some human Donkey Derby. He could hear Morris's voice, "Chinatown, big eats. No Lavender Street. Jowdy, jowdy."

Chapter 3

As the yellow Ford taxi horned its way to Raffles Hotel, *Grey Seal*'s three officers enjoyed some leisurely sight-seeing. Apart from the occasional V-for-Victory poster, there were no visible signs that Singapore was part of an empire fighting for survival. No sandbags protected official buildings as they did in London, and there were no air raid shelters marring the appearance of the wide streets, nor signs pointing to underground ones. They were not considered necessary; in any case, underground shelters had been ruled out as impracticable; the ground was too swampy for deep excavation. Throughout Britain's major towns and cities there was a rash of posters warning that careless tongues cost lives and urging everyone to be like Dad, keep Mum, but such alarmist advice was not needed in Singapore. What posters there were advertised household luxuries, or goods and clothing which had long disappeared from shops at home. Neither were the well-stocked windows of the bigger stores blighted by unsightly strips of sticky paper to avoid deadly splinters.

Even the solidiers who thronged the bazaars and street stalls resembled cruise tourists ashore for a short souvenir hunting expedition. Australians with wide brimmed hats flattened at one side bartered furiously with wood carvers over the price of enormous water buffaloes with small boys perched precariously on their backs, and elaborately patterned camphor wood chests which would look incongruously out of place in an out-back shack, assuming that their sheer bulk had not resulted in them being jettisoned long before the time came to return home.

Carnac had suggested that a rickshaw was the best way

33

to see the town, but Paton had overruled him and offered instead to pay for the taxi. He did not, he had said, see any point in subscribing to a man's early death, and even Phelp's tactful reminder that he would die that much earlier if he could not earn a living, had failed to budge the Commander.

As they were in no hurry they had instructed the driver to make a wide detour and point out the more prominent landmarks. After so long at sea it was a rare luxury to be able to lean back and enjoy the sights of the bustling city without having to maintain constant vigilance. Occasionally the Sikh driver removed one hand from the wheel to gesticulate vaguely at some building and mutter something incomprehensible, but in the main he was too preoccupied in seeing how close he could drive to the shuffling pedestrians before they were forced to jump aside.

At first sight, the three-storey hotel looked as if it had been lifted bodily from a Paris boulevard, for it contained all that was best and worst in French Renaissance architecture. It resembled a wedding cake made by a self-indulgent pastry chef who did not know when to stop; it was surrounded on all four sides by wide ornately decorated verandas and topped by a pagoda-style roof while the building was coloured dark green and white with matching striped awnings above the windows.

The taxi had hardly come to a halt before the turbanned jagger on duty at the entrance was twisting the door handle and saluting. They went up a flight of stairs into the T-shaped Tiffin Room paved with Carrara marble, with elegant galleries supported by graceful columns and arches, which gazed down from the upper floors. An ornamental skylight which also provided extra light and ventilation canopied the whole area. At the end stood the famous Long Bar which writhed snake-like between the columns. Overhead the punkhas creaked rheumatically, their blades stirring the humid air like gargantuan food whisks. The bar was already thronged with army officers in their best blues, and civilians in dinner jackets or tight-fitting bum freezers. Above the steady drone of conversation could be heard the music of a palm court orchestra mounted on a dais nearby. The young officer who had boarded *Grey Seal* earlier detached himself from a group at the bar and welcomed Paton. "Glad you were able to make it, Sir." Paton introduced Phelp and Carnac to the welcoming committee of naval officers, and a two-and-a-half straight ringer said, "What'll it be? I'd personally recommend the Singapore sling."

"What is it?" asked Paton.

"A head-blowing concoction created by Ngiam Tong Boon, the barman, in 1915. Really exotic. You just mix one half of gin, a quarter of cherry brandy, some mixed fruit juices – the local fresh lime is a must – some pineapple, a few drops of Cointreau and Benedictine, a dash of Angostura, and top it up with a cherry and more pineapple."

"Sounds lethal."

"It is, but some of the locals have a remarkable capacity for them. I'm told the record is held by three men who knocked back over a hundred of them in a couple of hours, then celebrated by going on to something else."

Paton said, "I'll try *one* later, but if it's at all possible I'd like a beer." When he saw the amount of fresh lime that was put into each sling he could not help thinking of the vast amount of bottled lime juice in *Grey Seal*'s rum locker. The Admiralty were obviously fervent believers in taking coals to Newcastle.

As their hosts raised their glasses and welcomed them to Singapore, the lieutenant-commander scribbled his signature on a chitty; cash, it seemed, never changed hands in the city, it was not the done thing.

A rubber trader already slightly tipsy joined them and said, "Newcomers? Any of you dab hands with the willow? I'm on the cricket club committee and we can always do with some good bats. Demand for tin and rubber is growing so acute we're finding it difficult to field elevens."

Paton replied that if his duties permitted he would like nothing better.

"You won't find Singapore too demanding, Commander. You'll have plenty of time to relax. The Nips will give this place a wide berth if they know what's good for them." He gestured with his head to the barman for drinks to be served all round, and a voice from the group he had deserted called out, "Look at all pencil-shy Jardine pushing the boat out! When it comes to buying drinks he's usually like a Jew with

35

no arms." The remark provoked guffaws of laughter, for the worst accusation that could be levelled at anyone was that he was slow with his signature. Mr Jardine took it in the spirit in which it was meant, for he knew he enjoyed a reputation for generosity.

After a couple of beers Paton switched to the sling which he found marvellously refreshing, but it did not prevent the sweat from trickling down the collar of his tight-fitting shirt and he felt the need for some fresh air. On the pretence of going to the Gents he walked through a collonaded arcade that ran alongside the dance floor and led into the garden. Tables were laid out on the lawn, ice floes on a sea of green, and several women in long dresses were sitting down enjoying the faint breeze that came in from the sea, barely stirring the leaves of the fan-shaped travellers palms and crimson flame trees which acted as sunshades although the tinted sky warned that nightfall was not far off and would descend with the abruptness of a curtain on a lit stage. The air was heavy with the fragrance of frangipani and hibiscus.

A voice, unmistakably American, called, "It really is as Maugham described it. Begins to pall after a while though. Like candy floss for breakfast."

He turned and saw a tall, slim woman in a white dress seated at a table tossing scraps of bread to a horde of chattering, yellow-beaked mynah birds who squabbled noisily over the titbits. She patted the vacant seat beside her. "Come and join me. I could do with some fresh company."

He sat down smiling slightly, for he had heard that Singapore women were rather snooty and conventional and seldom spoke to any male until he had formally dropped his card and been introduced as someone socially acceptable. He held out his hand, "Crispin Paton."

She took his extended hand and replied, "Commander RN, DSO and Bar. I'm Kate Hollis."

"You seem remarkably well informed about naval ranks and decorations."

"Just part of the job. Being in a British garrison I had to gen up on service ranks and medal ribbons. Let me get you a drink. You can't sit there without a glass in your hand. It's not allowed in Singapore."

He wondered if she had already had a few which would

account for her unconventional behaviour. "Let me get you one. Although I'm not sure they'll accept a chitty from me. Only arrived today."

"Out of the question. You have to be introduced to the manager first. Anyway, I'll put it down to expenses. Interviewing high ranking naval officer for off-the-record information about future strategy," she said with a laugh.

He smiled in return. "I'm afraid you'll be ploughing unfertile soil. I'm a complete ignoramus as far as Singapore goes."

"Don't worry. A lot of the people I wine and dine are fictitious. I won't ask one leading question."

"I'm intrigued. I thought you must be a tourist. I'm obviously wrong."

She heaved a mock sigh. "Such is fame! Somebody else who has never heard of me!"

"Should I have?"

"Of course not. I'm a war correspondent for the *Chicago Banner*, so there's no reason why you should."

He started to apologise, "I don't get much time for reading newspapers . . ." but she stopped him. "You don't have to be polite. My stuff is strictly for home consumption in the States and Canada where I'm syndicated. Just as well because what I've been writing hasn't made me too popular with the powers that be here. Seems it gets filtered back, probably by your embassy in Washington. As a result I've been branded as anti-British."

"Are you?"

"Ask me again in a couple of weeks time."

"That sounds evasive."

"All right; the answer is yes when it comes to the tuan besars and colonial dinosaurs who run this shooting match. They fell asleep when war started and set their alarm clocks for armistice day."

"Everyone says that nothing will happen."

"Let's hope their crystal balls haven't been fogged by over optimism."

"Isn't your title a trifle provocative?"

"No. Before I arrived here I covered Dunkirk and spent quite a few nights in your Underground writing about the Blitz."

"That seems a dangerous occupation for a young woman."

"There're a number of us around: Clare Luce, Molly Panter Downs and Eve Curie, to mention only three. The woman's view carries a lot of weight in America. While it's not petticoat rule back home we demand a hearing. Anyway, don't you have women in your armed services?"

Paton detected an abrasive edge to her voice. "Sorry, I didn't mean to sound patronising, Miss Hollis."

She noted his determination to remain formal, but accepted it as typical British reserve. She studied the young man opposite; the face was strong and quite good looking but for the bent beak of a nose that could do with a little cosmetic surgery, and apart from the badger's streak of grey the hair was dark and plentiful. He was not at all like some of the effete men she had met in London who affected a rather bored kind of langour. But there was a hardness around the mouth and eyes that had nothing to do with age and reminded her of the young soldiers she had met returning from the Dunkirk beaches, and the East Enders she had encountered during the bombing. They had witnessed and experienced things that time would never erase and which had made them prematurely old. From his speech she assumed that he was what Americans called upper crust; the kind of young man who accepted without question that he had been born to lead, but it was something not born of affectation but a genuine sense of duty.

He saw in turn a very attractive woman with a wide mobile mouth and a figure that was amply curved but needing no corset. Her fringed hair was cut short below the ears reminding him of Claudette Colbert and Benares brass. A little hard boiled and self-assured perhaps compared to most of the women he knew who worked hard to be ornamental rather than practical. A bit like a celluloid depiction of a girl reporter as seen through a Hollywood camera.

She signalled to a waiter who was gliding past on castored feet. "What'll it be, Crispin?"

"I'd better stick to a gin sling."

She ordered it from the boy, adding, "I'll have another bourbon on the rocks with plenty of soda. Put it down to room 23."

"What is it in your writing that has upset the authorities here, Kate?" he asked, finally breaking the thin sheet of ice that separated them.

"I've had the temerity to say that the people here are cocooned from reality, and while their countrymen and women are dying they're enjoying a continuous round of boozing, tennis and tiffin dances. Fiddling while Europe burns. They are so sickeningly complacent."

"The British are renowned for muddling through."

"If it was that I wouldn't mind. It's the total *indifference* they display whenever anyone mentions the war. Let me give you an example. I recently interviewed the wife of your Commander-in-Chief, Lady Brooke-Popham, who told me she was struck by the deadly inertia of the place; the people are utterly dormant. Apparently she had asked a certain women to give two hours help with ARP work and the reply was, 'I'm awfully sorry but I've already entered for the tennis tournament and ARP will interfere with that'. Since then I've met scores of women with exactly the same attitude. I wrote about it, but your censor refused to pass it. So I simply gave it to a buddy who was flying to Manilla and he cabled it from there. As a result I was accused of being deceitful and anti-British."

"I can see their point, I'm afraid."

"But the authorities are being deliberately misleading themselves. They encourage the torpor by stressing the non-existent readiness of the place in the unlikely event of an attack. The civilians justify their hedonism by emphasising the important role they are playing by earning dollars to finance England's war effort, but make no mention of the inflated salaries they pay themselves. Patriotism, my foot! When they screened 'Target for Tonight' to raise cash for the RAF it was virtually boycotted. It wasn't considered good enough entertainment. I felt like throwing up. The papers here blazon headlines across their front pages announcing the arrival of each fresh batch of troops, all well trained and equipped, when observers like myself know they are little more than kids and don't know a thing about real fighting. Is it wrong to point things like that out?"

"Perhaps they don't think that you're the right person to do it."

She detected the resentment in his voice; something she had encountered among most of her critics. It was understandable; America had remained on the sidelines while Europe had been conquered, and it was no secret that there were many influential voices in America, like Lindbergh, a national hero, who openly supported Hitler and saw Britain as doomed. But even worse, as far as Singapore's whites were concerned, was that while her country continued to sell war materials to Japan they still felt entitled to sit in judgement over *their* conduct. But, she reasoned, that was no reason for her not telling the truth; that was her duty to her profession. Aloud she said, "I can't afford to alienate any more people, Crispin, especially someone like you who has seen the worst of the war so far. Tell me about it. I've unburdened myself. It's your turn."

"There's not a lot to tell. I'm an anachronism. I've been trained all my life for war, and I've grown to hate it. It brings out the best and worst in men, but I'm not sure the former compensates for the latter."

She waited for him to continue, but that seemed as far as he was prepared to go. "Tell me about your decorations, Crispin. I really would like to know."

"I don't look upon them as mine. I consider they represent the joint efforts of my ship's company. Those still with me and those who aren't. But I'd willingly toss away a strip of ribbon if it would bring one of them back."

She realised he was not indulging in false modesty but speaking from the heart. It was a question she should not have asked. Perhaps her job with its incessant probing had made her insensitive to other people's feelings.

Paton finished his drink. "I really must go, Kate. I've left some fellow officers at the bar. I don't want to establish a reputation for being a round dodger. Unforgivable sin here, I gather. So please excuse me, unless you'd like to join us?"

"I'd love to. Being seen in your company may help re-establish my tarnished image. I don't have the nerve to go in there alone."

They threaded their way through the tables where salivating early diners were scrutinising the long menus like children confronted with a box of chocolates and unable to make a choice because each one seemed so enticing.

The crowd at the Long Bar had been swollen considerably by home-going businessmen and others who had already showered and dressed in readiness for a typical Singapore night of drinking and eating, and the group of traders had become markedly more boisterous. But their conversation came to an abrupt halt when Paton arrived with the newspaper reporter.

The rubber man Jardine who earlier had been so anxious to demonstrate his generosity, remarked in a loud voice meant to be overheard by her, "Watch your tongues, chaps, the great American depression is about to descend on us," while to her he said, "How is our expert on indecent exposure?"

Kate smiled amiably, determined not to be drawn into a rancorous argument and glancing down at her own low-cut dress said, "I hadn't realised I was revealing so much."

"I'm not talking about your tits. I'm talking about the scurrilous rubbish we hear is being circulated all over your country. Bloody disgraceful," said Jardine vehemently.

One of his colleagues said, "Knock it off, Clive; that's no way to talk to a lady. She's only doing her job."

"And what's that? Encouraging the American anti-war lobby? Not that they need much. Kept out of the last lot till the very last minute, and they're doing the same again, at the same time putting their own economy back on its feet at our expense."

Paton said coldly, "The young lady is here at my invitation, Mr Jardine, not to be insulted. Maybe it would be wiser if you didn't provide grounds for so much criticism."

"I see she has managed to get at you already, Commander."

Paton took hold of her elbow. "I'd like you to meet my ship's officers, Kate," and he steered her to where Phelp was trying to catch the barman's eye. "This is Lieutenant Phelp, my first lieutenant. Brian, meet Miss Hollis."

As they shook hands Paton asked, "Where's young Carnac? He disappeared?"

"No, Sir. He's dancing with a most pretty young girl he introduced himself to. Let me get you a drink, Miss Hollis. I've managed to establish my bona fides with the manager."

As Phelp ordered the drinks, she said to Paton, "That was very tactful of you, Crispin, but really I can take care of myself. I don't need naval protection. In my job one learns

41

not to get rattled. Next time I meet him I'll lecture him on Lend-Lease."

"It's what we call in the navy evasive action. Not cowardice but strategy. I would have punched him on the nose if we had stayed to hear any more of his rudeness."

"You can understand now why I was sitting alone. Meeting them professionally is bad enough without suffering them socially," she said.

Carnac was moving slowly round the small dance hall behind the Palm Court with a girl who could not have been more than nineteen or twenty, and who seemed determined to keep him at arm's length. A prominently displayed notice board stated: No dancing except in formal dress. It was a rigidly enforced rule; the orchestra had been known to stop in the middle of a number until an offender left the floor, although the more likely approach was from a uniformed "Buttons" who would discreetly slip a card into the hand of anyone improperly dressed asking him to leave. But such incidents were relatively rare; people soon learned that to survive in Singapore one had to conform; rebels were ostracised socially. If a person really overstepped the mark punishment was swift and severe, as more than one new arrival had discovered by attempting to take a "native" girl onto the floor. They were quickly packed off home in disgrace.

"Hell, the band is playing like a rundown gramophone that needs winding. The last time I danced to this tune it was a quick step," complained Carnac.

"We do things differently here, Terence," she said impishly. "One mustn't appear to be enjoying it." She laughed softly and added, "I'm only joking, there's a serious reason behind it. It's slow to avoid excessive perspiration, just as we don't hold each other too close for the same reason. *Real* gentlemen are considerate enough to hold a handkerchief against a lady's back, but you can't be expected to know that."

The sub-lieutenant did not really mind the funeral pace for it was clammily hot, even though the dance floor was open to the sea, but he would willingly have endured a blow lamp if he could have drawn her closer to him. It had been a long time since he had enjoyed the company of such an attractive girl.

"It was very forward of you coming up to me like that," she said in feigned rebuke. "If Daddy had been here you'd have got a flea in your ear. He's an awful snob, but if you are tuan besar you're expected to be."

He studied her carefully wondering if she was being serious or merely teasing, but there was nothing in her expression that conveyed her real feelings. Her father, Mr Jardine, she told him was one of the island's biggest rubber men, apart from his other lucrative business interests, and was a stickler when it came to etiquette. Fortunately, he was at the bar having a drink with some cronies until her mother arrived for dinner.

When the music stopped she led him to her table. "You can sit with me till they come in. I'll ask Daddy if you can stay for dinner. Don't want you wandering off to Cad's Alley." That, she explained in answer to his question, was where men sat hoping to catch the eye of one of the girls in the dance hall.

Dan Hopkins' orchestra began to play a hotted-up version of "Smoke Gets in Your Eyes", which was politely applauded, although no one attempted to dance to it preferring to "sit it out". It was the first time the musicians had shown the slightest indication that they enjoyed their work; for most part it had seemed a tiresome chore. Despite the description "Raffles' Celebrated Orchestra", it was little more than a collection of itinerant musicians, for the Far East was filled with displaced persons – White Russians who had fled the revolution, and more recently Jews from Hitler's Germany – several of whom were classical musicians forced to take up work in clubs and hotels in order to survive.

Hopkins, a red haired Irishman, had been a company sergeant major in the regular army in India until he was bought out for £28 in 1922 by a touring Dixieland band who were short of a drummer. After a nomadic career he had been spotted in the Savoy in London by Arshak Sarkies, one of the family which founded and owned Raffles. Now his band was the most famous on the island.

Their boredom was understandable for they churned out music to unemotional dancers and diners with scarcely a break. On Mondays, Tuesdays, Wednesdays and Fridays there were cocktail dances followed by dinner dances, and every Thursday and Saturday there were concerts followed by another dance. Singapore could not have enough.

Like the other women present she was wearing a long evening dress and Carnac thought she looked stunningly attractive, although a more mature man might have found her features a little too doll-like and her attitude that of a spoiled child who needed a good spanking.

From time to time she rummaged inside a sequined handbag and produced a battery-operated fan with which to cool herself. He thought it very sophisticated.

"What do you do for a living, Jo?"

She seemed genuinely surprised by the question. "Nothing! Daddy would never dream of letting me work, much as I would like to. He just says, 'What on earth could you do?' as if that settled the matter."

"But surely there's something? Your father sounds as if he has a big company."

She smiled wistfully, "The only women he employs are chi chi's and Asiatics. It would *never* do to allow his daughter to take on a menial task. The whole system would collapse if the memsahibs were allowed to do something useful."

"What on earth do you do with yourself?"

"Do! Singapore has more to offer than anywhere else, or so they say. The one thing it doesn't have is a cure for boredom. So I play tennis, golf, swim and dance, and ride my horse. But I'm not entirely content with chocolates for breakfast, tea and dinner, so I also help to roll bandages and attend First Aid lectures twice a week, although I've been assured I'll never use what I've been taught. But it's nice to feel you're doing your bit, especially when one realises what they're going through at home."

"It all sounds very hectic," he said, immediately regretting the discernible sarcasm in his voice.

"You're being unkind, Terence. It's not our fault we've missed the war, any more than it is the soldiers here who do nothing but drink and fight among themselves. Or would you rather we *were* at war?"

"Of course not, but it might create a better impression if the whites didn't make such an ostentatious display of enjoying themselves."

She retorted irritably, "Don't let Daddy hear you talk like that. He'll deliver his favourite lecture: 'You people come out here and in five minutes think you know the place. You don't, it takes years to understand the native mentality. Here face is everything. The natives must be shown that it is business as usual. We simply must not alter our way of life; otherwise the natives will think we've got the wind up.' I think he's wrong; we should play a more practical role, but you can't beat the system and so women are forced to act out this silly charade that we are here purely for ornamental purposes. No wonder there's so much bed hopping going on – despite the social whirl the memsahibs are bored to tears, bound hand and foot to the ruddy altar of conformity. We're like the characters in the Chinese theatres here, forced by custom to wear grotesque masks, never able to show our real selves."

Carnac was saved from becoming embroiled in an argument by the sudden appearance of her father escorting a dumpy, overdressed woman whose carefully enunciated words suggested she had taken elocution lessons to disguise an accent that hinted at origins she would rather not admit to. While "self made" was an accolade among men, the slightest suggestion that a woman was not really top drawer could prove a social albatross. When they had been introduced, the planter invited the sub-lieutenant to join them for a meal.

"I don't think he can possibly accept, Daddy. It would offend his conscience. He thinks it is quite wrong the way we enjoy ourselves," she said mischievously. Carnac caught a glimpse of the faintest suggestion of a wink.

Her mother rebuked her stridently, "You can stop that, Jo. Your father has had a very tiring day and he's in no mood for another lecture on how we conduct ourselves. He's had more than enough for one evening."

Mr Jardine said, "I've got broad shoulders, but Mother is right, darling. Enough is enough, even if you are joking. I've just had a brush with that awful American woman. She should be working for Goebels. Ought to be kicked off the island. Can't understand her sort. Expects us to put the bloody island under a state of siege. Imagine what effect that would have on native morale if the tuans besar were seen to be panicking."

"As the boy scouts say, Sir, there's no harm in being prepared," murmured Carnac.

Mr Jardine thumped the table. "We are, young man, we are. The navy's big guns can repel any attack from the sea, and that's the only way the Japs can come. Take it from me, I've been there, the mainland is impenetrable jungle. And that's not just my personal view, it's that of all the military experts."

Mrs Jardine coughed as if requesting permission to speak. "The island really is crawling with soldiers, and more are arriving every week. That's hardly being negligent." Somehow she managed to give the troops an insect-like quality.

"That's why we get so sick and tired of these bloody know-all Yanks who turn up telling us how to run the place. We've even had that Ernest Hemingway's wife telling us what a shower we are. Now we've got the damned Hollis woman taking up where she left off. *We* can shrug it off, even ignore it, but not all of their anti-British propaganda falls on deaf ears. There are lots of reds here who can't wait to kick us out. There was even an uppity naval commander in the bar who actually tried to defend her tonight."

Mrs Jardine patted his hand. "Don't get so upset, darling. It'll ruin your meal."

Carnac decided it would be tactful to change the conversation; he had a feeling that the commander was none other than his own commanding officer. He accepted the invitation and explained that he would have to apologise to his captain who was expecting him to join him at the bar. As soon as he saw Paton he realised the woman with him was the one who had set Mr Jardine's temperature soaring like a thermometer in a heatwave. He would have to guard his tongue when he rejoined the Jardines, otherwise he could jeopardise the chances of further meetings with Jo. He called Paton aside and explained that he had been invited to have dinner with a young lady, tactfully refraining from mentioning her father.

"Trot along and fill your boots, Sub, and don't worry about what time you return aboard. You never know your luck. I've read that the tropics have a tendency to make women a little amorous."

46

Carnac who missed the broad wink Paton gave his first lieutenant, said, "She's not at all like that, Sir", fervently hoping he could be wrong.

Paton and Phelp had had more than their fill of gin slings and feeling the pangs of hunger were wondering how to break away from their hosts without causing offence. It was Kate who saved them from their dilemma. "How would you like to have a Chinese meal? Not the rubbish served up in New York or London, but the genuine article."

Both readily agreed for they did not relish the idea of eating in the same room as the belligerent planter for fear that he could continue his assault on Miss Hollis.

"Good. I'll pop up and change into something more appropriate."

As they entered the high-ceilinged foyer, Kate was accosted by an immaculately attired Japanese who bowed formally, shook her hand, and said with a pronounced American accent, "Not leaving already, Miss Hollis? I was just coming to see you. I have an excellent little story for you."

"Can't it hold fire, Isao? I've just promised to show them Chinatown."

"It will only take a few minutes. Knowing the Royal Navy which always puts duty first, I'm sure they will not object."

Kate made a despairing gesture and followed the American-speaking Japanese to a gilt-legged table where he engaged her in earnest conversation.

"I have two juicy tit bits for you, Miss Hollis, which typify the British colonial inefficiency. You would hardly credit it. They reveal yet again how America is wasting her much needed resources in helping the decadent whites here."

The two naval officers saw her take out a notebook and begin to write. Twenty minutes later she rose and walked up the wide ballustraded staircase to her room.

The man named Isao came over and joined them. "We newspaper people work hand in glove with each other," he explained. "I help the Americans and British, and they in turn help me."

He gazed round the column-lined vestibule. "One can almost hear the echo of the feet of Somerset Maugham, Noel

Coward and Rudyard Kipling. They all stayed here, you know."

"You seem well versed in English literature," said Phelp.

"I am a great admirer of all three. Kipling who realised East was east and West west; Maugham the acid cynic who saw the Europeans here as they really are, and Coward the sparkling wit. Did you ever hear his crushing retort to a woman who said only the best people were allowed in the Tanglin Club? No! 'After meeting your best people now I know why there is such a shortage of good servants in London'. Isn't that delightful?"

"Apocryphal, more likely," said a smiling Paton.

"No, it is true," said the Japanese earnestly. "It is too good a story not to be true. Sadly it perfectly describes the British here. Scrubwomen are now ladies, and men are sent out here because they are failures at home. Like one of our senior detectives who was a bobby pounding a London beat until he came to Singapore. But you will discover that for yourself. Meanwhile, enjoy your stay in Raffles."

"I'm afraid we're simply guests for the evening," said Paton.

"What a shame! One should be a resident here, it is a great experience. A law unto itself. Do you know that when Mr Arshak Sarkies was asked why this hotel was so successful he replied 'Because there is only one rule here. We ring the bell at 6 o'clock in the morning and everyone goes back to their own room'."

"That's a hoary old story that has been told about most of the best hotels in the world," said Phelp.

"But there is a grain of truth in it."

"Are you speaking from experience?" said Paton good-humouredly.

"Good heavens, no. I'm afraid a white woman would never contemplate sharing her bed with a man of my complexion." He looked towards the stairs. "Here comes Miss Hollis. Enjoy your visit to see how the other three quarters live. I hope I shall have the pleasure of meeting you again. I have a high regard for the Royal Navy, it taught our own so much."

Paton could not be sure whether or not the smiling man in the perfectly tailored dinner jacket was being humorous

48

or serious.

As he turned to walk away he paused and said, "Commander, you must visit the billiard room here. You will learn a lot about the mentality of the colonial. There is a graphic account of how an intrepid Englishman shot and killed a wild tiger which was hiding beneath one of the tables. He is a great local hero."

"Sounds as if he deserves to be," said Paton laconically. "Tackling a man eater in a refined space needs guts."

"That is exactly what the story intends to convey. The calm phlegmatic tuan protecting the natives who were scared out of their wits. The truth, however, is less epic. The tiger was a tame one which had escaped from a circus and was cowering there in fear. The hunter was still drunk from a Government House ball. His first shots hit a pillar, the third was lethal."

"I think I prefer the true version," said Paton. "A much better story."

"That is only because you do not live here. The white man in question must be seen as an heroic figure, not a comic."

As he viewed the retreating figure of the newspaperman, Paton wondered why he was not bent double with the weight of the chip he carried on his shoulders.

In the dining room, Carnac sat studying the menu, wondering what to order, there was so much to choose from. He had existed so long on tinned tomatoes, tinned herrings, corned beef and other equally unappetising meals he was in a quandary. He eyed the waiter wheeling the silver roast-beef trolly perfectly balanced on delicately curved legs, decided against it and pondered on the merits of steak au poivre and sole meunière against those of lobster and scampi marinara.

Mr Jardine said, "Let me make your mind up for you, Terence. For starters I recommend a dozen Sydney rock oysters, followed by fresh salmon. It really is. Direct from Australia. To round off, what about some of our home-grown Cameron Highlands strawberries? The mangoes and paw paw are delicious, but only to be eaten in the bath."

Carnac nodded assent. With a bit of luck he would be invited back when he could try some of the other dishes which had made a personal decision so difficult.

"After we've eaten, perhaps you'd like to come home for a stengah or whisky ayer?" suggested Mrs Jardine. "You can fill us in with all the gossip from home."

"I'm afraid I haven't been home for quite a while," he apologised.

"Never mind. We'd still love you to come. And don't worry about getting back, the syce will run you to the ship. He just loves driving. Never a word of complaint about the hours he works."

"Better hadn't," said Mr Jardine jocularly. "There's a queue of men who'd sacrifice their own mother for his job."

"Don't take any notice of Daddy, he's not as hard as he makes out," said Jo.

Carnac could not help thinking that that would be very difficult.

Mr Jardine studied the comprehensive wine list with pursed lips; there was Chianti at $3.50, and Sauternes for the same price, and numerous Hocks and Moselles. He decided on the Chateau Yquem 1924, the most expensive at $12.

Kate who had changed into a dark blue cotton skirt and jacket, drove the small car fast and skilfully without being unduly reckless. Both officers were still a trifle confused to be driving through streets ablaze with lights after so long in a ship where "darken ship" had been piped every night.

"Who was the cocky little gentleman who button-holed you, Kate?" Paton enquired from the rear seat.

"Isao Okamoto, a top man with the *Singapore Herald*. A prize shit, but not to be underestimated. He calls his paper the voice of Nippon."

"He seems to have acquired a passable American accent," said Phelp.

"Ought to have, he was born in the States. Holds an American passport. I suspect he's a Jap spy."

"That doesn't seem to trouble your conscience," said Paton.

"Why should it? Every dentist, masseur, photographer and barber is engaged in passing on information to the Jap Consul. They photograph military installations with complete impunity while the Jap fishermen use their Kampang at

Bedak as a base for charting all the lesser known approaches, and no one stops them. Do you know, the *Herald* actually published top secret pictures of a defence conference sold to them by an army officer? No one took any action because his father held a high rank. Just as bad was when Pan Am wanted a photograph of the airport when they opened a new office. They were told it was a hush-hush establishment, until they learned the official photographer was a Jap who had pictures on open display in his studio window. They just bought one."

Both men had encountered a lot of blundering and ineptitude during the war, but what they were hearing seemed entirely different; the authorities seemed to go out of their way to encourage it.

"I find what you say difficult to believe," said Paton. "It's tantamount to criminal negligence. Why doesn't anyone do anything about it?"

Kate kept her eyes on the road ahead as she replied, "Some try, but they are voices in the wilderness. *The Straits Times* – admittedly through vested interest – repeatedly warns about the *Herald*'s activities, but its circulation soars with every edition. Special passes have even been issued for the *Herald*'s news boys to visit the barracks because it is so popular with the troops. They won't close it because they feel it would do more harm than letting it continue."

Paton said that from his short conversation with the Japanese he had not made any effort to be discreet.

"Why should he? He despises the British. To be honest, he has good reason to. Brooke-Popham couldn't wait to grant the *Herald* an interview, and promptly put his foot in it by seemingly supporting the paper's policy. He's so goddam dumb he hadn't realised it was Jap owned. Of course, curbs are put on the paper now; reporters are permitted to attend conferences but not allowed to ask questions. They get around that by simply asking one of the American or British newsmen to put them for them. Make no mistake, Isao has the best contacts on the island and he's very free with his information. In return some people allow him to reprint their own by-lined despatches, which enables the *Herald* to publish stories about inefficiency by well known writers."

"And you don't find that distasteful, Kate?" said Paton.

"Not if it will result in people removing the blinkers. If I'm chronically ill I don't want a doctor telling me I'm hale and hearty. I want treatment. I'm bored to tears hearing about an empire on which the sun never sets. Unless someone here pulls their finger out, they'll wake up one morning and find the Rising Sun fluttering from the flagstaff of Government House. Not every Jap is so open in their contempt for the whites as Isao, but make no mistake it's there, smouldering below the surface. They want Asia for the Asians."

Paton was experiencing a feeling of growing unease. He had seen enough of Singapore to make him wish that the people would shake off the lethargy. At the same time he could not understand the mentality of people like Kate who seemed to be playing into the hands of the Japanese by stressing the wide gulf that separated whites from natives and continuously drawing attention to the lack of leadership. Things might not be perfect, but the time to put them right was when the war was over. Creating dissent among the various communities could have a boomerang effect, and if war did come to Malaya the natives might find, too late, that the devil they knew was infinitely better than the one they did not.

Kate swung the car into the kerb outside a restaurant festooned with paper lanterns and decorated with gaudily painted dragons with popping eyes and forked tongues belching fire.

As they got out she announced cheerfully, "We'll have this on Isao. I'll bill the office for the two stories he passed on. They don't know he wouldn't accept a cent."

Paton and Phelp were mystified by the topsy-turvy ethics of journalism; it seemed a profession that had no qualms about openly collaborating with a possible enemy. They were even more bewildered when at the end of the meal Kate said that before taking them back to *Grey Seal* she would have to stop at the censor's office to hand in the stories the Japanese had passed on. "We've discovered it's best to call about 11.30 because the office closes at midnight and the duty man is so anxious to get to his club for a final drink before going home he doesn't bother to read anything. That's fine because he can't complain when our stuff gets fed back. He has to pretend he passed it."

52

After a gargantuan meal, Morris and Miller had found their way into The Happy World. The ornate arch at the entrance had been the gateway to a sprawling complex dedicated to the pursuit of pleasure. Australians rubbed shoulders with Scotsmen in tartan bonnets, and Indian troops in pugris, and Malays and Chinese in spotless white duck suits. A pall of blue tobacco smoke hovered over the sweating medley while the smell of cooking tantalised the nostrils. There were stalls selling all kinds of native foods, and a fairground that contained everything from shooting galleries to freak shows. For a dollar one could see an Indian with a jewelled turban and naked but for a lion cloth, belching fire and swallowing long curved swords and snakes. In the Chinese Theatre, a mainly Chinese audience sat expressionless and impassive as men in grotesque masks stamped and growled and made exaggeratedly menacing gestures to girls with doll-like rouged faces. Scene shifters moved about the open stage shifting props entirely unnoticed by the performers. There were booths offering cures for impotence, venereal disease, and tuberculosis, and fortune tellers who guaranteed a rosy future.

On a raised ring, oil-coated Sikh wrestlers tied each other in impossible knots which were only untied after much furious pounding of the canvas. There were also boxers who used their feet instead of their fists while a vast tented area presented animal acts which included tigers, lions, and elephants that seemed almost human.

Now, as Sub-Lieutenant Carnac was guiding Jo sedately around the dance floor at Raffles, Morris was also dancing, although his surroundings were vastly different to the plush opulence of Singapore's premier hotel. He was on a high stage supported by stout bamboo canes in the centre of The Happy World. The rough planked floor was so crowded with gyrating soldiers, sailors and airmen, that it seemed in imminent danger of collapse.

The Chinese and Malay taxi-dancers were all dressed alike so that they too could have been in uniform, for they all wore skin hugging ankle length cheongsams with slits up the side to display their proudly owned silk stockings. If the troops considered themselves fighters for democracy, the girls were strictly mercenaries in the battle for survival. They charged the equivalent of 7d a dance, and even then they remained more aloof than the white women in Raffles. They stood well away from their partners, jerking awkwardly like badly manipulated marionettes, not quite in time with the westernised music blaring brassily from the trumpet-shaped loudspeakers perched high above each corner of the dance floor. The dances though hectic were of short duration, with only the briefest of intermissions; to the girls this was not pleasure but work, as their expressionless faces indicated.

Morris, his stomach bubbling with too much Tiger beer on top of an enormous selection of Chinese stall food, was becoming more and more angry at the distance his partner insisted on maintaining between them. He had bought an entire book of tickets, more as an insurance for the end of the evening than a love of dancing, and was beginning to fear he would run out of cash before he had a chance to get around to his ultimate intention.

"Amy" – he had already discovered that much about her – "I don't have leprosy. There's a gap between us wide enough to berth the *Nelson*. Come a bit closer."

"No, sailor. I do not like the smell of beer all the time in my face. Why must you men always have so much?" she protested.

He liked the lilting intonation of her voice which was almost Welsh. "Don't be a spoil sport. We hold girls real close at home when we dance."

"Not enough tickets for jig jig," she said. "Some men buy three, four, sometimes five books."

"Listen Amy, don't go away. Me get more tickets," he said lapsing into pidgin English in the belief that it would make him better understood. She moved away, indifferent, to the chairs lining the perimeter of the timber oblong. If he returned with more tickets she would continue to dance with him; if not there were plenty of others willing to throw their money away.

Morris scrambled down the stairs to a nearby bar where his oppo Dusty Miller was staring morosely at a line of empty, sweating beer bottles.

"Dusty, sub me for twenty dollars. You know I've got a load of back pay piled up aboard."

"Not so much you can throw it away on a Chinkie bint. You don't even get within a nob's length of her. If you're feeling randy, why not join the other lads in the knocking shop?"

"First, she's not a Chink, Dusty, she's half English. Her old man is a sergeant in the army."

"Pity he isn't here to keep an eye on her."

"He was posted back to Blighty before the war started, but she's certain he'll come back."

"No soap, Isaac, I'm not throwing good money down the scuppers."

Morris's voice took on a pleading note. "Look, Dusty, I've been around long enough to know when I'm on to a promise. Stake me till I have a word with Jimmy-the-One, and you've got my tot for the next three days."

The promise of extra rum was enough to make Miller unbutton the purse attached to the waistband of his belt and produce the necessary note. "Like pissing to leeward, you never get your own back. Those bints are all prick teasers." Nevertheless, he handed over the money.

Morris purchased more tickets and waved them in front of the girl. "Plenty more where that came from, but no more of this arm's length stuff."

As they danced he pulled her roughly towards him, hoping she would feel the hardness beneath the buttoned-up fly of his trousers, but if she could she remained expressionless, which only made her more desirable. The colour of a person's skin never entered into his thinking; he automatically accepted that abroad white women were wardroom only; in any case, the girl's elfin features struck him as being much better than the horsey-looking Europeans he had so far seen. She reminded him of Dorothy Lamour in "The Road to Singapore" which he had seen in Calcutta, and a distinct improvement on the gutting girls in Grimsby who had been so generous with their knee-tremblers when he was a trawler-man.

At midnight precisely the music stopped, and as the National Anthem blared out in quick time, everyone stood to attention. As the last note died away, Amy was already scampering down the stairs with the other dancers and heading towards the long row of rickshaws where patient amahs were waiting to escort their charges home. There was a sudden transformation in Amy's movements; the uncoordinated jerking which had marked her dancing was replaced by a gazelle-like grace.

As the rickshaw, hauled by a thin-legged coolie, disappeared in the mêlée of departing dancers, Morris yelled, "See you tomorrow, Amy."

If she heard she showed no sign, for her eyes remained focussed on the coolie's heaving shoulders. As the rickshaw threaded its way through a maze of narrow streets, Amy considered the bleak future that lay ahead; something she did every night. Anywhere else she would probably be able to pass herself off as a European, but in Singapore she would never shed the taint of mixed blood. As a class they were unacceptable to the whites, Chinese and Malays. A few escaped by marrying white drop-outs who had succumbed to the bottle, or a garrison soldier as her father had been. It was the highest they could aspire to, for the white half of them was totally predominant, so that they often talked of an England they had never seen as home. It was a torment made all the more agonising by the knowledge that the whites they sought to emulate eschewed all responsibility for a situation they were responsible for creating. It was only at The Happy World that she dressed as a dancer; elsewhere she wore the clothes of a real lady. The Happy World was purgatory to her.

She thought of the sailor who was just the same as the others; all he wanted was to treat her like Lavender Street trash. If she saw him again she would show him a photograph of her father in uniform.

Chalkie White sat in a smoke-laden bar surrounded by empty bottles and imprisoned in a crysalis of misery from which he would never emerge, and deaf to the revelry going on around him. Some sailors were singing at the tops of their voices to the tune of "The Vicar of Bray", a bawdy song that was a mess deck favourite:

> Two tom cats, by the fireside sat,
> In between was a bucket of charcoal,
> Said one tom cat to the other tom cat
> Let's charcoal each other's arseholes . . .
> So one took a lump and the other took a lump
> And they charcoaled each other's arseholes.

White, who had sung the words with great gusto many times in the past, now found the words banal and extremely childish. Earlier he had gone with some of his shipmates to a brothel, which they had been assured was perfectly safe, and he had paid the Chinese girl, but had been unable to do anything in the cubicled claustrophia. He craved for love, but that was not purchasable and all he could see when he looked at the passive childlike whore was his wife's face.

He ordered more beer and fervently wished that the Japs would start something, for he had an aching desire to kill and be killed. That would teach her a lesson she wouldn't forget. Her betrayal was beyond comprehension; he had made a generous contribution on top of the normal marriage allowance, had remained reasonably faithful and never missed writing. Now he had nothing to show for it. It just wasn't fair. Some of his shipmates treated their old women like dirt, dipping their wick at every opportunity and never sending an extra penny home. Yet their wives remained as steady as a battlewagon in a calm sea.

He wondered why he wasn't drunk. He paid for his drink and staggered out into the street where he was violently sick. An open sports car driven by a young man with two girls in the back, narrowly missed him.

The man yelled, "You drunken bastard, and you've got the nerve to ask why you're ostracised and the best places are out of bounds."

White felt like explaining that it wasn't the drink, but decided it just wasn't worth the effort. No one would listen, let alone understand. He staggered to a rickshaw. "Keppel Harbour. *Grey Seal.*" It was now his only home.

Carnac sat in the rear of the Rolls Royce open Continental Phantom 11 wedged between Mrs Jardine and Jo. He watched Mr Jardine remove his black tie, then loosen his collar and belch contentedly.

He had never experienced such mechanical luxury before, although he had read about a similar model which had been ordered by an Indian prince who wished to add it to his collection of classic cars. The body and wings were a delicate shade of saxe blue which had been coated with an artificial pearl lacquer produced by finely grinding down herring scales which made it actually shimmer. The interior woodwork was sycamore, and the seats the softest calf hide.

"It's a wonderful car, Mr Jardine," he called out. "I've read about this model in a magazine but never dreamed I'd ride in one."

"Had it custom built and shipped out. Needed certain modifications for the climate. It'll have to see me through. Can't afford a replacement, especially now they're talking of increasing income tax."

The sub-lieutenant thought that wouldn't be such a bad idea; at least it would put Singapore on a greater parity with England where tax had reached an almost penal level. But judging from what Jo had told him earlier of the indignation it had aroused in the Letters column of *The Straits Times*, it was legislation that would not get very far. At present, only eight per cent tax was paid on incomes above £2,400 a year and higher, and that was still considered exorbitant. Many felt they were fully entitled to enjoy the boom; no one had worried unduly about the depression in the thirties when rubber had slid from 34 cents a pound to 4.9.

Mr Jardine's voice interrupted his thoughts. "Don't get the idea that I think I'm some Hollywood film star, Terence. I'm a hard-headed businessman, and the car is a symbol. It commands respect and attention, and when I turn up for a meeting people know it's a waste of time bartering with me. I state my terms and this car tells everyone they can take them or leave them."

He wondered whether Mrs Jardine was aware that one of his hands held Jo's while the other was resting gently on her thigh. So far she had made no attempt to curb him, and he felt encouraged to become a little more adventurous. She rested her mouth close to his ear and whispered, "Not now. Wait till we get home. Daddy might be watching."

She was unaware that her father was too absorbed in thinking ahead to bother to observe what was going on behind him. He had to admit, if only to himself, he would be immensely relieved to see her safely off his hands and settled. One of his closest friends had hinted, none too subtly, that Jo was playing fast and loose with a couple of fellows from the swimming club who were not exactly admirable types. He had hastily added, so as not to offend him, that he was sure it was harmless and she was just being a little hotheaded.

Unfortunately, he had managed to give the impression that he had got his extremities mixed. While he had no objection to his daughter having a little innocent fun, he had no desire to stand with a twelve-bore prodding an unsuitable and unwelcomed son-in-law up the aisle of St Andrew's. She really did worry him at times; although she shouldn't have a care in the world there were occasions when he suspected she was unhappy. And she could be so scathing about the established order of things. There simply wasn't room for rebels in the European community, and he did not want her to learn it the hard way.

He had tried to discuss it with his wife but she refused to entertain such thoughts, although he believed she secretly shared them. She had said, "We must do our utmost to see that she meets a thoroughly acceptable young man, although that is a bit difficult at the moment." And that was where the matter had rested, for neither had the courage to raise it with Jo who was quite capable of storming off and doing the one thing they dreaded.

Having heard something of the young officer's background, and provided Jo liked him, Mr Jardine had decided he would be eminently suitable as a prospective son-in-law. It was, he knew, rushing things, but in these unsettled times it wasn't a bad thing to contemplate the future. He would not be in his present position if he had not planned his business ventures well ahead. It was a fact that had to be recognised: Singapore did not possess many eligible bachelors, most of them were a trifle raffish and couldn't earn a decent living back home, while those who were acceptable had already been earmarked. It had always been his intention to send Jo to England to finish her education and then work in his London Office and be introduced to the right people. Who knows, she might have made a really worthwhile catch. Money opened a lot of doors back home. But the war in Europe had scotched that plan, and Jo was stuck in Singapore for the duration now. He dare not risk sending her to the bombings and blackout, or even worse, invasion. He would, however, have to have a word with Mrs Jardine and get her to whisper a discreet word of warning in Jo's ears that she was not to do anything foolish with the young man; there had to be some firm guarantee for the future before that.

Undeterred by Jo's own whispered plea, Carnac's hand moved until it was resting against the mound between her legs. He could feel the soft fount of hair and realised she had nothing on beneath the dress. He began a gentle stroking movement. Mrs Jardine began to snore.

The syce stared straight ahead into the headlamps as they illuminated the darkened Bukit Timah Road, the peak of his grey cap pulled down over his eyes like a guardsman's. He had driven Mr Jardine long enough to know that survival depended on ignoring what went on in the back of tuan's Rolls.

Without pre-warning, the Rolls swung off the road and swept under a wide, curved archway bearing a timber sign on which was burned in dark letters Cotswold Cottage. The syce pumped the horn which emitted a trumpet blast announcing the master's home coming. The beams of the headlamps illuminated vast trees which canopied the drive and the multi-coloured flowers and shrubs at their base. The sound of the horn set up a fierce chattering in the branches, and some monkeys, their eyes caught in the lights, scampered across the road.

Carnac removed his hand and gazed out of the window; the drive seemed unending. If this was a cottage, he wondered what the approach to a house was like.

The car crunched into a semi-circle of white pebble and halted outside a rambling house built in mock-Tudor style, which could have been lifted bodily from a Surrey stockbroker belt, except that it was surrounded on three sides by covered verandas. Standing at the entrance were three or four white-uniformed houseboys.

Mr Jardine said, "Shall I tell the syce to hang on, Terence, or would you prefer to stay the night?"

"I couldn't put you to all that trouble, Sir."

"No trouble at all. Place is full of empty rooms. Anyway, the syce will be grateful for an early night. Gather he's got a bit of fluff in the compound at the back of the house, but I'm the three monkeys where that kind of thing is concerned."

Once inside, the house abandoned all pretensions to alien architecture; the climate dictated how the occupants should live. The floors, like much of the furniture, was made of

Burmese teak to offset the voracious appetite of the white ants. The chairs were white rattan and covered with chintzy cushions and several had extending foot rests. The walls were white plaster for coolness and lined with gharishly coloured prints of famous Scottish and English golf courses, and line drawings of vintage cars. In the centre of the far wall was a fire place complete with inglenook and piled high with ornamental logs. Above the mantel was a coloured photograph of the King in Admiral of the Fleet uniform, and the Queen in a flowing gown with a train that covered several feet of the carpet on which they posed. Fans revolved overhead dispersing the sullen air.

Mr Jardine bellowed something to Chang the Chinese headboy who appeared with a trolley filled with bottles and a large bucket of ice. They sat drinking for half an hour or more, until Mr Jardine got up stiffly, stifled a yawn, and said, "Bed for me. Heavy day ahead." His wife dutifully rose saying, "Chang will show you to your room, Terence, whenever you are ready. Don't stay up too late, Jo darling. Must have your beauty sleep." She made it sound like a command instead of a trite remark.

The young couple sat side by side on a long cushioned settee, and Carnac promptly resumed the explorations he had started in the car, and when he encountered no resistance and remembering her whispered words, was encouraged to go further. He kissed her firmly on the mouth and felt her tongue, hot and moist, probing deeply into his. His right hand began fumbling clumsily with the eye hooks at the back of her dress until she said, "You're all thumbs. Better leave it to me; you're making a right mess of things." She let the dress fall down to her waist and as her bare breasts lay exposed he realised the dress had a built-in support. He caressed the small dark nipples until they became hard acorns, then took them into his mouth.

She pushed him away and pulled up her dress, like a girl caught by a peeping tom. "One of the boys could come in, then it would be all over the servants' quarters. You'd better go up."

As soon as she had re-arranged her dress she called for Chang who showed Carnac to his room. He was bitterly disappointed that he had got so close to what had been occupying his thoughts all evening. He hoped she wasn't just another girl who worked a bloke up and then left him feeling frustrated. Inside the mosquito net a pair of freshly laundered pyjamas lay on the pillow. He showered in the adjoining bathroom, then lay on the bed, his hands behind his head, listening to the sough of the wind in the palms and the orchestration of the insects in the lawn. The waves brushing the nearby seashore sounded like muffled drums. In the total darkness he experienced a serenity he had forgotten existed.

He heard her lowered voice cautioning silence as her fingers fumbled with the tapes of the mosquito net and as her naked body, scented with toilet water, sidled into the bed beside him, she whispered, "Don't you dare let me fall asleep. There would be all hell to pay if I was found in here in the morning."

As they resumed their love making he murmured, "I wasn't expecting this, Jo. I'm not at all prepared."

She sat up and said scoldingly, "I should hope *not*. I would be offended if you had been. I don't like to be taken for granted. But don't worry, the girls out here learn at a very early age not to take chances."

She slid down the sheets to the cleft in his loins and her tongue aroused him to tumescence, then guided him into her with a skill that suggested familiarity. When they both lay back exhausted, she giggled and said, "Beats all the Sydney rock oysters."

They made love repeatedly throughout the night as only the young can, and when he was awakened by a shaft of sunlight beaming through the shuttered windows he realised he was alone.

He breakfasted with Mr Jardine on one of the verandas where his host, despite the already oppressive heat, tucked into bacon and sausages and fried eggs. Like the imitation beams fronting the house, the traditional English breakfast was another reminder of home. Neither Mrs Jardine nor Jo it seemed put in an appearance till just before noon.

Jardine escorted him to the waiting car. "If you're free one weekend, I'll pick you up and take you to the Sea View Hotel. Something you can't afford to miss. It's become something of a ritual among us."

As he leaned back on the plush upholstery, Carnac relived

the night and realised there was no other person for him but Jo; he was going to like Singapore. In his contentment, it did not occur to him that Jo was remarkably precocious and experienced for someone so young, and a little too eager.

Chapter 4

Commander Paton sat on a hard-back chair in the crowded conference room of the General Headquarters which Air Chief-Marshal Sir Robert Brooke-Popham, Commander-in-Chief Far East, had established near the naval base on the northern side of the island. It seemed an inappropriate place as it was some fifteen miles away from the RAF and Army Headquarters at Ford Canning, and only served to underline the rivalry which existed between the three services which worked together like hounds following individual scents.

Paton had been ordered to attend the conference which was aimed at giving newcomers to the island a detailed briefing on future strategy in the unlikely event, it was stressed, of an attack. He had listened intently for more than an hour, but the humidity in the overcrowded room made concentration difficult and he felt as though he was trying to breathe through wet cotton wool. He glanced around and saw that he was not the only one who was struggling against the temptation to doze off. Sir Robert, sitting at a raised table with General Percival on one side and Rear-Admiral Spooner on the other, had given up the battle and was snoring gently with only a perceptible flutter of his lips which made his straggling red moustache quiver like a leaf in a gentle draught. Paton had heard that he had a fatal propensity for nodding off at all times of the day, even over dinner; it was a weakness which was readily seized upon by his critics at crucial discussions to pass decisions he would otherwise have opposed, so that when he awoke he found he was faced with a *fait accompli* because he could hardly say he had been asleep. He was, Paton conceded, a far from ideal choice to conduct the defence of Malaya and his appointment could only be construed as a further indication that no one seriously contemplated war. Sir Robert, a tall gangling man of 63, had retired from the RAF in 1936 to become Governor of Kenya, but had been recalled to service and now commanded Malaya, Burma and the Bay of Bengal. In the First War, he had been a pioneer aviator and the first man to fire a gun from an aircraft. His denigrators said his concept of war had never progressed beyond that era. Incredibly his command did not embrace the Royal Navy, which some said was ludicrous and others just as well. The more cynical said he was the ideal man to control the navy, having spent most of his career entirely at sea.

Lieutenant-General Arthur Ernest Percival who sat beside him pretending not to notice he was asleep, was a rabbit-toothed man whose thin arms protruded like broomsticks from the neatly rolled sleeves of his tunic; he commanded the 85,000 Indian, British and Australian troops in Malaya and Singapore. No one questioned his personal bravery for his tunic bore the ribbons of the DSO and Bar, the MC and Croix de Guerre, but he was a colourless individual totally lacking in charisma. Although he had proved his ability at waging war on staff college paper, he now seemed totally out of his depth in an active command. He vacilated to a depressing degree, and although he saw dangers when they were pointed out to him, he immediately closed his eyes for fear of making any decision which might lower the morale of the civilian population. The need to maintain the spirits of the people had been drummed into him by the Governor, Sir Shenton Thomas, who saw it as the number one priority, until it had become his overriding consideration.

It was the third conference Paton had attended since his arrival two weeks ago, as many others present had, but no one was excused on that ground so that at each successive briefing the audience grew larger and larger. The same ground was covered with monotonous regularity like a contested strip of Flanders' mud in World War I, until familiarity had begun to breed despondency if not contempt. The optimism which prevailed made the complacency that pervaded the island understandable.

If one really wanted to know what the officers who would

have to do the actual fighting felt, one had to go to Raffles or the Cathay Restaurant for a realistic appraisal, for only when out of the hearing of their commanders did they feel free to express their views without fear of being severely reprimanded for being defeatist. Paton had heard many officers complain that airfields on the mainland had been constructed in areas where there was no hope of defending them. The pilots in return bitterly protested that all the aircraft they possessed were obsolete, yet Brooke-Popham stubbornly insisted that the tubby Brewster Buffalo fighters, which the men who flew them described as death traps, were more than a match for any Japanese fighters. It was all part of a calculated policy of denigration; Japanese pilots were myopic men who wore corrective glasses, couldn't fly at night or shoot straight. The same applied to the soldiers.

Paton had listened appalled when one veteran army officer at the Cathay had described attending a meeting when Colonel G. T. Ward, an expert on the Japanese army, had lectured officers of the Singapore garrison and warned them that contrary to what they had been told the Japanese army was a first-rate fighting machine whose men were supremely fit, and who could move by night or day, and for whom the jungle had no fears. It was fatal to underestimate them for they were fanatics who would rather die than be captured. They had, he stressed, a mission to fulfill.

At the conclusion of his talk he had been roundly rebuked for being defeatist by the then General Officer Commanding, Major General L. E. Bond who had stood up and said, "This is far from the truth and is only his opinion."

When the speaker had protested he was right, Bond had told him that such talk was bad for the island's morale and he had adopted the same attitude to Ward's warning of a flourishing spy network.

When Percival had replaced Bond, those who had heeded Ward's warnings had hoped for an improvement, but he had adopted exactly the same ostrich-like attitude, so that when Brigadier Ivan Simson was sent out with instructions from the War Office to improve the fixed defences he had encountered a wall of indifference when, having toured the entire country, he had stressed how ill-prepared it was: the troops up country were abysmally ignorant of how to deal with tanks and pamphlets concerning vital information about defensive measures which had been sent out months earlier still lay in neat bundles at military headquarters. Further, when he had presented proposals for the installation of anti-tank obstacles, the setting up of defensive positions, the laying of minefields, the recruitment of civilian labour and contingency plans for a policy of demolition, Percival had not approved. Apart from being convinced that tanks would never be used, he saw the implementation of such plans as extremely damaging to morale, his number one priority.

As nothing remained confidential for very long in Singapore, such clashes were openly discussed in the clubs and bars with conflicting results. Whilst the civilians saw Percival's negative attitude as an assurance that life should continue as before, it created among servicemen the one thing Percival feared most.

It was understandable, therefore, that the regular conferences were viewed with mounting cynicism.

This particular briefing was, however, different to the others Paton had attended, for it was graced by the Governor, Sir Shenton Thomas, and Sir Alfred Duff Cooper who had been sent out as Churchill's Special Envoy to co-ordinate civil activities. Paton had been told by Kate, who had interviewed them both, that the two men were incapable of working together in harmony. No two men could have been more dissimilar; Duff Cooper was a short, dapper, wily politician with a brilliant incisive brain that was capable of grasping the most complex problems and reaching swift decisions, and who did not suffer fools gladly or silently. Unfortunately, he let it be known that the Governor and Brooke-Popham both fell into that category. It was common knowledge that he was planning to have Brooke-Popham replaced and was using his personal friendship with Churchill to achieve his object.

Now the three men sat near each other to convey an impression of common purpose, but even the suffocating heat of the conference room could not conceal the frostiness which existed between them.

Sir Shenton, the son of a Cambridge vicar, was in his sixties and should have been relieved, but his term of office had been extended when war broke out in Europe. Paton who had met him briefly at an official function, had found him an amiable man who cut a striking figure in his white uniform and plumed helmet; the perfect figurehead. But he had a lack-lustre personality and some said his brain had been dulled by too many years in the tropics. His concern for the welfare of the native population was genuine and heart warming, although Paton feared he was too preoccupied with Singapore's role as a dollar earner to the exclusion of everything else. Nothing must be allowed that would alter the status quo.

Duff Cooper found him a ditherer who was too easily influenced by the last person he spoke to and, tact not being one of his strongest qualities, made little effort to keep his opinions to himself. Although he had been told by Churchill that the war was not expected to extend to the Far East, he nevertheless believed in being prepared for such an eventuality, but he had found that many of those closest to the Governor were openly anti-military with a tendency to encourage over optimism.

Unfortunately, Sir Shenton was only too willing to listen to them. His marked animosity towards the politician was due to a large extent to the firmly held belief that the unwelcome envoy was trying to usurp some of his authority, and he made this clear when he had declined to meet him and his celebrated wife, Lady Diana, when they arrived in Singapore. Since then their relationship had deteriorated sharply.

Paton tried to cast all this from his thoughts and concentrate on the soporifics he had heard so many times before, as if the speakers believed that sheer repetition would give them validity.

Captain John Hewitt, a young officer whom Paton had got to know quite well, having arrived in the convoy which his trawlers had escorted, and who seemed to be a mine of information where the latest row was concerned, leaned towards Paton and whispered, "I hope to Christ the navy's right when it predicts any attack will come from the sea. If it doesn't we'll be up shit creek without a paddle. Despite all the pleading, nothing has yet been done to repel a possible attack down the mainland. Just positioning thousands of men there with no co-ordinated plan of action is about as effective as sticking pins in a map, which they excel at. If only those silly old buffers would stop squabbling among themselves just long enough to read the writing on the wall!"

The voice of the latest speaker droned on like a blue bottle trapped against a pane of glass, stressing that the mere presence of so many troops was an effective deterrent to any potential aggressor. "As we have witnessed, the Japanese cannot even defeat the Chinese army which is little more than a rabble in arms. They more than have their hands full without looking towards Singapore . . . "

The captain said, "Silly arse. Can't he see they're using it as a training ground for their so called short-sighted, can't-shoot-straight troops?" As he spoke Paton saw him put his thumbs to his ears and waggle his fingers like antennae in some secret signal to a fellow officer seated a few rows away.

Brooke-Popham woke up, puffed noisily, and said with great emphasis, "There are clear indications that Japan does not know which way to turn. Tojo is scratching his head."

The conference dragged on to a merciful close and there was an audible sound of wet cloth being detached from wood as the weary, sweat-soaked audience rose from their seats and stretched their cramp-stiffened legs.

The captain said, "Come and join me for a drink, Commander. I need to get the taste of bilge from my mouth."

Paton accepted, thinking how depressing it was that so many young officers were so openly critical, but their attitude was understandable even if not pardonable; they were the ones who would be called upon to fight and die if trouble did come, yet no one in authority seemed to care. For himself, he disliked such open criticism; it went against everything that had been instilled in him since his cadet days at Dartmouth. There he had been taught to accept orders without question and put his trust in his superiors, but it was difficult for young men who had not experienced that training to remain silent if the men commanding seemed singularly lacking in the qualities demanded by their position. He had encountered a similar attitude from Phelp when he had first joined *Grey Seal*, and it was only action and the guidance he had been able to give that had made him alter his view. If Singapore was attacked he had no doubt that the young officers who were so critical would rise to the occasion, as history had so often recorded, and fight to the last round; but would it all be to no avail because of the dilatory attitude adopted by those who had been entrusted with the task of commanding the battle? Bravery had not been enough in so many theatres of the war so far, but the seemingly endless routs would have to be halted some time, or defeat was inevitable.

Over their drinks, Paton asked Hewitt what was the meaning behind the signal he had transmitted. The young captain laughed and said, "It's the latest joke that's going the rounds of the mess. It's about an officer cadet who did it when his class was lectured to by a brigadier who should have been put out to grass years before. The brass-hat spotted it and wanted to know what it signified, and the cadet described how an army of ants were moving a ball of dung up a steep incline when it became in imminent danger of rolling back, and the chief ant who was watching the operation began to work his feelers feverishly. 'Now to you, general, that may not mean a thing, but to a million ants it means, for God's sake stop that bullshit.'"

Against his better instincts Paton could not refrain from smiling. "It's a good joke, but I'm not at all sure that we should be telling such stories. Denigration is a bit like rising damp; once it's started it's awfully difficult to halt."

"I know it goes against the grain for you professionals, Sir, to hear amateurs being so bolshie, but you must remember we were brought up in an age when our fathers constantly reminded us that war was too serious to be left to the generals. We laughed at it when kids, now it seems true. Honestly, it's a bloody disgrace the way everyone seems to be pulling in opposite directions. We volunteered, or were conscripted, to win the ruddy war, not stand back and see old men determined to achieve the opposite. Naturally we never express our innermost thoughts to our men, but they aren't blind or daft. They're prepared to fight and die for London, Glasgow and Manchester – Delhi too for that matter – but not to preserve a way of life they have no hope or wish to share. They see people scoffing and drinking to excess in places that are out of bounds to them, while the women react as if they're about to be raped whenever a soldier passes."

71

Paton knew that much of what he said was true, for he had been told by Kate of the regular off-the-record briefings at which correspondents were invited to ask questions, which they did with alacrity, and although the island's British controlled newspapers were discreet in what they published there was no such reticence on the part of the *Herald* which readily seized upon anything that would highlight differences of opinion among the services and the strained relations between them and the civil administration. It was difficult, therefore, to accuse any officer or man of disloyalty when the most popular newspaper among the forces was a blatantly anti-British one which delighted in headlining the continuing follies.

Paton recalled the invitation from Jardine, the bellicose rubber trader, to play some cricket if the opportunity presented itself and decided that he would go out of his way to volunteer, for he remembered that Sir Shenton was a talented player himself who loved nothing better than to turn out for the Singapore Club. It was a practical illustration of his philosophy that life should continue in the same untramelled way. It would provide a wonderful opportunity to pass on, in the most tactful way, the feelings of so many of the men in Singapore. The battle of Waterloo, he reminded himself, was said to have been won on the playing-fields of Eton. Perhaps the future of the island could be decided on the padang overlooking the sea.

The drinking session was short and relatively abstemious, and within a short time it broke up with people drifting back to their units, airfields or ships. The audience no doubt were anxious not to be guilty of the over-indulgence they found so reprehensible among the civilians, although they secretly accepted that come sundown they too would be filling the bars and clubs.

Paton walked back to *Grey Seal*, now moored alongside with the other trawlers at the naval base on the Johore Strait, the base on which so many hopes were pinned. It was certainly an impressive achievement, made all the more remarkable by the fact that it had been a political shuttlecock since it was first envisaged in 1925. Progress had been stuttering, first slowed by the economic depression, then actually halted by Ramsey Macdonald who wanted it abandoned on the altar of pacifism. Eventually it had been completed at a cost of £60 million and it sprawled over an area of one-and-a-half square miles with 22 miles of deep-sea anchorage. Millions of tons of earth had been quarried and large areas of swamp land reclaimed to provide underground stores, ammunition dumps, workshops and dockyard facilities. The base itself, encircled by high walls and massive iron gates, was a self-contained town, veined with streets lined with neat bungalows and houses. The Fleet Shore Accommodation alone was capable of housing 3,000 sailors when their ships were being refitted or repaired. The King George VI graving dock was one of the largest in the world, while the floating dock which had been towed out from England at a cost of £250,000 was capable of taking the Queen Mary. There were churches for all denominations, open air cinemas, canteens, and no less than seventeen football pitches. Enough food had been stockpiled to feed the entire island for months, and the dockside was lined with towering cranes, one so powerful it could lift the 500-ton gun turret of a battleship, while the oil tanks held enough to refuel every ship in the Royal Navy. It had finally been opened with great ceremony by Sir Shenton Thomas in 1938 and hailed as the Gibraltar of the East.

But it was on the big guns which bristled along the coastline that everyone relied to defeat a potential enemy. The Changi Fire Command to the east consisted of three 15-inch guns, three 9.2-inch guns, and eight 6-inch. In the south west the Faber Fire Command had two 15-inch, three 9.2-inch, and ten 6-inch. They were equipped with sophisticated range finders and an elaborate fire control system which enabled them to cover east and west entrances to the base, Keppel Harbour, and the commercial heart of Singapore. Just along the coastline was the vital Johore Causeway which linked the island to the mainland and over which trundled a non-stop stream of rail and road traffic delivering essential tin and rubber to the waiting ships. Although the traverse of the big guns was limited, they *could* fire inland.

Paton experienced a feeling of comforting relief when he saw their gaping barrels like yawning mouths ready to belch fire. With their enormous range they could pin down any army that attacked from the mainland. Viewing the base he felt his confidence restored. It was like having a concrete battle fleet anchored ashore; no invasion fleet could get within landing distance before it was blown out of the water. The knowledge went a long way towards dissipating the criticisms he had heard at the conference.

As he crossed the gangway he saluted the quarterdeck, and Jolson, who had adopted his customary role of additional quartermaster, wagged his tail in greeting. Paton's eyes strayed up to the flag locker at the rear of the bridge anticipating what he feared to see. Chalkie White was sitting alone and inconsolable; probably the only man in Singapore who did not give a damn whether or not the island was defendable. Paton paused momentarily, undecided whether to go up and attempt to ease the grief that gnawed at White's insides like a maggot in a wind fallen apple. But he continued his way to his cabin knowing that no words he could utter would have the slightest effect. White's recent request for compassionate leave which Paton had argued with fervour and tenacity, stressing his long stint of active service, had been turned down flatly; he had been told that there was no finer place than Singapore for a man to get over a marriage problem. The trouble was that White showed no inclination to drown his sorrows in drink or with visits to Lavender Street. He was only too willing to brood aboard and stand watch for anyone who wanted to go ashore, and no one took more advantage of his generosity than Morris who was firmly convinced that if there was such a place as heaven it couldn't be better than The Happy World where his personal angel, in the form of Amy, was at last showing that it wasn't just his money she was after. Not that he wasn't sorry for White – he was, for he was a shipmate, but it was an unwritten law of the mess deck that you did not interefere with a man's private misery unless he asked, and Chalkie had made it clear to everyone not to poke their noses into what did not concern them.

With that Morris wholeheartedly agreed, for only recently he had discovered the importance of privacy; his friendship with Amy had resulted in endless leg pulling about the tragic change in his way of life. They ribbed him about coming back aboard sober, and the way he steered clear of the red light area and never fell foul of the shore patrols. He was not, they lamented, a shadow of the man he once was.

He had wondered what they would say if they knew he had even got into the habit of having afternoon tea with her in a sedate tea room where they ate refrigerated pastries with fancy forks. Not that they would, he had assured himself; it was the last place they would venture into. On reflection, he had decided that he didn't really care for they would get the shock of their lives seeing Amy all togged up in clothes that would prove she was a cut above the other girls at The Happy World. That is if they even recognised her.

Paton thumbed through the pile of signals which had been delivered aboard, but none of them directly concerned *Grey Seal*; they were repeated for information only. Although the ship's company were revelling in the idleness, he wished he could get some sea time in, but since the group had moved to the base the trawlers had remained tied up. *Grey Seal* had been painted from stem to stern, her decks and steel work chipped clear of rust flakes, her whalers and Carley floats checked and rechecked, and gunnery practice carried out every morning, until the stage had been reached when Phelp and Tiger Read were actually looking for jobs to keep the hands occupied. So it was just as well to grant shore leave as soon as sunset was piped and the ensign lowered.

He himself was becoming a trifle bored with the endless round of parties, and had it not been for the pleasure he derived from Kate's company he would have declined some of them. Which reminded him that they had been invited to the exclusive Cricket Club the coming Sunday. That at least would provide him with the opportunity to fix up a game. He wondered if White played; he must ask him. It might prove to be the tonic he needed. Just as important, there was also the possibility of meeting the Governor.

He washed from a jug of tepid water, then knocked on the wardroom door and waited to be invited in. Carnac and Phelp sat shirtless playing cribbage and cursing as the cards stuck together in the sweaty heat.

"How did the conference go, Sir?" enquired Phelp.

"It was depressingly predictable, Number One. Nothing for us. It seems we'll remain alongside until the weight of the barnacles sinks us."

Carnac picked up his box and began pegging his score.

"Fifteen two, fifteen four, fifteen, six, and three makes ten, and one for his knob." Then in answer to his captain he said, "Can't say the thought of that fills me with gloom, Sir. I'm quite happy to see the war out here."

Phelp laughed. "Better watch yourself, Sub. Before you know it that Rolls will be flying white ribbons from its bonnet."

The sub-lieutenant flushed and said, "It's not as serious as that," though he admitted to himself that he would not object if it was – one day.

Chapter 5

Sub-Lieutenant Carnac felt as conspicuously out of place as a guest who turns up in dinner jacket only to find everyone else dressed informally. He had heard so much about the ritual of Sunday lunch at the Sea View that he had automatically assumed he was required to dress accordingly; instead he had found the planters and businessmen adorned in gaudy flower-patterned open necked shirts, shorts known as "Dhoby dodgers", long socks and sandals, while the younger women wore the scantiest of beach suits which consisted of a halter top and the briefest of shorts or skirts which barely covered the tops of their thighs and showed off their tanned legs to advantage. Jo was wearing a pinkish coloured outfit, and to Carnac she was easily the most attractive girl there, although he experienced a twinge of jealously at the thought of others seeing what he now considered his personal property.

The *pahits* kept arriving in an endless stream served by tireless waiters who were the only ones who seemed unaffected by the heat, and the quantity was only matched by their variety; there was scotch and soda, gin slings, rum and coke which seemed the latest craze, and pints of ice cold beer. Mr Jardine, "in honour of the occasion", insisted that his party should drink nothing but the best champagne, so that Carnac was left wondering what was the special event they were celebrating.

Mr Jardine seemed well intentioned, but he did wish he would not flaunt his wealth quite so openly; his own father who was an extremely successful Lloyd's broker, would have been appalled, for he had always drummed into him that ostentation was vulgar; a sin that, in his eyes, was as ungentle-manly and reprehensible as the wearing of check suits and bow ties. While Mr Jardine did not quite fit into that category, with his plain blue shirt and long white flannels, he was nevertheless what his father would categorise as "flash". Admittedly his father was a bit old-fashioned, possible *too* conventional, but he had been acutely embarrassed when the chauffeur-driven Rolls arrived to pick him up from the ship. Morris, the killick who had a way of being cheeky with-out overstepping the line, had remarked disarmingly, "Nice to see they've put the roof down, Sir. You'll be nice and cool. You can also wave to the people as you pass." That had made him blush and only when the car was well away from the base had he thought up a suitably witty retort. Next time he would ask the captain for permission to wear mufti, and casually tell Mr Jardine that it might be better if he made his own way as sailors did not always appreciate the need for the tuans to maintain appearances, even less for sub-lieutenants to travel like visiting royalty.

When he had joined *Grey Seal* as a raw snottie in his new Gieves uniform with its maroon tabs on the lapels, Paton had told him that while they might command a salute they could not command respect; that was something that had to be earned. He liked to think that he had achieved that by sharing danger and privation with the ship's company, and he did not want to risk losing it by appearing to have moved away from them by becoming some sort of playboy.

Unlike the majority of clubs, there was no strict colour bar at the Sea View and the gathering consisted of representa-tive collection of the island's wealthy: Chinese, Malays, Eura-sians – many of whom seemed to be vying with each other as to who could carry the most and costliest jewellery – British, Australian and Dutch. They all sat at numbered tables around the small wooden dance square which although open to the air was shielded by a canopy to protect them from the sun or a possible shower. Nearby an orchestra was playing the latest American and English hits.

By tradition, husbands never sat with wives and Mrs Jar-dine made it abundantly clear that Carnac should sit on one side of her with Jo on the other. In between dances he attempted to shift seats and be with Jo, but Mrs Jardine invariably patted the seat beside her in a way that had the authority of a sergeant major giving an order to a lowly private. He found her proximity rather daunting for she kept dropping hints which suggested his friendship with Jo had assumed the stage when an official engagement was in the offing. Carnac began to feel that nothing short of the entire front page of *The Straits Times* would satisfy her. From time to time Jo tried to curb her enthusiasm. "Do stop it, Mummy. Terence will feel he's got a shotgun pointing at him. Don't rush things, please." But her voice lacked conviction, so that Carnac felt that while she was not exactly encouraging her mother, she was not really trying to dissuade her. Not that he had any strong objections to asking her to become Mrs Carnac, although the thought of having Mrs Jardine as a mother-in-law was not at all appealing. He felt he had known Jo long enough now to accept that she was the only girl for him, although he was not totally blind to her more obvious flaws. He wished she was not quite so pleasure-loving, and despite her father's objections, would take a job, not necessarily for money, perhaps with one of the volunteer services. Just a gesture that would indicate a sense of purpose. But he realised she was not to blame, she was a victim of her environment. If they did marry they would naturally live in England where those faults would be easily remedied. There she would quickly discover there was no one to come rushing when you clapped your hands. But that was all in the far too distant future to worry about. First the war had to end. Apart from that major obstacle, he had not even mentioned the possibility to his parents, or discussed it with his captain whom he admired so much he could not contemplate such a momentous decision without first seeking his advice. In any case, he felt sure there was some regulation that stated junior officers had to obtain the permission of their commanding officers. The Andrew had a regulation for everything. He would have to tactfully point out all these obstacles to Mrs Jardine.

Like most of the older European women present, Mrs Jardine resisted the temptation to expose herself to a sun that could darken a complexion, preferring to wear a long-sleeved dress and a wide-brimmed straw hat festooned with artificial cherries which would not have been out of place at Henley or Ascot. The heat and the champagne had turned her face into a colour that matched the cherries, and she was becoming increasingly more voluble.

"Terence, dear, has my husband ever mentioned the great opportunities that exist for an enterprising young man here in Singapore? He doesn't want to work himself into an early grave – certainly, I don't want him to – and he's hinted more than once since you appeared on the scene how splendid it would be if he could groom someone to take over the reins. Of course, he would never contemplate such a step while dear old England needs our rubber and tin and the dollars we earn for them, but its worth thinking about. Life back home will be very precarious when all the young soldiers, sailors and airmen return and start fighting for jobs. Clive remembers the end of the last one when officers were only too grateful to take jobs as billiard markers and brush salesmen."

"I'm pretty well too pre-occupied with the present to give much thought to the future, Mrs Jardine. For all I know, I may not be around when the war ends. People do get killed you know. *Grey Seal* has lost a fair number of good men. In any case, I think my father expects me to join him."

Mrs Jardine's hand flew to her mouth. "I honestly don't think I could bear to lose Jo. She is all we have." Carnac feared she was about to burst into tears, but he was relieved when dismay turned to feigned anger. "I don't want to hear you talk any more about dying. It's very wicked of you. As long as you remain in Singapore you will be perfectly safe, and there is no earthly reason why you shouldn't until it's all over."

Carnac smiled and said, "We would all like nothing better, but I'm afraid we go where the ship is ordered."

Mrs Jardine sounded quite huffy. "Father has many influential friends here, both at Government House and among the top brass. I wouldn't put it past him to pull a few strings if you ask him nicely."

"I wouldn't dream of . . ." he began, but Jo tactfully intervened by asking him to dance.

As they moved at arm's length round the crowded square she said, "Don't take her too seriously, Terence, she's like most mothers out here; desperately anxious to make a good match. They're haunted by the fear that their daughters may end up being married to an alcholic tin or rubber man from up country. After all, there's not much to choose from here. The more acceptable bachelors are all a bit long in the tooth or are chummery boys with a reputation as rakes and a string of Chink tarts in tow. Good fun, but not to be taken seriously."

With the feel of her bare flesh under his hands he was reminded of her capacity for passionate love-making, which was something he had every wish to continue. "I don't have any objections to becoming engaged, Jo, but it isn't that easy", and he went on to explain the problems which confronted him.

She moved away and stared him straight in the eyes. "You're not looking for excuses, Terence, are you? I'm beginning to think I've made myself cheap and foolish. I thought perhaps you shared my feelings."

"I do, Jo, honestly, but let's not rush it."

"Tell me then."

"What?"

"You know damn well what I mean."

"Here! On a crowded dance floor?"

"Why not? You don't have to bellow it out."

Carnac drew her close to him and whispered, "I love you, Jo, honestly." A couple glided past and the man whistled and said, "Watch it, Jo, you're asking for a touch of the old pork dagger." His partner shushed him loudly and said, "Don't be so vulgar, darling. This isn't the club snooker room." She turned to Jo and smiled, "Sorry, Jo, his mind never rises above his fly buttons."

Carnac thought to himself: Christ, they make some of the lads on the lower deck sound positively refined.

When they returned to their table, Mr Jardine had ordered more champagne and as they sat down he said, "I'd like everyone to rise and drink a toast."

Carnac's heart began to sink, but Mr Jardine only raised his glass and said, "To victory", and everyone repeated dutifully, "To victory", adding, "and damn quickly".

It was as if the toast was a cue to the musicians who began to play the opening bars of "There'll Always be an England".

Everyone – British, American, Chinese, Malay and Dutch

– picked up the sheets of cardboard piled on each table bearing the words of the song, and began to sing what had become a second national anthem in Singapore.

They sang with gusto and conviction, somehow managing to convey to the sentimental words a threatening tone as if challenging anyone to contradict them.

As the orchestra struck the closing notes, Mr Jardine pronounced, "No Sunday is complete without that. Now for lunch."

Lunch turned out to be an enormous curry consisting of at least a dozen different dishes. There was fish, enormous prawns the size of small lobsters, eggs, beef, chicken, and an incredible variety of vegetables, some swimming in rich aromatic sauces laced with hot chillies, cardomans, coriander, cinnamon and cloves. Others were dry-fried in the Chinese style. Huge platters of saffron-flavoured rice were dotted along the centre of each table. For side dishes there were hot curry puffs and an assortment of pickles and chutneys which ranged from palate – searing limes and mangoes to cooling cucumber and tomato raetas and fresh coconut, and sardine-sized fish that crumbled like crisps. For desert there was pineapple and banana fritters, and fresh tropical fruit salad. The champagne was replaced by beer, for Mr Jardine said it was the only drink to take with curry.

The tiffin lasted until well into the afternoon and several of the men denoted their pleasure by emitting loud belches which did not draw any criticism from the ladies, and Carnac assumed it was all part of an eastern custom for he had read somewhere that what might be considered extremely rude was accepted as complimentary in some parts of the world.

Several people had retired to the long chairs stretched out on one of the verandas like recliners on the promenade deck of a cruise liner, and were snoring gently.

Mr Jardine said, "Time we headed for home and a quiet nap. You two can have a swim later. Then we'll just have time to dress for dinner at the Cricket Club. It'll be a pleasant way to round off the day."

Carnac's mind could think no further than the promised swim, for the secluded changing room near the pool had become a regular and safe place for their love-making.

A ripple of applause echoed across the padang as a batsmen made a delicate late cut that sent the ball rattling against the boundary palings, and Paton felt himself transported back to his native Hampshire and the village green where he had so often played during periods of leave. Kate dutifully joined in the clapping, but confessed to him that she would never understand the finer points of the game which seemed to abound in total contradictions. The entire contest seemed to be governed by the two words out and in, and Paton had confused her even more by humorously giving examples when they meant the entire opposite. Eventually he had given up in mock disgust and taken her into the pavilion where an illuminated panel had the basic rules of cricket set out in gilt lettering with the object of being deliberately misleading.

Adjoining the cricket square were a series of tennis courts where several couples were playing doubles. Small boys bent almost double scampered across the manicured grass to retrieve the balls. The hollow plonk of rubber on cat gut sounded soporific in contrast to the harsh click of leather on willow.

They sat together on the veranda of the pavilion surrounded by flannel-clad cricketers waiting their turn to bat; some were already padded up, others were indulging in some mild horseplay with a group of young ladies. "A corner of some foreign field that is forever England," she murmured.

"As a matter of fact that's true; if the British haven't accomplished anything else in their empire building, they've at least transported the greatest game to many parts of the globe," he said.

The medium-pace bowler at the sea end of the ground was making the ball seam and swing in the heavy atmosphere, and there was a burst of clapping at the end of his over which prompted Kate to ask, "What are they clapping now? Nothing has happened."

"He just bowled a maiden over," said Paton, which provoked a peel of laughter. "I didn't realise this game had sexual overtones, Crispin. I'll take a renewed interest in it now, but I don't think it'll ever usurp baseball in my affections. Now that really is a man's game, but you don't play it, do you?"

"Men don't, Kate, but they do at girls' schools, only they call it rounders."

They had been indulging in a gentle banter throughout the game and thoroughly enjoying it, and for the first time neither of them had even mentioned the war.

A young officer in a resplendent uniform introduced himself as one of the Governor's ADCs with an invitation to join HE's party for a drink. Paton had noticed the presence of Sir Shenton but accepted that protocol prevented him from making a personal approach, and he was extremely grateful for the opportunity to meet him and tactfully raise some of the points he had heard from disgruntled officers.

Sir Shenton, who was informally dressed in a well-pressed linen suit yet still managed to look as if he were in uniform, acknowledging Paton's salute with a brisk nod of his head said, "Admiral Spooner was telling me a little about your exploits, Commander. I thought I would hear at first hand a little about the war we are mercifully being spared." He then introduced him to Lady Thomas, who shook hands politely and said, "When we hear of what others are going through it makes us feel quite guilty, but it is not our fault that we are destined to remain on the sidelines; but as His Excellency never ceases to point out, our task here is so vital to the successful conduct of the war. Sometimes I think that is overlooked." Paton wondered if the remark was aimed at Kate whom he felt was being deliberately snubbed.

"May I introduce Miss Hollis, Your Excellency."

The Governor smiled coldly. "I'm awfully sorry, Paton, I didn't think introductions were necessary; I have met Miss Hollis on numerous occasions. I'm afraid she rather belittles our efforts here, but the sun has thickened our skins. But I realise she has a job to do. In a way our tasks are not dissimilar, we must do our utmost to increase production, just as she must increase the circulation of her newspaper. Understandably she engages in a little journalistic licence."

Kate, conscious of the harm she could do to Paton by offending the island's most distinguished personage, refused to rise to the fly and instead said, "I'm off duty today, Your Excellency. Commander Paton has been trying without success to explain the compexities of your national game."

Sir Shenton mellowed tangibly, for he was an ardent cricket

84

fan, and in his younger days had been a player of considerable talent. "It is not just a game, Miss Hollis, but more a way of life. If we conducted our affairs, as indeed we try to do, according to the laws of cricket the world would be an infinitely better place." he paused and said, almost as if to himself, "When the one great scorer comes to write against your name, He'll write not that you won or lost but how you played the game." He spoke as if he was making a formal declaration.

Lady Thomas said, "This is the first time he has been able to watch a game for goodness knows how long, but today I insisted. All work, etc."

The Governor said, "I wish I was out there myself, Paton; that wicket was made for stroke play, yet those lads do nothing but prod and probe. Did you every play?"

Paton modestly replied that he was able to turn his arm over and was a reasonable but not brilliant number four. He did not mention that in peacetime he had played for Hampshire on the odd occasion, and regularly for the Royal Navy.

As the atmosphere visibly lightened, Paton gave an accurate but rather colourless account of the war as it had affected him personally. He mentioned the boredom of the Northern Patrol in the icy waters of the northern Atlantic, the campaign in Crete and the evacuation of Dunkirk. As he spoke he was able, without appearing at all critical, to broach the subject of a possible war in the the Far East and the misgivings expressed by some servicemen.

"We may give an appearance of complacency, Commander, but I can assure you that every authority has assured us that there is no danger here, and that it is best for everyone if it is shown that it is business as usual. The slightest sign that we are worried would have disastrous consequences on the native population. I'll tell you something, providing Miss Hollis will give me a solemn undertaking not to publish it before it is officially announced?" He looked towards Kate, who replied, "You have my word, Your Excellency", and he continued, "Within a matter of days, two of our most powerful and modern battleships will be arriving in Singapore. They have been sent on the personal decision of Winston Churchill, not as an aggressive gesture but purely as a deterrent to any Japanese thoughts of extending the war to here."

Kate said, "I hope I shall be able to visit them."

"Don't worry, Miss Hollis, there will be a grand showing of the flag. Every newspaper reporter will be invited to the ships. Even that detestable *Herald*. We want to get the maximum publicity out of it."

As soon as the shadows began to lengthen over the ground, the Governor announced that it was time to leave as there was a formal dinner party at Government House which was not entirely social, but more in the way of an unofficial conference between the service chiefs and the top civil servants.

As the Governor and his lady rose, everyone on the balcony stood rigidly upright until they had left the building and got into their official car.

Darkness descended with tropical suddenness resulting in the game being drawn, and Kate and Paton went into the bar just as Mr Jardine and his party arrived. Paton noticed how tenaciously the young girl clung to Carnac's arm, almost as if she was making a public pronouncement that this particular commodity had been purchased, and no further bids would be considered. He hoped the sub was not being bulldozed into anything. He had met Jo a couple of times, and although he had to admit she was extremely attractive and had some charming points in her favour, she was rather vacuous and had too readily absorbed some of the less pleasant characteristics of the colonial. But he had no doubts that if Carnac was serious he would eventually approach him and seek his advice, then he would tell him quite blatantly that he would have to treat her as he would a stroppy rating: firmly, if necessary harshly, for that could only be to their mutual benefit.

Mr Jardine automatically assumed that they would be delighted to join his party, for he was already poised over a chitty and asking what everyone wanted. Mrs Jardine immediately button-holed Kate and began to regale her with problems she was encountering with a new servant and telling her, on the assurance that she wouldn't breath a word to anyone, that two enormous battleships were due to arrive in Singapore to show the Japs that the lion was not asleep and toothless.

As Carnac and Jo joined some of the younger set, Mr Jardine attached himself to Paton. "I had hoped to see a few overs but my siesta became a little over-extended; too much curry and champagne. Speaking of cricket, have you thought any more about turning out for us?"

Paton said, "Quite a lot. Especially as one of my ratings tells me he won a Jack Hobb's bat at school and regularly played for a club back home until he joined the navy. He would love a game, and I would be grateful too, because he's going through a rather rough patch of sea at the moment. Wife trouble."

Mr Jardine pursed his lips. "We could, as I've said, do with some fresh talent, but it could be very difficult. This place is out of bounds to ors, and you can't ask a fellow to play then banish him from the bar. Not cricket. Smacks too much of that stupid gentleman and players thing you have back home. Using different entrances and all that rubbish. No, I honestly don't think we can bend the rules to that extent. But I'd love you to turn out for us."

Paton said, "I'm afraid I'm not good enough", and left it at that.

Shortly afterwards, he politely declined an invitation to join him for a meal. He had had more than enough of Mr Jardine's company without extending it to breaking point. Apart from that, he could see that Kate was trying desperately hard not show how boring she found Mrs Jardine. Furthermore, he sensed that his presence was also inhibiting Carnac's amatory intentions.

When they had finished their dinner, Paton said to her, "Fancy a nightcap before I head back aboard?"

Kate said, "Not in the bar, Crispin. I've had enough of Singapore society for one day. Let's have one in my room. I'd like to kick my shoes off and change into something more comfortable. All this formal dress for dinner may be very uplifting, but it is also remarkably tedious."

Kate's room was spacious and overlooked the sea front. A small desk accommodated her typewriter and a row of reference books which included a dictionary, a guide to Singapore, and a telephone. An ornate brass-nobbed bed canopied by a mosquito net occupied a large proportion of the room, and against one wall was a bamboo trolley containing bottles of drink.

"Help yourself, Crispin, and look the other way whilst I change. Pour me a real dry Martini – lots of gin and just a whiff of vermouth. Back home my father says any host who can make a bottle of vermouth last a year has mastered the art."

Paton poured himself a generous measure of scotch which he topped up with water, then poured her drink. When he turned he saw that Kate was standing in front of her wardrobe wearing only pants and brassiere, and pondering on what to wear. "It wasn't feasible to keep looking the other way," he said as he handed her the drink.

"I'd have been offended if you had. While it could be considered gentlemanly, Crispin, it would hardly have been flattering. Anyway, you can see more at a swimming pool."

He gently kissed her bare shoulder, more with affection than passion. "You're a very beautiful woman, Kate, but I'm not sure we should let things develop further."

"Is that a rejection?"

"Of course not, just a little common sense. You've never even asked me if I'm married."

"The same applies to you. Like most men you've assumed I'm not because everyone refers to me as Miss Hollis."

"Are you?"

"As a matter of fact I'm not, but I won't pursue the subject with you."

"You ought to know though. There are two women who expect me to return to them, but I've been cowardly about it and left it to time to sort out."

"Do you want to stay the night, Crispin? I'm inviting you. There are no strings attached."

"I'd be lying if I said I wouldn't like to, but I'd hate for you to get hurt."

"I won't, and don't look so darned shocked. If you'd asked if I would go to bed with you that would have been perfectly all right, but when a woman suggests it a man gets all prudish and feels he has been trapped by a harlot."

She slipped into a dressing gown. "Let's not analyse it, but simply enjoy ourselves. That's all I want to do."

He awoke in the morning relieved to find that he experienced neither remorse nor a sense of betrayal. He wondered whether this was due to the fact that he was obviously not the first man to make love to her, or because of the sheer pleasure she obtained from physical sex. In peacetime he had encountered a number of promiscuous young navy wives, and although he had occasionally succumbed to their overtures he had invariably felt guilt at betraying a fellow officer; but Kate's approach was so thoroughly healthy and emancipated that he saw no reason why they should not continue to be lovers.

He felt across the bed but the space beside him was vacant, and he heard the sound of the shower and her voice called out through the open door, "Would you like to ring down for breakfast, Crispin, or perhaps you'd prefer not to be caught in *flagrante delicto*."

He laughed aloud as he recalled the Japanese reporter's story of Raffles having only one rule.

"It might be more tactful if we went down, Kate. Think of your reputation."

She laughed loudly. "When you sit down to breakfast in your uniform, Crispin, people will draw their own conclusions." She emerged from the bathroom vigorously towelling herself. "It's all yours," she said.

He lay back looking at her naked body with two whitish patches which her bra and pants had protected from the sun and felt himself become erect. He swung his feet out of bed. "A cold shower is what I need. At Dartmouth when I was a kid that's what they told us was a cure for feeling randy."

She saw his erect penis and said, "Stay there, Crispin. You look like you are on parade, standing to attention like that . . . I'd better help you stand easy."

Over breakfast she said, "Let's dispense with the need for future invitations. You just stay whenever you want to. We obviously both satisfy each other's needs."

Back aboard *Grey Seal* Paton was checking through a list of wanted stores which Phelp had drawn up, when Steward Hall entered the cabin and said that a gentleman wished to see him. "Didn't give a name, Sir. Said it was personal."

"Better show him in, Hall, and rustle up some tea."

A tall, overweight man with a florid complexion and cheeks blotched with ruptured veins that a deep tan could not entirely hide, and dressed in a neatly pressed white suit and sporting a topee, came in and extended his hand. "Superintendent Nolan, Special Detective Branch. Didn't tell your man on duty. No reason to make him jump to conclusions."

Having invited him to sit down, Paton asked, "One of my men been in trouble ashore?"

"No, Commander. I wanted to have a word with you about the American, Miss Hollis."

Paton looked puzzled, and said, "Why not talk to her yourself. I'm sure she's better placed to help. She's a very forthcoming person."

"That wouldn't be very tactful, Sir. The job of my department is to keep an eye on people we suspect of trying to undermine our efforts here."

"And Miss Hollis falls into that category?"

"To be frank, yes. I suspect she is a supporter of the Keep America out of The War lobby. Neutrality at any price. What she writes certainly indicates she is not one hundred per cent behind us."

Paton suggested that she was so outspoken in the hope that something would be done to remedy the shortcomings so apparent to visitors. "Personally I think you're aiming at the wrong target, Superintendent. If I were in your shoes I'd be looking at some of the Japanese here, especially those on the *Herald*."

"We have tabs on them, don't worry, but they are a limited danger. If the balloon goes up they'll all be interned in double quick time. We can't do that to an American though."

Paton thought it was a classic example of shutting stable doors much too late, but said aloud, "Why come to me with your suspicions?"

There was a barely concealed smirk on the detective's face. "Well, you're in a privileged position." He winked. "Don't worry. I wouldn't kick her out of bed myself. Would like the opportunity to, I must admit."

Paton spoke harshly, "Look, I've no intention of discussing my private affairs with you, Superintendent. Neither do I like your crudeness."

The policeman was completely unabashed. "I have a job

to do, and I intend doing it, Commander. If I sound offensive, that's too bad. You are a naval officer, and if you shack up with someone who has given us grounds for suspicion, then it isn't your private life any more. We're not talking about a young sensitive girl, but a mature woman who is happy to nip into bed with the first good looking officer who comes along. She may want to pump you."

Paton had taken an intense dislike to the man opposite and wondered how such a person could occupy a position of responsibility, and he found himself recalling the words of Okamoto.

"Are you suggesting that I should stop seeing her?"

"Christ, no Sir. You take whatever she offers. After all, a slice off a cut loaf is never missed. All I'd like you to do, Sir, is combine business with pleasure. You pump her, instead of the other way around. Then pass on anything you think is suspicious." He guffawed loudly. "Pump her. I like that, Commander. An unintentional pun, I assure you, but apt. You can do it two ways."

"If you weren't aboard my ship, Superintendent, I'd punch you on the bloody chin. Now if you don't mind I have ship's business to attend to."

The policeman remained unruffled. "Don't get hot under your collar. It'll get you nowhere. Lay a finger on me and I'll have you up on a court martial charge before you can say fuck. I carry a lot of weight around here, and I'm not worried about chucking it about. You'll do what *I* ask, or your name will make shit smell like lavender. I've got the ear of everyone from His Excellency down."

Paton handed him his topee and summoned Hall. "See the Superintendent over the side."

Paton was completely unconcerned about the policeman's threats; if he did draw his conduct to the attention of anyone it could hardly affect his career. Sailors were expected to have a girl in every port. but he had no wish to become involved in deceit or to have his privacy invaded by someone acting like a professional snooper looking for divorce evidence. Even more important, he had no intention of subjecting Kate to such an ordeal. He would tell her exactly what had occurred in his cabin.

His dislike for the policeman did not blind him to the fact

that he obviously did have considerable authority and backing, otherwise he would not conduct himself in such an oafish manner or with such supreme confidence.

Chapter 6

Paton stood on *Grey Seal's* bridge physically feeling the small hairs at the nape of his neck begin to prickle as he viewed through his binoculars the awesome spectacle of the battleship *Prince of Wales* and the battle cruiser *Repulse* escorted by destroyers sailing majestically along the Johore Strait towards the naval base. The decks of the two capital ships were lined fore and aft by hundreds of sailors standing stiffly to attention while the strains of "A Life on the Ocean Waves" played by the band of the royal Marines on the battleship's X-turret wafted jauntily across the glass-like surface of the water. He looked down to where his own ship's company were fallen in on the quarterdeck and forecastle ready to snap to attention as the warships were piped.

Nearly all of Singapore seemed to have turned out to welcome the ships, and the foreshore was lined with thousands of people of all nationalities cheering wildly and waving their hats, handkerchiefs and small Union Jack flags.

It was a timely arrival, for only the day before a State of Emergency had been declared, although no one could see any reason for the sudden alarm; nothing had happened to their knowledge to account for it.

Without warning, notices had been flashed on all the cinema screens ordering all troops to report to their units immediately. Similar announcements were made in the three Worlds – the Happy, New and Great – and other places of entertainment, and within a matter of minutes there had been a mass exodus from dance halls, restaurants and brothels. Understandably, the Press contingent had been anxious to find out the reason, for it had created a state of near panic in White Singapore, but to their surprise they had been asked not to report it to their newspapers as it was merely a precautionary measure and did not imply that anything serious had occurred. Even so, the presence of the warships bristling with guns acted as a soothing balm to people who had experienced a temporary fit of the jitters.

The Singapore Free Press welcomed their arrival with a headline, "Bad News for Japan", and was almost euphoric about the contribution they would make to the already impregnable fortress. The *Malaya Tribune* was even more ecstatic and hailed them as an invincible force, while the radio gave the impression that any possible threat of attack had now been removed for ever.

As *Prince of Wales* drew abeam, Tiger Read's bosun's pipe warbled the Still and the ship's company came to attention while the officers saluted. The band had now ceased playing and the bridge bugler on the battleship returned the salute with a brassy fanfare which reverberated across the separating stretch of water.

When *Repulse* came abreast, the salutes were again exchanged and they continued until the last destroyer had passed.

The 35,000-ton *Prince of Wales*, one of the navy's most modern warships, still bore the scores of her encounter with *Bismarck*, a comforting reminder to those ashore that the massive turrets housing the ten 14–inch guns were not ornamental. Although their muzzles were now tampioned, they could be removed within seconds and ready for action. Originally it had been intended to fit her with 16-inch guns, but the 1935 Naval Treaty restricted the calibre of guns aboard new battleships to 14-inch. Ironically, Japan which refused to sign it had, unknown to the Admiralty, equipped her battleships with 18-inch. On either side of the main deck were eight twin 5.25 turrets, sixty-four pom-poms known to the crew as Chicago pianos, plus numerous 40-millimetre Bofors, Oerlikons and light machine guns to deal with high and low level air attacks. She had been dubbed "Churchill's yacht" by the lower deck for she had carried the Prime Minister across the Atlantic to Placentia Bay for his historic meeting with President Roosevelt. She looked what her designer intended her to be – indestructible.

In contrast, *Repulse* was one of the navy's oldest ships, having been launched before the end of the First War, although she was still considered the most elegant ship in the Royal Navy with her classical lines and sweeping bow, and had been chosen to take the King and Queen on their pre-war visit to Canada. Her armament consisted of six 15-inch guns in twin turrets fore'ard and a single one aft, six hand operated 4-inch guns, two pom-poms, two four-barrel two pounders, and machine guns.

Amid a flurry of upper deck activity and the rattle of capstans and winches, *Prince of Wales* was berthed alongside the West Wall of the naval base, while *Repulse* was moored offshore in the stream, as if to emphasise the flagship's seniority. It was not strictly accurate; Captain W. G. Tennant of *Repulse* was the senior officer, as Admiral Sir Tom Phillips had flown ahead from Ceylon to enquire about air cover. Even so, *Prince of Wales* had led the Fleet in.

It seemed unimportant to Paton at the time.

A special platform had been erected on the quay which swarmed with dignitaries, newsreel cameramen, radio and press reporters. Looking resplendent in his official uniform was Sir Shenton Thomas, who was flanked by Air Chief-Marshal Brooke-Popham, General Percival, Air Vice-Marshal Pulford, Commander of the RAF, Duff Cooper, and Admiral Sir Geoffrey Layton who was soon to be ousted by Admiral Phillips.

An hour later, Paton was sitting in the stern sheets of one of *Repulse's* motor launches on his way to pay his respects to Captain "Bill" Tennant, known to his crew as "Dunkirk Joe", for he had been the Senior Naval Officer Ashore during the epic evacuation and had been one of the last to leave. It was there that Paton had last met him.

He found Tennant literally living like a king for he was using the quarters occupied by George VI when he visited Canada. They greeted each other with affection, for each had a high regard for the other's qualities. Tennant had been the man largely responsible for seeing the bulk of the British Army escape from France to fight again, and he recognised that his efforts ashore would have counted for nothing but for men like Paton who had repeatedly endangered their ships and men to ferry the weary soldiers back to England.* A truly modest man, as he offered Paton a drink he hastily assured him that it was not his usual custom to occupy the royal quarters; he preferred his sea cabin but had been told to expect a virtual avalanche of VIPs who wanted to see over the ship when it was opened to visitors.

He talked enthusiastically about his ship and the fine crew who manned her. She was a "guz" ship, which in naval parlance meant she came from the Devonport Division, and her men had salt in their blood. Most of them were regulars, although a number had been called back out of retirement to provide the necessary stiffening for the untried "hostilities only" ratings. Tennant exuded a calm confidence that they would give a good account of themselves in action, even though her guns had only been in action once since the outbreak of war when German bombers had attacked her at Rosyth. Prior to that the last time her big guns had fired in fury had been towards the end of the First War when she had scored a direct hit against the German cruiser *Konigsberg*. But the men were proud of their gunnery and openly boasted of the formidable rate of fire they had achieved in practice shoots.

Before leaving the ship, Paton was invited to the wardroom where he renewed acquaintance with a number of friends he had known in peacetime. Not all exuded the same confidence as their captain, although they all shared his faith in the ship, which was not only happy but efficient. They had reservations about *Prince of Wales*. For some unaccountable reason the battleship had acquired a reputation on the lower deck as a Jonah, for her short career had been blighted by misfortunes, and there was a genuine, if unfounded, belief that she had let down *Hood* in the battle with *Bismarck*. *Hood* had been the navy's pride and understandably no one could accept that she had been sunk so quickly and so easily, and a scapegoat had to be found. Unfortunately, the choice had fallen on *Prince of Wales*. Although badly damaged, she had in fact scored three hits on the pocket battleship even though there had been continuous trouble with her guns and new equipment. Eventually she had been forced to withdraw from the action.

* See *The Restless Waves*

Coupled with these misgivings was the resentment at always having to play poor relation to the more modern battleship, and the men saw further evidence of this in the way *Repulse* had been moored in midstream while the *Prince* went alongside. The crew had even got to the stage of calling their ship *HMS Anonymous*, for throughout the voyage east the censors had only allowed the Press and radio to refer to *Prince of Wales* "and other heavy units". As a result, the battleship had hogged all the headlines wherever they were halted. Tennant had even raised the matter with Captain Leach, the Prince of Wales' commanding officer, who promised to address the ship's company and explain the strategic and political reasons for the anonymity, and dispel any feelings that it had anything to do with her antiquity.

Paton knew from experience that there was always intense rivalry between ships, but this was different; he could detect a degree of hostility which was not entirely healthy. But given time he was sure it would all be ironed out as the crews of the two ships had hardly had time to get to know each other; most of the time they had been together had been spent at sea. But what Paton found most disturbing was the lack of confidence true only hinted at, in Admiral Tom Phillips, the man chosen to lead the newly formed Fleet. Paton had only met him briefly when he was Vice-Chief of Naval Staff under Admiral Sir Dudley Pound, the First Sea Lord, where he had established a well earned reputation for efficiency and as a planner, although he had not been an easy man to get on with. Because of his diminutive stature he was known throughout the navy as "Tom Thumb"; behind his back he was described as having "all brains and no body". Churchill, it was rumoured, had not been too upset to see the back of him. They had worked harmoniously together since the outbreak of war when Churchill was First Lord, and their association had blossomed into a close personal friendship. but Phillips had disagreed strongly with Churchill's policy of the strategic bombing of German cities; not on moral grounds, but in the firm conviction that it would not destroy the enemy's morale. And because they were so alike in many ways, dogmatic, iron willed and intolerant, they had reacted like similar poles, or rather Churchill had. The invitations to Chequers had ceased, and it became a business-only relationship with the Prime Minister just biding his time until a suitable opportunity arose to get rid of him. Now he had, although many felt it had been unnecessarily cruel and unfair to Phillips who had not seen action since 1917, had not been to sea since 1939, and had never commanded a capital ship. Layton, whom he was replacing, was far better qualified to do the job. Apart from his capabilities he was popular, whereas Phillips was not, lacking both personality and humour.

The views Paton heard expressed were not out-and-out criticisms but vague doubts, preceded by words such as "I wonder if...", or "Their Lordships know best, but...", and 'Between you, me and the gatepost...'. None of their apprehension, they hastened to add, had been allowed to percolate to the lower deck, but Paton, knowing the navy, felt sure that the inevitable buzz had reached it that Phillips' appointment was political.

So he was not sorry when the time came for him to return ashore; he had heard enough about the lack of confidence in men entrusted with the defence of Malaya and Singapore without the rot spreading to the navy. He hoped his fears would be dispelled when he went aboard *Prince of Wales* later in the day when the ships would be open to visitors and the Press.

When Paton stepped onto the deck of the battleship with Phelp by his side he was transported back to the navy he had forgotten existed. The brass work gleamed, the decks were spotless, the decorative rope work freshly blancoed, and the boats glistened as if for a regatta. A bugle frequently commanded attention, while a disembodied voice issued orders over the tannoy. Nothing, it seemed, could be achieved without a bugle call; it summoned cooks to the messes, boats' crews to their stations, working parties to their posts.

The upper deck was already crowded with visitors: women in their smartest dresses and hats, and men wearing their best suits and topees, walked under the huge canvas awnings as if engaged on a Sunday morning promenade. Petty officers and Marine sergeants in spotless uniforms acted as ushers as they conducted groups around the various parts of the ship where officers explained in great detail the intricacies of a certain piece of equipment or the lethal qualities of a particular gun. It was all reminiscent of a peacetime Fleet Review. Paton contrasted it with the grime and squalid conditions aboard *Grey Seal* where, with a minimum of fuss, the most complicated tasks were carried out with efficiency born of long practice, and realised to his relief that he was far happier away from the spit and bullshit than he ever could have imagined. It was as if some form of telepathy existed between him and his first lieutenant, for Phelp whispered, "Can't say I'd want to swop berths, Sir. That ruddy bugle regulates their life. I bet it sounds when someone wants to go to the heads."

Yet again *Prince of Wales* was the centre of attraction, to the deteriment of the battle cruiser, for none of the reporters saw any point in visiting a ship they could not name. Across the crowded deck, Paton caught sight of Kate with a party of reporters who were standing below the towering bulk of one of the 14-inch turrets listening to a gunnery officer talking about muzzle velocity, range, and angle of trajectory. He was surprised to observe that Okamoto was among them, and he assumed it was a deliberate piece of Press relations to invite him to see for himself what his adopted country would be up against if it decided to do anything stupid. A little further away, he saw Mr and Mrs Jardine engaged in conversation with General Percival. No doubt, he thought cynically, he was giving the Army Commander some sound advice. Carnac was with Jo who, to his surprise, was wearing the uniform of the Medical Auxilliary Service. It seemed that anyone who was anybody in Singapore had managed to get invited to the flag showing. Some, like the Jardines, seemed more preoccupied with seeing who they could meet than looking over the ship. He felt a slight tap on his shoulder and turned to see the unwelcome face of Superintendent Nolan who jerked his head in the direction of Kate and said, "I see your bosom friend has managed to wangle her way aboard, Commander." He managed to instil some sexual connotation to the word bosom. Despite the hour his breath smelled of last night's whisky which the odour of peppermint failed to hide. "but even she will be hard put to try and find something derogatory to write about. Which reminds me, Sir. You don't seem to have given much thought to my little proposition."

"As a matter of fact, I've not given any to it."

"You should. But with or without your co-operation I'm determined to expose her for what she is . . . a bloody Fifth Columnist. Frankly I can't understand how a man like you can let a bit of crumpet cloud his judgement. What she writes doesn't matter a toss to intelligent people like you and me, but it does make an impression on the uneducated rank and file, and even some raw young officers. Cyrano's restaurant in Orchard Road has become such a hot bed of gossip it's been placed out of bounds. Officers are also being discouraged from going to the Coconut Grove at Pasir Pantang, which is the centre of the American community's social life, for the same reason. So you can see I'm not a dog that barks at shadows."

Paton deliberately turned his back on the policeman and pointedly made his way towards the group she was attached to. It was, he realised, a studied snub that Nolan would not forget. But the policeman seemed to have a fixation about her loyalty, forgetting that there were others equally as critical.

He had told Kate of the first meeting with Nolan, and she had been quite blunt; she had no intention of tempering anything she wrote if she felt it needed saying and, much as she valued his friendship, she would understand if he decided that it would be better if they stopped meeting. He assured her that no threats by Nolan would have the slightest effect on him, and he had no intention of even speaking to him. Nolan was perfectly capable of acting on his own to confirm or deny any suspicions he may have. She had bridled at this, saying that it seemed to her that he himself wasn't too sure of her intentions. He had with some reluctance pointed out that perhaps it wouldn't be unwise to exercise a little discretion in some of the things she wrote, if only to make life a bit more tolerable for herself. They had come dangerously near to an out-and-out row, and wisely agreed not to mention the subject again.

When the conducted tour was completed, the anonymous voice announced over the loudspeaker system that visitors were invited to the wardroom for drinks where they would

100

be able to meet Admiral Phillips who would answer any questions the journalists might wish to ask.

Admiral Phillips, a short square-jawed pugnacious looking man with close set eyes, sat in the centre of a long table with Captain John "Trunky" Leach, who commanded the flagship. Leach's nickname derived from his largish nose and the sight of him gave Paton a feeling of renewed confidence, for the broad shouldered West Countryman was one of the navy's finest officers and certainly among its most popular. He was what men called "a sailor's sailor", thoroughly professional yet not lacking in the common touch. He still smouldered over the criticisms levelled at him, his ship and his men over the *Bismarck* encounter and was determined to make their denigrators eat their words.

In addition to being a gunnery expert, he was a superb athlete and had been the navy's squash and tennis champion and a mainstay in the ship's cricket team. His ship's company felt no sense of guilt, feeling justifiably that if their shells had not inflicted so much damage, which included the severance of a fuel pipe which left a tell-tale trail on the ocean, *Bismarck* would never have been tracked down and sunk. In their own crude expression, there was no better man to be in command, "When the shit hit the fan".

As the mess stewards dispensed pink gins and sherry among the guests, the Admiral dressed in a crisp white uniform with a clerical collar relieved only by a single row of brass buttons and a double row of medal ribbons, looked ash-grey with fatigue and close to breaking point. Only the ship's senior surgeon knew that he hardly slept and was being kept going on pills. He gave a brief outline of the purpose behind the arrival of the fleet, assuring everyone that it was not a provocative gesture but purely intended as a deterrent to *any* would-be aggressor. He spoke of the close harmony that existed between the ships of Force-Z and the high peak of efficiency attained by their guns crews, especially those of *Prince of Wales* who had achieved a record rate of fire with their big guns. While they were not looking for trouble, they were more than capable of meeting, and defeating, any force they encountered. He spoke with quiet determination without adopting a threatening tone.

101

When it came to questions, a reporter asked him if he was not worried that the fleet had no aircraft carrier accompanying it, and the Admiral explained that it had originally been intended to include the carrier *Indomitable* in the force but it had run aground when leaving Jamaica and was unable to join them. But, he stressed, he was not unduly worried; he was a firm believer that well armoured battleships with sufficient anti-aircraft guns manned by well trained crews were a match for any bombers. His personal opinion was that the Japanese were not particularly air-minded. "Her air forces, both naval and military, are of much the same quality as the Italian and markedly inferior to the Luftwaffe." And he went on to assure his audience that despite the absence of the carrier the RAF was capable of providing adequate air cover. This, he knew, was a deliberate untruth for Pulford had explained the true situation: Malaya had a totally inadequate air force, but repeated requests to Whitehall for more and better aircraft had gone unheeded. But he saw no wisdom in repeating it.

Even so, as Paton listened he realised that Admiral Phillips was too steeped in the traditions of the past to accept that times had changed; his conviction that battleships could defend themselves against determined air attacks had surely been exploded by the success bombers had had off Norway and Crete. Phillips, however, remained an unashamedly big gun man.

Paton's thoughs were interrupted by the sound of Kate's voice. "Talking of air cover, Admiral Phillips, I have recently returned from a visit to the airfield at Kota Bahru and I can't share your optimism. The Brewster Buffaloes should have been pensioned off years ago. I should know because my own country produced them and couldn't get rid of them quick enough to anybody foolish enough to want them. It's an open secret that the ones operating here needed no less than 27 modifications before they were passed as safe or battle worthy." Her remarks were greeted with laughter, and the Admiral smiled and said, "I am a sailor and can only reiterate what the Commander-in-Chief is on record as saying, namely that they are more than a match for any Japanese fighters. And he should know."

Kate was tempted to ask him if he was aware of the conditions under which the pilots and airmen were living, in the hope that something might be done about it. There was no point in telling her American readers that they were living in appalling camps, constantly wet, and eating food which the visitors to Raffles wouldn't feed to their animals. They had no influence. But before she could mention it Okamoto raised his hand and asked politely, "Am I permitted to ask any questions?"

The Admiral directed his gaze upon one of the official censors in attendance to rule out of order any questions he thought were better not answered.

"I see no objection. He has been invited in an official capacity", and to Okamoto he said, "You may not be our best friend, but I see no reason why your readers shouldn't be enlightened about the Fleet's potential, or, for that matter, purpose."

The Japanese smiled and said, "Does the Admiral not know that Japan has built up one of the largest air forces in the world with aircraft of matchless quality, whereas the entire air force in Malaya consists of 17 Hudson bombers, 34 Blenheims, 27 flying boats, four Swordfish, and five Sharks. All obsolescent."

The Admiral replied courteously, "That sounds more like a statement than a question. If you have ever read about the sinking of the Italian ships at Taranto you would not write off the Swordfish in such a contemptuous way. But I do think you should address your remarks to someone in a better position than myself to comment on our air resources.

Okamoto said "I have no wish to be alarmist, Sir, but like many who live and work here, I am anxious to see we are adequately protected in the extremely unlikely event of an attack."

Phelp whispered to Paton, "Crafty little bastard; pours poison down everyone's ear, then makes it sound as if he's genuinely concerned for their safety. Notice how those scribes gratefully accepted the information about our air force?"

The censor interrupted, "I don't see that any useful purpose will be served by repeatedly retreading that grape."

But the subject of air cover refused to be ignored, and

another questioner returned to the vulnerability of capital ships against bombers.

Phillips said, "I can only reiterate my unshaken belief that adequately armed ships with well trained guns crews *are* capable of defending themselves. Whatever anyone says *no* British battleship has yet been sunk by enemy aircraft, and heaven knows the Germans have tried their darndest. As we have against their pocket battleships. We have mounted massive air strikes, at a grievous loss in men and aircraft, but they are still afloat. Of course, there are some who think otherwise. I remember my friend Bomber Harris remarking jokingly to me, 'One day, Tom, you will be standing on a box on your bridge and your ship will be smashed to pieces by bombers and torpedo aircraft; and as she sinks your last words will be, "That was a ... great mine".' As you can see, I am quite capable of telling that story with a smile. It is I assure you not prophetic."

His remarks earned a ripple of applause and laughter, for they showed that contrary to what was said he *did* have a sense of humour and could tell a joke against himself. But more important, they underlined his supreme confidence.

Once again, Paton heard Kate's voice, this time with taunting innocence. "Can the Admiral answer one final question from me? Has he ever heard of Assistant Chief of the American Army Air Corps, General William Mitchell?"

Phillips pondered momentarily before replying. "I must confess, it's a name with which I'm not familiar."

Kate said enigmatically, "Sailors tend to ignore his existence". and left it at that.

Paton was relieved; it did not do to bait an admiral in public, even in fun. He reminded himself to ask her who Mitchell was.

Admiral Phillips looked towards his audience. "Are there any more questions? If not, I suggest we replenish our glasses and get to know each other a little better."

When there was no response from the Press, Captain Leach stood up to indicate the conference was over. When the Admiral got up he was dwarfed by Leach. Even so he managed to give the impression of strength and tenacity, as if silently reminding those present that Nelson and Napoleon were both men of small stature.

He sank back into his seat almost immediately, as Mr Jardine took a sheaf of notes from his pocket, adjusted his glasses, and said, "May I trespass on your valuable time for a few minutes, Admiral, and welcome you and your gallant sailors, on behalf of the business community of Singapore. I have been asked to do so, and it is a task I regard with pleasure and as a high honour. I know I speak for everyone, irrespective of race or colour, when I say the sight of the white ensign flying so proudly and defiantly from your ships is a guarantee of our total protection. Anyone who has the temerity to doubt that Britain does rule the waves is in for a rude shock." He paused and referred to his notes. "Singapore has its doubting Thomases, and that has been evident today, but to them I say this is an island, very much as home is" – the walls of Harfleur rose in his mind – "and to echo Winston's immortal words, we will fight on the beaches, in the streets and, on the hills if we had any; we shall never surrender."

A burst of loud applause echoed through the wardroom, followed by shouts of, "Well said", deliberately cutting short the speaker who still had a lot more to say. Phillips nodded briskly and looked away to hide his obvious embarrassment. Above the noise the voice of Nolan was heard to say, "Put that in your pipe and smoke it, Miss Hollis."

As people withdrew in small groups to drink and pass pleasantries, Paton asked Kate who Mitchell was. "He was an outstanding combat flier in the last war who became Assistant Chief to our air force and who predicted the demise of the battleship. What's more, he demonstrated it by sinking five empty ones with bombs in Chesapeake Bay, but far from being heeded he was court martialled in 1925 for his unorthodox views and insubordination, for accusing the War and Navy Departments of incompetence, criminal negligence, and what amounted to treasonable administration of the national defence. His court martial had little to do with the charges, it developed into a battleship versus bomber debate, his critics arguing that the ships he had sunk were unarmed, without power and therefore incapable of evasive action."

"A valid point."

"He replied that if loaded with ammunition and depth charges they would have been that much easier to send to the bottom. He lost. He was suspended without pay from rank and duty for five years for doing what he considered his duty. He understandably resigned. His supporters argued that the wrong man was in the dock. But only time will tell if he is right. Now he's only remembered as the man who coined the word doughboys."

As she spoke they were joined by Okamoto. "I should imagine, Miss Hollis, that you and I are the only ones present who have heard of Mitchell, although I am reliably informed, he is highly thought of in Japan." He immediately turned away to join a group of reporters who were talking to Leach, and Paton felt his dislike for the man intensifying. He seemed like an actor who always made his exit on a telling line.

Gradually the visitors dispersed and made their way ashore, and Paton walked with Kate to her car, arranging to meet her later in the evening. On the way back to *Grey Seal* he met Carnac and Jo and complimented her on her smart appearance. "I suppose you two will be dancing the night away?"

"Afraid not, Commander, I'm on duty at the hospital. I'm a full time nurse now. Nothing much to do but fetch and carry bed pans, dish out medicines to malaria cases, and comfort soldiers who've sprained an ankle falling down the stairs in Lavender Street."

Mr Jardine's voice boomed impatiently across the quay like a starting cannon. "Come along, Jo. Remember mother and I have people in for bridge tonight. The hospital is miles out of my way. You'd have been better occupied making up another table instead of holding hands with lead swinging soldiers."

As she hurried towards the waiting Rolls, Paton said, "You know, Sub, I think this could be the making of your young lady. Sadly I don't think there's much that can be done to improve her father."

Carnac flushed, torn between conflicting loyalties. "He's all right, Sir. It's just that Europeans here have a totally different set of values. But I'm glad for Jo's sake that she's done something off her own bat. It'll do her good to have some responsibility."

"What made her change her mind?"

"She said she liked the uniform, Sir. I think she was joking;

at least I hope so."

That evening Paton stood by the flag locker on the bridge flat gazing up at the white ensign and waiting for the bugler of *Prince of Wales* to sound the Alert signalling sunset. The blast when it came echoed mornfully over the Strait, and every ensign was lowered as if hauled down by the same halyard, while countless bosun's pipes contributed their individual salute. Every sailor and marine on the upper decks stopped dead in their tracks, pinched out cigarettes and turned towards their ensigns and saluted. Only when the "Carry On" was sounded did they continue with their duties. Paton knew that a similar routine was being enacted at sunset in every port where the navy was stationed. It was an imperishable tradition, and as much part of naval lore as the proud claim that once in action the white ensign was never struck.

When he arrived at Raffles, Paton was dismayed to discover that far from arousing a sense of urgency the arrival of the fleet had only fostered an even greater apathy than had existed before. The Long Bar was just as crowded and toasts were being raised to, "The Navy", which invoked cries of "God bless it", while the band was playing a nautical medley with songs such as, "All the nice girls love a sailor". No one seemed aware of how incongruous it was that they should laud men who were not allowed inside the hotel.

He ordered a drink and sat alone until Kate joined him. When she did she handed him the story she intended filing. "I want you to read it, Crispin. You might want to change your mind about dinner. I'll understand if you do."

He read it carefully, then handed it back. "Our friend, Nolan, isn't going to like that at all. I can't say I do. You've made poor Admiral Phillips sound like a maritime dinosaur – the naval equivalent to a First War general who insisted that cold steel was better than any tank."

"I'm sorry, but he does remind me of an ostrich, only his head is under the water, not sand." She lit a cigarette and blew the smoke towards a slowly revolving fan. "I wish I could dispel my fears as easily as that fan disperses that smoke. I can't. I gave a lot of thought to it, Crispin. I wasn't going to write it, just for your sake, then I realised I had

107

to; it's what I think and what the people back home need to be told."

It was a hard-hitting, well-written piece of journalism which concentrated on the Admiral's fervent conviction that the two mighty ships were capable of surviving the most intense aerial attack. She had recounted the unfortunate mishap involving *Indomitable* and said the British Admiralty should immediately send out a replacement carrier. And once again, the name of Mitchell was mentioned to emphasise the strength of her argument.

Paton said, "Okamoto would be quite proud of that himself, Kate. Do you have to send it?"

"Yes. When I got back here you'd have thought the threat of war had gone for ever. It hasn't. Last night I spoke to my office and was told Japan is becoming increasingly belligerent and the feeling is growing in the White House that it won't be long before the balloon goes up. But my editor said the majority of Americans just refuse to accept the fact that they might soon be involved. We are as smug and complacent as the people here. My story may not enhance my popularity in Singapore, but maybe someone at home will sit up and take notice and see we don't make the same mistakes. If Nolan approaches you, pass my views on."

"It will only endorse his suspicions that you aren't entirely with us, Kate."

"I see the seeds of doubt are beginning to germinate in your own mind, Crispin."

"I'm just a trifle confused, that's all. Those ships have been sent here as a deterrent, a bluff if you like; what useful purpose does it serve to tell people they are toothless tigers? You saw them for yourself. They're anything but that, so why go out of your way to be alarmist?"

"If you smell smoke you sound the alarm. It's my job to report the facts and interpret them accordingly. I happen to know that the RAF has asked London for at least five hundred more aircraft, bombers as well as fighters, and not the obsolete rubbish they've been fobbed off with so far, but Hurricanes and some of the bombers which have been pounding Germany. Our friend Mr Okamoto was telling the truth about Japan's air force."

"I've said from the start that they're daft to let him continue his policy of journalistic sabotage. They should close his paper down."

"I agree, but that won't make the Japanese air force any weaker. Look, our man in London has said that your Air Ministry agree there is a crying need for reinforcements to be sent here, but the war in Europe must have top priority so nothing can be spared. That just doesn't make sense to me if they're taking seriously any threats to Far East safety."

Paton found himself wondering why he could not entirely agree with her; she was only stating what every commander should in theory advocate, namely, that in order to defeat an enemy you had to know and exploit his weaknesses. Why then did it smack of disloyalty when you reversed the position and pointed out your own? To put it another way, in a sporting contest, he told himself, no fight promoter would ever contemplate putting a light weight into the ring against a heavy weight. Grudgingly he had to concede that the fault was really with him; it was a British characteristic not remotely to consider the possibility of defeat.

"Let's go and eat, Kate," he said resignedly, "But just promise me one thing; let's stop at the censor's on the way so that you can hand in your story and not wait till 11.30."

"If it'll make you happier, of course."

When Kate came out of the censor's office she was smiling wryly. "We can both sleep with an easy conscience tonight. My copy went all the way to the top man who reluctantly refused to pass it. As a State of Emergency now exists, he considered it unnecessarily alarming."

"You could fly to Manilla?"

"I could, but won't. You know, what upsets me most is the knowledge that the *Herald* will be allowed to get away with it. They don't bother to pre-censor the local papers."

"Tell me honestly, Kate, do you want America to keep out?"

"I'm not mad keen to fight to preserve this colonial bastion. But let's drop it. I've had enough for one day."

Again he experienced confusion. It was not the answer he had hoped for, but it was one he could appreciate.

Chapter 7

Kate Hollis sat in the shade of a fronded tree in the garden of the Palm Court sipping a glass of ice cold lime juice. The smell of curry from the nearby kitchens reminded her that it was Sunday and the chefs were preparing the inevitable curry tiffin. It was a hotter and more sultry morning than usual with a Sumatra blowing in off the sea, an indication, according to one of the boys, that the monsoon was not far off. But her discomfort was forgotten as she opened her copy of the *Malay Tribune*, noted the date – December 7 – below the strap head then read with a sickening feeling in the pit of her stomach the headline blazoned across the front page announcing that twenty-seven Japanese warships and transports had been sighted off Cambodia Point. The story below said that the Point was at the southern tip of Indochina and the ships were steaming towards the east coast of Malaya or southern Siam. Her concern mounted when she saw on the same page an official announcement advising people not to travel, and those on holiday to return home.

She wondered why the news had not been passed on to the Press contingent; if true, it would have menacing overtones. Leaving her drink unfinished she hastened to her room and telephoned the *Tribune* office and asked to speak to the news editor.

"Is your front page splash true?"

"Of course. It was put out by Reuters and passed by the censor. Apparently the plane which spotted them was fired on. We heard that too late, though, to make the edition."

"Why the hell wasn't a statement issued? I could have missed the biggest bloody story since I've been here."

"You should consider yourself lucky you didn't file it. Our editor, Jimmy Glover, got a hell of a rocket from Brooke-Popham for running it. He told him it was most improper to print such alarmist stuff. The position isn't half as serious as we've made out."

"Jesus, it could mean war!"

"Sure, but the C-in-C doesn't like anyone to rock the boat. Nothing must upset the Sunday ritual. Look, I'll have to hang up, the switchboard is jammed with callers. I've had orders to allay any fears."

Kate decided to call personally at the Service Public Relations Office in Union Buildings on Collyer Quay to see if there was any official confirmation of the story. It proved a fruitless and frustrating journey for she was told that a statement would be issued in due course; in the meantime, she was advised to take the *Tribune*'s story with a generous pinch of salt. She reflected with a certain amount of bitterness that it was understandable why the Press corps referred scathingly to the office as Aspro; it was the perfect anodyne.

As she walked back to the hotel she glanced at her watch; it was nearly 11.30 which meant Paton, who was joining her for lunch, would already be waiting at the hotel – that is unless he had received information which had not been made available to her.

She experienced a feeling of immense relief when she saw him sitting in the garden; clearly there was no emergency or he would not have been allowed to leave his ship. When she showed him the newspaper he whistled silently and said he had better ring naval headquarters, but when he returned a few minutes later he smilingly assured her that there was no panic. Reuters had got it all wrong. But throughout lunch she sensed that he was far from relaxed and she was not at all surprised when he said he would feel much happier if he returned aboard. "I'm sure it's a false alarm, but I'd rather not take any chances."

She readily understood his anxiety, for somehow the totally relaxed atmosphere of the curry tiffin had the effect of heightening not lessening the tension she felt gnawing at her intestines.

Everyone was carrying on as if they did not have a care in the world. When they had sung their usual quota of patriotic songs they would drift off for a short nap, followed by a round of golf, tennis, or a swim at the club or in the sea. She studied their faces; if any of them had read the *Tribune* it had no visible effect. What was even more depressing for her was the feeling that no one was putting on a bold front: they clearly believed that nothing had happened to upset the cherished routine of the Sabbath.

Sir Shenton Thomas was aroused from a deep sleep by the incessant ringing of the telephone in his bedroom at Government House. He swung his feet out of bed, shuffled into his slippers and glanced at the bedside clock and noted that it was 1.15 a.m. He lifted the receiver to hear the agitated voice of General Percival informing him that Japanese forces were landing at Kota Bahru, a coastal town near the Siam border. Sir Shenton consulted a mind's-eye map of the country and felt comforted; Kota Bahru was more than four hundred miles away. "Well, shove the little men off," he said casually, and hung up. He was further consoled by the knowledge that the landings did not constitute a serious threat, for the monsoon was due shortly and any military movements woud be brought to an abrupt halt in the roadless, impenetrable barrier of forest.

The call had also awakened Lady Thomas who asked him what was happening and he assured her that there was absolutely nothing to worry about, Percival had worked himself into a tizzy over nothing. He then telephoned police headquarters and belatedly gave instructions for the rounding up and detention of the 1,200 Japanese in the city. It was, he consoled the officer on duty, purely a precautionary measure.

Lady Thomas roused the servants and asked for tea to be served on the verandah where they usually breakfasted. Government House, perched on a hill like a limpet on a rock, commanded a panoramic view of the city, and below them they could see Singapore twinkling like a fairground. The streets were brilliantly illuminated by millions of lights, while spotlights shone on the frontages of the more prominent landmarks such as the white Cathay skyscraper and Municipal Buildings. At Fort Canning, where the senior army officers pored over maps, light streamed from every window. It was a reassuring sight to Sir Shenton and his wife, and

113

when they had finished tea he told her to go back to bed. "There's nothing you can do."

At Fort Canning, General Percival was ruminating on his brief conversation with the Governor, not sure whether his remark indicated unruffled calm in a crisis or sheer complacency. His own confidence, already shaken, was badly dented when an emergency call from Brooke-Popham was cut off by a zealous operator who announced matter-of-factly, "Your three minutes are up, Sir." Percival returned to the map spread out on a huge table and tried to visualise what was happening, and wondering how serious the situation was, for communications with the battle area were extremely poor as there had not been time to get the field telephones operating efficiently. His two prominent front teeth moved in agitation like a rabbit nibbling lettuce, as he looked at the pins with coloured heads which represented real men and wondered where to move them. The Governor's words echoed in his mind, "Shove the little men off". He would dearly like to do so, but he was not at all sure where they were.

The Governor meanwhile changed into casual clothes and took a moonlit stroll through the beautifully tended gardens, absently picking off dead heads and making mental notes to pass on to the mali, for there was little he could do to influence events. The city itself was not threatened, and although entitled to the courtesy title of Commander-in-Chief, it was a purely titular appointment. He had no authority over the service chiefs.

It was shortly after 4 a.m. that he was again summoned to the telephone, this time to hear even more disturbing news from Air Vice-Marshall Pulford commanding the RAF: enemy aircraft were rapidly approaching Singapore and were only twenty-five miles away. Sir Shenton, now seriously alarmed, barely had time enough to contact the Harbour Board and alert ARP Headquarters, which was virtually unmanned. It was only after an urgent personal appeal was made by one of the few officers present that he gave permission for the sirens to be sounded. But before their stomach-churning wail was heard the first bombs were already falling on the helpless city.

Kate was hurled from her bed by the shock waves from an exploding bomb which momentarily deafened her. In a half sleep, she confusedly imagined she was still in London, until she saw the floor was carpeted with shattered glass. As she hurried to the verandah there were a whole series of explosions and fires began to flare up in various parts of the brightly lit city. Soon ambulances and fire engines, their bells clanging wildly, were racing through the streets which were thronged with thousands of onlookers gazing skywards at the tracer shells which looped lazily towards their clearly visible targets, and the gun flashes and shrapnel bursts, as if watching a firework display. The solitary gun outside the hotel cracked and more glass was shattered. Searchlights tentatively fingered the sky and the barrage intensified as the high-angle guns of the two capital ships which everyone such a short time before had been confident would deter any attack, joined in. At the same time, an onlooker telephoned RAF headquarters and reported, "Someone's opened fire. Who is it?" The officer taking the call said, "Us, I think", then hastily corrected himself, "No, it's the Japs."

Kate cursed loudly as the city remained brilliantly lit, providing a perfect target for the bombers which flew in a tight formation as if on a practice run. Robinson's, the regular venue for morning tea, received a direct hit in its newly opened air conditioned restaurant, and Kate decided it was foolhardy to remain on the balcony. When she reached the foyer it was crowded with irate residents, and one woman was protesting volubly that she had telephoned police headquarters and been told that it was a practice alert. A harrassed man at the reception desk was trying his utmost to convince her, without much conviction, that it was, for he had visions of panic stricken residents rampaging through the hotel seeking shelter anywhere that offered protection.

Kate said caustically, "You'd better look at my windows if you think those bombs are dummy ones."

Throughout the city people were asking the same question; why doesn't someone switch the lights off?

Unknown to them, as the bombs continued to rain down, a frantic search had been launched to find the official with the master key for the city's lighting system for like so many others he was not on duty. Apart from it being the weekend, no one had contemplated an air raid, least of all at night, for the propaganda about the poor eyesight of the Japanese had been eagerly swallowed. Even if the official with the so-called master key had been found, it would only have been a partial solution for in the older parts of the city the street lamps were gas and could only be turned off by cycling natives equipped with long staves. In addition, some areas had their own generators and in the ensuing chaos some districts were plunged into darkness only to light up again a few minutes later.

Unable simply to stand idly by as an observer while men, women and children were probably being killed and maimed, Kate decided to see what help she could give and drove to Chinatown where the flimsy buildings offered no protection and where the streets were totally devoid of shelters. She arrived to a heart-rending scene; many of the wooden buildings had been flattened by blast and direct hits. Women wandered aimlessly calling aloud for missing children, while others crouched cowering with fear in the monsoon ditches. Ironically, slit trenches had not been dug as shelters because the authorities feared they would be a breeding ground for malarial mosquitoes. Now, wisely, people preferred to risk catching it in the ditches than being blown to bits. Bodies, some terribly mutilated, lay unattended in the streets, while the undermanned fire brigade fought manfully to put out the ever-increasing number of fires. Hordes of people, their few most precious belongings tied to sagging bamboo poles, or piled into hand carts, were streaming towards the special camps which had been established outside the city in place of air raid shelters which had been considered impractical to build. Animals bellowed in pain from gaping shrapnel wounds, and a dog with a bloody stump of a hind leg howled at an uncaring sky.

Kate helped lift three badly burned Chinese women and two injured children into her car and drove them to the nearest hospital, for there were insufficient ambulances to deal with the casualties. As soon as they were placed on stretchers and carried inside, she returned to the scene of devastation.

It was the crack of *Prince of Wales*'s secondary armanent opening fire which sent Morris, the duty quartermaster, hurrying to Paton's cabin. He burst in without bothering to knock and shouted, "The *Prince* has opened up with her ack-ack guns, Sir. Must be an air raid."

Paton was already struggling into his trousers; the first salvo had awakened him immediately. He raced to the bridge and sounded the alarm bells before realising it was a needless gesture; the upper deck was already crowded with seamen rushing to their action stations. At the same time, he noticed that *Prince of Wales* had slipped her moorings and was heading into midstream where her guns would be more effective. The high-angle guns of *Repulse* were also firing at a steady rate.

Paton looked down at the closed-up gun crews and reluctantly conceded that they could not contribute anything to the barrage as their Oerlikons and Lewis guns did not have the range, and it was too risky to fire the twelve-pounder as long as the ship was alongside. He wondered why no fighters had taken off to engage the enemy aircraft, unaware that Buffaloes were actually warming up on the tarmac when they were grounded by RAF headquarters who feared they would be shot down by the inexperienced anti-aircraft gunners.

Paton, his steel helmet set squarely over his eyes, deliberated on whether to follow the battleship's example and anchor in midstream where he could bring his main armament into action, when a three-ton lorry braked to a sudden halt alongside the gangway, filling the air with the smell of scorched rubber. The petty officer driver jumped out, hurried to the bridge and saluted. "You are to send a working party into Singapore and see what help you can give, Sir. There's a chronic shortage of ambulances and fire engines, and every extra hand is needed. Bloody streets are full, Sir. Some silly sod told them it was a practice."

Paton needed no further bidding; anything that removed the sense of impotence was welcomed. "Sub, rustle up a dozen hands, including some stokers, and get them aboard that lorry without delay." He turned to Phelp, "You can look after the ship, Number One. Keep the Oerlikons and Lewis guns closed up. You may have the chance of taking a pot at them."

The sailors and stokers selected for the job clambered over the tail board and squatted on their haunches among a heap

117

of shovels and fire extinguishers. They wore a motley of ill-assorted clothing, but every man had remembered to collect his tin hat. Paton hammered on the roof of the driver's cabin. "Right, off you go." One of the stokers stared dismally at the shovels and remarked, "Don't tell me we're going to stoke the bloody fires."

Paton snapped, "You're going to dig, lad, till you drop."

"Only joking, Sir," he said disconsolately.

"I know, but I don't think we're going to find anything to joke about."

As the lorry approached the city, the sky had turned a fiery red from the reflection of the numerous fires, while the shell bursts continued to pock-mark it and the searchlights to probe for the aircraft whose presence was emphasised by the steady drone of their engines.

The streets in Chinatown were latticed by hoses and hissing steam rose to reduce visibility to a few feet as the jets were directed onto the blazing shanties with their inflammable attap roofs.

As Paton bellowed orders for his men to grab their shovels and start to clear the rubble of one demolished house where a warden said some people were buried, he cursed the sense-less loss of life brought about by penny-pinching policies.

Several bodies were recovered and put into the lorry and driven to hospital. The rescuers hoped for the best although they feared the worst.

Soldiers from nearby barracks and sailors from the shore base were visible everywhere as they cleared rubble, loaded ambulances and lorries, and assisted the fire brigade. Scots toiled alongside Australians, forgetful of the fact that earlier in the day the military police had been called out to stop them fighting, and that imagined grievances had been shelved when they found a common target in the detested red caps. Most of the rescue work was confined to the Indian and Chinese quarters as little help was needed in other parts where the more substantial brick buildings provided greater protection.

As soon as the dead and wounded were extricated from one house, Paton and his men moved to another to repeat the same grisly process. Beside the blazing pyre of what had once been a restaurant, Paton waited patiently until the fire

118

was brought under control and his seamen could start digging. He felt a slight tap on his shoulder, and turned to see Nolan clad in a blue battle dress and wearing a steel helmet, a rarity among the ambulance and ARP workers. They had been ordered but not delivered. The detective gestured towards the fire which emitted crackling bursts of sparks as if fanned by an invisible pair of bellows. "This is due entirely to the alarmist reports of people like your American friend. What she's been writing was tantamount to an invitation to the Japs to attack."

Paton said harshly, "I don't think this is a suitable time to discuss it."

"Quite agree, Commander, but maybe you'll now agree that it would have been better if you had co-operated."

"A few bloody shelters and some steel helmets for the ARP, not to mention a black-out, might have been a little higher on your list of priorities than trying to blame your shortcomings and criminal irresponsibility on the Press. The place is so full of Jap spies there was no need for anyone else to tell Tokyo how unprepared you were."

"Don't worry your head about them. At this very moment they're being arrested. Tomorrow the *Herald* will be in the hands of the Custodian of Enemy Property."

Paton turned away in disgust and began to supervise the loading of more casualties aboard the lorry which had returned; the detective's mind was as closed as the stable doors he had just shut.

A voice screeched through the mist of enveloping steam, "Can we have more help over here."

Paton turned to Carnac, "Take some of the lads over and see what you can do."

Carnac and half a dozen of the working party, their mouths covered with wet cloths or handkerchiefs, ran in the direction of the summoning voice, stumbling over fallen cables, tripping over the hoses, and dextrously avoiding burning carts and rickshaws.

Several of the rescued people had been laid out in a row, resembling piles of discarded clothing, while a doctor and three nurses gave blood transfusions and administered tourniquets to mutilated arms and legs. Carnac was surprised to see Jo, her face a blackened mask, her hands covered

119

in blood, moving from body to body with a lipstick which she used to write symbols on their foreheads to denote a tourniquet had been applied or a morphine injection given.

"I didn't expect to see you here, Jo ..." he began, but she cut him short and said brusquely, "Help get these people into one of the ambulances and take them to St Andrew's Hospital. The General's too overworked."

He was amazed that she could bear the sight of so much injury and suffering with such calm detachment and efficiency. "You're doing a marvellous job, Jo," he said with sincerity.

"I'm not," she retorted angrily, "but I'm doing my best."

The raid was of short duration and was over well before the first pink hues of dawn began to compete with the reflection of the fires. But it was not until 5.10 a.m. that the "Raiders Passed" was sounded. It had not been a particularly heavy raid; only seventeen bombers had taken part, for simultaneous raids had been carried out on airfields on the mainland and more important military objectives. It had been a purely terror raid, but despite the surprise casualties had been relatively light: 61 killed and 133 injured, most of whom were Chinese.

As Paton and his men relaxed with a cup of tea by the side of the mobile canteen, he saw the dishevelled figure of Kate appear and gratefully accept a steaming cup of tea.

With the guns no longer booming and the sky silent of the unnerving throb, throb, throb of the bombers, an uncanny silence settled over the city although several fires still glowed, and a canopy of black smoke rose high into the starlit sky.

"This should provide you with some good copy, Kate," he said bitterly.

"I'm in no mood for sarcasm, Crispin," she said flatly.

"I didn't mean it that way. Someone deserves to be court martialled."

"I didn't come here looking for a story," she said wearily. "I've been trying to help. Afraid I've been more of a hindrance."

He noticed her torn and scorched clothing and the encrusted blood. "Write every damn word, Kate. The failure to sound the sirens, the total lack of blackout. The sheer incompetence of the civil authorities. You might just as well, because our friend Nolan has already selected you as a scapegoat."

It was not until much later in the morning that Singapore first heard of the landings at Kota Bahru; no mention was made of the fact that it was only one tine of a four-pronged attack. It was the first war communiqué issued from GHQ and it was a complete travesty of the truth, stressing that the attempt to land had been successfully repelled. A later communiqué went even further to encourage a sense of wellbeing by stating that only a few bombs had fallen on the airfield at Kota Bahru, and all invasion ships were retreating at full speed, while the few troops trapped on the beaches were being slaughtered by machine guns. It was a deliberate deception; the truth was too disquieting. Enemy warships had heavily shelled the defences before troops poured ashore, and the ships retiring at high speed were doing so because they were empty. And such had been the confusion ashore that the RAF pilots had been uncertain whether to attack the warships or the transports until they were told, "The transports, you bloody fools". Despite the suddenness of the assault, the defending troops had fought stubbornly, often in fierce hand-to-hand encounters, but someone had panicked and a rumour spread along the line that the enemy had broken through and the airfield at Kota Bahru was threatened. In the ensuing chaos an order was given to abandon the airfield and everyone fled, leaving behind stocks of bombs and petrol and other equipment which the Japanese had readily seized. One flight-lieutenant was so eager to get away he blew the lock off his car with his pistol rather than lose time unlocking it.

Incredibly, a mood of extreme confidence pervaded the city for earlier that morning news came over the radio that relegated the landings into virtual insignificance; a powerful force of carrier-based planes had attacked the United States fleet at anchor in Pearl Harbour without warning. America had been caught as totally unprepared as Malaya, and the scenes had been just as unedifying. The losses were extremely high as the attack had been carefully timed for Sunday morning when it was known that most of the ships would be at anchor or alongside for, as in Singapore, the Sabbath was religiously observed. But what mattered most was that America, the most powerful nation in the world, was now at war and victory was assured. Against that a scuffle up country counted for little.

A rash of Stars and Stripes began to appear on balconies and in shop windows, and toasts were raised in every bar and club to the American community who a short time before had been considered harmful company because of their alarmist views.

At Raffles, Kate threw a champagne party at which Paton managed to make a token appearance having made a duty call at Ford Canning. He raised his glass and said jocularly, "There's no time now for the dispassionate objective reporter, Kate."

"I never was," she said earnestly. "They never fed back *everything* I wrote, only what seemed critical. Since the start I've urged that it was *our* war as much as yours. How could anyone with a Jewish mother have any option?"

"You never mentioned that."

"I didn't see it was relevant. I didn't need to justify my actions because of personal reasons. I'm not out for revenge. I just wanted to make sure that if anything happened here, Malaya would be ready and not overrun like the Low Countries."

Nolan, slightly tipsy, came over and extended his hand. "How about letting bygones be bygones, Miss Hollis? I won't apologise for my suspicions, but now that events have made them superfluous, it doesn't matter. All water under the bridge. After what has happened to your fleet you'll probably want to forget some of your criticisms. Case of the pot calling the kettle black."

Kate took the proferred hand. "I don't regret a word I've written, Mr Nolan. If I'd been at home I'd have said the same about our own shortcomings."

Nolan stiffened visibly. "Apologies obviously don't come easily to you. I'd hoped this party was more than a tongue-in-cheek gesture."

Paton, anxious to avoid an unpleasant scene, enquired, "How did the round-up of the Japanese go, Superintendent?"

"Very well indeed, most of them are now safely incarcerated in Changi Prison, awaiting transportation to India. Unfortunately, one or two eluded the net, must have been tipped off. Okamoto was among them. Seems the bastard was really a colonel in their army. We weren't to know that, of course. Came here on an American passport, like Miss Hollis." Before Paton could comment on the snide remark he added hastily, "He wasn't the only wolf in sheep's clothing. When we searched the houses of some of them we found that quite a few were officers in the armed forces, including that smarmy bugger who made a fat living out of photography and some shopkeepers who've lived high on the hog for years."

"Any news from the front? Reliable I mean?" asked Paton.

Nolan tapped the side of his nose. "I shouldn't tell you this, Commander, but I know the silent service will live up to its reputation. The little slit-eyed bastards are so poorly equipped they're stealing bicycles from the natives. And we were worried about tanks!"

It occurred to Paton that that form of transportation was ideal for the narrow, uneven roads which ran through the rubber plantations, but he remained silent. Kate put down her empty glass and said, "If you'll excuse me, it's back to work. But you carry on drinking. Put it all down to my account. I'm going to Fort Canning to plead with General Percival for permission to visit the front."

Nolan said, "You'd better hurry. There might be nothing to report by the time you get there. We've got them well and truly on the run." As he observed her retreating figure he said, "I'm glad about Pearl Harbour, Commander. Apart from dragging the Yanks in, it's comforting to know the brash buggers have been caught with their pants down."

"It may not be long before you're regretting those words; some of those ships which have been sunk might have been welcomed here."

"I'm surprised to hear a navy man say that, Commander. Those two battleships at Johore will see off any Nips."

Kate went up to her room and changed into the khaki drill uniform of jacket and slacks which she had had made by a Chinese tailor in the remarkably short time of twenty-four hours and which sported the shoulder flash of an accredited American war correspondent. She hoped her semi-military appearance would influence General Percival in his decision.

As she drove through the crowded streets which still bore the scars of the raid, patrols of military police and navy shore patrols were touring the city announcing through loudspeakers that all leave had been cancelled. She was astonished that any had been granted.

At Robinson's store a long queue had formed of people anxious to buy black-out material and mattresses to provide extra shelter in their homes in case the bombers returned. A temporary tea room had been set up in the basement so that the ladies of Singapore would not be deprived of their regular morning refreshment and gossip.

When Paton returned aboard *Grey Seal* there was an urgent signal informing him that his ship and the other trawlers in his group should be made ready for sea immediately.

In the oven-hot heat of his cabin, Admiral Phillips called an urgent meeting of his senior officers, Rear Admiral Palliser, his Chief of Staff; Captain Leach, Captain Tennant, and several staff officers. The Admiral looked very ill and his brow was beaded with sweat, for despite its modernity the battleship was poorly ventilated. In tense tones he outlined the present military position; far from being repelled the enemy landings at Kota Bahru, Singora, Tepha, and Patani had all succeeded and the army was falling back, while the RAF had also suffered heavy losses. Furthermore, the Japanese navy was known to have a large force of capital ships and cruisers in the Gulf of Siam on protective duty; a sure indication that further landings were planned.

Phillips was in a quandary: to remain in Singapore was inviting disaster and the most sensible course would be to sail his fleet to safety, but that was contrary to everything ingrained in him. With the army fighting for survival he could not run away; the only noble course open to him was to sail in search of the enemy and inflict as much damage as possible to the warships and transports.

The junior staff officers were dismissed, and when they had gone he outlined his plan of action. For security reasons,

Force Z would sail shortly before dusk and head for the Anambas Islands, avoiding possible minefields, then steer for Singora where hopefully they would inflict crushing damage to ships and shore bases before returning to base. Speed and surprise, he emphasised, were essential to the success of the action. It was also vital to have reconnaissance aircraft and fighter cover over the scene of the proposed attack. No one demured when he asked if his plan met with approval, although everyone present was aware of the grave risks involved. To have opted for sense and safety was something they would never be able to live with.

When the meeting broke up, Phillips contacted Pulford and requested the necessary reconnaissance aircraft and fighter protection, but to his dismay the air chief told him that while he could provide the reconnaissance aircraft he was not at all sure about the fighters. His uncertainty arose from the sudden evacuation of Kota Bahru.

It was just after 5 in the evening when Paton who was standing on *Grey Seal*'s bridge became aware of the frenzied activity on the upper decks of *Prince of Wales* and *Repulse*. Through his glasses he could see dripping manillas being hauled inboard on the battleship and her decks being cleared for action. In the stream he could hear the clatter of *Repulse*'s anchor cables rattling through the hawse pipes. Then at 5.35 precisely *Repulse* passed, her sleek bow cutting a swaithe of white foam through the smoked-glass surface of the Strait. Her decks were lined fore and aft, the white ensign flapping briskly astern as she increased speed. Then *Prince of Wales*, flying the flag of a full admiral, steamed past her to take up position at the head of the fleet. As the two ships came abreast, salutes were exchanged and Paton could clearly see Admiral Phillips and Captain Leach wave their caps in greeting to Captain Tennant. Astern of the capital ships were four destroyers. Paton waved his own cap, although he knew that no one could see him. As the fleet passed through the anti-submarine boom, a signal was run up on *Prince of Wales*'s halyards ordering paravanes to be streamed.

Paton thought how different their departure was to their arrival. No cheering crowds lined the shoreline where the setting sun silhouetted the palms which swayed in the gentle breeze as if waving farewell. For some unaccountable reason the clandestine departure reminded Paton of hotel guests slipping furtively away without paying their bill.

Aboard *Repulse*, a personal message from Captain Tennant was pinned to the notice boards in the wardroom and messdecks: "We are off to look for trouble. I expect we shall find it. We may run up against submarines or destroyers, aircraft or surface ships." He went on to remind his officers and men that although they had sailed 53,000 miles in the past nine months without meeting the enemy, the opportunity now awaited them. "I know the old ship will give a good account of herself. We have trained hard and long for this day."

When the ships reached the open sea, a slight drizzle began to fall reducing visibility to a minimum; a good omen for the dry-mouthed and tense sailors; it meant they were unlikely to be spotted. Speed was increased to seventeen knots with the two big ships four cables apart while the destroyers took up station ahead and on each flank. The high angle guns of the fleet were already pointing menacingly towards the star-canopied sky.

Shortly afterwards, Admiral Phillips sent a message to *Repulse* to be relayed to the ship's company. Exuding confidence it informed them that further landings had been made on the east coast and they would soon have the chance to attack enemy warships and transports. "So shoot to sink."

At 0629, shortly before dawn, one of the destroyers reported sighting an unidentified aircraft through a break in the clouds, but it had quickly disappeared. No further sighting was made and Phillips felt confident they had remained unobserved, for heavy rain squalls and driving mist continued to envelop the fleet like a comforting cloak.

The evening that the fleet had slipped from its moorings, the dining room at Raffles was crowded and there was the usual dance in progress. A crude attempt had been made to black out the dance floor, but it was a half-hearted effort, the management preferring to rely on dimmed lights. It did not make for easy dancing as couples kept bumping into each other, but they remained good humoured and remarked cheerfully, "This really *is* an 'excuse-me' dance", and "Whoops, pardon my big feet", while diners and drinkers cursed the brown-out with no great animosity as they were forced to use the beam of torches to sign their chits.

Kate sat alone at a rattan table, deliberately avoiding company. Her visit to army headquarters had produced nothing definite; her request to visit the front would be given due consideration along with similar ones from every reporter on the island. A rather pompous brigadier had reminded her that there was a war on and the army was too hard pressed to wet nurse reporters. Her irritation was further increased by the discovery that two pressmen, one English and the other American, had been invited to sail with the fleet on a secret mission. When she had protested that she should have been given the opportunity to go, she was sharply reminded that apart from being a woman she had not helped her chances by some of the things she had written. It was hardly fair to men who could be sailing to their death to be foisted with someone who doubted the value of the two mighty ships.

Having suffered that rebuff she was handed a copy of an Order of the Day issued by Brooke-Popham which was laughable in view of the events of the past twenty-four hours, and although she disputed nearly every word of it she knew she would have to file it if she wanted to go to the front; failure to do so would be taken as further evidence of her disloyalty.

"We are ready," it proclaimed. "We have had plenty of warning and our preparations are made and tested." Kate recalled the slaughter in the totally unprepared city, the fiasco of the lights, and the ill-equipped ARP service, yet she forced herself to read on. "We are confident. Our defences are strong and our weapons efficient."

She was amazed that the Commander-in-Chief could have the effrontery to foist something so blatantly untrue onto a population which had witnessed evidence of his incompetence. The enemy, he went on, was exhausted by its long war with China and was no match for the defending army and everyone who set foot on Malayan soil would be destroyed. The empty rhetoric and talk of truth, justice and the defence of freedom sickened her. She would have been even more incensed if she had know the Order had been prepared six months before.

Her reverie was broken by the mournful, blood-chilling howl of the sirens, and as if by some incredible act of legerdemain waiters disappeared while the diners and dancers hurried for their cars. She saw several halt on their way out and grab whisky bottles by the neck and take a long swig. But within a short time the dance floor was once again crowded and the smiling waiters were moving among the tables as silently as cats; the "All Clear" had sounded. It was a false alarm.

Two hours after the fleet had sailed, *Grey Seal* and her sister trawlers were passing through the boom with orders to engage a small force of reinforcements which were said to be approaching Mersing on the east coast. Paton was glad to feel the movement of a ship beneath his feet and hear the steady pounding of the triple expansion engine; he had been tied alongside far too long. He studied the chart and was surprised to see how far south Mersing was; if the report was true the enemy was becoming very audacious. He secretly wondered what his small group could contribute, poorly armed as they were, but if they encountered nothing but transports they had a good chance of sinking some.

Chalkie White's voice reached him through the darkness. "It's been a long time since we last saw any action, Sir. Thought we'd missed out on it."

"Don't be so depressed, Bunts, we still may have."

"Don't worry about me, Sir. I'm looking forward to it."

A few minutes later he heard the signalman's West Country voice singing softly, "Cheer up my lads 'tis to glory we steer". It sounded like an audible death wish.

Morris, closed up at the starboard Oerlikon, turned to Miller his loader. "I keep wondering what my Amy is doing. Don't like slipping off like this without letting her know."

Miller, obscured by a shiny sou'wester to keep off the incessant drizzle, grunted. "I'll tell you what she's doing, Isaac. She's fleecing some poor sod of his hard earned pay. She won't even be thinking about you. You're just last week's meal ticket."

"That's just what you *like* to think, wack. I know better. She's eating her little heart out. I just hope we come across some Jap planes." He patted the huge coiled spring circling

128

the barrel. "Remember what this old gun has done in the past to the Jerries and Wops. By the time we've finished there'll be a few less of the buggers to bomb Singapore."

Miller noisily cleared his throat, spat and ground the gob of spittle with the heel of his boot. "You piss me off proper with your death and glory crap. If they attack I just hope it's at night, because the bastards can't see in the dark."

He began to sing in a dirge-like toneless voice:

> I don't want to join the navy,
> I don't want to go to war.
> I want to knock around Piccadilly Underground,
> Living off the earnings of a high born lady . . .

Morris, said, "Christ, Dusty, the last thing I want is you to serenade me. Save it for the Japs; they'll run like a cat with a scalded arse if they hear you."

Chapter 8

Duff Cooper sat in the lounge of his home in Dunearn Road sipping a scotch and soda and re-reading the personal telegram from Winston Churchill which had elevated him to Resident Minister for Far Eastern Affairs with Cabinet rank. When he received it he had been delighted; it provided him with teeth at last and the authority to make important decisions without referring back to London. Now, at the end of a particularly arduous day, he was ruefully reflecting that it took more than a sheet of paper to shift the military and civil authorities from their hide-bound convictions. On receipt of the telegram he immediately summoned the first meeting of the War Council over which he would preside, determined to put an end to the ditherings of the Governor and the bickering inter-rivalry between the service chiefs. He was further determined to ignore the warning that he should not usurp the function of the Commanders-in-Chief or the Government representatives.

Unfortunately, soon after the commencement of the meeting at his house, he was forced to accept that those around the table had different ideas. Sir Shenton had pointedly told him that he had no intention whatsoever of being dictated to by a politician, while Brooke-Popham pronounced scornfully that he would continue to take his orders from the Chiefs of Staff in Whitehall. A flaming row developed, and the sour relations which already existed became even more billious, and he found himself pounding the table and insisting that as far as he was concerned the purpose of a War Council was to wage war, and that was what he was going to do. Inwardly, he admitted as he studied the sullen faces around

131

him, that was not going to be easy, and his resolve to get rid of the obnoxious Brooke-Popham hardened. If he had been sacked earlier the war would not be going so disastrously. As it was, nothing but bad news emerged from the front. Although the troops were fighting with dogged tenacity, there seemed no definite strategy and they were being forced continuously to retreat, although Percival insisted they were strategic withdrawals. It just would not do, he stressed, to admit publicly that the troops at the front felt they were fighting an invisible army who moved with the stealth and cunning of tigers. And he stubbornly refused to concede that the jungle, which he had confidently predicted was impassable, presented no difficulties to the Japanese who on the contrary used it as an ally. And he refuted any suggestions that the war effort was lacking in leadership at the top, bottom and middle.

"It would be unforgivable to encourage that view, which happens to be totally untrue. We cannot allow the morale of the army or the civilian population to be undermined. These are only temporary setbacks and will soon be reversed."

And as the meeting dragged on, Percival still would not agree that there was a need for strong defensive positions to be set up on the other side of the Johore Causeway. It was ludicrous to suggest Singapore was endangered.

He looked towards Brooke-Popham for confirmation, but he had dozed off.

Paton stared at the slowly rising and falling bow of *Grey Seal* just visible through the heavy drizzle and morning sea mist, and wondered whether to be grateful or disappointed. If the weather continued to remain as foul there was little hope of sighting any enemy vessels, but it also meant they would not be spotted by enemy aircraft or warships. But as dusk approached the weather changed with tropical unpredictability. The low cloud cover lifted and the rain ceased, so that the horizon all around was clearly visible, while to the westward the sky was already assuming a pinkish glow. The lookout on the starboard bridge wing bellowed, "Unidentified aircraft bearing Green five-0."

Paton swung his glasses in the direction of the bearing and was just able to pick out a minute dot high in the sky and well out of range of his guns. "Well spotted, lookout," he called. The aircraft came lower and flew directly overhead, still cautiously out of range yet clearly determined to identify the small force below. It was now near enough for Paton to identify it as a Mitsubishi G4M1 which was code named on the recognition charts as Betty. But details of the plane's performance, bomb load and defensive armament were lamentably sparse. His thumb pressed down hard on the alarm bells and in a matter of seconds men were rushing across the upper deck to take up their stations at the twelve-pounder fore'ard, and on the port and starboard Oerlikons. They had anticipated the alarm signals as it was normal practice to close up at dawn and dusk.

The seven-man bomber which had a maximum speed of nearly 300 miles an hour and was capable of carrying a 2,200 pound bomb load, dropped height and circled the trawlers still maintaining a safe distance, resembling a cat stalking a prey it was not quite sure it could devour. Then it came down in a steep dive and swept along the line of ships. *Grey Seal* was the first to be attacked; first by the 7.7-millimetre machine guns in the nose, then by those in the dorsal and lateral positions, and finally by the bigger 20-millimetre cannon in the tail. The funnel was pitted with bullet and shell holes, and the air was filled with the sound of splintering wood and the ping of steel against steel. Furrows were ploughed in the deck and stays parted with the twang of breaking piano strings. The speed of the aircraft caught the guns crews unawares and they only had time to loose off a few rounds before the ship astern was under heavy attack.

Paton yelled to White, "Signal scatter"; in an unbroken line the sluggish trawlers were perfect targets. At the same time, he grabbed his megaphone and called below to the guns crews, "He's bound to make another run. This time be *ready*."

As the ships swung out of line the Betty did a sharp wheel and Paton saw the bomb bay in her belly open. As the bomber swooped and came in nose on, the Oerlikons and twelve-pounder simultaneously opened fire. Shrapnel bursts from the fo'c's'le gun enveloped it, while tracer, armour piercing and high explosive shells from the Oerlikons seemed to be frequently striking home, but miraculously the bomber remained airborne.

Morris's shoulder ached as his Oerlikon yammered away, and when the decks received another straffing from the seeming invulnerable bomber already well out of range, he hammered the cylindrical magazine in frustration and shouted to Miller, "Who was the prick who said they were made of rice paper and chewing gum? The bastard's so fast our ammo can't catch him up."

The bomber set course for *Porpoise* which had taken up station well astern of *Grey Seal*'s port quarter, and as it flew overhead a dark object tumbled from the under belly and Paton watched in horror as *Porpoise* was enveloped in a cascade of spray which totally obscured her. A ball of bright orange fire emerged in the centre, followed by a deafening detonation. Whether by incredible bad luck or superb bomb-aiming, the bomb had fallen directly onto the bridge and penetrated the engine room. An even louder explosion rent the air as the boilers burst, and when the steam cleared all that could be seen was a white patch of turbulent water.

Paton glanced at the red, raw sun which was dropping into the sea on the horizon and prayed that it would sink as fast as *Porpoise*, and provide the protection of total darkness, their only guarantee of survival. But the Betty had clearly lost interest in further attacks; either its pilot did not consider the targets worthy of risking his aircraft, or he had spotted something better, for it climbed rapidly and disappeared into the thickening gloom.

"Bunts, signal all ships: Report damage and casualties." As the Aldis blinked, he called to Phelp on the fo'c's'le. "Number One, check our own damage and casualties and report as soon as possible."

He leaned over the voice pipe, "Hard a starboard", and Read's disembodied voice floated back, "Hard a starboard, Sir", followed seconds later by, "Wheel hard a starboard."

The trawler curved a wide, white arc and headed for the small patch of sea littered with the wreckage of *Porpoise*. He knew that it was a hopeless task; there was no possible chance of survivors, but every effort had to be made in the few minutes of light remaining. He called to the engine room,

"Stop engine", in the forlorn hope that there could be some-body floating on the surface and who would otherwise be churned to pieces by the propeller. But the sailors who lined both sides of the ship peering intently into the rapidly darkening water could see no sign of life. A few baulks of timber, some hatch covers and a circular cork life-buoy bobbed up and down in the swell, the only reminders that a few minutes earlier a ship had existed.

Paton ordered the group to reform, and as the murkiness increased the reports of damage and casualties came flickering back on the night signal torches. The RNR skipper of *Heron* had been killed and the first lieutenant had assumed command. Several men had been badly wounded, but none fatally. *Walrus* had escaped with little damage and no injured, although her fore'ard gun had been knocked off its mounting.

Phelp clattered onto the bridge, breathless with exertion, "Able-seaman Task has had it, Sir, and one of the Lewis gunners is in a bad way. Hall has a nasty cut on his arm from a flying splinter, but otherwise we seem to have got off lightly."

"What about damage?"

"Superficial, Sir. A few holes and dents and one of the whalers looks more like a sieve, but we'll get home."

"The injured being attended to?"

Phelp shrugged. "As much as we can do aboard, Sir. They're on the mess deck being made as comfortable as possible." He grinned in the darkness, "Hall is acting like he's on the first stage to being Nelson, but it's only a graze."

Paton called out to White to signal the course he had set and ordered his group to steam at maximum speed.

Morris and Miller carried a stretcher to the fo'c's'le and laid the corpse of the gunner on it. "Poor old Task," said Morris. "He wasn't such a bad mucker. Still, he didn't feel anything. Should have been Chalkie. He'd've been grateful."

The stretcher was placed on the deck by the cable locker and they waited for Phelp to give them instructions about burial, hoping they would not be detailed to sew him inside a canvas shroud or hammock.

"Put some blankets on him," said the first lieutenant. "We're near enough home to give him a decent burial ashore." He had seen too many bodies, resembling Egyptian mummies, tipped over the side and carried to the bottom weighted by furnace bars and shackles to want to repeat it if it was avoidable.

As Morris and Miller returned to their gun, Morris said, "It was the same kind as the bombers which clobbered the Yank fleet. They're real lethal."

Miller said dismally, "Some bright spark had a sense of humour when he called them Betty. That's my old lady's name. They frightened me more than she can, and that's saying something."

Far out to sea and well away from the coastline, Force-Z steamed steadily on. The Anambas Islands were well astern and the weather continued to be benevolent with low cloud, rain and mist. Once again the high-angle guns and pom-poms swivelled on their mountings as another aircraft came into view through the swirling wet fog, but there were audible sighs of relief when it was identified as a Catalina flying boat which had been despatched on reconnaissance patrol. The pencil-shaped, cumbersome plane banked and flew low over the bridge of the flagship like a winged duck, as its Aldis flickered out the information that the enemy was making landings north of Singora. It was just the news that Admiral Phillips wanted; although his force risked destruction, it was in a position to deal a lethal blow and bring the invasion to a halt, and that alone justified the possible loss of the two capital ships.

But as the weather had proved the undoing of Paton's group, so it altered to put the fleet in grave danger. As dusk approached conditions improved and the entire force was silhouetted on the empty ocean. High above, the first enemy aircraft made their appearance, content to observe the ships below. They resembled vultures, wheeling lazily in a thermal over their prey, patiently awaiting the moment to swoop.

As Admiral Phillips observed them through his binoculars, he realised that the one thing he most needed for the successful accomplishment of his mission – secrecy – was no longer available. What transports there were would already have received orders to scatter while the warships would be grouping for a counter attack. Reluctantly, he decided to return to Singapore. It was a bold, almost heroic decision; he knew his action would be wrongly interpreted; furthermore, it was against all the traditions of the service he loved.

As Phillips used all his skill and knowledge to confuse the enemy, a desperate game of hide and seek developed. As the fleet repeatedly changed course to shake off the shadowing aircraft, the pilots signalled loss of contact only to be brought back into the hunt by stalking submarines radioing the position of the fleet.

Then the flagship received an urgent signal from naval headquarters in Singapore – fresh landings were being made at Kuantan. It was a vital position, for if taken a large number of the troops fighting in the north would be cut off and isolated.

Phillips and Leach pored over the chart and made a series of rapid calculations; by altering course and steaming at full speed, the two capital ships could be off Kuantan before dawn, the ideal time for a surprise attack in which to inflict massive damage to the invasion forces. For the first time in hours, the semblance of a smile flickered across the Admiral's anguished features, and there was no hesitation in his voice as he gave the orders to alter course. Instead of returning like whipped dogs they could, with a modicum of good fortune, return in triumph.

As they approached the target area, their battle ensigns fluttering like plumes on a knight's helmet, a Walrus seaplane was catapulted into the sky, but it returned with the shattering news that there was no sign of any activity. In desperation, Phillips despatched the destroyer *Express* to investigate, but she too returned with the same frustrating news. Even so, Phillips decided to continue to search out the enemy.

As Paton's badly bruised force steamed at full speed for Singapore, Fishy Pike the telegraphist burst onto the bridge and thrust a sheet from a signal pad into Paton's hand. "Just intercepted it, Sir," he stammered in a voice that was taut with anxiety. "Sorry to be so slow, it took some time to decode."

Paton read the message and experienced a feeling of total dread: "From *Repulse* to Any British Man of War. Enemy aircraft bombing. My position 134nYT w 22×09." It was timed 11.58.

Paton hastened to the chart table; his immediate reaction was to retrace his steps and steam towards the fleet, but he realised that it was a worthless gesture. With a maximum speed of fifteen knots there was no possible hope of reaching them before the outcome of the battle had been decided. He recalled Phillips' confidence that his ships could repel any attack and sincerely hoped he was right, for at the same time he could hear Kate's voice asking him about General Mitchell.

"Don't leave those headphones for a second, Sparks. Sub, you go with him to the wireless room and help with the decoding, then bring up any signals as fast as your legs will carry you."

Half an hour passed before Carnac hurried onto the bridge with a signal from *Prince of Wales* which had also broken radio silence:

"Emergency. Have been struck by a torpedo on port side." It gave her position, and added the chilling information: "Four torpedoes. *Repulse* hit by one torpedo. Send destroyers."

From that moment on, neither Pike nor Carnac had a minute to spare, and there was such a flurry of signals that Paton laid on a chain of messengers from the wireless room to the bridge.

Soon after the first attack another was received from Senior Officer Force-Z to Any British Man of War appealing for all available tugs to be sent to her position. The destroyer *Electra* followed with: "Most Immediate: HMS *Prince of Wales* hit by four torpedoes. *Repulse* sunk. Send destroyers."

Paton wondered why no urgent request had been made for fighter cover; destroyers could do nothing to ward off the swarm of bombers and torpedo aircraft. He crumpled the sheet of paper into a ball and let it fall to the deck. It was beyond belief that so much damage had been inflicted in such a short passage of time. He had never felt so impotent as his mind's eye saw men fighting to remain afloat in the oil-scummed water and repeatedly being machine gunned by low flying aircraft. If he had not been so far away he would have turned and gone to the aid of any survivors, but he realised it would be no more than an empty pointless endeavour that would commit his crippled group to certain

138

annihilation.

A breathless Carnac pounded up the bridge ladder and passed the latest signal, "Looks like the end, Sir." He read aloud, "From Commander-in-Chief Eastern Fleet to Chief of Staff Singapore. Most Immediate. Am disembarking men not required for fighting ship. Send – something missing, Sir – fast as possible."

Minutes later the flagship signalled that she was disabled and out of control.

A deadly silence descended over *Grey Seal* as the men waited at their posts for the latest information to be relayed to them.

Prince of Wales and *Electra* continued to call for all available tugs to be despatched, until the destroyer sent a final message to: Any British Man of War. It was the shortest of them all – "HMS *Prince of Wales* sunk."

A powerful armada of bombers and torpedo aircraft had finally exploded the myth of the invincibility of the battleship. Torpedoes, far smaller than her gun barrels, and bombs little bigger than her massive shells, had turned Bomber Harris's prophesy into a horrifying fact.

By the time the first Buffaloes appeared it was too late; the enemy aircraft were on their way back to base. All that remained of the big ships was the upturned hull of *Prince of Wales* lying in the swell like a stranded leviathan. It was still dotted with the ant-like figures of men who had remained at their posts until the final order Abandon Ship, and were now waiting for a convenient moment to leap into the sea. Then the bows rose high above the water like an accusing finger, revealing the gaping torpedo wound. A terrible rending noise came from her interior. It was the ship's death rattle, for almost immediately she slid below the surface.

When the news was announced over the radio, it was greeted by the stunned silence of disbelief in the clubs, hotels and bars. At Raffles it was so catastrophic it cleared the dance floor. Apart from the sound of a shattering glass, dropped from a nervous hand, the only other sound in the Long Bar was the whir of the punkahs. Mr Jardine who had dropped in for a beer said, "A bloody fine protection they turned out to be." Someone counselled him to watch his tongue, and he stalked out shouting over his shoulder, "The shower running this war here couldn't organise a piss up in a brewery."

Kate Hollis heard the news on the portable radio in her room. When the awful truth had driven home she lowered her head and sobbed. Her thoughts were with the young sailors she had met during her brief visit to *Prince of Wales* such a short time ago. She saw too the tortured face of Admiral Phillips and experienced an overwhelming feeling of guilt as she heard her own voice taunting him. She poured whisky into a glass, not bothering to measure it. Her hand shook as she lifted it to her lips, spilling some of it down the front of her khaki jacket. She tried to tell herself that nothing she had said had altered the inevitable consequences of the action, but she remained unconvinced. She finished the drink, then drove to the naval base to try and obtain further information about the sinkings. It would make headlines throughout the world next morning, especially in America which was still reeling from Pearl Harbour. It was a blow to Allied prestige which would take a long time from which to recover. The tragic truth was that the Royal Navy no longer had any real presence in the East and her own country was impotent to do anything about it.

As soon as Paton's battered force had secured alongside, he went to report the loss of *Porpoise* and the damage and casualties inflicted on the other trawlers. Understandably, no one was particularly interested, and he was asked to submit a report in writing as soon as possible, request what replacements in men and equipment were needed, and specify what dockyard facilities were needed to effect repairs. Apart from a curt expression of sympathy, they might not have existed.

When he returned aboard, he summoned Carnac and Phelp to his cabin. "I know everyone is absolutely out on their feet, but no one is to turn in. The destroyers will be returning soon with survivors and they'll need every man jack there is to help them ashore as quickly as possible." To Carnac he said, "See that everyone who wants it gets a tot. I'll get Tiger to write it off as spillage."

He then went off to see the other commanding officers in his group and offer what empty solace he could. When he got back, Phelp said, "What shall we do with Task, Sir?"

Paton said, "Jesus Christ, I deserve to be flogged round the base. I've been so preoccupied thinking about the *Prince* and *Repulse* I'd forgotten one of our own lads was lying fore'ard. Send for an ambulance. Tomorrow we'll have a pusser funeral, complete with firing party."

A feeling of total chagrin engulfed him and he sent for Tiger Read to see him in his cabin. When the coxswain appeared he poured him a stiff drink and said, "You'd better let me have all Task's personal belongings and if you know anything about his home life please let me know. I'll have to write to his next of kin."

Half an hour later, Read appeared with a small navy issue suitcase containing all the dead man's personal belongings: there was his pay book, a bundle of grimy letters, a few faded snapshots, some Malayan dollars, and a lock of hair in an envelope.

"Not much to remember a man by, Cosx'n. Thank God he wasn't married and had no children."

"Not that he's admitted to," said Read, but Paton knew it was not callousness but merely an attempt to disguise his grief, for the old salt considered every man on the lower deck his personal responsibility.

He refilled his glass and said, "I suppose one man is nothing compared to the numbers who went down with *Repulse* and the *Prince*. But Task wasn't faceless to us as most of them were."

When Read had gone, he thumbed through the pay book and found that Task's mother was his next of kin and he sat down and wrote a letter to her full of the same stilted phrases he had employed so often in the past. He will be deeply mourned and missed by me, my officers and his shipmates . . . he was a popular and well liked man with whom it was a privilege to serve . . . Although it is no consolation, I know you will be relieved to hear that he died without suffering and with immense gallantry . . . He was buried with full naval honours . . .

He paused, sickened by the glibness, yet knowing the words would be treasured by the recipient; his letter would

141

be passed around with immense pride until it had to be held together with strips of transparent tape. He signed it Commander Crispin Paton, RN, DSO and bar. It seemed sordidly arrogant, but he knew from past experience that it added dignity to someone's death if it was felt he had died under the command of someone with some tinselled trappings, for no doubt Task had never referred to him as anything other than "the old Man". Anyway, it was far more intimate than the formal telegram his mother would receive informing her that he had been "killed in action", as if he was some piece of readily replaceable equipment.

Below deck the traditional mess deck auction of the dead man's clothing and other items he had collected during his time aboard, was already in progress. Someone bought a collar they did not want, another bid for a pair of shoes that were too big, a cap tally worth a few pence fetched a pound. The money would be sent to his mother with a carefully worded letter from Read which avoided any suggestion of the stigma of charity.

It was just before midnight and most of the men aboard *Grey Seal* were dozing on the upper deck, unable to keep their eyes open through sheer fatigue, when a voice from the quay called excitedly, "Stand to. The first of the destroyers is about to come alongside." Men who seconds before had been sleeping where they sat or where they were leaning against bulkheads, immediately became alert and staggered ashore to give what help they could. The dockside was lined with ambulances, both civilian and military, along with teams of doctors and nurses and mobile blood banks.

Heaving lines thudded ashore, and within minutes panting sailors were hauling the dripping manillas onto the quay and securing them to bollards. In a short time the three destroyers, *Electra*, *Express* and *Vampire* had secured alongside. Between them they had rescued 2,081 men.

Grey Seal's ship's company was split into three groups with Paton in charge of one, and Phelp and Carnac in charge of the others. "We'll take a ship each," he called out, "and see what help we can give."

Paton led his men aboard the Australian destroyer *Vampire* and was jolted by what he saw; every inch of the deck

142

was crammed with burned and wounded sailors and marines, many of them so oil-coated with diesel fuel that only their teeth and the whites of their eyes gleamed in the semi-darkness. Several were completely naked, while others wore just underpants and vests. Rows of blanketed figures indicated that a great many had not survived the voyage back to base. In the mess decks and wardroom, every inch of space was occupied and vomit and discarded soiled bandages and field dressings stuck to the stanchions and rigging. The sickly smell of chloroform clung like a fog to the bulkheads.

Those incapable of walking were carried ashore on stretchers and planks or were given piggy backs, while the walking wounded groped their way over the gangway on the shoulders of the helping sailors.

Paton was surprised to see Kate assisting a boyish looking sailor ashore; he was grimed with oil and his face was hideously burned, yet he was protesting that he did not want to ruin her clean clothes.

Waiting doctors gave morphia injections to those in agonising pain for the stocks of the pain killing drug in the destroyer's sick bay had soon been exhausted and many of the wounded had had to endure great suffering throughout the long voyage home.

There were stokers with the skin of their hands hanging in strips like biltong where they had grasped red hot rungs of ladders to escape being entombed in the sinking ships. Others had been badly scalded by fractured steam pipes. There were men without arms and bloodied stumps where legs had once been, and machine gun wounds stitched across their torsoes. Some found relief from their pain by moaning softly, while others did not utter a word. Several although badly wounded insisted that there were others far worse off who should receive attention before they did.

Soon the night was filled with the clamorous ringing of ambulances as they sped off to the hospitals where surgeons waited in the operating theatres to save as many lives as their skill would allow.

In one of the vast cavernous warehouses, a temporary reception centre had been set up with urns of steaming tea, sandwiches and cigarettes and limitless rum. The latter was not issued as a generous gesture, but to make the men vomit and rid their stomachs of the oil they had swallowed while in the sea.

In another large shed the base staff established a reporting centre with rows of chairs and tables where survivors capable of giving a coherent account of the attack could be interviewed.

Kate asked Brian if he could obtain permission for her to sit in on some of the interviews, and when this was granted she sat unobtrusively behind one of the interrogating officers with a note pad resting on her knees. Each man stood before an officer and gave his name, rank and number, and then related what he could recall of the battle. Stories emerged of great heroism coupled with incidents which reflected badly on the standard of equipment aboard the ancient battle cruiser and the modern battleship.

One young gunner said, "We didn't stand a chance, Sir. The bloody sky was full of high level bombers with low level torpedo planes skimming the surface. We didn't know where to direct our fire. They came in from all directions, giving us no chance to take evasive action. But we got a few of the bastards, Sir, and would have got more if the pom-poms hadn't kept jamming. Duff ammo." When he got up he noticed Kate and grinned, showing white teeth in a minstrel face. "You don't look like a matelot to me, Miss."

"I'm not," she said, "I'm a reporter."

"Well, just you see you give us a good write up. A lot of folk are going to make out it was our fault."

Kate said, "I'll see no one gets that impression." She winked, "And good luck."

The young sailor fumbled inside his filthy shorts and produced a rabbit's paw which he ran over his stubbled chin. "This ain't let me down yet."

Stokers told of being trapped below decks in total darkness and escaping along uptakes and ventilator shafts, only to find that they were imprisoned behind heavy metal grilles. "A couple of my oppos tied ropes round the mesh and had a tug of war to haul them away. Christ, they pulled hard, Sir, before they came adrift," said one engine room artificer gratefully.

A young officer from *Repulse* seemed totally unconcerned with his own injuries and kept stressing that not one man had left his post until the order "Abandon Ship" was given, while what guns there were still in action remained firing to the very end. "It was like farting against thunder," he said dejectedly.

Paton, who had been detailed to arrange for their transportation to the Fleet Shore Accommodation as soon as they had finished being interviewed, was amazed that anyone had survived the slaughter. The torpedo bulges had offered little protection against the salvoes which had been fired by the wave-skipping aircraft, while the bombs from the high flying aircraft sliced through the armour plated decks like tin openers.

Many of the survivors related how they had actually walked down the side of the stricken *Prince of Wales* to jump into the water. But the most tragic tales were about shipmates trapped below in total darkness in magazines, shell handling rooms, boiler and engine rooms, to await a slow and inevitable death. A young petty officer who had survived by clinging to a lashed hammock, solemnly swore that he had seen an officer treading water and saluting as the ship went down.

As men from *Prince of Wales* sat down, they were repeatedly asked if they knew what had happened to Admiral Phillips, but their answers seemed conflicting. He had been seen walking down the side of the ship; he had last been seen sitting calmly on the bridge having asked for his best cap to be sent up ... Paton guessed he had gone down with his ship, for he would never have survived the inevitable Court of Inquiry if he had been rescued. As it was, a man who could not accept that war had altered had chosen a traditional and pointless way of dying. It was movingly appropriate.

Outside the hut a solitary midshipman, looking extremely boyish, walked along the quay asking if anyone had any news of his father, Captain Leach. But those he stopped hurried past, none of them had the heart to tell him he had gone down with his ship.

Dawn was beginning to lighten the Johore Strait before the last survivors had been interrogated. It might have seemed unnecessarily harsh but the Royal Navy had been struck the most grievous blow in its long honourable history, and its future very much depended on what light the officers and men could shed on the disaster and what lessons could be learned.

When the last man had departed and the lights in the Reporting Centre dowsed, Paton invited Kate aboard for a drink. He sent a message for Hall to rustle up some tea, then cancelled it when he remembered the steward had been injured. "Maybe you'd like to be mother," he said to her with a grin.

"Make it a tot of that grog which seems to cure everything, and I'm with you," she replied with a grim smile.

"Can't do that, Kate. Every tot has to be accounted for, and apart from that the wardroom doesn't get an issue. But there's plenty of scotch and brandy."

Inside the wardroom they found Phelp and Carnac sitting exhausted around the small table, their uniforms black with oil and red with dried blood. Both made as if to rise, but Paton waved them back into their seats. "We can dispense with the formalities; Miss Hollis is as whacked as we are." He slid a chair towards her and said to Phelp, "Got the key to the spirit cupboard, Number One? This calls for a ruddy wake."

Phelp produced glasses and bottles and poured out heavy measures of whatever they wanted.

Kate said, "I've got enough to write a book, but this is one story I would happily have missed. Those poor kids – they are that. Some of them are little more than boys." She raised her glass and said, "Let's drink to the navy; I really mean that", and they could see that she did.

It was bright daylight when Paton escorted her ashore. The decks of the three rescuing destroyers were littered with the recumbent forms of men who had dropped asleep where they stood; orders had been given not to disturb them for twelve hours. They had accomplished far more than the wildest optimists could have hoped for. Ninety-one of *Prince of Wales*'s 110 officers and 1,195 out of 1,502 of her men had been rescued. The losses aboard *Repulse* had been much higher: even so, 42 of her 62 officers and 754 of the 1,240 men had survived.

As Paton walked with Kate to the car she said, "I can understand why you're so fiercely proud of the navy, Crispin. So many of those men must have known they were being led to certain death by a stubborn old bigot, yet they fought to the very last."

He said quietly, "Maybe Admiral Phillips was the last of the old school."

She paused as she was about to get into the car. "Do you really think so? Do you know what I overhead one staff officer say? The survivors looked like a drunken undisciplined rabble."

"Wellington was supposed to have said something like that before Waterloo."

"I think the staff officer meant it."

Paton waved as the car drove off; he was out on his feet but he feared that as soon as his head touched the pillow he would be tormented by the screams of men trapped below the decks of the stricken ships. He looked into the wardroom where Carnac and Phelp had fallen asleep on their bunks, still clothed in their filthy uniforms. Hall poked his head round the door, his right hand encased in an enormous sling. "I've put a jug of hot water out for you, Sir, and a pair of clean pyjamas. Can't have the captain crashing his head in that state, can we?"

Paton smiled wryly; Hall was like a fussy old hen, but he made sense. He needed sleep before tackling the job of getting *Grey Seal* fit for sea again.

"How's the arm?"

"One of the sawbones stitched it up and told me I'd had a narrow squeak, Sir. Another inch or two and I've had been with Davy Jones."

Paton could not suppress a smile. "Drowning in your own blood, Hall." He knew the steward would make as much as he possibly could out of his slight injury. He would grunt and grimace at the slightest exertion but would always be available. Like a schoolboy with a bandaged grazed knee, he would wear his sling like a medal ribbon.

He went on deck to take a final look round before turning in and saw Tiger Read sitting on a coiled hawser smoking one of his thinly rolled ticklers and staring unseeingly ahead.

"Time you turned in, Coxs'n." He detected an unexpected air of weariness in the old sailor and tried to sound jocular. "You need to catch up on your beauty sleep."

"Don't need so much at my age, Sir. Not like the youngsters. Five minutes watch and they want to crash their

147

swedes."

Paton sat beside him. "Something on your mind?"

"I was just thinking, that's all, Sir. A few nights ago I was having a couple of beers in the petty officers' wet canteen with an old mucker of mine in *Repulse*. Like me he'd been called out of retirement around Munich. We were yarning about the days when I was a green-arsed killick in *Repulse* and he was an AB. That was in peacetime. They were going to tow her to the scrapyard, she was so old, but they changed their minds and gave her a refit. Christ, she had so many we called her HMS *Repair*."

"Maybe it was better she went as she did, instead of ending up as razor blades."

"He's gone, and so has the old ship, but that don't worry me over much. Ships have always been sunk and men lost. My gripe is that this could have been avoided. All the years I was in the peacetime Andrew, Sir, there was a row whenever the navy estimates came out and always the men who held the purse strings at the Treasury won. And the politicians were no better. If it meant taxes going up a penny they'd rather scrimp and scrape and risk the lives of good men rather than chance losing a few votes. We've been paying the price for that since the first day of the war, Sir."

Paton remembered how Churchill had been forced to barter part of the Empire for fifty obsolete American destroyers because the navy was so short of ships, and he realised there was a lot of truth in what Read said, but it would be fatal to agree with him. He was the essential buffer between the wardroom and the mess deck, and it was vital not to admit to sharing his pessimism.

"There's nothing wrong with our ships or the men who man them, Cox'n. We've just got to learn that things have changed and no one arm of the forces can survive without the support of the others."

Read flicked his cigarette with a dexterity born of years of experience so that it was caught by the wind and carried over the side. "Don't worry, Sir, I don't ever let my personal feelings become known to the lads, but you and I know full well, Sir, that things aren't going the way they should and we'd be half baked if we didn't recognise that."

Paton patted him gently on the shoulder. "We'll be going

into dock soon and with a bit of luck there'll be a spot of leave for everyone. It'll give us time to relax and be ready for the next round."

He returned to his cabin, washed and changed into the clean pyjamas, then lay down on his bunk and began to ponder on how things were going up country, but within minutes he drifted off into a deep and dreamless sleep.

Chapter 9

Paton sat in the Long Bar at Raffles waiting for Kate and fretting over his enforced inactivity. *Grey Seal* and the other damaged trawlers were in one of the smaller floating docks undergoing repairs which were taking far longer than he had anticipated, for despite the urgency to get them seaworthy as quickly as possible there was trouble in raising sufficient coolie labour; Whitehall, it seemed, could not agree on new rates of pay which were being demanded by the men who did the bulk of the heavy manual work on the island. The ships' companies had meanwhile been housed ashore in the base and were enjoying unprecedented freedom, being allowed to do more or less as they pleased, with the result that most of them spent much of the day playing football and most of the night in Singapore or in the base's wet canteens. All the latest Hollywood films were on show in the cinemas, providing perfect escapism, for none of them even remotely dealt with the war. If the sailors experienced a feeling of guilt it was shortlived; when they glanced around they saw that the audiences consisted of many of the city's better known figures.

Earlier that morning before the heat became too intense, Paton had been invited to play a round of golf on the island's exclusive course with a set of borrowed clubs. He had even had the unaccustomed luxury of two caddies, one to carry his bag, another to walk well ahead and spot his ball, but it had not been an enjoyable experience. The unreal atmosphere of the clubhouse had only served to make him more aware of his own idleness and the indolence which existed despite the dangers that confronted the island. The calmness of Drake's game of bowls in the face of impending danger had much to commend it, he thought; at least he had gone out and destroyed the Armada when his game was over, but on the mown fairways and manicured lawns there seemed no sign that anyone would shake off their lethargy. In the bar he overheard a heated argument among some committee members about the outrageous request from the army that it should be turned into a fortified position. The course, they bemoaned, boasted the finest fairways and greens in the East and it would be sacrilege to desecrate them; apart from spoiling their sport it would take years before they could be restored to normal. Naturally, they argued, an emergency meeting would have to be called to discuss it, but the general feeling was that it was totally unnecessary, a panic measure that should be rejected out of hand. It would be interpreted by the natives as a visible sign that morale was crumbling.

As they argued he looked out through the clubhouse windows and saw an army of people tending the spacious lawns and flower beds, while the fairways were being hand weeded by a line of women on their haunches carrying wicker baskets. Yet there was a shortage of labour to unload much needed supplies in Keppel Harbour.

Now as he waited for Kate, he wondered what was needed to jolt the city awake. The bar was as crowded as ever and the telephone rang incessantly as people called to reserve tables for dinner. The only indication that Raffles was making some contribution to the war effort was a sign in the restaurant announcing that two meatless days a week had been introduced, but this was no hardship as chicken, duck, game and fish were not considered meat, while in the dance hall the notice still insisted that dancers must be formally attired.

For a short period the city had been subjected to almost continuous air raids, but they had virtually ceased and with the lull had come an air of false security. But as a precaution a spotter remained on duty on the hotel's roof and everyone felt confident he would give ample warning of approaching aircraft with four blasts on his whistle. Such interruptions, however, were rare and most of those were false alarms and came to be considered a confounded nuisance by people who had to abandon half-eaten meals, or others, prepared to face the bombs, who had to forage for their own food when the waiters and kitchen staff fled. The less scrupulous diners forgot to sign their chits.

When Kate came down she said, "Sorry I'm late, but I've just been talking to a colleague from UPI who's just arrived from Penang. The place has been overrun."

Paton said disbelievingly, "Are you sure? There's been no official communiqué. In fact, things seem to be going quite well up country."

"A rigid censorship has been imposed. No one is allowed to report it yet. Seems the whole thing was a total shambles."

He sat in numbed silence as she recounted what she had been told. It had been a repetition of the surprise raid on Singapore only with much more calamitous results.

Although the streets of George Town, the main city in Penang, the idyllically beautiful island off the west coast four hundred miles from Singapore, had been plastered with Brooke-Popham's Order of the Day stressing the state of preparedness, no one expressed any alarm over the fatuity of the stirring words for the simple reason they could not believe it would ever be the object of an attack. The unlikelihood of such a thing happening was underlined by the limited anti-aircraft defences which consisted of two antiquated six-pounder guns. No one, they reasoned, would knowingly leave them so nakedly exposed to danger, if there was a genuine risk.

And such was their confidence that they turned out in force to watch a Japanese bomber force attack the airfield at Butterworth on the nearby mainland. That they could understand, for it was a military target whereas George Town was little more than a holiday resort.

"Next day the bombers were over George Town and everyone turned out for another free show. There wasn't a British fighter in sight and not a single gun fired as the bombers released their cargoes simultaneously and the fighters cruised up and down machine gunning. A thousand died and many more were injured. The army had to organise mass cremations to prevent an outbreak of pestilence," said Kate, her voice tinged with disgust.

"Christ, I can understand them wanting to keep it quiet."

"They can't do that for long, Crispin. The first survivors will be arriving here soon and the cat will really be among the pigeons. You'll be lucky if there isn't a mass exodus of civilians from Singapore."

"Why do you say that?"

"Because," she said with evident scorn, "some silly arse gave secret orders for all the European women and children to be evacuated along with the military garrison. The native population woke up to find they had been abandoned by the very people to whom they looked for leadership. Understandably, they feel betrayed. It didn't help when the military pulled out in such a panic they left behind vast quantities of war materials and a fleet of small boats for the Japs to seize and use against us. If I have to go down on my hands and knees to Percival, I'm going to get to the front before it's too late. Nolan was right, but for the wrong reasons; there won't be anything to report soon."

As they spoke, Clive Jardine came in and said jovially, "I was hoping to bump into you, Commander." He winked like a lecher. "Trust I'm not interrupting anything private, but I wonder if you and your officers are doing anything for Christmas? Thought you'd like a taste of real home from home. My wife is planning a traditional English dinner, turkey, roast beef, mince pies, brandy sauce, the works." He sat down without being invited and signalled to one of the waiters. "You are more than welcome to come along, Miss Hollis. I expect you'll be at a loose end."

Paton tried to conceal any suggestion of relief in his voice. "Thanks for the invitation, Mr Jardine, but I'm afraid I'll have to decline. In the navy we too have a hallowed tradition on Christmas Day when the officers wait on the ship's company at dinner. They in turn try to get us drunk on their illegally bottled rum. It's a challenge I dare not refuse." He added with mock seriousness, "It's a question of face, so I'm sure you'll understand."

Mr Jardine signed for the drinks like a rich man anxious to avoid embarrassing his less well-to-do friends, and said, "I suppose you must be quite bored, Miss Hollis, with nothing to do. But then, no news is good news. All the war stuff seems to be coming from the desert and the Russian Front where the Germans are getting a taste of their own medicine. Nothing happening here but the strategic withdrawal to well prepared positions. As the Chinese say, slowly slowly catchee

154

monkey."

"I have nothing to write, Mr Jardine, because I'm not allowed to go anywhere, and those who are are not permitted to write about it."

"Frustrating, I agree," he said solemnly, "but it makes sense. No point in letting the enemy know what you have up your sleeve."

"I wish that was the case, but I suspect lack of information is deliberate policy in order to put a smoke screen over what is really happening."

There was a note of exasperation in Jardine's voice. "Come now, Miss Hollis, I thought you were pulling with us now. Don't wish bad luck on us."

She had no wish to reopen old wounds and replied tactfully, "Perhaps you're right. I'm probably looking on the gloomy side because I'm so frustrated."

His voice mellowed, feeling he had scored a valid point and that she had recognised it. "If you really want something to write home about you can point out that unless something is done about coolie labour, Singapore will cease to be a dollar arsenal. We'll be skint. Ships are lying unloaded and the roads full of much needed military equipment, while rubber is piling up in the godowns, and trees are untapped because London can't agree on paying the coolies more."

"You can always increase it yourself," she said innocently.

"That just isn't on. We can't fix rates of pay. Has to be done officially otherwise every bugger'll be leap frogging in order to get their own stuff away. Apart from that, the war isn't going to last for ever. Once you've opened the sluice gates there'll be no closing them."

Paton who had read of the series of crippling strikes which were affecting the plantations, tin mines and docks, said, "Maybe they have seen how the price of rubber and tin has rocketed and feel justified in asking for a share in the profits."

"Don't take this as a rebuke, Commander, but I'm afraid you just do not understand the real reason behind the labour disputes. The coolies are very simple people, expecially the Tamils, and their imagined grievances are being exploited by Commies and Bolsheviks who don't give a damn about the war. They just want to end colonial rule. Stabbing us in the chest."

155

"I thought the Communists were doing a great job in fighting the Japs with guerrilla tactics, Mr Jardine," said Kate who had been told by a colleague with leftist tendencies that while the Communists wanted to see the end of tuan supremacy, they had no desire to replace it with domination from Tokyo. "Maybe they *are* fighting for *their* freedom."

"Misguided nonsense. Take it from me, if they ever did manage to kick us out Singapore would revert to what it was when Raffles stepped ashore – a useless swamp. The plantations and mines would be allowed to go to pot while the docks would grind to a halt. They lack two essentials we have, enterprise and initiative."

Paton sensed it was time to switch the subject for he was fully aware that America favoured the end of colonial rule every bit as much as the most rabid Communists. "They are problems that can wait until we've sorted out the Japs. Meanwhile, you ought to be concentrating on the labour situation."

"I quite agree. Pity we can't use some of the survivors from the two battleships. They're just sitting on their backsides doing nothing. I hate to say this, but people are sick and tired of the word survivor. They've had their moment of glory, but you can't live on that for ever. Everyone has got to pull their weight these days."

Paton said as calmly as he could, "If there were ships available, those lads would volunteer to a man. It doesn't help them to be idle, especially when they see how little effect the war is having on Singapore."

"Hold on, old chap," said Jardine, genuinely aggrieved. "That's not fair. We're certainly making sacrifices all across the board. Partial food and petrol rationing for a start. Not that the food worries me, but the petrol ration doesn't make life any easier for those of us still running businesses. You wouldn't think there was a shortage, though, if you saw all those brasshats piddling around doing nothing with their staff cars except drive to and from the clubs for drinks and tiffin."

"Have you heard that Penang has been captured?" said Kate.

"Good grief!" said Jardine. "That"ll choke the Governor, and many others for that matter. They have holiday homes there." He glanced at his watch and hastily stood up. "*Tem-*

156

pus fugit. Must get down to the docks." He winked slyly.
"I've slipped a few backhanders to my coolies, nothing in
writing, to get some stuff loaded. Goes against the grain,
but the wheels of war have to be kept rolling." He paused
just as he was about to leave. "I was serious about Christmas.
Would love to have you."

Paton thought about the soldiers who were being forced
to unload their own equipment from the ships which had
brought them half way across the world to defend Malaya
because of the reluctance to increase the pittance the coolies
were paid, and conceded to himself that the social barriers
which had been erected in Singapore were not such a bad
thing after all. If the soldiers were able to meet people like
Jardine they might lose all heart for the battle.

Sub-Lieutenant Carnac sat on a low wall beside the single
storey rambling hospital building smoking a cigarette with
Jo who seemed tired and utterly listless. It had been days
since they had been able to go out together, and now she
seemed to have lost all enthusiasm for social life. He was
just urging her to go with him to Sea View and get away
from the heat and suffering of the wards; she would feel
so much better for a short break.

"When I come off duty, Terence, all I want to do is go
to bed. It's as much as I can do to kick my shoes off, I'm
so whacked."

"You can't carry on like this, Jo. You'll crack up," he
said with genuine concern. "You're not used to this. You've
got to learn to pace things."

"Have you seen inside one of our wards?" she asked
angrily. "If you had you wouldn't be so bloody smug. There
isn't an inch of room to spare. The spaces between the beds
have stretchers on the floor, and every corridor is filled with
wounded. The fans are inadequate and the place stinks like
a thunder box. The doctors complain that we just can't take
any more casualties, but fresh trains keep arriving each day
across the Causeway. Come on, I'll show you. Then ask me
to take time off."

She led him into a long narrow ward that reeked of rotting
flesh. Men, swathed in bandages, lay groaning softly as nurses
administered morphia, applied tannafax to scorched bodies,

and changed foul smelling dressings, while doctors stood waiting patiently by the beds of freshly arrived cases as nurses carefully removed maggots from infested wounds with tweezers before they could stitch them up.

"They have to do it here," she whispered, "because the operating theatres are overflowing with more urgent cases. They say the maggots are good, they help to keep the wounds clean during the long train journeys. Some of them have had their bandages on so long they have to be cut off. Often it's too late. They're dying so quickly we've had to build an extension to the mortuary. And you want me to go dancing."

Carnac felt his stomach beginning to contract and he hurried out into the fresh air, afraid that he would vomit. A sense of guilt overwhelmed him which even an awareness that his own idleness was not his fault did nothing to assuage. As soon as they were outside she lit another cigarette from the round tin of fifty Gold Flake which she carried, forcing him to say, "You're becoming a chain smoker."

"I know. They help to keep me going. Anyway, I need to carry a big supply around with me. It's the first thing the Tommies ask for when they come in." She glanced down at her grimy uniform, stained with blood and pus, and grimmaced. "Before I came here I'd never washed so much as a handkerchief; now I do my own dhobeying. The dhobies here are too busy washing sheets and what not to get around to our stuff."

"You could send them home."

"The Asian nurses can't do that, and I don't want to appear superior. Anyway, one gets used to it. Talking of home reminds me, just because I'm not getting away very often I hope you aren't snubbing Mummy and Daddy. They're very fond of you."

Carnac felt a slight flush reddening his cheeks; he had been rather reluctant to see too much of them. "I have been home for the odd meal and had a drink or two with your father at the club, but frankly it's not quite the same without you. Anyway, the club life is not my scene. I feel out of place among the tuans." He tried to make it sound like a joke.

"You'll have to get used to it if we're going to have any kind of life when this is over," she said.

Carnac remained silent; he did not want to reopen the argument about what they were going to do when the war was over. As far as he was concerned, Singapore did not figure in his plans, but there was plenty of time to sort that out. After a suitable pause he said, "The last time I saw your father he raised the subject of Christmas again. He's so touchy about it. I *explained* why I had to be aboard, but he couldn't see it. If I knew you'd be there, though, I'm sure the captain would let me sneak off later."

"I'll do my best, Terence, because I know how much it means to Daddy," but her voice lacked conviction. "It may be as hot as hades but nothing is permitted to alter our Christmas. He insists on all the trimmings, even down to the paper hats and those ridiculous silver things you choke on when you eat the pudding. It's silly really when you think of it. Crackers and a Christmas tree and those soppy mottoes. Even the servants have to sit down to a meal they secretly loathe. We really do dream of a white Christmas although I've never seen snow, except on cards."

"So you'll be there," he asked hopefully.

"Depends on matron," she said absently. "She insists that priority will be given to the married women. We have quite a lot, believe it or not. So you see we aren't all totally indifferent to what is happening, as you like to think." She realised she was becoming serious and said with a laugh, "Mind you, they still play cards every day, only instead of bridge they play solo with the soldiers."

"I admire them, Jo. It must be quite a wrench to give up the luxury they're accustomed to."

"Between you and me I think they revel in the opportunity of getting away from their boring husbands. They enjoy washing down some of the lovely young men who aren't too badly hurt and who readily respond."

Carnac had a vision of her beautifully tanned lithe body and firm thighs and the two whitish patches which were protected from the sun by her swim suit. It seemed so long since they had last made love behind the pool. "I hope," he said earnestly, "that no one tries anything on with you. Remember, we are more or less engaged."

"More, or less," she said vacantly. "It doesn't seem to matter all that much just now."

"It matters a great deal to me," he retorted with some heat. "Maybe we should announce it at Christmas."

"That would be lovely, Terence", but he detected a singular lack of urgency, and he said, "You don't seem over the moon about it."

She grasped his hand. "I am, honestly, but it seems rather pointless to think of the future. There may not be one. If you could hear some of the things I have to listen to you'd wonder if anyone at Ford Canning has any idea what is happening at the front. The soldiers say it's one ginormous cock-up." She giggled girlishly at her lapse into vulgarity. "At first I thought they were talking about something much more enjoyable than a mess, but I've discovered soldiers can't refer to anything without prefixing it with the word for fornication. Though to give them their due they do try not to swear in front of us." She glanced at the small watch pinned to the breast of her white tunic. "I really must dash. I'm due back in five minutes."

Carnac kissed her gently on the mouth, feeling immensely proud of her but regretting she had become so self-reliant; she had shed her girlhood too quickly. For a fleeting moment, when she had referred to a cock-up, he had been reminded just how young and naive she really was.

"I'd better shove off too, I'm duty officer," he said, although he knew he was only trying to sound as if he was doing something useful. But the feeling of guilt again assailed him, and he added, "Not that there's anything to do. I sleep aboard but do everything else ashore, even to going to the heads."

"I'll come along with my bed pan," she chuckled. "I've become quite an expert."

She walked with him to the main gate, her fingers possessively entwined around his left arm.

"At least your father has stopped sending the Rolls to pick me up," he said for lack of something to say.

"That's not to save your feelings, it's to save petrol," she said teasingly. "He's a cunning old devil; he collects the ration for all three cars and only uses the smallest. Not very patriotic, but he's a businessman to the soles of his shoes."

As Carnac walked away he wondered how such an unlikable man could have such a beautiful daughter. His mind

160

reverted to thoughts of Christmas; it would not be so much hades but purgatory, but he would willingly suffer the carols, Mr Jardine's boorishness and his wife's cloying attention if Jo could be there. He imagined Mr Jardine singing "Away in a Manger" with a voice choked with tears and could not suppress a shudder of revulsion.

Isaac Morris lay stretched out on a beach of egg-timer sand feeling the hot sun beat down on his bare chest, and although his eyes were closed he could still see the brilliance of the sun through his lids. The swish of the sea on the shoreline provided a comforting background music. He reached out a hand and rested it gently on Amy's bare thigh, and sighed contentedly. He felt her hand squeeze his in response, and sat up and leaned over her. The old fashioned one piece swim suit was carrying modesty to extreme, he thought, for most of the other women bathers wore the scantiest of costumes. He kissed her greedily and felt her mouth and body eagerly responding. "This is the life for me," he said. "One continuous holiday. People pay a fortune to do this."

Unlike his captain or Sub-Lieutenant Carnac, he had no qualms about his enforced idleness; instead he revelled in it. Most of his life had been spent at sea, and like many sailors he adopted a simple philosophy of taking the rough with the smooth. He had happily endured since the age of fourteen the hardships of trawling for cod in some of the most inhospitable waters in the world, and later with the outbreak of war the risk of death during action. Similarly he had enjoyed the runs ashore which consisted of drinking as much as he could and fornicating as often as the opportunity arose. And while he stoically accepted that his present idyllic existence would not last for ever, as long as it did he would seize every precious moment of it.

Since the ship had been laid up, the afternoon swim on the relatively secluded beach had become a regular part of his routine, his one regret being that Amy was not more accommodating. He would dearly have liked to take her hand and wander off into some tree sheltered spot where, unobserved, he could make love to her. Her skin was the most beautiful he had ever seen, reminding him of honey, while her almond-shaped eyes with their long lashes made him think of a frightened fawn. He saw nothing incongruous in the comparison for they both brought a lump to his throat. But he accepted that the idea of making passionate love to her was wishful thinking; Amy had made it abundantly clear that she would allow nothing more than heavy petting. If he loved her, she insisted, he would agree that that was the right and proper thing. Only bad girls were naughty, and no man would wish to marry a bad girl. The logic did not escape him, although he did not agree entirely with her. In his home town of Grimsby many a girl walked up the aisle clutching a huge bouquet to hide the ominous bulge in her white dress.

It had now been established that she was his regular girl, although there was no question of her giving up her job at The Happy World; the money was vital for there were now extra mouths to feed at home as three of her mother's relatives had descended without warning, having been forced to leave their kampong up country, and insisted on being given accommodation. The question of refusal did not arise. He could only take her word for it; so far all requests to meet her mother had been met with a polite refusal. He suspected she did not wish him to see the conditions in which she lived, even though he repeatedly assured her that it didn't mean a thing to him; if she wanted to see squalor she should visit *Grey Seal*.

"I wonder how many afternoons like this will be left for us, Isaac," she said in the lilting voice he found so attractive.

"Nothing will ever change this place," he replied in a burr that carried the wind-swept flavour of the Humber estuary. "The war won't reach here. You've just got to read the papers to realise that."

"I do not think they tell the absolute honest truth. My mother's relatives say we are losing the war. One after another kampongs are being abandoned. People cannot grow food because the Japanese drive them out, and fishermen cannot fish because their boats are stolen from them to take soldiers over the rivers."

A solitary Blenheim flew low over the palm-fringed shoreline and several of the bathers sat up and waved. It was a reassuring sight. The only aircraft the islanders saw these days were RAF. The Japanese, after relentlessly bombing the

162

city, seemed to have lost interest in Singapore as a target; an indication that they now accepted they could not subdue the population by terror tactics. As for gunfire, the only shots they heard were the occasional practice rounds loosed off by the shore batteries, whilst at night the searchlights ceaselessly probed a sky devoid of infiltrating bombers.

"Individuals never see the entire picture, Amy; they only see a bit of the jig-saw, the bit which affects them, so they tend to think that what they've been through is happening to everyone else. It isn't as gloomy as they like to make out. Every day more ships are arriving with reinforcements. We're just building up for the big push. Then the tide'll turn."

It was quite a profound observation for the simple reason that he did not pause to think about the progress of the war, preferring to leave such things to his superiors and betters, such as Commander Paton. His thoughts never encompassed such figures as admirals and generals; they were mere shadowy figures who simply commanded his destiny. But he did have an unquenchable, unreasoned belief that everything would turn out right in the end.

He got up and walked across the scorching sand, as tentatively as a fakir on hot coals, to the stump of a tree where Jolson was tethered. The dog seemed dead, and Morris experienced a heart seizing moment of panic when he saw the flies crawling unmolested around his closed eyes and mouth, but he was reassured when he observed the slow rising and falling of the Labrador's diaphragm, as imperceptible as a hibernating animal. Jolson sprang to life as soon as he felt the restraining piece of rope being removed and he dashed down to the sea, barking joyously in anticipation of their regular game. Morris found a dried husk of coconut and threw it into the water for him to retrieve. Jolson was perfectly content to repeat over and over again the same pointless routine, happy in the knowledge that he was making his master happy.

Ever since *Grey Seal* had been in dock, Morris had got into the habit of taking the dog with him whenever possible. It was not an ideal arrangement, as the animal was not welcomed in most places, especially restaurants and The Happy World where he had to be tied to the nearest post, but Morris had no alternative.

Deprived of his customary berth aboard and barred from the quarters Morris occupied in the shore base, Jolson had got into the habit of roaming wild and often a whole day and night passed before he returned ravenous, panting and filthy, but clearly delighted with his foray ashore. But the fear of air-raids and an awareness of the lethal traffic had forced Morris to keep a closer watch on him.

They stayed on the beach until the sun began to wane, then they changed, awkwardly hopping from foot to foot as they slipped out of their costumes under the cover of large towels.

Morris had become bored with The Happy World and no longer bought books of tickets, preferring to observe Amy from one of the seats. She in turn did not accept all offers to dance and with them the much-needed dollars, but sat out some of the dances to hold his hand.

When the National Anthem was over she walked with him for half an hour through the bustling congested streets before getting a rickshaw to a place he could only visualise.

As Christmas neared, an atmosphere of renewed confidence invaded the city, much of it brought about by the news that Lieutenant-General Sir Henry Pownall was to replace the buffoon Brooke-Popham; at least he had the reputation of being a fighting soldier.

It also brought an unexpected mood of urgency into the dockyard, although Paton doubted if the events were related, but the coolies seemed motivated by something and worked hard so that *Grey Seal's* repairs were completed and she was able to leave the dry dock.

There was also a flurry of activity as preparations were made aboard for the Christmas lunch. A lorry was despatched to the Cold Store in Singapore and loaded with turkeys, tinned Christmas puddings and hams and other delicacies the crew had not seen for years, while a victualling party under the discerning eye of Hall descended on the open air market to buy fresh vegetables, fruits and nuts with the money the crew had been hoarding in readiness for the festive season.

On Christmas Day, in mess decks festooned with bunting from the signal locker, Paton, Phelp and Carnac served lunch and resigned themselves to having "Harry sippers" and "Harry gulpers" forced on them. The period immediately before the holiday was the only time a blind eye was turned on the furtive storing of grog on the mess deck, although no such rule was enforced in the small mess shared by Tiger Read and Harry Reynolds – exemption was one of the few privileges accorded to their rank. The reason for the navy custom of prefixing almost everything with Harry had been lost in the passage of time, but sippers and gulpers were self-explanatory. Men reluctant to be too generous with their tots offered the former, while those of a less miserly disposition proffered the latter. But the object was the same; to try and get the officers drunk.

The meal ended with a rousing sing-song in which a remarkable variety of songs was sung ranging from the obscene to the sentimental, and terminating with "For Those in Peril on the Sea" as if it was a shanty and not a plea to the Almighty.

Then the officers presented the men with their own present, several crates of Tiger beer, before retiring to the wardroom – proudly still vertical and sober – to enjoy their own modest celebration.

Sub-Lieutenant Carnac, having slept his head clear, was waiting on the upper deck for the warning toot announcing the arrival of Mr Jardine's syce; it came at 6.30 precisely, and he was relieved to find that even on such an auspicious occasion he had not sent the Rolls. Carnac was not looking forward to the ordeal, but felt he could not go back on his word having promised Mrs Jardine he would be there. His acceptance had been due entirely to Jo's confidence that matron would release her for the day, but at the last minute she told him she would be needed at the hospital.

As the car stopped outside the house, Mr Jardine was waiting to ladel out a glass of hot punch from a silver bowl held by one of the houseboys. He reminded the sub-lieutenant of a master of the foxhounds dispensing hot toddies at the Christmas Hunt.

"In normal times the whole drive is ablaze with red, white and blue fairy lights, but the black-out has temporarily put an end to that," his host said apologetically.

The lounge was milling with men dressed in dinner jackets

with starched white shirts, and women in dresses that swept the floor. Everyone looked uncomfortably hot. Houseboys in blue satin jackets and red trousers weaved as silently as nuns among the guests with trays laden with drinks and canapés. A Christmas tree, the tip of which almost touched the ceiling, stood in one corner, its branches sagging under the weight of parcels wrapped in paper decorated with holly leaves and berries. Against one wall was a buffet of oysters, prawns and other sea foods.

Mrs Jardine introduced him to group after group with the words, "I would like you to meet Terence, almost one of the family now." But as soon as he moved on he had already forgotten their names. The one person he wanted to see was not there. When he had been introduced to everybody, Mrs Jardine paused below a huge sprig of artificial mistletoe which hung from the chandelier in the centre of the room. She looked up and said, "I'm sure if Jo was here you'd know what to do. As it is, I shall deputise." Carnac kissed her perfunctorily on the cheek, but clearly a more ardent display of affection was expected for Mrs Jardine turned his head and kissed him on the lips, an act which was greeted with a ripple of applause. Carnac detected the sickly odour of cachou tablets, and removed it with a long swig of whisky.

The drinking went on for an hour or more before a gong reverberated through the room and Mr Jardine announced that dinner was ready.

The long banqueting table was laid for forty guests with each seat confronted by a formidable array of glistening silver and sparkling crystal glasses for the various wines Mr Jardine had uncorked to enable them to breathe. Along the centre of the table were bowls of highly scented flowers. A succession of boys, some hired for the evening, began to serve the food; an ice cold consommé to start with, then beef, turkey, stuffing, roast potatoes, peas and chipolatas.

Carnac, dutifully wearing a paper hat, ate his way untasting through course after course, grateful that Mrs Jardine's full mouth prevented her from engaging in endless chatter. He raised his glass to seemingly endless toasts, only feeling emotion when it came to "Absent Friends", even though Mrs Jardine did squeeze his hand in a manner that somehow managed to convey both affection and sympathy.

166

After they had pulled crackers and blown paper whistles which shot out long curling tongues, and cracked nuts and finally passed the port, they retired to the lounge.

Mr and Mrs Jardine stood beside the tree, while the guests formed a large semi-circle. Mr Jardine took down a parcel and handed it to his wife who solemnly read out the names "Gladys and George", and looked up expectantly as the couple came forward like children at a prize giving to receive their present. The process was repeated until everyone but Carnac had been given a parcel.

Mr Jardine took the two last remaining parcels down, handed them to his wife who said, "Last but not least, dearest Terence". She handed him the parcels and he mumbled his thanks. Mrs Jardine gave him another kiss and Mr Jardine shook his hand with a vigour that would have been more appropriate to a reunion between dear friends who had not met for years.

He held up his hand, although no one was talking, and said, "We had hoped there would have been something rather special to announce this evening, but Jo has been called to duty. Without her presence it would be rather like trying to play Romeo and Juliet without the leading lady."

There were stifled sighs of disappointment, and he added, "But, God willing, we pray it won't be too long before she is standing here amongst us. I know Terence is as anxious as we are that that day is not far off."

There was a rustling of paper as people untied their gifts, and oohs and aahs of surprise at the generosity of their hosts.

Mrs Jardine said, "Open ours first, Terence. It isn't much, but it's the thought that matters."

He untied the parcel with fingers that seemed all thumbs and could not suppress a gasp of surprise when he opened the leather case inside and saw a set of diamond cuff links and shirt studs for evening wear. Inside was a note, "Fondest love, Clive and Olive Jardine".

He thanked them profusely, muttering that they should not have been so extravagent, at the same time thinking that there were many things he would have preferred as he did not possess the necessary clothes to wear them with.

"That's from Jo," said Mr Jardine. it was a solid gold cigarette case engraved, "From J to T with love".

167

Mr Jardine felt inside his jacket and produced an envelope. "She asked me to give you this too. Pop off and read it."

He moved into the dining room, deserted but for the boys clearing the table, and sat down and read the letter in school-girl writing of thin up and thick down strokes:

Dearest Terence,

I really did try and make it, but in a way I'm not too sorry I couldn't. This may sound strange coming from me but I think such parties are a bit out of place at a time like this. I'll be happier serving the lads Christmas dinner in the ward instead of being waited on hand and foot. I'm sure you feel the same regarding your ship. Mummy is naturally upset that we did not announce our engagement, but she does like to *rush* things. I know I love you enough to be prepared to wait. I won't change my mind. I wrote instead of telling you because I found it so much easier to put my thoughts into words this way. A voice is yelling for the BP. Hope you like the pic.

There was a double row of crosses below her name. He looked at the enclosed photograph of her in uniform and suddenly felt tremendously elated; if her absence was the price he had to pay for the letter, he was more than content.

He went back to the lounge where Mr Jardine said, "Apologies for absence, Terence?"

"That's more or less the gist, Sir." The contents were too precious to disclose to him.

A space had been cleared in the centre of the lounge and a few couples were dancing rather lethargically to a small group of musicians who had materialised from nowhere. Others were strolling through the gardens or resting on chairs on the mosquito-screened verandah. Several, with their host's permission, had removed their jackets.

Mrs Jardine said, "Having a nice time, Terence?"

"Wonderful. I really ought to be going now. It's nearly 2 o'clock."

"Go! We've only just got going. We'll keep it up until breakfast is served."

"I'm afraid my captain insists I'm back aboard by 3. I don't want to end up doing jankers." It was a blatant untruth; Paton had issued no such order, but he had an urge to get back aboard. The discomfort of the ship would make him feel much closer to Jo than the ostentatious comfort of her home could.

As he was driven back to the docks, he could actually feel the letter in his pocket.

As Carnac slid down into the leather comfort of the Jardine's car, Kate Hollis was experiencing a far less comfortable ride in the back of an army Humber scout car that jolted and jarred every bone in her body. But she was happy.

She had managed to avoid the party without being churlish, having at last obtained permission, albeit grudgingly, to visit the troops at the front. She left Singapore early on the morning of Christmas Eve and travelled in convoy across the Causeway. Now after hours of driving, punctuated by the briefest of halts to eat a hasty meal of bully beef, biscuits and hot tea, she was at last approaching the battle line. A young army captain who spoke excellent Malay was assigned as her guide and interpretor, and she only hoped he would become more loquacious as the journey continued. So far he had hardly said a word and it had been a considerable achievement to extract the fact that his name was Charles Brent.

He hardly seemed well equipped for the trip for he was dressed as if he was due to attend a formal parade. His boots gleamed like polished ebony and his leather Sam Browne glinted like a horse chestnut. He carried no weapons but clung tenaciously to a swagger stick which he rested on his bare knees.

Kate on the other hand wore a bush jacket with ample pockets, long sleeves buttoned at the wrists, and slacks which were tucked into a pair of stout lace-up boots with thick rubber soles. She had been advised about her dress by a regular tippler in the Long Bar who had spent long periods in the jungle on hunting trips. The long sleeves and trousers were essential if one did not want to be bitten to death, he told her, while the boots were the best protection one could devise against the ever-present leeches.

She thought that if the old man's advice was correct the captain was in for a rough time.

She smiled to herself as she recalled the Christmas menu at Raffles and compared it to the army rations, and reflected cheerfully as she was bucketed from one side of the vehicle to the other that she would much rather have her by-line alongside a dateline "At the Front" than to have spent her time with the Jardines who, no doubt, had contributed most generously to the soldiers' fund organised at Raffles and sloganned, "Make their Christmas a memorable one".

Chapter 10

They drove late into the night in almost total silence, the Sepoy driver peering intently from below the peak of his cap at the black ribbon of road ahead, conditioned to speaking only when spoken to, while the captain displayed the soldier's enviable ability to sleep in the most uncomfortable conditions. Eventually he was awakened by an internal alarm clock and decided it was too hazardous to continue; with only the side lights to light the way there was a grave risk of wrecking the car.

"There's a plantation just up the road, we'll stop there," said Brent.

"That's pretty good forward planning," said Kate. "How on earth did you manage to contact anyone in this remote area?"

"I didn't. We'll just drop in and ask for somewhere to sleep. Even though we're unexpected we'll be welcome. The Europeans up country don't often get visitors."

They drove slowly for several hundred yards until the captain saw a large sign which said "Meredith's Estate" and he instructed the driver to turn into the rutted track beside it.

They stopped outside an attap roofed bungalow in a small clearing, hemmed in by thousands of straight trunked trees perfectly aligned like soldiers on a parade ground. From inside came the sound of Beethoven's Pastoral Symphony.

A Malayan jagger was lying on the floor of the verandah blocking the doorway, and at the sound of their footsteps he sat bolt upright. Brent spoke to him in his own tongue and he scuttled inside, and a few minutes later the European overseer appeared and invited them in. To Kate's astonishment he was attired in a rather shabby dinner jacket. He led them into a spacious room cluttered with an odd assortment of catalogue furniture. The legs of the chairs and tables all rested in tins filled with parafin to keep off the ants which would otherwise munch them to sawdust. Rows of mildewed books, most of them related to cricket, rested on a long shelf, and there were piles of old *Illustrated London News, Horse and Hound,* and *Punch* on a casual table. The music was coming from a handcranked gramophone with an enormous trumpet-shaped speaker. Kate half expected to see a black and white dog, ears cocked, listening intently to the music.

The overseer gently lifted the needle head and stopped the record before speaking. "To what do I owe this unexpected pleasure?" he asked. "Is there anything I can do for you?"

Brent introduced himself and Kate and said that he wondered if it was at all possible for him to put them up for the night.

"Delighted to, but I'm afraid the accommodation is pretty rugged. Don't get callers here; surprised you knew of my existence."

Brent explained that prior to joining the army he had worked in a shipping office where part of his duties included arranging the loading of rubber cargoes. In that way he got to know the whereabouts of most of the plantations although he had never visited any.

The overseer who introduced himself as Bob Cresswell showed them into an adjoining room which, apart from a crude table made of lengths of bamboo lashed together and two charpoys, was devoid of furniture. "It's all I can offer, I'm afraid," he said apologetically. "I'll have my boy rustle up some blankets. You'll need them."

"I don't know about Captain Brent, but it'll suit me fine," said Kate. "I could sleep on a clothes line."

When they returned to the lounge, Mr Cresswell produced a bottle of whisky and poured three large measures. "It's nice to have someone to drink with," he said. "Solitary drinking has been the downfall of many a good rubber man, so I have to watch myself. Alone I limit myself to two strengahs a night." She noticed that the label had pencil marks on it so that it resembled a medicine bottle on which the dosage was measured.

When Kate had finished her drink she got up and said, "If you don't mind, I'll say goodnight," but before she could protest Mr Cresswell had refilled her glass, clearly intent on enjoying the unexpected company for as long as he possibly could. Apart from the occasional trip to Singapore, he explained, when he let his hair down, he hardly even saw another European; the periodicals, he added rather touchingly, were his only contact with home and civilisation. He also apologised for wearing a dinner jacket. "It was considered the done thing when I first arrived out here and habits die hard. It was stressed upon us that if one did not maintain standards it was too easy to slip into unfortunate habits." And he recounted how when he was first interviewed for his job in the firm's London office he was given a list of items considered essential for the appointment, among them was a morning suit. "They're not so rigid these days," he said, "but one has to advance with the times."

Inevitably the conversation turned to the war, and Kate was amazed how little Mr Cresswell knew of what was happening in Malaya. "I have the radio, of course, but I tend to forget to charge the accumulator and I lose touch with things."

Eventually she managed to excuse herself, and when she lay down fully clothed on the charpoy she fell asleep almost immediately.

Sunlight had barely begun to pierce the endless rows of trees before Captain Brent was gently shaking her awake. "Time we got cracking. We've still got a fair trek ahead and the road doesn't get any better. The bathroom is at the end of the verandah."

Kate made her way along the verandah to a small outhouse which contained the Shanghai vase, a large earthenware pitcher with a tin ladle suspended from the lip. She stripped off her clothes and poured the water over her hot flesh, and was surprised to find how deliciously cool it was.

After a welcome breakfast of tinned sausages, tinned bacon with fresh eggs, they bade farewell to Mr Cresswell who urged them to make sure they dropped in on the way

173

back when he would be prepared to entertain them properly.

The driver who had slept in the car was already behind the wheel and had the engine running. They continued along the narrow road which was lined with towering trees which almost shut out the sunlight so that it seemed as though they were travelling down an endless unlit tunnel. Occasionally the driver was forced to swerve violently to avoid the craters caused by enemy bombers, and they were hurled across the car before they had time to grab hold of something firm.

Kate cocked her head and listened intently; in the distance she could hear what sounded like the rumble of thunder.

"Guns," said the captain in a voice totally devoid of any expression. "Long way off though. Sounds like our own twenty-five-pounders."

"How far?"

"Hard to say. The jungle does funny things to noise." He consulted a fold-up map covered with protective transparent perspex. "We'll be halting soon. But not to worry, the Japs are a long, long way off."

"Where do we stop?"

"Fraid I can't tell you that. Didn't they tell you that no place names are to be used? Neither must you name units. Security."

Kate nodded. It was an understandable request, although it had not been mentioned when the visit was arranged. It did not, however, made for authentic reporting, and readers would suspect that, like one of Evelyn Waugh's fictional correspondents, she had not left the comfort of Raffles.

Soon afterwards, the road petered out into what was little-more than a bullock track and the rubber plantations gave way to thick, dense jungle. The trees were enormous and as perfectly proportioned as the Grecian columns of a ruined yet limitless temple. High above a canopy of green foliage shut out the sun, and vines and creepers as thick as a man's thigh entwined the trunks, while the ground was carpeted with dead mouldering leaves and patches of impenetrable thorn scrub and sickly smelling wide-leaved palms. In Kate's eyes it certainly looked impassable.

Without warning they emerged into a wide clearing dotted with houses perched precariously on stilts, the verandahs of which were crowded with dejected looking soldiers, their eyes dark with fatigue, cigarettes drooping from their lips.

Captain Brent tapped the driver on the shoulder with his stick and shouted something in Urdu, and the Sepoy braked and brought the car to a juddering halt. They had stopped outside one of the huts which seemed fractionally bigger than the others.

"This looks like the officers' mess," said Brent. "Not exactly the Ritz, but not too bad in the circumstances."

Kate gazed around her in bewilderment. "It looks a strange kind of barracks to me."

"It's a deserted kampong. The natives have skedaddled. Doesn't take much for them to bolt. We're still a long way from the actual fighting, but it's as far as I'm permitted to take you."

They went inside a largish room containing several tables which had been pushed together to form one large one, and littered with an assortment of chairs which ranged from crude wooden ones to car seats.

A lieutenant-colonel who looked as if he could do with a night's sleep, rose from one of the chairs and listened politely as Brent explained the purpose of Kate's visit. "She has permission, Sir, to talk to any of the men she wishes to, although they must not be named. If you wish you can draw her the general picture, without of course revealing anything that could assist the enemy," said the captain.

The colonel who introduced himself as Graham, smiled and said, "I don't think you're going to learn a lot, Miss Hollis. This is turning out to be a rather confusing war. Didn't prepare us for it at Sandhurst, but I'll do my best. You've seen the kind of terrain we're fighting in; the enemy can be twenty yards away and you don't know he's there till he starts shooting. It's pretty unnerving to men who haven't been trained for that kind of thing. To be honest, the Japs are teaching us a thing or two, but we learn quickly. They don't stand and fight, they skirmish and use encircling tactics so that you find they're behind you instead of ahead. That's rather disquieting when you're fighting a strategic withdrawal."

Kate looked across at Captain Brent and saw his mouth pursed in disapproval; he clearly did not approve of the gloomy picture the colonel was painting. "It isn't quite as depressing as Colonel Graham suggests," he said stiffly. "The withdrawal is going exactly as planned. We're falling back to well prepared positions in order to choose our own field of battle. When the time is ripe we'll counter attack in force. Isn't that so, Colonel?"

"I can see you haven't seen any of the fighting, Captain, otherwise you wouldn't be so bloody smug. This, believe it or not, *is* a well prepared position; there's nothing here but some slit trenches and primitive barricades made of sharpened bamboo which we hope the enemy will obligingly impale himself on. Whereas the position we have retreated from had pill boxes and proper fortified dug-outs. I'm still trying to find out why we pulled out," he said wearily.

The captain tapped his cane against the palm of his hand like a schoolmaster about to administer six of the best to a wayward pupil. "With due respect, Sir, I can't see that it serves any useful purpose in talking like this to Miss Hollis. Extremely lowering for morale. The last thing we want to do is cause despondency among the civilian population." He turned to Kate and added, "Incidentally, it is not permitted to mention the word retreat. That is not a request but an order, direct from Churchill himself."

"I'm not writing for local consumption, Captain, but for American readers who have an uncanny ability to read between the lines. They have many faults, but candour is one of their virtues."

Tactfully, Colonel Graham produced a bottle of whisky. "If Miss Hollis has permission to talk to my men, then I'm entitled to prepare her for what to expect. If you think I'm being too frank, just wait till you hear what they have to say. What respect would she have for me if I glossed over difficulties? If she writes what she hears, then maybe some of the top brass at Fort Canning will realise they've got to alter their entire strategy before it's too late."

"I shan't be able to ignore your remarks, Sir. I consider it my duty when I submit my report," said Brent petulantly.

"You can read it aloud in Raffles Place for all I care, Captain. If I'm relieved of my command, I'll look forward to a spell in Singapore fighting for a drink."

Kate realised the tremendous strain the colonel was under for she could not envisage such frankness in normal circum-

176

stances; at the same time she sympathised with him, remembering the criticisms she had been subjected to because of her efforts to arouse a sense of urgency. Graham, she suspected, was trying in the only way available to let outsiders know the true gravity of the situation.

The colonel picked up his cap and said, "Miss Hollis didn't come all this way to hear us argue, Captain. Let me show you round."

They walked out of the hut with Brent a pace or two behind like a dutiful dog.

Kate said, "Stop me if I'm being too inquisitive, but what *is* the present situation?"

"Grim. Our troops, and that includes Australians, Indians, Gurkhas, the lot, are fighting like hell, but the army is spread too thinly over the penisular without air cover and we've got our priorities topsy-turvy. We've just fought a stubborn action to defend an airfield which has no aircraft, they've all been flown back to defend Singapore Island. As a result of these panicky decisions and abrupt evacuations, we're being chased by planes using our own fuel and dropping our own bombs."

As they walked through the deserted kampong, she noticed that many of the shops were filled with merchandise, indicating the speed with which the villagers had fled. It made the obsession with morale seem laughable; the natives were not likely to remain tight lipped when they reached the relative safety of Singapore.

All over the compound men were huddled in small groups around fires made from damp wood which had required an immense amount of patience to get started, and over which they were cooking a stew of bully beef and vegetables collected from the abandoned gardens. At regular spaces around the perimeter armed sentries stood guard and she was amazed at the amount of equipment they carried: packs, haversacks, folded great coats and gas masks, and she wondered who in their wisdom had feared gas attacks in the jungle.

Kate squatted beside half a dozen men and explained the reason for her visit and enquired if they would co-operate. She had come well prepared with tins of cigarettes with which to loosen their tongues, and they were greedily but thankfully accepted. She noticed that most of them had hideous, festering sores on their arms and legs and asked what had caused them.

A sergeant said, "Leeches, Miss." He shuddered in an exaggerated manner. "Give me the Japs any time to them little buggers. Doesn't matter what you do, they find a way of drinking your blood. They could get through the eye of a needle. Somehow or other they wriggle through the lace-holes of your boots, up your nose, and in your mouth if you fall asleep with it open. A hot fag end is the only thing that'll make them drop off. Salt's good if you have any, but we don't. The little perishers inject something which stops the blood clotting, so what with the heat and the flies they soon turn septic."

A young private said with a laugh, "You ain't told her where else they crawl, Sarge."

"That's quite enough from you, lad. The lady isn't interested in your private parts. Pardon me, Miss, he's a vulgar little so and so."

Kate laughed and said, "Don't worry, Sergeant, I haven't come from a convent. As they say back home, I've covered the waterfront." The sally raised a good laugh and she was encouraged to ask, "Tell me about the actual fighting."

The sergeant raised his eyes and looked questioningly at Colonel Graham who nodded, while Captain Brent scuffed the ground with a well polished boot, his mouth curved in disapproval at the other ranks being almost encouraged to grouse and express opinions on a subject on which they were not qualified to speak.

The sergeant encompassed the small band with a sweep of his head and said, "I wouldn't say it to their faces unless you were here, but even though I say it myself there are no finer soldiers in the world. They'll stand and fight to the last man and the last round if ordered to but they aren't. We fell back for no reason and without explanation. That's against all the traditions of our regiment which was at Corunna, the Somme and Christ knows where else. So naturally we are confused. When I joined as a lad my RSM drilled into me that a good soldier never looks behind, but out here that's all we seem to do."

The voice of Captain Brent, bridling with irritation, interrupted him. "Don't think your feelings aren't appreciated,

Sergeant; they are. But you cannot be expected to appreciate the overall strategy that is being employed. What may appear chaotic, even misguided, to you, is the result of infinite study and planned with the utmost precision."

The sergeant replied, "Sorry, Sir, but the young lady asked me how I saw it, and what I've told her is only my personal honest opinion."

A cockney private who could not have been more than nineteen, said hesitantly, "Everyone gasses on about morale, Sir, but we heard on the grapevine that some general or other has said we ain't fighting with the proper spirit. That don't go down too well considerin' what we've been through. None of us reckoned on this kind of caper. The Japs don't fight like real soldiers. They dress up as wogs and the next thing you knows they is lobbing a grenade at you or banging away with an LMG. That, of course, is when they give you a sight of 'em, and that ain't too often. If only they'd come out in the open and fight like men we'd 'ave the lickin' of 'm. They wouldn't know whether to shit, shave or shampoo, if you'll pardon the expression."

The sergeant wagged an admonishing finger, and Kate put him at his ease by saying, "Don't worry, Sergeant, I have a grandfather whose language really does turn the air purple. A Bostonian." But she realised the joke was lost on the soldiers who would know little about her country.

Another soldier fortunately broke in, "Sleep's the thing I miss most, Madam. Half the time you're fighting to keep your eyes open. Then no sooner do you get your head down than you're up and off, falling back to some place that isn't even on the map. It's hard to fight for somewhere like that. It doesn't mean nothing to you. Maybe they ought to give them names like Hammersmith, or Oxford Street, or even Glasgow, and that's an..." he paused as he sought for a suitable word before blurting out, "armpit of a place."

"Well done, son," said the sergeant. "I thought for a moment you were going to let your tongue get the better of you."

Kate laughed and said, "Don't apologise for him, Sergeant. I've heard the word anus before."

It brought loud guffaws of laughter from the soldiers who realised that the lady reporter was one of the lads at heart, and it encouraged them to be even more forthright.

Kate moved away and spoke to several more men, some of whom were shaking uncontrollably with malaria, but their eyes although hollow and dark-shadowed gleamed with hope for they had been assured they would be evacuated to Singapore on the next available ambulance train. She garnered their comments like a squirrel hoarding nuts, happy to dispense with a notebook because she knew she was unable to quote names, yet happy in the knowledge that the appearance of a pencil and notebook tended to make people much more reticent to speak openly.

Then without warning it began to rain, at first in sparse penny-sized drops that were cool and refreshing, but which quickly developed into a torrential downpour that stung the bare flesh it was so harsh. Kate hastily put on the steel helmet she had been issued with, but it felt as if her head was being pounded with a hammer, while men who only minutes earlier had been sweating now shivered with cold, and there were loud choruses in the foulest language as the rain doused the precious fires which had taken so long to get started and which the ground sheets no longer protected.

Colonel Graham said, "Better call it a day, Miss Hollis, and go inside. This could last for hours."

It required great effort for Kate to trudge back to the mess for the earth had turned into a porridgy morass that rose above her insteps and almost sucked her boots off. And with the rain the distant gunfire ceased as if the opposing foes had given up hope of competing with nature's artillery which rumbled and growled in company with flashes of lightning no guns could match.

Inside the improvised mess, Kate rubbed her hair with a towel handed to her by Colonel Graham, who said, "The monsoon was our only real hope of stemming their advance. But it doesn't bother them. They've done their homework pretty thoroughly. They don't worry about roads but just drive down the wide avenues between the rubber trees. I suspect their agents prepared maps a long time ago, whereas we looked at survey maps and saw only the jungle. And we scoffed at the way they relied on cycles, not realising that they had learned from the natives that it was the finest means of transportation here."

That evening she dined with the officers at the long table. It was an unappetising, spartan effort consisting of the inevitable corned beef, hard biscuits with some sweet potatoes and vegetables "borrowed" from one of the deserted stores, and livened up with chillies. It was hard to imagine that she was in the same country where fresh strawberries were still available, and oysters flown in from a prodigious distance.

The officers, most of whom looked remarkably youthful, had clearly made every effort to look their best for the unexpected guests; their khaki was newly pressed, although obviously not freshly laundered. Over drinks which were meticulously logged in the mess account, they relaxed and talked enthusiastically about sport and their plans when the war was over, their voices drowning the noise of the rain battering the roof like muffled drums.

Colonel Graham drew her aside and said, "Fancy a breath of fresh air?" He led her out onto the narrow verandah and they watched the rain pitting holes in the mud which now resembled the bubbling crater of a volcano and beating a frenzied tattoo on the steel bonnets of the transport concealed among the trees and camouflaged with branches and foliage. "You don't know what a tonic you've been, Miss Hollis. The men really enjoyed the opportunity of having a good moan. They can't complain to me, and they daren't to the NCCS who won't listen. But you gave them a golden opportunity to unburden themselves with official approval."

"I'm not sure that was the intention at Fort Canning. What's more, I'm not sure Captain Brent will go along with you."

"Frankly I don't care too much for his type. Officers like him with a knowledge of the country and the ability to speak the language should be up here where they can be of use, not stuck at headquarters. If we're to win this show we'll need to thin them out a bit. Far too thick on the ground at the moment."

"He could be vindictive."

"Not a hope. I've just been recommended for an MC, two of my officers for Mentions, and one of the sergeants for an MM. Even Percival can't quibble with that record."

"Perhaps, but he won't take too kindly to your criticisms."

The colonel smiled, relieving his face of some of the tension. "My indiscretions were not entirely motiveless, Miss Hollis. I know the censor will delete anything he considers damaging in what you write, but the captain will dutifully report my outspokenness, which suits me because that's the only way we can let them know just how disastrously things are going."

The rain stopped as suddenly as it had started, and a new sound invaded the night as millions of unseen insects began to croak and screech, competing with the mournful howls of Gibbon monkeys and the shrill calls of birds. In the far distance the sky was brightened by the renewed flashes of gunfire, followed by the ominous thunder-like rumble.

"They've started up again," said the colonel laconically. "Much closer now. They keep moving, no matter how much it rains. It might not be such a bad idea if you set off first thing in the morning. I have a vested interest in you getting back."

After a fitful night in which she tossed and turned, tormented by invisible mosquitoes which pinged around the room and bit with a relentless savagery and abetted by sand flies which stung like red hot needles, she rose and prepared for the return journey to Singapore. Much of the time was spent in silence, for Captain Brent was discinclined to converse and the few occasions when he did were only to urge her to be cautious and circumspect about what she wrote.

"Lieutenant-Colonel Graham is a fine courageous soldier, but he could do with a spot of leave. Tends to let his tongue run away with him and give a completely false impression. Doesn't understand this country."

"I won't rely on simply what I heard," she said. "I did *see* quite a lot for myself. Frankly, it wasn't all that comforting. Some of those soldiers are acting like automatums, they're so whacked."

"That, I might say, is the time when they need to be gingered up. Bit like a horse that's flagging, they need a touch of the whip and spur, not mollycoddling."

Kate closed her eyes, not because she was sleepy but merely to bring the melancholy conversation to a halt. Captain Brent reminded her too much of the red-tabbed staff officers who habitually frequented the hotel bars and clubs and who all spoke with the same voice, echoing their ignorance and

182

insufferable complacency. She felt like shaking him and saying, "Wake up, for God's sake. Your cosy little dream world is falling apart."

When she arrived back at the hotel she luxuriated in a bath of warm, scented water, feeling the aches and bruises from the uncomfortable journey gradually seep away. As she lay stretched out with the water lapping her breasts, she thought of the soldiers in the jungle, soaked and shivering one minute and huddling together for warmth, then baking hot when the sun began to rise, and mentally began to compose her story.

Two hours later she sat anxiously across the desk from the censor who was reading her typed cable with a furrowed brow. He was a slightly built man with sparse hair slicked down with water who enjoyed a comfortable living as a solicitor and had recently been appointed as a part-time censor with the acting rank of major. Long years in the tropics had given him a wizened, jaundiced appearance which made him look much older than he was. "It is an extremely well written account of conditions at the front, but are you sure it is the kind of thing that's needed just now? It is, if you will pardon me, somewhat depressing and hardly gives the impression of resolute men who are holding the line with determination and skill. When I read material like this, I always think of my beloved daughter back in England and ask, 'What effect will this have on her?' I don't want her to worry unnecessarily. You could substitute her for the wife or sweetheart of any soldier." He leaned back and said gravely, "I'm afraid I can't approve it in its present form."

Kate sighed wearily, if irrationally; it was exactly what she had feared.

"If you would mark the passages you don't like, I'll rejig it."

"I can't possibly do that, Miss Hollis. I can't *dictate* what you write. There's a world of difference between censorship and imposing my own views. It's rather similar to my work as a solicitor. I cannot *tell* a client what his defence should be. That is quite unethical."

"I'm afraid I don't see the relevance."

"I know you must think this harsh, especially in view of the considerable hardship you have endured. But morale

183

is paramount at this moment in time."

That same terrible word, thought Kate. The unvarying excuse for concealing the truth.

She returned to her room and rewrote her despatch, but when she read it through she wondered whether the trip she had been so anxious to make had been worth the effort; her story now resembled an official communiqué, but she knew her editor would much prefer some news to no news at all.

When she had resubmitted it and been praised for its content, she filed it then drove out to the naval base, but when she arrived at the quayside the berths occupied by *Grey Seal* and her sister trawlers were empty.

Grey Seal's blunt bow rose and fell imperceptibly in the gentle swell of a sea that was almost aquamarine in colour, while the sky above was entirely devoid of cloud. Hardly the ideal weather, thought Paton, for a clandestine operation, the success of which depended on remaining undetected. He glanced over the bridge parapet to the deck below which was crowded with an assortment of nationalities; there were British soldiers in jungle green, Malays, Chinese and Indians, and Europeans who until a short time ago had worked in the tin mines, rubber plantations and timber forests. They possessed one thing in common, a love of Malaya and a detailed knowledge of the language and conditions up-country. Around them the deck was cluttered with wooden crates containing wireless equipment, grenades, explosives and detonators. Wrapped in grease-covered canvas and sealed in large oil drums were rifles, Tommy-guns, pistols and ammunition which would be used to arm a secret army.

They were all products of the Special Training School which was set up in Singapore Island where a handful of specialists in guerrilla warfare trained them in the arts of demolition, intelligence gathering, and silent killing. The instructors were officers and NCOs who had undergone courses at commando schools in the Highlands of Scotland and were shipped to Malaya to establish a secret centre aimed at defeating the Japanese at their own game.

At the start, the idea of such a place had met with total indifference then outright opposition from Sir Shenton Tho-

184

mas, and the equally unimaginative Percival, who fell back on their time-worn excuse that such a force would be bad for morale as it conceded the possibility of enemy occupation. Furthermore, Percival still saw war as some kind of sporting encounter, and an illicit force trained in hit-and vanish tactics smacked a little too much of cheating to his liking. But belatedly, as conditions worsened, they had grudgingly conceded that it might conceivably have a useful function, and specially recruited men, with outstanding talents and whose reliability was assured, had been trained in the Forest Reserve at Bukit Timah, which contained jungle comparable to that on the mainland and in the foul-smelling mangrove swamps and little known creeks around the island's coastline. They were also taught to hunt and fish and literally live off the land by being instructed on which plants, berries and fungi were edible.

A cosmopolitan force, it was stressed, was essential if the scheme was to succeed, for no European, purely on the grounds of his appearance, could hope to survive without the active support of natives.

Some of the men assembled below were known Communists who had been released from detention in order to undergo the hazardous training. At first, the idea of Chinese being trained to fight and allowed to carry arms was greeted with total astonishment by Fort Canning and Government House, despite the fact that the Chinese had been waging war against Japan for years. Even appeals by interned members of the Malay Communist Party to be allowed to contribute to the war had met with a flat rejection because they were considered to be dedicated to the overthrow of white supremacy. But events progressed so rapidly and so disastrously that the defeat of the common enemy became supreme, and all barriers were removed and their help readily accepted.

Now *Grey Seal* escorted by *Walrus* and *Heron* were heading for Bagan Datoh on the west coast where the men would be landed under cover of darkness to create as much havoc as possible and impede the progress of the advancing Japanese who were now pressing towards the vital line of the Slim River, the last reasonable defensive position barring the way to Kuala Lumpar. Once ashore they would divide into small, compact groups to vanish into the jungle and if necessary remain as stay-behind groups monitoring intelligence back to Singapore, and continue their work of sabotaging roads, railways, bridges and other installations to prevent the enemy using them.

Because so many obstacles had been set up to prevent the establishment of the School, much of the equipment they carried was far from suitable for the tasks which lay ahead, especially the wireless sets which were too heavy and bulky for speedy transportation and concealment. But it was all that was available, and the special squads of volunteers were prepared to accept the risks entailed; after all their problems were no different to those of the army who had to rely on inferior equipment.

Far on the starboard beam, the green blur of the coastline of the peninsular was clearly visible, making Paton uncertain as to whether he should be further out to sea or closer inshore, for he was bedevilled by the difficulties of the course he should steer for their ultimate destination. If he sailed too close to the mainland he was in danger of being spotted by enemy patrols or Fifth Columnists, yet he dared not be too far out for risk of being sighted by enemy ships or aircraft. He had decided on a compromise, tormented by the knowledge that only time would prove if he had made the right decision.

So far they had remained undetected, presumably because the Japanese could not envisage such a move when the army was falling back so quickly. The old adage that the pursuer seldom looks behind was proving its worth. It was Paton's intention that as nightfall approached he would make a sudden alteration of course which would set their bows directly towards the target and enable them to unload the equipment and disembark the men in secrecy. An advance force with its own transport of lorries and private cars had already reconnoitred the area and established contact with loyal Malays who would provide extra boats to complement those of the trawlers in transporting the men and equipment ashore. Once they were safely landed, Paton and his ships were to return without delay to the naval base, leaving the volunteers to their own ingenuity.

He glanced anxiously at the sky and then astern to where

Walrus and *Heron* were positioned, and called to White to signal them to close up in order to provide maximum fire cover if needed. The choice of the trawlers to carry out the mission was an indication of just how acute the shortage of ships had become; ideally the task should have been given to destroyers, or even better, fast coastal craft. But none were available and Paton recognised that if the occasion arose they would have to fight in a very tight formation and use their limited fire power to maximum advantage.

Paton moved across to the chart table and calculated that if everything went according to plan they would alter course in roughly half an hour when for the short time before dusk they would be exposed to the maximum risk from shore observation. He called to Phelp to take over and went below into the wardroom for a final consulation with the major who was in charge of the army side.

"By my dead reckoning we should be off the landing zone by 1900 at the very latest. How long will it take to get your men and equipment ashore?"

"If there are no hitches and we get the recognition signal from ashore telling us the boats are ready, we should complete it in about three hours. We've done it in less in training, but I'm erring on the safe side. Practice and the real thing aren't always the same."

Ideally, Paton wanted to be able to leave with darkness still providing a comforting cover, but that was the last thing to worry about, he had been told. The most important thing was to get the force safely ashore, no matter how long it took, and only when that had been achieved was he to concern himself with the problems of departure. The most perilous time, he realised, would be if he and his trawlers were caught in daylight, for then they would be a target for any shore batteries which might be in the vicinity. He asked for aircraft to cover his withdrawal, but that had been ruled out on the grounds that there were far more important things to defend than three old trawlers which were low on the list of priorities once their mission was accomplished. Although not stated in so many words, at the briefing he got the impression that they were considered a justifiable sacrifice and no great loss when measured against the plight of the retreating army. It was a situation he accepted without too much rancour; it was not the first time *Grey Seal* had been cast in the role of sacrificial lamb and still managed to survive. And, given a reasonable toss of the dice, they would again. He craned over the voicepipe and gave Read the order to alter course towards the land.

Leading Seaman Isaac Morris sat on the deck beside the Oerlikon thoroughly dejected and deep in thought – totally indifferent to the dangers that lay ahead. He had far more important things to occupy his mind. His philosophy was simple; if it had your name on it, then your number was up and no amount of worrying would alter that, but he was unable to adopt such a phlegmatic view over the two shattering blows he had received just before the ship sailed.

Dusty Miller offered him his tin of cigarettes. "Fag, Isaac?" But Morris did not even bother to answer, causing Miller to reflect that his oppo had hardly uttered a word since leaving harbour and nothing he said or did had lifted him out of his depression.

"You are a wet and no mistake, Isaac. An oyster's good company compared to you. You're making my life a misery. So your dog's done a moonlight and your girl friend has hopped it, but that's no reason to be like a wet weekend in Blackpool. You see, when we get back they'll both be waiting on the jetty. Jolson's a real bad penny, and the girl ain't going to ditch you if what you say about her is true."

Miller would have done most things for his oppo, but he could not bring himself to sympathise with him over what seemed to him so trivial; the dog was just a dog, while The Happy World was full of surrogate Amys. In another forlorn effort to cheer him up he said, "If you'd been married as long as me you'd buy her a single ticket to anywhere and not give a fart."

Morris said surlily, "Why don't you belt up? What do you know about it? It's not just *any* old dog you're nattering on about, neither is she an ordinary bit of skirt. She's *my* girl, and Jolson's as much a mucker as you are."

The tragedy, and it was very much that to Morris, had started shortly after the ship left dock and the crew returned aboard, and he had assumed that Jolson would settle down into his normal routine. Confident of this, he had not kept him under constant surveillance with the result that one evening the dog had nipped ashore, an event which did not worry him unduly for Jolson had done it before but had always returned, even if looking the worse for wear. But two days passed and still there was no sign of him. By then *Grey Seal* was under sailing orders and Paton who shared his concern for the ship's mascot gave permission for Morris to go ashore and search for him. He visited the Beach, the tea room, and all the other places he had gone to with Amy, but there was no sign of the Labrador. His final call had been to The Happy World where he hoped to see Amy and tell her to keep an eye open for Jolson and hang on to him until the ship returned to port, but to his added dismay he learned that she had not been to work for two nights. She gave no reasons, a friend told him, for the sudden disappearance, neither had she given any indication of when she would return. She merely stated that she was going up country.

He tried without success to obtain her address and even offered bribes to two rickshaw boys he knew had taken her home, but for reasons known only to themselves they feigned ignorance and pretended they did not know who he was talking about.

Eventually he was forced to abandon his search as it was getting perilously close to sailing time. Since then he had lapsed into a morose silence, his thoughts concentrated on the fate of the two most important beings in his life, and on the rare occasions when he managed to snatch some sleep he was invariably awakened by a nightmare in which the most terrible things had happened to them.

Miller tried yet again to open the conversation. "You know this little caper we're going on isn't going to last long. We'll be in and out like a pawnbroker's parcel. Then when we get back I'll help you find them, honest. The Old Man will give us the time."

"If I knew they were all right I wouldn't worry, but for all I know he could be on sale in one of them markets where the Chinks buy them to eat. As for Amy, she must have a bloody good reason for nipping off without telling me. Everyone else is tail-arsing it away from the fighting, not heading towards it. It's got to be something serious."

Paton glanced at the luminous dial on his watch and turned

to the major standing beside him. "I'll be dropping anchor in fifteen minutes. Your lads all set?"

The soldier nodded in the darkness. "Ready to go over the side as soon as I give the order."

Paton turned to Chalkie White and told him to flash the code signal on the shaded night lamp and watch for the reply which would signify the advance party were in position and everything in order for the operation to go ahead.

The hollow thump of *Grey Seal's* engine sounded alarmingly loud, although she was barely making way and the splash of the anchor hitting the water seemed so deafening Paton was convinced it could be heard ashore.

White's voice called out excitedly, "There it is, Sir. Dead ahead."

From the invisible shore a dim light briefly flickered the response and almost simultaneously Carnac gave the order for the two whalers to be lowered and the wireless set and other equipment to be winched overboard and secured to the thwarts.

As the boats' crews pulled on their oars, the whalers vanished silently into the gloom, the rowlocks muffled with canvas eliminating the slightest creak of wood on metal. Barely visible in the enveloping darkness, Paton could just make out the murky hulks of the two other trawlers, although he could hear the sounds of boats being lowered.

Half an hour later six or more small boats were bumping against *Grey Seal's* hull and soldiers began clambering over the side into them. An hour later all the men and equipment had safely disembarked. Paton shook hands with the major who was the last to leave, and wished him the best of luck, and he stood listening to the throaty phut, phut of the boats' engines until they were out of hearing before giving the order for the anchor to be hauled inboard. It had all gone off without a hitch. He called down to the engine room, "Maximum revs, Chief. We're off home," and to the wheelhouse he said, "Hard a port."

As *Grey Seal* carved a luminous wake on the surface of the star-dappled water and headed for the open sea, he could see the other trawlers already taking up station astern. Several hours of darkness still remained which would give them ample time to be well away from the scene of the landing and so give no hint to the enemy, if they were spotted, what they had been up to.

When dawn come, the sea was clear as far as the horizon; there was not even a smudge of smoke to indicate the presence of any other vessels. The ship juddered underfoot and vibrated with the strain as full speed was maintained, and Paton could imagine the curses being uttered by Chief Reynolds who was always loathe to push the ancient engine to the utmost, but every hour was invaluable; it was vital to be within the shelter of the numerous off-shore islands that fringed Singapore as quickly as possible.

Several hours passed and he was convinced they had made it when the starboard lookout bellowed, "Aircraft approaching Green three-O". Paton swung his glasses in the direction of the bearing and spotted two minute dots high in the sky, too far off for positive identification. His thumb jammed down on the alarm bells; it was too much to hope that they were British.

It took an unmercifully long time for them to get closer, and when he was at last able to identify them he was relieved to see that they were cumbersome Swordfish bi-plane torpedo bombers, known in the navy as "Stringbags" because of the profusion of struts and wires. They were due to be pensioned off at the outbreak of war because they were so slow and lumbering, but they were reprieved owing to the acute shortage of front-line aircraft.

He called to the signalman, "Signal who we are, Bunts. Can't be too careful." The signalman flashed frantically with the Aldis, but evoked no response. He called out, "Buggers must be blind or something. Either they can't read morse or they don't want to."

Paton stared anxiously at the two planes as they circled warily at a safe distance. Then they began to gradually lose height and head for the ships, almost skipping the wave tops at around ninety miles an hour, and when they swept overhead he could see quite clearly the huge torpedoes weighing 1,610 pounds suspended from their undersides, and he realised that the pilots were determined to have a really close look before accepting they were friendly ships.

"Keep flashing," he called to White, as he dashed across the bridge to the locker containing the Very pistol and flares.

He fired a succession of red and blue flares which would immediately identify them as Royal Navy vessels. He watched the two Swordfish turn together and come in again at little more than mast height. Christ, he muttered to himself, they take some convincing. It momentarily crossed his mind that they might have been captured at one of the airfields overrun by the Japanese, or the pilots were so suspicious because they could not imagine that any vessels other than enemy ones would be in that particular stretch of water.

Once more they roared harmlessly overhead, only to make a tight turn and head towards them again. They reminded him of huge prehistoric birds in the last stages of an evolutionary process in which they would eventually lose the ability to fly. Behind him he could hear the signalman clicking away feverishly at the trigger of the Aldis.

"Don't bother with that, Bunts. Signal to the other ships to make smoke", and almost in the same breath he called to the quarter deck, "Sub-Lieutenant Carnac, get some smoke floats over the stern." He also told Pike, the telegraphist, to break radio silence and inform base that he feared he was in imminent danger of attack from aircraft bearing RAF markings, and to contact them immediately informing them of their error. Despite their ungainly appearance, he knew that "Stringbags" piloted by men determined to press home an attack with little or no thought to their own survival could be extremely lethal; they had proved that at Taranto, against *Bismarck*, and in the U-boat war. He wasn't prepared to let them underline the point.

He was in a quandary; he was perfectly entitled to retaliate with gunfire if he was attacked, but the problem with that was that the pilots might take it as confirmation that they were enemy ships, whereas a smoke screen would completely obscure them and make a torpedo attack impossible. Furthermore, it would provide the necessary time for RAF headquarters to warn off the Swordfish.

Carnac and four seamen with axes cut through the lashings securing the huge cannisters and tumbled them overboard, and almost immediately the fuses began to activate the chlorosulphuric acid and a dense curtain of whitish smoke swirled and spread astern, as impenetrable as the thickest London pea souper fog. At the same time, Paton gave a helm order that brought *Grey Seal* steaming back into her own screen and he could see the seamen aboard the other ships manhandling their own cannisters overboard. But those of *Walrus* steaming just ahead of *Heron* seemed defective for they floated harmlessly on the surface without emitting the faintest puff of protective smoke. Just before *Grey Seal* was enfolded in a cotton wool mist he had a momentary glimpse of the first Swordfish releasing its torpedo. The subsequent explosion told him that it had scored a direct hit, and minutes later there was an even louder one, followed by a terrible sound of grinding steel, like a massive tin can being crunched by some gargantuan boot. This was followed by a red, raw flash which was visible through the choking smoke that shrouded the ship, and the deck was peppered with splintered planks of wood and pieces of jagged edged metal.

Although it meant exposing his own ship to danger, Paton realised he had no alternative but to break clear of the screen in order to find out what had happened and pick up possible survivors; it was out of the question to abandon them to their fate. As *Grey Seal* emerged into brilliant sunshine, the second Swordfish attacked, the Pegasus radial engine making an incredible din as it skimmed overhead, its forward machine gun chattering madly. It was so low he could see the heads of the helmeted and goggled pilot and observer. it was obviously an unsatisfactory run in or a sizing-up one, for the torpedo remained firmly anchored to the underbelly. Once more it turned and commenced a fresh run in, and this time Paton saw the torpedo drop, pancake on the water, then disappear, leaving only a creamy wake which was heading straight amidships. He gave an emergency helm order that swung the bow directly in the line of the approaching wake, presenting the smallest possible target, and he whistled softly with relief as he watched it pass harmlessly down the starboard side less than twenty feet away.

"Open fire," he shouted, and the Oerlikons began hammering away at the receding aircraft which was still firing the machine gun mounted in the rear cockpit. Several bullets pinged and ricocheted off the deck and superstructure, and the guns crews expressed their opinion of the Royal Air Force in obscene phrases of frustrated fury. But the two aircraft, content with the success of their mission and without any tin fish left with which to inflict further damage, climbed high and headed towards their distant base. Their range, he knew, was only 546 miles and by now they would be perilously low on fuel.

Grey Seal steamed slowly and cautiously in a wide circle waiting for the smoke screen to clear. Despite his mounting impatience, Paton refrained from steaming into it for fear of running down any survivors and churning them to pulp with the massive propeller. "Christ, it's taking its time," he said to himself.

As if by some divine intervention, a stiff breeze began to blow and the smoke started to disperse into wispy drifts that were quickly carried away. There was no sign of *Walrus*, but listing crazily at a precarious angle was *Heron* which seemed in imminent danger of capsizing; her mainmast was gradually dipping towards the sea and the portside bulwarks were already lapping water. The sea around was littered with Carley rafts and the one whaler which it had been possible to lower was filled with seamen, while just as many were clinging to the ropes along its hull. A number of corpses were floating face down in the water, kept buoyant by inflated lifebelts. There were also several men swimming frantically towards the rafts and one of them was good-humouredly making the gestures of thumbing a lift. Mercifully, because the two ships were coal burners, the surface of the sea was not coated with killing fuel oil.

Carnac and Phelp were already supervising the lowering of their own boats whilst seamen were cutting adrift the Carley rafts and launching them down their sloped racks. Paton gave the order, "Stop engine", and allowed the wind to drift the ship towards the survivors. Unable to wait, a number of men began swimming towards the ship, and as they neared heaving lines were thrown and they were hauled alongside and helped inboard.

In a remarkably short time, all the survivors were safely aboard, many of them badly burned and wounded. Hot cocoa laced with rum was handed round along with the inevitable cigarettes. Almost the last man to be rescued was Lieutenant Jimmy Hamilton, the RNR "skipper" of *Heron*, whose right arm hung limply by his side, bent at a grotesque angle, but he refused any medical attention until everyone else had been

194

treated.

Grey Seal cruised around for more than an hour to make absolutely certain there were no more men in the water before ordering full steam ahead and setting course for Singapore Island. Paton stared resolutely ahead; rising and falling, rhythmically like lillies in the wind-stirred swell astern, were the dead. He hated the thought of abandoning them, but the heat which caused such quick decomposition left him with no alternative. They would present a health hazard before he reached harbour.

He handed over the conning of the ship to Phelp and went to tour the messdecks to see how the injured were being cared for, and when he saw that Tiger Read was personally supervising the first aid he knew his own presence was not needed. During his long career, the coxswain had witnessed every conceivable form of injury and picked up an extensive if basic knowledge of how to treat them.

He went to his own cabin where Hamilton was lying on the bunk grey with pain yet stubbornly silent. He looked at the shattered arm and grimmaced, there was little he could do until they reached port except relieve the pain with morphia.

"What a ruddy turn up for the books, Sir. We put the pongoes safely ashore, then get clobbered by our own aircraft. *Walrus* got a tin fish dead amidships."

"I know, I caught a glimpse of it. But what happened to you?"

The lieutenant closed his eyes as the pain seared through him like a hot knife. "*Walrus* just stopped dead in her tracks and went down almost immediately, and I had no way of avoiding her and must have gone over her. Ripped a hole in my side you could have driven a Liverpool tram through. No hope of keeping her afloat, so I ordered abandon ship. Grateful so many of my lads managed to get clear. Do you know exactly how many?"

"My Number One is making a list. I'm afraid quite a few have gone, although we mercifully picked up a few of *Walrus's* crew. Must have been blown overboard by the explosion."

"I'd better nip down and show my face, Sir."

He groaned aloud as he tried to get up, and Paton gently

195

pushed him back onto the bunk. "You stay there. I'll tell them I refused to let you leave the cabin."

Paton gave him a morphia injection before returning to the bridge, where Phelp announced with incredulity, "Sorry Sir, but White has had it."

Paton heard the words with total disbelief. "What! How? He was perfectly all right when I last saw him."

"When I relieved you, Sir, he was sitting behind the flag locker and I thought he had dozed off. I called out to him to wake up, and when there was no response I shook him. He just keeled over and when I looked he had a wound right through his neck. Must have been a stray one from the Swordfish. Million-to-one chance. They've carried him down to the mess deck."

Paton was so shattered at the news he just wanted to be alone, and although he had the utmost confidence in his first lieutenant he said, "I'll take over. You go down below and see if they need a hand."

He slumped disconsolately into his bridge chair; a number of good men had been lost, but he had thoughts only for White whom he had known for so long. Ironically, he had survived the early days of the Northern Patrol, then in quick succession Norway, Malta and Crete, only to be killed by his own side. White who had so silently nursed his own grief may have lost the will to live, but even he would not have accepted such an ignominious fate. He had hinted at glory with his tuneless singing, but died senselessly and needlessly.

As soon as they returned to base he would have to submit a formal report and no doubt there would be some form of inquiry, but he doubted whether anything would come of it. It was not the first time ships had been attacked and sunk by friendly aircraft, or infantry shelled by their own artillery, and it would certainly not be the last. More than likely the unfortunate incident would be conveniently hushed up on the grounds that the publication of such a costly blunder would be deeply damaging to morale.

Grey Seal tied up at her normal berth close to the spot where not so long ago he and his ship's company had helped the survivors of *Repulse* and *Prince of Wales* ashore. In response to his wireless signal, several ambulances were waiting to take the wounded to hospital, but this time there was no reception centre to question the survivors. The loss of two trawlers amounted to little against the greater disasters which were unfolding on the mainland, and it would not do to reveal yet another blunder brought about by lack of co-ordination.

An hour later a staff captain from naval headquarters came aboard and saw Paton in the privacy of his cabin, where he extended the sincerest sympathies of the navy's Commander-in-Chief. "I know how bitter you must feel, but it just did not happen as far as the navy and air force are concerned, and I want you to impress that upon your men. It isn't a cover up, just common sense. No possible good can come from broadcasting it, especially when things aren't going too well. It was a genuine, if lamentable, error on the part of the pilots, but they have been flying such long hours their judgement has become impaired. But they are doing a wonderful job in impossible circumstances, and it would be disastrous if the impression was given that they are unreliable. So no idle gossip in the wet canteens or ashore. If I get the slightest whisper that anyone has let his tongue run away with him, everyone will be confined to ship. Is that clear? Imagine the effect it would have on morale. As it is, there are too many unfounded rumours going the rounds that British bombs are being dropped on our troops. Mustn't add to them."

Paton nodded wearily. "I'll do what I can, Sir, but I'll explain it to them in my own way. I've heard a lot about morale, but I know one thing, If your men lose their respect for you, their morale disappears with it."

"I'm not sure I understand you."

"I'm simply saying, Sir, that I will not tell my ship's company they must pretend it never happened. I'll appeal to their common sense, and for White's sake and for the others who were killed. They deserve a better epitaph."

"As you wish, Paton," he said stiffly. "I don't care as long as the outcome is the same. You must see my point?"

"With respect, I don't, Sir. I'm not worried about the morale of my men, but I am concerned about the gradual erosion of it among the civilian population. There I concede you have a point. But I believe it is due entirely to the false optimism which has been deliberately encouraged. Obviously people will be demoralised when they find out they have been repeatedly misled. It would be better if they were made to face reality as we did back home after Dunkirk."

"I know you've been under severe strain, Paton, so I'll overlook your insubordination. I did not hear it. But God help you if I hear you've repeated it."

As Paton saw him over the side, he thought to himself that the ability to gloss over unpalatable truths was reaching epidemic proportions.

Only Morris found their homecoming an occasion for smiles. Sitting forlornly on the quay, his coat matted and filthy, was Jolson. His ribs were sticking out and countable, and there were several deep lacerations on his head as if he had been involved in a ferocious fight. He limped slowly towards Morris, his stomach almost touching the ground, his tail wagging feebly as if unsure of the welcome he would receive. A shore-based sailor said, "He's been sitting there for ages. I tried to smuggle him into camp but he wouldn't budge, turned real nasty. Better give him some nosh because he refused to eat a thing, and a tot for his tonsils, he's been throwing his head back and howling like a bloody timber wolf. You're lucky a sentry hasn't put a bullet up his backside."

Morris raised a clenched fist at the dog but withheld the blow, thinking of those occasions when he was a child and his mother had vented her relief by striking him when he had narrowly escaped an accident or injury. Instead he slipped a length of string through his collar and said, "Come on, you daft bugger. Better get you cleaned up before the Old Man sees you and puts you back ashore, you bloody scruff."

He led the dog along the deck to the galley where Hall gave him a fanny of hot water into which he poured disinfectant before carefully bathing the wounds. "I'd hate to think what the other bloke looks like," he said. Then he slipped into the galley and surreptitiously opened two tins of corned beef. "You don't deserve it, going AWOL like that. I only hope it was worth it."

Jolson wolfed down the food, then raised his head and licked Morris's hand, his tail beating furiously on the deck. Then he limped wearily into the wheelhouse, circled round

198

once or twice before settling down and falling into a deep sleep punctuated by deep growls and twitches.

Morris stood watching him, then patted him affectionately before going to the wardroom to report the dog had returned aboard in one piece. At the same time, he requested permission to collect the mail which would present him with the opportunity to go to The Happy World. But when he got there, unlike Jolson, there was no Amy to welcome him, and all he could obtain in the way of information was that she was helping the army as an interpreter in their difficult task of evacuating people from villages where strong defensive positions were being established. it sounded to him as if the army was really on the run, because it wasn't so long ago that he had read an official announcement in one of the papers urging people to *stay* in their kampongs.

Chapter 11

Kate Hollis sat staring at the blank sheet of paper in her portable typewriter, facing what had become an almost daily quandary, a weary reluctance to work; it was not, she realised, a writer's block but the feeling that it was a sheer waste of time. She knew *what* she wanted to write, but realised it would never get past the censor. From wounded officers returning from the front and disgruntled staff officers from Fort Canning, she had gathered that the orderly withdrawal had developed into an almost disorderly rout, yet the official communiqués continued to give a rosy picture that implied everything was going according to a well-conceived plan. Every correspondent in the city knew it was totally untrue and deliberately misleading, but they were powerless to say so. The much vaunted stand on the Slim River had turned out to be a débâcle; the enemy had overrun it with comparative ease and the army had abandoned several heavy guns, anti-tank weapons, anti-aircraft guns, fifty armoured cars, more than five hundred vehicles of all types, along with mobile artillery, and enormous amounts of equipment, rations and medical stores. These the Japanese eagerly seized, using them against their foe, and gleefully describing them as "Churchill's rations".

The roads were choked with long, straggling columns of troops who were so dependent on mechanised transport that a single breakdown quickly developed into a gigantic traffic jam.

True the soldiers continued to fight with tenacity and courage, but they were confused and bitter, and many had lost faith in their leaders. The Indian troops were literally leaderless because the enemy had concentrated on their officers as prime targets and the Sepoys, many of whom were poorly trained, felt at a total loss.

And at night the army was haunted by the fear that the Japanese, who moved with a reptilian stealth, would capture them and subject them to the most hideous torture, for they had revealed an unimaginable barbarity. Furthermore, at night as they lay up in the jungle, they could hear what they took to be the rumble of tank tracks which added to their fear, although the sound in fact came from the rattle of tyre-less cycle wheels; the enemy was advancing so rapidly they did not have time to repair punctures and rode on the bare rims.

As the bewildered and utterly fatigued men fell back towards Singapore Island, a scorched earth policy was embarked upon which was pitifully inadequate; vital bridges were only partially destroyed and quickly repaired, while some fuses were rendered inoperative by the torrential rain. Entire villages were razed to the ground, which did little to impede the enemy although it had a disastrous effect on the native population who could not understand how the destruction of their homes and livelihood could be equated with the pledge that the British were fighting to defend Malaya from the invaders.

Kate was aware of all this, but was impotent to say so; Army Headquarters was adamant – it was vitally important that no hint of despair should be allowed to escape. It was a laughable assertion because there were hundreds of people who had fled from the mainland and were only too eager to talk about their ordeals and air their grievances to any willing listener.

Despite this, official announcements were made almost daily that fresh reinforcements had arrived and more were on the way. The arrival of one particular convoy was given added prominence; not only did it contain crack troops, but fifty crated Hurricane fighters. No mention was made of the fact that the men were inadequately equipped and only partially trained, or that the pilots lacked combat experience. But it produced the desired effect, and people were lulled into thinking that the crisis was over because one had to probe and question to find out the truth, something the majority of Europeans were disinclined to do, preferring to accept the repeated reassurances. Any doubts they may have had were quickly dispelled by the sight of newly arrived tough-looking Australians who exuded confidence as they toured the bazaars for souvenirs, and talked eagerly of their enthusiasm to encounter the enemy. No one imagined that most of them had only undergone two weeks basic training and had never fired a rifle at the butts, let alone in anger, or that the weapons they had been issued with were obsolescent. The British troops were only marginally better trained, and they were flabby from weeks at sea and ill-prepared to be thrown into the cauldron of battle. But their mere presence was enought to bolster morale.

And so the city carried on unruffled and unworried, although the enemy had renewed their aerial assault and barely a day passed without a raid. Sometimes there were as many as three or four. In a depressingly short time, the Hurricanes were exposed as no real match for the Zeroes, and most of them were shot down, allowing the enemy to concentrate their attacks during daylight when scores of bombers would appear over the city in perfect formation and simultaneously drop their bombs on a signal from the leading pilot. Inevitably, the casualties were greatest in the native areas where the population had more than doubled with the number of refugees who had arrived from the mainland. With no identity cards it was impossible to keep a check on the casualties, and at least 150 were killed each day; but that was only a rough-and-ready estimate, people just disappeared. But they were not purely terror raids; the docks and warehouses were also prime targets.

Although the ARP and fire service were operating without pausing for sleep, and often going without food for hours on end, they were quite incapable of coping with the damage and the mounting casualties. Some bodies were never dug out of the ruins, and the sickly odour of putrefying flesh filled the streets in Chinatown. Sewers were fractured and many streets flowed with effluence, and to counter the threat of disease the people were offered free injections. As the death roll mounted, mass graves were dug to avoid pestilence as corpses decayed so quickly in the heat and humidity, and next of kin were barely given time to identify relatives before they were filled in.

Kate, her arm aching from a booster jab, walked away from her desk and stood looking out of her window. Below, white-coated waiters were darting about smoothing fresh table cloths and taking orders for drinks and meals. Surprisingly, White Singapore was still considered relatively safe, for not only were the buildings stouter, but it had not been subjected to a relentless pounding, the enemy preferring to concentrate on the docks, the remaining airfields and other more strategic targets. In the distance she could see some syces calmly mowing the grass of the tennis courts, while immediately below a procession of cars was arriving with the first diners. She lit a cigarette and drew deeply; it was hard to accept that martial law had been proclaimed. That evening, she knew, the bar, restaurant, and dance hall would be teaming as usual with officers in smart uniforms, men in dinner jackets, and women in fashionable dresses. But it was not comparable to the manner in which she had seen Londoners cope during the Blitz. They had learned to *live* with it; here the people simply closed their eyes.

She returned to her typewriter and started to write without enthusiasm until the sirens began to emit their mournful howl. She visualised the scene that was taking place outside her room; the waiters would scurry away, the shops, banks, stores and offices would close until the "Raiders Passed" was sounded, when it would be business as usual.

She recrossed to the window and saw the bombers, escorted by fighters, flying overhead, resembling cruising carp in a pool of blue. She watched almost hypnotised as the leading pilot jettisoned his bombs and the others promptly released theirs. The black objects seemed to tumble down incredibly slowly, as if they were weightless. Once more the target was the dock area, and in a short time great columns of acrid smoke soared above the city as warehouses filled with rubber were set on fire. The bombing, she knew, would not be disciplined or too accurate, and Chinatown would inevitably get a share of the high explosives and framentation bombs. Once again the streets were filled with the familiar clamour of clanging bells as ambulances, fire engines and rescue squads careered recklessly towards the target areas.

One bomb fell with a deafening explosion in Raffles Place, and she decided the time had come to seek shelter. She made her way to the lobby which was crowded with European women and children who had been evacuated from the mainland. Homeless, penniless, and without clothing, they chose Raffles as a base where they wandered around aimlessly, hoping to bump into a friend who would lend them money or provide temporary accommodation of some kind, no matter how primitive. Many of them spent hours window shopping, gazing at the luxury goods on display they could not purchase, conscious of the hunger pains gnawing at their stomachs. At some time during the day they would go to one of the swimming clubs to wash their clothes in the changing rooms, then bask on the lawns until they were dry. Others queued for hours outside one of the many cinemas, and once inside would sit through the same film several times because they had nothing else to do, and the screened world of make-believe at the end of the dust-choked funnel of light took them away from reality.

The raid although heavy was fairly short, and Kate found herself automatically walking towards the Long Bar. It had almost become a ritual for people to down a coule of *stenghas* after a raid as if to celebrate their survival. The usual air of forced joviality pervaded the bar which had filled with incredible speed. There were rubber men trying to sound unconcerned over the loss of more rubber and a warehouse, and businessmen grabbing a couple of stiff ones before returning to work. She wondered whether Paton would be dropping in. She had not seen him for some time and only knew from asking some naval officers that he had been to sea, although they were unable, or reluctant, to elaborate.

Above the hubbub of conversation she heard the unmistakable voice of Mr Jardine who stopped talking as soon as he spotted her and invited her over. "Come and join the school, Miss Hollis," he boomed.

She had no wish to join him, and her reluctance increased when she saw that Nolan was one of the group, but it occurred to her that Jardine may have news of Sub-Lieutenant Carnac which she could relate to Paton's whereabouts.

As he ordered her a drink, he asked, "Any news to pass on? You newspaper people are always the first to hear the latest gen."

"Nothing encouraging, I'm afraid. Like everyone else, I have to rely on official handouts. Not allowed to report any unconfirmed stuff, but the army is continuing to fall back and there's still no sign of the long promised counter attack. All rather depressing."

Nolan growled, "You're a born pessimist. Like all reporters you look for disaster. Good news is bad news as far as you're concerned. But I'll let you into a little secret. Another big convoy is due any time now. Percival is just biding his time until they land, then wham, he'll shove the slit-eyed bastards all the way back to Tokyo."

"I've heard *that* whenever reinforcements have arrived, but they seem to be left kicking their heels in Singapore. However, it's true that I'm beginning to think good news *is* bad news. I don't believe a word of those cosy communiqués·that emanate from Fort Canning."

A man she had not met before interjected. "You've got something there, Miss Hollis. I don't think things *are* going as well as they make out. Know why? This morning my wife went shopping, and the Chinese owner of the shop we've been going to for donkey's years told her no more chitties, from now on it's cash. The Chinese are smart devils; maybe they can see the writing on the wall."

Nolan snorted. "Bloody fair weather friends. Probably want to get as much cash together as possible before scooting. Loyalty is not their strong suite. When the going's tough they lose themselves in a cloud of ruddy opium."

Kate said amiably, "That's hardly fair, the ARP and fire services would collapse but for the Chinese. They're doing a wonderful job." Because she had no wish to start an argument she promptly changed the subject. "How is your daughter, Mr Jardine? Seeing much of her young man?"

"See hardly anything of her, let alone Terence. She's become a proper Florence Nightingale. Can't say I'm not proud of her, but she does tend to overdo things; always has done. Bit to headstrong, won't listen to advice. Thinks the ruddy hospital will grind to a halt without her. My personal opinion is that the volunteers are being exploited. You can drive a willing horse too far. There're plenty of army nurses around without taking advantage of our own girls."

206

The anonymous man said, "We're all in this together, Clive. My wife is exactly the same as Jo. If I see her twice a week I'm lucky. Odd thing is I've never known her more contented. Says she can't understand why see wasn't bored to tears with her previous way of life. That's all very well, but she doesn't realise how much she's needed at home. Half the servants have decamped and I'm forced to bury the night soil myself because of the coolie shortage."

Jardine said scornfully, "I told you *years* ago to move with the times and invest in flush sanitation as I did. When I find myself digging a hole in the garden after a good clear out, it's time to think of leaving. Christ, we're supposed to be civilised and setting an example to the natives who know no better than to squat and do their business anywhere that's convenient. Worse than animals."

The men finished their drinks and apologised for having to leave her alone, and as they were going Kate said, "If you hear from Terence, Mr Jardine, I'd be most grateful if you gave me a ring. I'm rather worried about Commander Paton."

"I'll do that, promise, but I expect they're pretty well tied up at the base. I gather they had a rather nasty brush with the Japs. Lost quite a few men."

Kate felt the prickling chill of fear spread through her body, and wondered if the reason he had not been in touch was because he had been injured, and she decided to drive out to the base and find out. But when she arrived at the gates and showed her Press card, the armed sailor said, "Sorry, miss but no one who isn't on official business is allowed in. New orders."

"Is *Grey Seal* in harbour?"

"'Fraid I can't even tell you that. There's a big security clamp-down."

She drove back to the hotel wondering why security at the base had suddenly been given top priority; it seemed a little late in the day. She went straight to her room and wrote a letter to Paton explaining that she had tried to see him and would he get in touch as soon as it was convenient. As she wrote it occurred to her that the reason for the secrecy might have something to do with events on the mainland, and she decided on the spur of the moment to go to the front again. She knew it was a waste of time to make a formal application to revisit the battle area. Days could pass before she got a decision.

She dressed in the same clothes she had worn for her previous visit, filled her car with petrol, then called at a nearby food store and purchased several bottles of purified water, some packets of biscuits and an assortment of tinned sardines, corned beef and fruit; enough to last her for several days should it be necessary. The Chinese proprietor helped her to carry everything to her car, repeatedly apologising for insisting on cash.

She drove slowly across the island finding it hard to believe that a short time before people had been cowering in terror from falling bombs. A handful of golfers was playing a leisurely round, seemingly indifferent to the groups of soldiers sitting beside their machine guns sited in the bunkers. A little further on she saw a huge herd of cattle peacefully grazing in some pasture. Several times she had to pull off the road to let long convoys of military vehicles pass her, but no one stopped and asked her where she was going. As the last lorry passed she tagged on to the end, and as she crossed over the Causeway she decided to follow them until she was ordered back.

General Percival stared intently at the pin-dotted, large-scale map of Johore and Singapore Island, but it remained as blank as the sheet of paper in Kate Hollis's typewriter. It told him nothing. He thought wistfully of his days at Staff College when his tactical ability had been renowned, and his acute perception the envy of everyone. Then he had been able to anticipate the intentions of the enemy as if he had been endowed with second sight, but they had been an imaginery foe who did exactly as he thought, but the Japanese were totally unpredictable. They did not do any of the things he expected them to do. Now, as he studied the map, he was incapable of seeing solutions, only problems that had no answer. His two prominent incisors nibbled at his lower lip as he forced his brain to function. He felt unutterably tired. It had been a long time since he had enjoyed a night of uniterrupted sleep; he was invariably awakened with news of some fresh calamity. In fact it had become so difficult to cope with the constant changes that he no longer slept at Flagstaff House but spent most nights on a camp bed in his office.

With the departure of Brooke-Popham and the appointment of Pownall in his place he thought that life would be a lot easier, but Henry had not really had time to win his spurs because, he suspected on the insistence of the Americans, General Archibald Wavell had been appointed Supreme Commander of all Allied Forces in the South West Pacific which, of course, included Malaya.

Archie, he conceded, was a brilliant soldier, but he was overworked, which accounted for the series of disasters in the Middle East, and needed a rest, something Churchill had observed when he replaced him with Auchinlech. Now he had been hauled back into harness and given the job of master-minding the campaign in Malaya, unfortunately, not on the spot, but from far-off Java, which was ridiculous. He was like a school inspector who popped in occasionally looking for faults.

Percival felt his cheeks glow hot and realised it had nothing to do with the heat. He was recalling the sudden visit of Archie to Singapore when together they had inspected the defensive positions along the Johore Strait and on the northern coastline of the island. He could still feel the chilling stare of reproach in Archie's glass eye, as penetrative as a knife, when he asked him *why* there were so *few* fortifications, and he replied that such a measure would have been extremely bad for morale. Archie, renowned for his taciturnity and economy of words, was genuinely shocked, and the little he had said made it abundantly clear that he thought he had fallen down on the job and, he had added with some asperity, that it would be a damned sight worse for morale if the mainland had to be abandoned.

Of course, he had argued his case at great length until Wavell had lapsed into one of his typical moody silences, and he had felt a glow, not of smugness exactly, more the warmth of confidence achieved when a point has been finally established. It was only later, to his chagrin, that he discovered that Archie had felt himself swept away in a meaningless torrent of words spoken by a man who could not see the wood for the trees, and who believed that monotonous

209

repetition was a substitute for clear thinking. It was not very comforting to know that he did not command the total confidence of his Commander-in-Chief. But he was sure *he* was right and Archie wrong.

He forced himself to study the map in detail. In the unlikely event of the island being attacked, he was convinced the enemy would land on the north east coast. Admittedly, the north west coast was far more suitable – it did not contain the awful mangrove swamps where the trees seemed to be walking on the water, and the beaches were better – but the Japanese would expect him to assume that they would select the easier side, whereas he was astute enough to anticipate they would do the exact opposite. That ability to checkmate the enemy at his lectures had always been his forte.

Wavell, however, had expressed the view that the north west was the danger area, and he had a supporter in Brigadier Ivan Simson who was proving to be a bit of a thorn in his side. He had misguidedly established a series of strong points on the north west coastline and built up stocks of mines, booby traps and petrol for setting fire to the water, and erected barbed wire obstacles and even stripped abandoned cars of their batteries and headlights in order to illuminate the "killing grounds". Well, he had scotched that absurd idea, and had most of the stuff transferred back to the north east, only to be overruled by Churchill himself who put his oar in with a long list of what he considered essentials if the island was to be turned into a citadel and defended to the end. Apparently he was shattered when Wavell cabled him expressing dismay at the island's vulnerability and that it had only been prepared to defend itself against a seaborne invasion. He was aware of the Prime Minister's faith in his own misconceived ability as a strategist, which caused him to muddle in matters best left to the generals, but he suspected that the devious Duff Cooper had also had a hand in the long list of instructions which amounted almost to a reprimand, for they were based entirely on suggestions submitted to Cooper by the interfering Simson. Now they had come back like a boomerang as a direct order from Churchill; booby traps *must* be installed in the mangrove swamps, strongpoints established with machine guns and artillery, and searchlights mounted on confiscated boats, to decimate the enemy if they tried to cross. And field batteries were also to be sited at each end of The Strait to sink any approaching ships and the big naval coastal guns to be provided with high explosive ammunition in addition to the armoured piercing shells which was all they had at the moment. Furthermore, mobile columns were to be set up, capable of moving at high speed to any endangered area. The entire male population should be enlisted to build fortified positions using, if necessary, picks and shovels. That, he mused, was entirely out of the question. One couldn't order white men to demean themselves by doing the work of coolies. The Prime Minister's cable – which Wavel passed on to him – left no doubt that *everyone* was expected to fight to the last. "No surrender can be contemplated", and if necessary nothing was to be left to fall into the hands of the enemy.

Well, he had done his reluctant utmost to comply, especially as Wavell had been so insistent and said, not very encouragingly, that it might be too late. Personally he believed Wavell and Churchill were being unduly pessimistic. His own opinion was that the Prime Minister was preparing to save his own face should the worst come to the worst, for he was undergoing a crisis of confidence in his own management of the war and had asked the House for their support. It really was unfair of him to express surprise at the lack of preparation; everyone had known about it for years, but all requests for improvements had been shelved in the sacred cause of economy.

As he moved some pins he felt his anger growing; it was *quite* wrong for Winston to dictate strategy from thousands of miles away. The man on the spot was really the only person capable of making rational decisions. Despite what everyone else said, he still adhered to the opinion that the landings, if any, would be made in the north east and had wisely concentrated the bulk of his troops there.

One of the many telephones jangled noisily disturbing his thoughts, but he left it to one of his staff to answer. The news from the front was bad, the enemy had completely overrun Johore, and there had been fresh landings on the east coast of the mainland. His gloom mounted as he calculated that the army would have to withdraw to the island within a few days. Well, he had prepared for a prolonged siege by storing enough food for at least six months. Several thousand head of cattle had been brought over the Causeway and there were a quarter of a million pigs on the island, while two of the largest cinemas had been converted into food stores. But, he told himself, he would have sacrificed half of it for a couple of squadrons of modern fighters; the air force had now been whittled down to a mere handful. Mercifully, he did no have to worry about water, the island's reservoirs were capable of providing enough for years, not months.

Kate followed the convoy feeling uncomfortably like an uninvited mourner in a funeral cortège; no one paid the slightest attention to her presence. The comparison, she thought, was not entirely inappropriate; the convoy was proceeding at a funeral pace, interrupted by frequent halts when the officers would jump out of their vehicles and herd together to head-scratch over a map spread out on the bonnet of a scout car, before moving off with a vagueness and indecision that was far from comforting. The vacillation had been transmitted to the soldiers who wore an air of dejection as they sat upright in the backs of the lorries, looking for all the world like condemned men in tumbrils who had given up all hope of a reprieve. The sky reverberated to the incessant din of gunfire, and occasionally a fighter would appear, as if from nowhere, to machine gun the column. The soldiers, their faces masked with scarves and scraps of cloth, were grateful that the roads which shortly before had been a porridgy morass were now coated with inches of dust which the wheels churned into fog-thick clouds which clogged the throat and brought tears to the eyes, and reduced visibility to a few yards. But it also helped to conceal them from the fighters. As the lorries ground on in low gear they were increasingly aware that the sound of the guns was becoming louder and louder.

To add to the confusion, they frequently encountered columns of troops moving in the direction from which they had come, and in the ensuing jumble officers shouted to each other from behind cupped hands that each was going the wrong way. An hour later the convoy halted at a deserted village and the vehicles were speedily dispersed in the undergrowth fringing the perimeter. it seemed to Kate pointless to continue to tag behind in hopeful anonymity, and she got out of her car and walked determinedly to the wireless van where several officers had assembled waiting for instructions to reach them from Singapore. She introduced herself to the colonel who seemed to be in charge, and lied with unruffled calm. "I was told to follow you if I wanted a good story. So far I haven't learned a thing."

The colonel looked at her appraisingly and smiled. "Whoever gave you permission to cross over wants his head examined. Those units which have just passed us have received orders to withdraw to the island. Seems as though General Percival has given up all hope of holding on to the mainland. It's crazy seeing as how we were sent to hold the line. We've just radioed for clarification, and until we get it there's nothing we can do but kick our heels here. No point in looking for a line that doesn't exist." He turned to a sergeant and said, "Take Miss Hollis over to the canteen and see if you can whistle up some tea."

She followed the sergeant to a mobile field kitchen where huge vats of tea were being brewed. A long queue of shuffling men had already formed, patiently waiting with their mugs in their hands for their turn to be served with the scalding, dark brown tea laced with condensed milk.

"It looks a trifle chaotic, Sergeant."

"That's putting it mildly, Miss. The Grand Old Duke of York would be at home here."

As he spoke, the air was filled with the shrill whistle of approaching shells, and the soldiers dispersed in all directions like rabbits at the sound of a shot gun. Some dived for cover in the undergrowth, whilst other began feverishly to dig slit trenches with their bayonets. Several of the lorries received direct hits and exploded with a deafening whoof as the petrol tanks exploded. Leaves showered down, and vast tree trunks were split as if struck by lightning. Men were writhing in agony on the ground as splinters of shrapnel tore through their flesh, inflicting the most hideous wounds and severing arms and legs. Kate, cowering beside the canteen, saw the head of one soldier sailing through the air like a well punted football. She was unable to stifle a scream of terror, and she felt herself being hauled upright and ferociously shaken

213

by the sergeant who then dragged her towards her car. "Listen, Miss, we're well and truly clobbered. We've got to break out of here somehow or other, but the chances are pretty slim. So no one will have time to keep an eye on you. My advice is, get in your car, put your foot down, and head towards the guns. They'll be increasing their ranges as we pull back, so you might be lucky. If they catch you with us they won't give a damn that you're a woman. On your own you might make it."

Kate jumped into her car, but the engine refused to respond to the starter and she accepted with a calmness that amazed her that she was experiencing her last minutes on earth. The ground was carpeted with screaming, mutilated men, crawling and writhing towards the surrounding jungle. Those incapable of moving were being carried sack-like on the shoulders of their comrades. Medical orderlies with no concern for their own safety were doing what they could for the wounded, and snatching off the identity discs from the dead. It was a kind of warfare she had never envisaged; the soldiers were caught in a trap of steel and fire by an unseen enemy. The sergeant bellowed for a group of soldiers to give him a hand with a push start. Some pushed from behind while others added their weight to mudguards and door handles. When the car was moving steadily the sergeant shouted, "Put her in second and let the clutch in." As she did so the engine fired and she careered down the dusty road without the vaguest idea of where she was heading. Behind she could hear that the barrage had intensified and the low crump of mortars added to the sound of exploding shells. As she drove she passed bewildered groups of soldiers looking as lost as she was, and once, when she halted to ask for advice, a corporal said, "Wish I could help you, Miss, honest, but we've lost all our officers and we don't even have a map or compass. We're just heading for the fight that's going on ahead in the hope we can team up with some of our own lads. Not many of us are going to make it to Singapore, but the Japs'll know they've been in a fight. You'd be better off on your own though."

She drove until the sound of battle was just a distant rumble and was astonished that she had not encountered the enemy; and when she came upon what appeared to be another abandoned village she concealed the car and carried her food and drink into an empty attap-roofed hut. She inspected it by the beam of her small torch, and in a darkened room found a primitive bed and an oil lamp. She lay down on the bed knowing that although sleep was out of the question it was vital to conserve her energy. She thought of lighting the lamp, but decided against it; the glow might attract attention. She opened one of the tins of corned beef, and as she did so she was surprised to discover how hungry she was. When darkness came she ventured out and saw the sky from the direction in which she had come was a fiery orange. As she stood there she became aware of sounds above the croaking of the frogs and the nocturnal chatter of insects, and she tilted her head, convinced that it was the whisper of female voices. Then she heard the soft crunch of stealthily moving feet, and as she withdrew into the room she saw a dozen or more dark shapes emerge from the darkness and move towards an adjoining hut. A voice, unmistakably Anglo-Malay, murmured, "We will be safe here", and another voice, obviously English, reply, "Are you sure?"

Kate padded softly in the direction of the hushed voices and called out, "It's all right, I'm American. Can I come in?"

The lilting Welsh-like voice replies, "Yes, we are all friends."

She slipped past a strip of canvas curtaining the door and went in, but could only make out vague shapes silhouetted by the moonlight filtering through the windows. "We must cover them up before we light a lamp," said the Eurasian. What light there was was blocked out by shapes covering the windowless windows with some material or other. An oil lamp glowed dimly then, as the wick was raised, she was able to see about half a dozen women and several small children. All except one of them were coloured.

Kate addressed herself to the white woman. "Jesus, am I glad to see *you*! I got caught in some kind of ambush and was told to get the hell out of it as fast as I could. No idea where I am."

The woman said, "I'm Vera Brooks. Thanks to Amy here, I'm still alive and kicking. I was with a small group of wives who were being evacuated to the island when we too got caught by the Japanese. They killed all the soldiers and the other women, but I was buried under a pile of bodies and the Japs didn't even stop to see if there were any survivors. I was the only one. If Amy hadn't turned up I don't know what I'd have done. I don't even speak Malay."

Kate felt her fear melting away like snow in warm sunlight, and she took out a tin of cigarettes and passed them round. Only Mrs Brooks and Amy took one; the other women declined, preferring to smoke small cheroots which they produced from beneath their shabby blouses.

Kate said, "I have my car here. Do you think we can all get in and make a dash for it at first light?"

Amy said, "No, the car is bad. Native people do not have them and the Japanese would shoot at it without challenge. We must go on foot. I have taken many people to Singapore. I know the paths well. In the morning we shall dress you two white ladies in different clothes, so that you can pass for our people. The Japanese are not harming them; they are our friends, they say. They are doing this for us."

Soon the women lay down on the bare floor and fell asleep, and Kate found herself alone with Amy who explained that she had been helping to get people to the island, but the army unit she was with had been called away to fight and she was left to get back as best she could. "I do not think it will last too long now. The war here is lost. Only in Singapore can we be safe."

As they talked deep into the night, Kate asked her why she continued to risk her life; she would be better off pretending to welcome the enemy. The girl seemed shocked at the suggestion. "Half of me is English, the other half is Malay, but I prefer the British half. My father is a soldier, and my boy friend is in the Royal Navy. A killick. That is very high. I could not stare him in the face if I turned around my coat. Now we should sleep; it is a long walk to Causeway."

Kate was awakened by a shaft of dust-clogged sunlight filtering through a chink in the makeshift curtains. She sat up and saw Amy standing over her with a bundle of clothing and a straw hat, shaped like a limpet, similar to those she had seen women wearing in the paddy fields. "Put these on, and please remember, if you are halted you cannot talk. I shall say you have lost your tongue."

216

Kate took off her bush shirt, slacks and heavy boots, and put on a ragged blue blouse that reached her waist, and a baggy pair of trousers and wooden soled sandals. "Some little dirt on your face will be good," said Amy.

As she smeared her face with dust from the floor she was aware of voices chattering excitedly in the next room. "What's that?" she asked anxiously, but Amy merely put a finger to her lips and said, "Remember, no talk."

Together they hurried to the window and made a cautious parting in the curtains and saw the compound filling with lorries crowded with men, but the churned up dust made it too difficult for them to identify them although Kate was able to recognise the lorries as British. "It's OK, Amy, I think the trucks are ours," but Amy had once more pressed a finger to her lips before murmuring, "Captured".

As they watched they saw men scrambling over the tailboards, and as the dust settled they were clearly recognisable as Japanese; they all wore ill-fitting uniforms and identical baseball-style caps. They stepped back silently into the semi-darkness, then heard the clump of boots on the verandah and the darkness became total as the doorway was filled with figures. Three soldiers with bayonets thrust them forward and began prodding menacingly at them. All had wispy moustaches and one screamed something unintelligible in a near hysterical voice, and although they could not understand a word, his meaning was clear. He wanted them to go outside. As they went out onto the verandah they were kicked and hit with the butts of the rifles, and as Kate was propelled down the small flight of steps she heard Amy whisper, "No speaking".

As she landed in the dust, Kate looked up and saw the other women and their children jabbering excitedly, being prodded across the compound to where an officer was standing upright in a captured Humber staff car. Unlike the soldiers he was impeccably dressed in a well pressed and starched uniform, his black boots glistened with polish, and a long sword dangled from his side. Despite the pig-bristle moustache and beard, she recognised him immediately as Okamoto. He drew his sword and pounded on the bonnet of the car like a summoning drum. "Pay attention! Does anyone speak English?"

As the other women threw a protective cordon around Kate and Mrs Brooks, so that they were out of sight of the officer, Amy stepped forward and said, "A little. Not too much."

Okamoto stepped down from the car and walked towards her. "Good. If you obey my orders you will come to no harm. We are here to help you. We are your liberators from the colonial yoke. Tell them that."

Amy translated his words, but the women stood there looking vacant, the unaccustomed phrases meaning nothing to them.

He shouted something to his men, who immediately began to push the women into the semblance of a straight line, and he again addressed Amy. "Are there any British soldiers here? If you are harbouring some you will pay dearly. Just tell me the truth and you will not be harmed. My soldiers are honourable men and have no quarrel with women."

Amy stepped forward, and in a remarkably calm voice replied. "There are no soldiers. We have been forced to leave our kampong and are trying to make our way to the island. We have no money or food, and we are hungry."

"I will see that you get some rice and fish. That is all we have to offer."

A soldier stomped out of the hut shouting excitedly, a tin of corned beef in each hand and Kate's discarded clothing under one arm. At the same time another soldier scuttled up to Okamoto, bowed, and pointed to where her partially concealed car was standing. Okamoto shrieked more orders and several soldiers lined up in front of the terrified women, brutally ripped off their hats, grabbed hold of their hair and yanked their heads back so that Okamoto could see their faces. He walked straight towards Kate, his face wreathed in a wide smile. "Miss Hollis, I didn't expect to meet you again. I thought you would have the good sense to be in America."

The lie came glibly to her lips. "I've been covering the final stages of the retreat. I had planned to return to Singapore and write a piece that would be a vindication of my earlier criticisms. I hope I'll still have the opportunity."

Okamoto muttered something to one of his men who ran over to the Humber. "Let us go inside for a few minutes.

218

I do not want my soldiers to know that we are friends. They are like all victorious warriors; at the end of the day they need to relax and a white woman is a great temptation. I cannot watch them all the time."

She followed him up the steps into a hut where he sheathed his sword with a dramatic flourish and gestured her to sit down on one of the crude chairs while he perched on the edge of a rickety table. "Just what were you intending to do among these natives, Miss Hollis."

She explained how the convoy she was with had been ambushed and how it was her hope and intention to return to Singapore.

"That is the last place you should be contemplating going to. It is doomed. Soon our heavy artillery will be in range of the island and we will reduce it to rubble until the white flag is hoisted. You would be better advised to think of an alternative."

"Do I have one? It seems as if I am your prisoner. Any decisions are yours."

He produced a tin of Players cigarettes and held it out to her, and when she had taken one he politely lit it for her. As he did so the unkempt soldier who had been despatched to the Humber clumped in, saluted, and handed Okamoto a bottle of Johnny Walker.

"The British are most considerate. When they run away, not only do they leave us ammunition and equipment, they provide us with generous gifts of cigarettes and whisky. The British officer it seems does not march on his stomach but on his hip flask. You must excuse me, Miss Hollis, they do not provide us with glasses."

"On the neck will suite me fine," she said as he handed her the bottle. She took a long swallow and felt the spirit burning through her, first in her throat, then her stomach. She swallowed far more than was advisable, but thought to herself that if she had to die she would rather do so in an alcoholic haze. She held up the bottle, "Mind if I exploit your hospitality?"

He nodded in assent, and as she hugged the bottle between her knees she saw that the level had dropped considerably and she was already feeling light headed and reckless.

"The ball's well and truly in your court, Colonel. It is

219

Colonel, isn't it? At least, that's what Superintendent Nolan said."

He smiled without humour. "Oh Nolan! I think I once hinted at my opinion of him. An incompetent, and the worst possible example of the colonial officer. Despises the people he was appointed to protect; but he is not a rare specimen."

He leaned forward and prised the bottle from her hands. "There is no need for the prisoner to drink a hearty breakfast. In any case, I would like one myself."

He drank greedily, spilling the spirit down his chin and rubbing dry the trickles on his tunic. "Contrary to what you may have heard, we are not barbarians; although my soldiers might strike fear into you, that is what is expected of them. They are taught to kill or be killed. They despise those who surrender. They prefer death to dishonour. But they do not make the decisions."

"I'm glad to hear that. They haven't been too gentle."

"That is only because they are mistrustful. Some of the natives, men and women, are secretly pro-British and they have learned to be cautious until they are satisfied they do not constitute a threat to our ideals and ambitions, and accept us as friends."

"Ripping their country to shreds is hardly a way of proving your good intentions, Colonel."

He smiled tolerantly, "I'm glad you have not lost your American sense of humour. Frankly it was something that always eluded me. The truth is the British have caused more havoc to villages than we have. We invariably give the people an opportunity to leave before we attack. We are not motivated by a desire for conquest. We want to liberate Asia and ensure that its riches are not exploited for the benefit of a handful of entrepreneurs. When the British have been driven out we will rule the country as partners."

The drink had made her bold. "If what you say is true, why the heck are you fighting the Chinese?"

Okamoto rapped his boots impatiently with his scabbard. "Let us please remain friends, Miss Hollis. I have promised that you will come to no harm; do not impose on our friendship. You helped me in the early days; I wish to repay that debt. I cannot if you continue to cross swords."

Kate mumbled, "Sorry. Just being facetious." She raised

her eyes towards the bottle dangling from his hand. "What about a final snort to cement our friendship?"

He passed the bottle. "Do you think it is wise? You will need a clear head."

"Before I decide on that you can tell me what you have in mind."

"Of course. I will see that you are escorted to the shore where a boat will be provided. You will in turn give me your word that you will not make for Singapore, but go to one of the kampongs on an off-shore island. That is necessary for obvious military reasons. Otherwise you will be heading into grave danger and where I can no longer help. I do not wish that. You are truly a friend, although it may be difficult to accept. You have served the Emperor well, even if unintentionally."

He rose stiffly and escorted her outside to where the other women had been shepherded together by the side of a truck. He shouted something in Japanese and the women were helped into the back. He handed the whisky to Kate and said, "Take it. I have plenty. You may also take your food and water." He leaned over the bonnet of the lorry and wrote something on a sheet of paper ripped from his notebook. "If you meet any Imperial troops, show them this. It will guarantee safe passage. I can do no more."

Kate shook his hand and said, "I'm genuinely grateful. I still think we'll win, and when we do I'll put in a good word for you, Colonel."

He smiled, this time with genuine humour. "When I was in America, I always enjoyed those films at which you excelled depicting tight-lipped heroes surmounting impossible odds. They were invariably British, having so little history of your own. But this is reality. The next Briton I see will be across the surrender table."

"Don't count on it. Remember Malaya is founded on rubber which has a habit of bouncing back."

"You are resorting to glib journalese. The rising sun is setting over the empire. Why should you, an American of all people, suggest that colonialism will triumph? Your own president has stated quite openly that American is not in this war to maintain the British Empire."

"That's true, but we aren't fighting to prop up the Empire.

221

We're fighting someone who attacked us without warning."

Okamoto sighed and dredged up a rueful smile. "You have had too much whisky. Perhaps we should not continue to talk as if we are equals. We are the conquerors, the British the vanquished. America soon will be too. But we shall be magnanimous. The world will witness that."

He shouted more orders and the sergeant at the wheel started the engine and four armed men climbed over the tail board. As Kate got in she said, "Whatever our differences, I really am grateful for what you're doing."

As the lorry drove off, she had a last glimpse of him standing in the clearing waving farewell, and wondered how long it would be before he lost his sense of fairness and chivalry.

As they rocked and bucketed along narrow, dusty roads, they passed scenes of sickening carnage; the burnt out shells of lorries, armoured cars and ambulances lay everywhere, surrounded by mounds of bodies in grotesque poses. Swarms of flies soared up as they passed, only to resettle immediately and continue their insatiable gluttony. And although they did not witness any fighting they were aware of its proximity; guns thundered all around.

The sergeant drove skilfully, clearly aware of his destination, and something like an hour later they arrived at a fishing village which was already occupied by soldiers squatting around the compound eating from bowls pressed close to their lips. The guards jumped out and herded the women together while the sergeant presented himself to an officer; a long conversation ensued which resulted in the women being marched to a small pier against which were moored a motley collection of fishing boats and sampans.

To Kate's surprise, the officer had a working knowledge of English and he explained that Colonel Okamoto had given orders that a fishing boat should be placed at their disposal with two fishermen to crew it. "You are free to leave, but it will soon be dark so you must delay here until day. That is safer. In darkness all boats will be fired at."

Then they were escorted into a hut with a sentry posted outside. Kate fell into a fitful sleep tormented by the sight and sound of the ambush, and when she awoke she imagined she heard the skirl of bagpipes followed soon afterwards by a series of shattering explosions. Jesus, she told herself, I'm so jittery I'm getting hallucinations.

Half an hour later the party was sailing down the Johore Strait.

Amy came up to her and said, "I have spoken to the fishermen. We will be safe where we are going. I know it well. When we arrive, have you any money for them? Otherwise they may talk about us."

Kate produced a wad of notes from her money belt. "That is probably more than they've ever seen at one go, but it's a silence worth buying."

Chapter 12

Paton sat drinking tea in the wardroom with Phelp and Carnac. Across the Strait he could hear the continuous clamour of battle and his thoughts kept straying to Kate, for he had received her letter and as the guns pounded away he repeatedly wondered where she was. It seemed extremely foolhardy to have ventured to the front when the situation was so delicately poised, but he could hardly criticise her for doing her job.

Grey Seal had remained alongside ever since the encounter with the Swordfish, seemingly forgotten and unwanted, and day after day there had been nothing to do but listen to the fighting getting closer and closer with the inevitability of an incoming tide. He spent hours on the bridge, glasses to his eyes, trying to see what was happening, but he saw no more than fires and great spouts of smoke climbing into the cloudless sky.

His thoughts were interrupted by a brisk rap on the door and the quartermaster poked his head in to announce, "Four ringer coming aboard, Sir."

He grabbed his cap and hastened to the waist of the ship, just in time to salute as the captain came over the side. "Let's go somewhere where we can talk in private, Commander," he said brusquely.

Paton led him into his cabin, closed the door and offered him a chair. The captain sat down, glanced anxiously around to make sure they could not be overheard, then said, "I won't waste time; there isn't any to waste. The base is being evacuated. Every manjack, including the labour force, is to be withdrawn as quickly as possible, and every item of equipment and machinery that might be of use to the enemy destroyed. Quite a lot of the men have gone already. Went last night. Wouldn't do to signal our intentions."

Paton could scarcely believe what he was hearing. "But the base is the sole reason for fighting. If we abandon it there's no point in staying here. Apart from the raids and some spasmodic shelling there's been no great threat. Anyway, Sir our troops are still fighting over there."

"I know it sounds cock-eyed, but the order came from London. All the European naval and civilian dockyard staff are to go to Ceylon."

"That means we've given up hope, Sir," said Paton in disbelief.

"Not at all, the island will be defended to the last. Look at it practically, Paton. What's the use of a base when we no longer have a fleet here. The skilled men will be better employed in Trinco. By the way, this is strictly confidential. Don't want everyone rushing to panic stations. Even Percival doesn't know yet."

As he spoke he produced a bulky envelope from his pocket and put it on the table. "Sealed orders. Not to be opened until you sail at 1700. I won't say anything; all you need to know is there. Some ERA's and men trained in demolition will be coming aboard soon. They know what they have to do. Your job is simply to take them to their destination and bring them back to Keppel Harbour. Good luck."

Paton saw him ashore, then returned to his cabin where he sat tapping the table top with the bulky envelope containing his orders; the news that the base was to be secretly abandoned filled him with a sense of shame; in his eyes it amounted to a betrayal of the army fighting so stubbornly on the other side of the Causeway, while the labours of sixteen years were to be tossed away without a struggle. For the first time in his career he deliberately disobeyed orders and opened the envelope.

Grey Seal was to sail at dusk and steam through the Strait at full speed and head for an offshore island to the south where several oil storage tanks were sited. There he was to remain until he received orders for the demolition of the tanks and installations. The orders were detailed and listed the role that would be played by the various parties who would soon be boarding. They reiterated that the demolition parties had been separately briefed and would, therefore, require no supervision.

He summoned his officers, Read and Reynolds, into his cabin and explained the mission they were to undertake. As he spoke the ship was lifted at her moorings by a massive explosion that caused a minor tidal wave. The row of photographs on his desk was hurled across the cabin and a torrent of upheaved water came through the open ports.

"What the hell's going on?" said Phelp, and they rose as one and hurried out onto the upper deck, all thinking that it was a surprise raid. Along the shore a great mushroom cloud of impenetrable smoke was climbing into the sky, almost blotting out the sun. The first stage of the evacuation had commenced with the destruction of the fuel dumps. They watched in amazement as the plumes writhed skywards, illuminated at their base by a glowing core of fire. Another explosion rent the air and the giant floating dock which had been towed all the way from England disappeared in a cloud of spray, and when it cleared the dock had settled, partially submerged, on the bed of the Strait. As the demolition continued, streams of lorries filled with sailors and workmen began to leave, but it was a panic departure rather than an orderly evacuation, and the policy of total devastation was disgracefully mismanaged. Huge cranes capable of lifting a gun turret were left intact, along with workshops, radio equipment and mountains of ropes, hawsers and food. In fact, everything needed to maintain a fighting fleet of hundreds of vessels. No attempt was even made to render huge replacement boilers useless, or smash the countless weapons in the armouries.

Paton, still with three hours remaining before sailing time, decided to go into the base and see for himself exactly what was happening. As the long queues of vehicles drove away, he walked across ground littered with all kinds of equipment from gas masks to clothing, and when he entered the mess halls it seemed to him that the base had been struck by an earthquake as suddenly as the one which had destroyed Pompei. Tables were covered with half eaten meals, and the unmade beds cluttered with partly cleaned items of equipment. Already swarms of flies had descended on the food and ravenous dogs emerged from nowhere to snarl and fight outside doors where they could smell food. Rats, normally stealthy and cautious, scampered across the floors enjoying the unexpected harvest.

Paton walked slowly back to the ship, appalled that so little effort had been made to salvage the vast quantities of food, clothing and equipment which would be priceless if the island was invaded. He would only have been marginally appeased if he had known that orders would be issued for the army to help themselves to whatever they wanted once the last man had gone, or that it would take more than a hundred lorries working a tight schedule to salvage everything that was portable, and that men who had worn the same filthy uniform for days, sometimes weeks, would now have new shorts and shirts.

As he stepped aboard, he saw that his own demolition parties had already embarked. The Chief Gunner's Mate who was in charge tossed his head towards the base and said bitterly, "Don't exactly make you proud of the Andrew, does it, Sir? Now we're going to add our little bit of mayhem so we don't feel out of it. Won't make the lads who went down in *Repulse* exactly sleep peacefully."

Paton detected an added note of bitterness. "What prompted that?"

"Well, Sir, I was in her, and we came out here thinking the naval base was important, and we fought till the water was coming over the sides because we believed they meant it."

By 7 o'clock on the morning of Saturday, 31 January, when *Grey Seal* was approaching her destination, the two remaining pipers of the Argyll and Sutherland Highlanders inflated their bagpipes and played, "Jennie's Black E'een", and "Bonnets over the Border", as the tail end of the 30,000 troops who had been fighting to stem the enemy advance crossed the Causeway. Then the Commanding Officer of the Highlanders, who had fought every yard of the way from the Siam border and been almost annihilated in the process, crossed the three-quarters of a mile long strip of concrete to the defiant strains of "Hielan' Laddie". It was the music which Kate had imagined hearing, and it signalled the end

228

of the fight to maintain even a toehold on the mainland.

Soon afterwards, Singapore Island became totally isolated as the delayed action fuses were fired, blowing an enormous sixty foot gap in the Causeway and destroying water pipes, lock gates, and other vital installations.

Grey Seal moored broadside on to the jetty on the southern side of the island and almost immediately a shore party under the Chief Gunner's mate set off to reconnoitre the oil storage tanks.

Paton meanwhile ordered every available hand to go with Leading Seaman Morris and collect as many palm fronds and other foliage necessary to cover the entire upper deck and conceal the ship from any enemy aircraft. It was a ruse that had worked well in the Norwegian fiords against predatory Stukas, and there was no reason why it should not be as effective now.

Camouflage was plentiful and easy to cut, and as the working party slashed away with machetes and axes, Morris set off, with Jolson at his heels, to see what could be picked up in the way of bunce, for it seemed to him at first sight that the island had been hastily evacuated; there was no sign of life at all. He went into several bungalows obviously used by European staff, for they were well constructed and comfortably furnished. He experienced a feeling of eerie unease as he prowled through the rooms; there were unmade beds, and floors stewn with clothing, tennis raquets and fishing rods, as if the occupants had been given a minimum amount of time to pack the most essential requirements. In a nursery he saw a clockwork Hornby engine and coaches stationery on a circular track as if someone had been halted in the process of winding it up. He spoke aloud to the dog, "Hell's bloody bells, it's like a ship that's been abandoned which is in no danger of sinking." He opened a refrigerator, then closed it in disappointment; clearly the departing occupants had placed alcohol high on their list of priorities.

He strolled on until he reached a much larger building surrounded by neat flower beds and lawns, and skirted by a wide verandah on which were lined, in neat rows, white cane chairs and tables. A flight of polished wooden steps led into a long cool room where punkahs revolved noisily and the walls were lined with photographs of men in cricket flannels and rows of women in floppy hats sitting on benches in front of pyramids of bowls resembling cannon balls. Old magazines lay on the tables and there were cigarette butts in the ash trays. He peered into a side room and saw two billiard tables, their baize covered by dust cloths; on the walls there were racks of cues, some of which were in black tin containers bearing the owner's names. He went through another door and found himself looking at a long wooden bar with shelves lined with hundreds of bottles. He rubbed his hands together and again addressed the dog. "Aladdin's ruddy cave. We'll be up here tonight, Jolson, and really fill our boots." Behind the bar was a zinc-lined ice-box filled with bottles of beer, and he opened one and drank without bothering to use a glass. He spotted a glass-fronted case containing cigars of various sizes, and he took several knowing Tiger Read's fondness for them. "Finders keepers," he said aloud.

When he returned to the working party Dusty Miller, who was stripped to the waist and glistening with sweat, said angrily, "You skiving bastard, Isaac. Here we are sweating our goolies off and you go sightseeing."

"Hang on sunshine, I've just discovered this is treasure island", and he explained what he had come across. "I'll get Tiger to have a word with the Old Man and see if we can nip up there tonight. No point in letting all that stuff go to waste."

"Where is it, Isaac?"

"Now as if I would be telling you that. If no one else knows, it means I've got to show the way, don't it?"

When they returned aboard, Tiger Read supervised the camouflaging and it was not until he had expressed his satisfaction that Morris handed him three cigars. "There's more where those came from, Chief. Just a question of getting permission to go there."

Tiger sniffed the cigars appreciatively. "These are the real thing, lad; haven't seen the inside of a woman's thigh. Now, don't go holding out on me."

Morris explained how he had come across the deserted club and how it would be a nice place for the lads to relax.

"I'll have a word with the captain. I'm sure he won't mind

so long as it's fair dos for all and no one comes back half seas over."

Paton was in his cabin listening to the Chief Gunner's Mate recounting his tour. "The tanks can be easily destroyed, Sir, but it'll involve a certain amount of risk seeing as we aren't exactly experts in the field. The same applies to the other installations we've got to put out of action. But there is a hill we can use as the firing point and detonate everything at the same time. I think it'd be wise to place the charges and run the wires out without too much delay. Then my team can doss down in one of the bungalows and keep an eye on things till we get the go ahead, Sir."

"You do what you think's best, Chief. I'm just running a bus service on this one. Draw what rations you need and get cracking as soon as you can."

When he had gone, he called in the coxswain and told him that he wanted sentries posted all round the island about a quarter of a mile apart. "They can patrol up and down and keep in touch with each other. Whilst I don't anticipate a landing, I'd hate to be caught on the wrong foot."

Read took the opportunity of mentioning the club, and to his surprise Paton raised no objection. "Just make sure no one rips the backside out of it, Coxs'n."

He then went up to the bridge where Phelp was gazing across the narrow strip of water that separated them from Singapore Island. They chatted for some time until darkness came with its tropical suddenness, and then it seemed as if nature was playing tricks by cutting the night short and bringing dawn forward by several hours, for the dark outline of the island was enveloped in a crimson hue and it took some time for them to realise that it was the fire from the still burning tanks at the naval base.

"How long do you think they can hold out, Sir?"

"I've heard various figures from six months to a year. Who can say? The real question is, does it still serve any useful purpose? If I had to make the decision, I'd evacuate it lock, stock and barrel while the troop ships are still there. Leave it too long and there could be a disaster."

Morris trod warily along the unlit road with the half a dozen or more seamen and stockers who had been given permission to visit the abandoned club, have a few beers,

231

then return aboard so that others could enjoy the unexpected pleasure of a drink in civilised comfort.

"You sure you know the way?" grumbled Miller. "This place isn't no bigger than a postage stamp, yet we've been going round like a dog chasing its own tail."

"Jesus, I saw the place for the first time in broad daylight; you can't expect me to go straight to it. I'm not a homing pigeon. Anyway, we're building up a good thirst."

As he spoke he caught sight of a faint glimmer of light and was convinced he was on the right track, but he was a trifle concerned as to whom could have put the light on. He pressed a finger to his lips at the bottom of the steps which he now recognised, and they almost tiptoed their way in. As they passed the billiard room they were surprised to see two men in shirt sleeves calmly playing billiards; they were so engrossed in the game they did not bother to look up.

"Just our fucking luck to find two Good Man Fridays," said Morris.

A Malay in a spotless white jacket was standing behind the bar polishing glasses and holding them up to the light to make sure that not even a speck of dust was visible.

Morris said, "Mind if me and my muckers have a drink? We've just arrived."

The steward nodded indifferently. "Make it beers all round then."

The steward began removing the crown corks with a badget attached to the bar, when a voice called out, "You can stop that, steward."

The sailors turned and saw the two men who had been playing billiards coming into the bar. They had now put on jackets and ties. The one who had called out said sharply, "Just what do you think you're up to, barging in like this?"

Morris said hesitantly, "We just dropped in for a couple of beers."

"But this happens to be a members only club."

"We thought the place was deserted..." Morris began by way of explanation.

"Well, you can see it isn't. Two of us are still here. We were due to play the club championship tonight and we were damned if the Japs would prevent that. Just as well, otherwise you'd have turned it into a four ale bar."

Miller tugged at Morris's arm. "Let's get cracking, Isaac. Clearly we ain't welcome", and with the diffidence he invariably displayed when he sensed trouble, added, "Sorry we intruded, Sir."

Morris, with the prize within such close reach, was reluctant to concede so easily. "I like your guts, Sir. Japs just around the corner and you still play your match! As a navy man I admire a touch of the old Sir Francis."

The man smiled. "Almost the identical words that Jim and I exchanged. We've both been here fifteen years, and one of us was determined to get his name on the cup. Been trying long enough. We'll take it to Singapore and make sure it's engraved."

"Who was the victor, Sir?" enquired Morris disarmingly.

The smile became broader, even smug. "As a matter of fact, I was. Touch and go though, but I got the balls tucked over a corner pocket and it was cannons till the cows came home."

"No doubt you'll be celebrating, and you deserve to. Well, we'll be taking up the anchor. As they say, two's a crowd. Also we have the hazardous job of keeping an eye on your property till you come back."

The man mellowed visibly. "We can sign in visitors. Nothing against that, so long as you don't try and buy any drinks."

"We don't normally approve of spongers, Sir, prefer to stand our own corner, but the lads'll see your point. Rules are rules."

The steward was told to produce the visitors book, and each of the sailors signed his name and under the column marked Address they wrote *Grey Seal*.

The two men – the other was introduced as Henry – signed for drink after drink, although they confided it was rather a waste of time in view of the circumstances, but there was nothing they could do about it as it was a club rule that money must not pass over the counter. "Anyway", said Henry, "it would only go into his pocket", and he gestured towards the expressionless steward.

They sat down at the cane tables with their boots resting on the extended foot rests, wallowing in the unaccustomed luxury and quite forgetting their promise not to over-indulge and to be back aboard in time for others to enjoy a break. Jim breathed contentedly and said with genuine feeling, "You don't know how pleasant it is to have an evening without the ladies. Count every drink you have and tear everyone's reputation to shreds. This is a real stag night. Pity we've got to join them so soon."

It was only after two hours solid drinking that Henry asked them what had brought them there, and when he was told he said, "Well, if Singapore does come under siege there'll not be a great need for petrol, the island isn't that big. Never mind. We'll be off first thing in the morning so you can tell your captain he can use the club's facilities as and when he wishes. The only thing I would ask is that he does get everyone to sign for what they have, purely a formality, no one will bring him to account. But this club has always prided itself on being run on very strict lines . . ." His words trailed off into silence as he realised the fatuity of his remarks. But they were gleefully seized upon by Morris who could see a way out of his dilemma for having stayed longer than he had promised, and as he walked back to the ship trailed by an unsteady and heavy-footed group of shipmates, he was already rehearsing in his mind the words he would say to Tiger Read in the morning.

The ship was in darkness when they reached it, and the only sign of life on the upper deck was the blurred form of the quartermaster pacing up and down trying to fight off the urge to sit down somewhere and doze off.

Morris whispered to the men behind him, "We're in luck. Nobody around. Let's nip down to the mess deck before anyone spots us."

He was halted by the booming voice of Tiger Read. "Not so hasty, Able Seaman Morris! I want a few words with you, lad."

Morris said with all the innocence he could summon, "What! *Me*, Chief?"

"Yes, you, unless there's someone else around here who answers to the same monica."

"Couldn't you sleep, Chief?"

"Oh, I could sleep alright, AB, but I've been forcing myself to stay awake till you decided to grace us with your presence,

234

Able Seaman."

Morris sounded aggrieved, "What's all this AB stuff, Tiger? I'm a killick and you know it."

"You were, before you decided to go on your jolly jaunt and leave all the work to your messmates. It's off caps for you in the morning. Captain's defaulters."

Through the corner of his eye, Morris could see his shipmates sidling off and slipping down the mess-deck hatch. He did not feel bitter at the way in which they were deserting him at a time when he could have done with their support; in similar circumstances he would have done exactly the same. But he was determined not to lose his hook without putting up some semblance of a defence, no matter how unconvincing. His voice sounded almost indignant at the unfairness of it. "Listen, Tiger, I was so long because I was trying to lay on something for the lads, and the officers," he added hastily. "I had to swallow a few jars which I didn't really want, but it worked out all right in the end."

Read sighed in a manner that suggested he did not believe a word he was hearing, but was prepared to let him carry on just to see how far he would stretch his credulity. "I'm listening, Morris, only cut out the violin accompaniment."

"Well, Chief, you won't believe this . . ." He waited for the coxswain to interject, but he remained silent and Morris encouraged to continue. "You know I said the place was deserted? I was wrong. When we arrived we expected to find it like the Marie Celeste, but there were two old codgers playing the club's billiard final. Wouldn't let us have a gargle because we weren't members. I didn't want you to think that what I had given you before was a lot of flannel, quite apart from knowing how disappointed you'd be, so I had to talk them out of it and they took some convincing, believe me."

"And you got a bellyfull while your chums were pacing up and down this earthly paradise watching out for Japs."

"That's where you're wrong. We all remembered that and couldn't help thinking they deserved some kind of reward. So, being the spokesman, I nattered on about how our chummy ships had copped it and how upset we all was. You know, lots of bullshit applied with a trowel. Anyway, you'll be glad to know the club's all ours. Any time we like we fill our boots. I thought it was worth risking jankers if I could do that for my muckers, Chief." He paused, feeling like a defence counsel who had made a brilliant closing speech.

Read, who had no intention of putting him on Captain's Report – he was too valuable a leading hand to have stripped – and had already decided to mete out his own punishment, said, "I'll tell the captain first thing in the morning of your noble gesture, and with a bit of luck he'll let some of us go up to this shangri la you rabbit on about. If it's all you crack it up to be we might even overlook things. Meanwhile, you take over the deck watch and stay awake till it's time to rouse the hands. If you so much as blink an eye I'll have you busted down to OD." He did not wait for a reply but went straight into the petty officers mess.

The quartermaster, who was being unexpectedly relieved, said, "Tough cheese, Isaac, but in the state you're in you won't feel a thing."

Morris walked slowly aft and sat on one of the depth charge racks. Staying awake presented no problem. He recalled times off Iceland when he had been on his feet for forty-eight hours chopping black ice off the stays to prevent the ship capsizing. This was a piece of cake. He felt Jolson's wet nose muzzling against his hand. "You know, Jolson, if I'd have known this was going to happen I'd have brought a couple of bottles back with me." His eyes turned towards Singapore, bathed in a man-made glow, and he could hear, quite distinctly, the detonations as the night bombers released their cargoes. "We don't know how lucky we are. They're being kept awake too, but at least we aren't having seven bells of shit knocked out of us." As he spoke his thoughts aloud, he was reminded of Amy and he wished he knew exactly where she was; for all he knew she could be buried under the rubble of a demolished building.

He realised the beer was beginning to take effect for his words were becoming slurred and he was getting maudlin. "Funny bloody war, Jolson. The blokes with silver badges are getting tin-fished in the Atlantic trying to get oil to England, while we're blowing the stuff up. In Pompey and Guzz matelots are tear arsing around from pub to pub tryin' to find one that'll sell two pints of boiler maker to anyone who isn't a regular, yet when I find enough free booze to flat the *Warspite* I get jankers. My old Mum, bless her, moans about having to make do on two ounces of meat, and here they're bitching about the shortage of oysters. Amy's gone AWOL, but no one gives a fish's tit because she's got a touch of the tarbrush. Makes you want to spit blood. Roll on my syphi doz, because it's going to take that bloody long to win this war, and if the likes of me aren't around it's going to take a ruddy sight longer."

In the morning as the hands turned to to clean ship, C.P.O. Read told Paton of Morris's escapade, making it sound as if he had been genuinely motivated by the noblest of intentions; and to his surprise the captain accepted the story and said that when the sentries were relieved they could make their way to the club. A strict and fair routine was to be observed, so that every man, and that included the explosive squads, would have an opportunity to relax for a short spell.

When the coxswain had gone, Paton thought: he knows I don't believe a word, any more than he was fooled. Morris is a skate, but if he fell into a barrel of manure he'd emerge smelling of lavender water. The inescapable truth was that the discovery of the club would make all the difference to his men who would otherwise become intolerably bored, and Morris deserved credit fo saving them from that.

He knocked on the wardroom door where Phelp and Carnac were having breakfast. "You two are having a night off," he said, and he told them of the open invitation. "You can keep your eyes on things and see they don't wreck it. Don't rush back, but if one of you feels like relieving me for an hour or so I won't object. A break will do us all the world of good. We've been cooped up aboard too long."

For three nights the club was to become a haven where the ship's company were able to enjoy a drink, play darts and billiards and shower in the well equipped changing rooms.

The next morning a signal arrived from naval headquarters with orders to commence the demolition at noon.

When the Chief Gunner's Mate assured him that everything was ready and that only he and an ERA need remain ashore at the firing point, Paton slipped *Grey Seal's* moorings and anchored a mile offshore.

He stood on the bridge, his glasses focussed on the hill,

while Carnac stood by his side with a pocket chronometer in his hand counting off the minutes, then the seconds. At 12 o'clock precisely a light blinked from the hill and seconds later the area of the oil base seemed to disintegrate in smoke and flames. Huge metal sheets soared into the air as the tanks were blown apart, and debris rained around the ship. "Crikey, Sir, they made sure of it all right."

Paton called to Phelp on the forecastle, "Shorten to three shackles, Number One." Phelps watched as the anchor cable was hauled inboard, and when it was almost vertical he called back, "Up and down, Sir."

"Weigh anchor," shouted Paton, and as the cable rattled through the hawsepipe he gave the order, "Slow Ahead" and moved closer inshore to pick up the whaler which had been left with the demolition squad.

As soon as the boat was hoisted inboard, he called down for "Full speed ahead", and Reynolds said, "For once don't worry about the revs, Sir. You can 'ave all you like. I can't see a fing down here, but it sounds 'airy."

Two hours later as *Grey Seal* was approaching Keppel Harbour the light on the signal tower began flashing. "Take it, Sub, and see what they want."

The sub-lieutenant spoke aloud each word as he acknowledged it with the Aldis:

Grey . . . Seal . . . will . . . proceed . . . immediately . . . to the . . . assistance of . . . *Empire . . . Crusader . . .* aground and . . . abandoned on Pulau . . . Sakra . . . stop . . . carrying . . . much . . . needed . . . ammunition . . . equipment . . . Ends.

Paton studied the chart and saw that Pulau Sakra was one of a group of thirteen minute islands – little more than coral reefs – off the south west corner of Singapore Island. He gave a wheel order and the ship swung sharply to port, and half an hour later he could see smoke billowing from a large merchantman which was beached bow on. Distress rockets burst in the sky above her bridge, and the jammed siren emitted a continuous mournful howl. As he got closer he could see quite clearly the falls and lifelines hanging vertically from the empty davits, suggesting that the crew had left in great haste. Dense clouds of smoke and steam were pouring out of the ventilators and a fierce fire was burning fore'ard

238

of the bridge.

Paton took *Grey Seal* within loud hailer distance, so close he could read the name of the ship on the stern above her home port of Tilbury. The stern was high above the water, although her screws and rudders were still submerged. He called over the hailer, "Ahoy, there. I have been sent to render all possible assistance."

A squat figure in a reefer jacket that was more green than blue and which sported four rings on the sleeves, appeared on the bridge wing and called back, "What I need are tugs. I'm well aground fore'ard. I keep asking for them, but sod all happens."

Paton could feel the intense heat, and some of the hull plates were beginning to blister. "What is the damage?"

"Got a bomb through the hatch of the fore'ard hold. We were tail end Charlie in the convoy when we got attacked in the Sunda Strait. I was well and truly brassed off; we've sailed thousands of miles without seeing a thing and we cop it with twelve miles to go. Thought I could make it, but the steering jammed and I had to beach her. The fire's bad, but it'll be a bloody sight worse if it reaches the ammunition."

"What else are you carrying?"

"Anti-tank guns, field guns, automatic weapons. Enough to equip an army. The shower I had as a crew couldn't wait to get over the side. Just pissed off. Couldn't care less how much the army needs this stuff. All I have is the chief engineer and half a dozen hands. Just to make things worse communications with the engine room have broken down and I'm reduced to using runners. That means a lot of things we ought to be doing aren't being done."

"Pumps all working?"

"Most of them. At the moment the Chief is trying to flood the fore'ard hold, but it's a slow job and if we fill it too much there's not a hope in hell of getting her afloat. Every inch of fire hose is being used, but some of it's being scorched."

"If I get a line aboard, can you take in a towing hawser? Also, ask your engineer if he can flood the aft tanks and pump out the ones fore'ard. That'll lift your bow and put the stern down."

"I'll see what can be done, but it's a question of having

enough hands."

He disappeared inside the bridge and a few minutes later four men appeared on the stern and gathered round the capstan. Paton noticed an ancient looking four-inch gun on a mounting above the quarterdeck still shrouded in its canvas cover. The crew, he thought, had clearly considered it an unnecessary ornament. He called down to Carnac, "Get a line across with the Lee-Enfield and prepare the towing wire."

There was a sharp retort as the line-throwing rifle was fired and a thin, but strong line curled through the air and landed on the deck of the merchantman. Morris expertly attached a thicker line which in turn was fastened to the heavy towing wire. The capstan on the merchantman began wheezing and clanking as it strained to haul in the arm-thick hawser. "Pay out handsomely," bellowed Carnac. "The sooner we get that aboard the better for everyone."

The master reappeared on the bridge with a megaphone. "Tow's secured. Let me know as soon as you're ready and I'll put the engines full astern."

Paton turned *Grey Seal* stern on and called to the engine room, "Slow ahead, and I mean slow, Chief. I don't want that tow snapping like a violin string. It'll decapitate everyone," and to the quarterdeck he shouted, "Sub, pay out more slack. I want the tow just touching the top of the water."

He heard someone hastening up the bridge ladder and turned to see Phelp. "Your place is on the upper deck, Number One," he said tartly. "There's nothing you can do up here."

"I was thinking, Sir, that with your permission I'd call for some volunteers to go aboard with me. They just don't have enough hands to cope, and without the extra help she's going to remain stuck there. I've served in a similar ship so I'm *au fait* with the equipment."

"I'm not enamoured with the idea, so let's see how the tow makes out first." He peered aft and called out, "How's it going, Sub?"

"Not budging an inch, Sir. She's well and truly stuck."

Paton gave an order to the engine room and increased the revolutions until the tow was taut and strumming with the tension, but there was not the slightest sign of the cargo ship moving.

Morris said, "We've got as much hope of pulling her off as we have of prising a stoker off a Wren virgin."

Paton turned to his first lieutenant and said, "Looks as if you were right. How many hands will you need?"

"Half a dozen seamen, a couple of stokers, and some of the ERA's we have aboard. Some can work the pumps and hoses while the artificers can help out in the engine room. The seamen can lend a hand on the upper deck."

"How do you propose boarding?"

"We'll lower the whalers and get them to put some rope ladders over the side, Sir. No great problem. I've done it before."

"All right, Number One. Go ahead. As far as volunteers go, make it you, you and you, if no one steps forward. I don't want to hang around with that ammunition in danger of going up."

He heard Phelp clatter down the ladder, and a few minutes later the bosun's pipe summoning the boat parties.

Phelp stood in the waist of the ship hurriedly explaining what he had in mind. "Now all I want are volunteers, or do I have to pick them?"

Morris stepped forward, "Me and Miller will go, Sir. if I'm there we'll get away that much quicker. Dusty'll come because he won't want to be left out." He grinned cheekily and said, "I remember once off . . .", but Phelp cut him short. "I know, Morris, you did a similar job with the tow held between your teeth."

Three stokers volunteered for no other reason than anything that offered a respite from the furnace heat of the stokehold was welcome. A wireman and three ERA's joined the group without saying a word. The Chief Gunner's mate said, "I know a bit about ammunition, Sir, and that might come in handy; apart from that, there aren't many jobs I haven't done in my time. I'm kind of responsible for my own lads, Sir."

When Phelp had finished counting heads, he had fourteen men. "That'll do. Any more and the whalers'll capsize."

Paton watched the boats pull away, carefully avoiding the turbulent wake which was being churned up by the merchantman's screws. The tow continued to twang with the strain, and he was fearful that if he increased speed it would part. Three ladders snaked over the side, and he watched anxiously as the men scrambled up and heaved themselves over the gunwale. He saw Phelps wave cheerfully before he disappeared onto the bridge to confer with the master.

An hour later the master appeared on the bridge and shouted, "Your men are doing a splendid job. The ammunition seems reasonably safe now, and we've got more pumps going. I'm still flooding the aft tanks and pumping out fore'ard. Keep your fingers crossed. I'm continuing to ask for those bloody tugs."

Two hours later, Phelp appeared at the stern rail and reported that the fire was under control, and Paton could see that the stern was now well down in the water and the bow riding high, but the ship stubbornly refused to budge.

When darkness was approaching and *Grey Seal* had been straining like a Clydesdale to free a farm truck stuck in deep mud without success, he summoned the master on his loud hailer. "We're getting nowhere, and I daren't put any more strain on the tow. I propose to slip it and try again at first light. By then the tide will be at its highest. You agreeable?"

"Perfectly. I've just heard the tugs will be here at dawn. They've got the same idea; waste of time to try until I've got more water below me. They know these waters like the back of their hand."

Phelp appeared at hs side and called out, "We've started to pump out the hold. The fire seems to be out, but one can never be sure. It's a risk we'll just have to take. We need the extra buoyancy. Ideally we should dump the ammo over the side, but we don't have the time."

"Stand by to slip the tow, Number One. As soon as I've hauled it inboard I'll lay off and drop anchor. Keep in touch."

When the trawler had anchored, Paton sat hunched on his bridge chair staring through the mounting gloom at the now barely visible bulk of the merchantman. Carnac came up and said, "Let me take over the anchor watch, Sir, while you grab a couple of hours sleep."

"No, Sub, you go and get your head down. I'll need you at full throttle in the morning."

Hall appeared a few minutes later with some hot cocoa and a plate of sandwiches. "Took the liberty of putting a

242

tot in the ki, Sir. Anything else you need?"

"I'd appreciate it if you'd bring up my greatcoat, there's a real nip in the air."

As he sat huddled into the upturned collar of his coat, he heard the coxswain's voice. "Permission to come on the bridge, Sir."

"Of course. Welcome the company."

Read said, "What are the chances, Sir? She seems to be stuck like a limpet."

"Depends to a large extent on the tide. An extra few feet can make all the difference. If the tugs turn up and do their stuff, I think we can get her off. Danger is the Japs might return. What with us and the tugs they might suspect the cargo consists of something extremely valuable to merit so much attention. An air raid would just about put paid to any hopes of success."

"Between you and me, Sir, my main concern is for Lieutenant Phelp and the lads we've put aboard. I know the cargo is important, but they've abandoned so much it strikes me they're getting their priorities a bit late in the day. What's aboard her is a drop in the ocean to what they've handed the Japs on a plate."

"I've been trying not to think about that, but it's difficult not to. Bit like a man who tosses away a sovereign and spends hours on his hands and knees looking for sixpence."

"Fancy a cigar, Sir? I took the liberty of helping myself to a few."

"Not just now, Coxs'n, but I'll take one and smoke it over a large scotch if we get that ruddy ship afloat."

"I'll take you up on that, Sir. Now I'd better nip down and see the lookouts are all awake. The idea of sitting here in a busy shipping lane without lights scares me more than the thought of that ammo going sky high."

Paton paced up and down, occasionally stamping his feet and flapping his arms around his body to keep warm, until the sun began to rise over the rim of the horizon; he had always been amazed at the speed with which it did so; now he thought he had never known it take so long. Reynolds' voice floated up the voice pipe. "Ready when you are in the engine room, Sir. Let's 'ope we 'ave better luck this time."

Carnac appeared on the bridge. "All ready aft, Sir."

"Good. We'll weigh anchor and I'll take her much closer this time. Save a lot of time passing the tow that way."

The procedure of passing the tow was accomplished in a fraction of the time it had taken before with more men now available on the merchantman, and as *Grey Seal* once again heaved and strained to prise free the 10,000 tons of stranded steel, Paton caught sight of the enormous waves being thrust up by the squat, heavy-fendered bows of the two ocean going tugs. He heaved a silent prayer of relief, the powerful ships were capable of moving the largest vessel, while their masters were expert in the art of salvage, as their bank accounts no doubt confirmed. They backed onto the stern of the beached ship until their sterns were almost touching and their tows were passed in a time that made Paton ashamed of his own efforts.

In a short time the two tugs and the trawler had fanned out and the water was thrashed into a turbulent froth as they hauled in unison.

Phelp appeared at the stern rail and held up two thumbs. "She's budging slowly, but she's moving."

The sound of grinding steel echoed across the water as the hull scraped against the coral, and the ship began to slide sternwards into the water. As the agile tugs shifted their tack, they reminded Paton of sheepdogs at work as they veered to port then starboard in order to create a yawing movement.

The master appeared on the bridge and announced through his megaphone, "No sign of holing, thank God. What wouldn't I have given for those tugs twenty-four hours ago."

Then Paton heard the warning that he had been dreading. One of the lookouts shouted, "Aircraft approaching, dead ahead." His thumb pressed hard on the alarm bells and he called out aft, "Cut the tow, Sub." With the tow intact *Grey Seal* was incapable of manoeuvring and as the tugs were unarmed the safety of all the ships depended on her guns.

As the deck echoed to the sound of the guns crews racing to their action stations, he studied the approaching aircraft through his binoculars. There were two Mitsubishi G4M1s and a single Zero flying in a leisurely manner that indicated their confidence.

244

He shouted down to the crew of the twelve-pounder, "Open fire as soon as you like." As if in response to his words the ship reverberated to the sound of the first shell, followed almost immediately by a second round.

Then to Paton's astonishment a louder bang came from the merchantman and he swung his glasses onto it and saw the Chief Gunner's Mate had mustered a gun's crew for the 4-inch. That, he said to himself, makes it a much more even match.

The three aircraft were soon enveloped in cotton wool shrapnel bursts, but they continued to fly on without the slightest alteration in height or course. The Oerlikons joined in, and their tracers could be seen looping towards their targets. The aircraft were well out of range of the 20-mm shells, but if they only made them maintain height they were serving a useful purpose.

The *Empire Crusader* had now slid clear of the coral and the tugs increased their speed and begun heading inshore in the hope that the shore batteries would join in. Paton regretted having had to use his smoke flats during the Swordfish attack; they would have provided ideal cover now.

The Zero side-slipped away from the bombers and went into a shallow dive towards the merchantman, its wings sprouting flame as the machine guns yammered furiously. The Oerlikon shells followed it as it sped towards the *Empire Crusader* where men were diving for cover on the upper deck to escape the hail of bullets. The barrel of the 4-inch was almost horizontal when it fired, and one wing of the fighter fell off and fluttered into the sea like a falling leaf. Seconds later what remained of the aircraft careered into the hull of the ship and was engulfed in a ball of burning petrol. When it cleared the wreckage of the fighter was seen tumbling into the sea. Miraculously, the ship appeared to have suffered no danger; it was still afloat and responding to the tugs.

The 4-inch swung skywards, and Paton followed it towards the two bombers. Their bomb bays were now open and dark objects tumbled down. The whistle of the falling bombs was discernible above the gunfire, and the merchantman was obscured from sight by columns of cascading water that rose bridge high. The aircraft had adopted the same tactics they had used over Singapore, releasing all their bombs at the same time. Whether satisfied with their achievements or deterred by the ferocity of the gunfire was hard to say, but they altered course and flew off to disappear over Singapore.

Paton took *Grey Seal* as close as he dared and called through the loud hailer, "Everything all right?"

The master replied, "I'm waiting for a damage report, but as far as I can make out it's only superficial."

"Any casualties?"

"I'm checking on that too."

As he passed close astern, he saw the Gunner's Mate and called out, "Well done, Guns. Whale Island would be proud of you."

"Glad they scarpered when they did, Sir. That old gun was so bloody ancient that last round split the barrel like a peeled banana."

They had passed Sentosa and Keppel Harbour was in sight when the master appeared on the bridge and summoned Paton. "I've just informed the tugs I'm making water fast. Pumps can't cope. One of the bombs must have sprung some plates below the waterline. They're coming alongside to nurse me in."

"Can you hang on? We're nearly home."

"Like shit to an army blanket," yelled the master cheerfully. But as he spoke the merchantman began to list violently to port and lose way and settle in the water.

One of the tugs came abeam of *Grey Seal*. "We've cast our tows, but we'll have to lay off a while. Daren't attempt going alongside, she might take us with her. If she looks like remaining afloat we'll move back in."

Paton watched, impotent to intervene, as the masts of the merchantman began to tilt seawards and the master appeared at the waist of the ship and threw the steel safe containing the confidential books over the side. He raised his megaphone. "She's had it, I'm afraid. Four foot of water in the engine room. I've told everyone below to come topsides. At least we gave it a try."

He watched as men began to assemble at the lowest part of the ship, calmly awaiting the order to go over the side. The master made a sweeping gesture with his hands and several men began to shin hand over hand down the lifelines attached to the empty davits, while others used the rope

246

ladders. The ship now seemed to have stopped listing and a number of men jumped straight into the water which was only ten or twelve feet below. In a few minutes the sea was a mass of bobbing heads.

"Get some scrambling nets over the side," yelled Paton. "I'll stop engine and drift down broadside. The water'll be that much calmer on the lee side." From the corner of his eye he could see the tugs were already hauling men inboard.

He craned over the bridge parapet and watched his own men helping swimmers over the side. He saw the Chief Gunner's Mate, Morris and Miller, then several others who had volunteered. The last man over the gunwale was the ship's master.

Grey Seal cruised up and down looking for any more survivors, and it was only when he was satisfied that no one had been abandoned that he called off the search. He then told Carnac to take over while he went below to talk to the rescued men. "Everyone accounted for?" A quick head count revealed that the only person missing was Lieutenant Phelp.

"Did anyone see the First Lieutenant?"

Morris said, "We went over the side together, Sir. He gave me a thumbs up salute. Must have been picked up by one of the tugs."

Paton took *Grey Seal* abeam of the tugs and requested the names of all the men they had rescued. Phelp's was not among them.

Reluctantly he set course for Keppel Harbour. It seemed incredible that Phelp could have vanished like that, the water was as calm as a mill pond, and there had been no internal explosions which could have injured him. Sharks could be ruled out, they would all have been frightened off by the bombs. It could have been a sudden attack of cramp, swallowing too much water, a heart attack. The permutations were endless and pointless.

Carnac said hopefully, "He might have made it to the shore, Sir. He's a fine swimmer, and it isn't far."

Paton thought it most unlikely that anyone would swim away from ships so near at hand, preferring to head for the shore, but he kept his fears to himself. "Let's hope so, Sub. It's a hell of a way to go after all he's been through."

He imagined Lesley's reaction when she received a telegram announcing that her husband was "missing presumed killed". It was so indefinite. And the vagueness made it doubly cruel, for so long as she did not hear anything concrete she would continue to hold out hope; much as he did with Kate, although common sense dictated that she gone out of his life for good.

When *Grey Seal* had secured alongside the quay, he went to naval headquarters to report on the abortive venture, and express the view that although *Empire Crusader* was still afloat she should be sunk by gunfire as she constituted a hazard to navigation.

The staff captain said, "You did everything that was possible, Commander. Pity we couldn't get the tugs there earlier, but they've had their hands full with the number of ships damaged in the harbour. Sorry about your Number One. Apart from having a splendid record, I gather he was extremely popular. It's not the way one likes to see a good man go. One is always reluctant to accept the worst. On the other hand, he may well still turn up. It's been known to happen. I'll see that the army along that stretch of coast is notified and asked to keep a sharp eye open. I'll let you know as soon as I hear anything. But, and I hate to say this, from my own experience it's best to look on the black side. Then any news must be good news."

Paton acknowledged the wisdon of the words, no doubt borne out by experience, and when he returned aboard he went straight to his cabin. Carnac knew better than to disturb him; he could tell from his expression he wanted to nurse his grief alone.

He lay on his bunk in the darkened cabin with his eyes wide open, wondering what he would say when he wrote to his sister. It would not be at all like the other letters he had written to next of kin. Most of them had just been names, whereas Lesley and he were as close as a sister and brother could ever be. The thought of expressing on paper his innermost thoughts appalled him. His affection for Phelp had been so genuine that any words would sound empty. Christ, he rebuked himself, you've already given up hope! He came back once, he can do it again. Then he realised it was just wishful thinking.

He got up and went into the wardroom. "Fancy a game

of crib, Sub, and a stiff scotch. We've earned one."

"Yes, Sir," said Carnac enthusiastically. He knew that his captain's mind would not be on the cards, but it was his way of saying there was a job still remaining to be done. He would not let his grief become infectious so that an air of gloom was cast over the ship.

Carnac went to the spirits cupboard and took out glasses and a bottle. "Let's drink to Brian, Sir. He wouldn't want us to wear long faces. He'd rather it was him than one of the volunteers."

Paton raised his glass. "You've got a wise head on those young shoulders, Terence. To Brian, may his shadow never grow less."

The acceptance that he would not see him again came as a relief. "I'll inform headquarters first thing in the morning that you've taken over as first lieutenant."

"That's a pretty tall order, Sir, but I'll do my best."

"That's more than good enough for me. I wouldn't have dreamed of it if I didn't think you were up to it. Your first box, Terence."

The sub-lieutenant sensed that his captain's casual words were a reminder that Phelp was already part of the past, and his name should no longer be mentioned. In the close confines of a small ship, that was the only way to survive.

Chapter 13

Sir Shenton Thomas, in a freshly laundered and starched white duck suit, strolled round the grounds of Government House noting with silent satisfaction the damage which had been inflicted on his official residence, and the houses of some of his more senior officials. The odd mound of upturned earth here and there marked the hastily dug graves of several devoted servants who had been killed by shells or bombs, some of whom had been so unmarked they appeared to have fallen asleep at their posts. While he deplored the tragic loss of life and hated to see the scarred and battered buildings which he had grown to love, and the churned up flower beds and uprooted trees, it comforted him to know that he was at last in the thick of things, sharing the same dangers as his loyal subjects. He imagined this was very much the same as the King had felt when Buckingham Palace was hit during the Blitz; no longer an observer but a warrior in the front line.

Soon after the army had withdrawn over the Causeway, the Japanese brought up batteries of heavy artillery and sited them on high vantage points, and for several days now the island had been subjected to a relentless barrage. It was a matter of great personal satisfaction that the enemy had selected his home as a prime target, considered every bit as important as the docks, the few remaining airfields and packed warehouses, and seldom an hour passed without hearing the sudden shrill whine, almost a demented scream, that heralded the arrival of the high calibre shells. They were so punctual he could almost set his watch by them. They arrived soon after sunrise and continued with brief respites until sunset. With a bit of luck they might be running short of shells, although he had to concede that so far there was little sign of it. From his balcony he could quite clearly see the observation balloon which floated gently above the Strait, enabling the gunners to fire with pinpoint accuracy. In some respects the shells were far more unnerving than the bombs which continued to rain down; at least the sounds of the sirens and the engines of the bombers gave you time to seek shelter, but the shells just arrived. Not that he spent his time cowering in the shelter; he wanted to be seen sharing the ordeals of the people he represented in the name of the monarch, and whenever possible he liked to show his face in the city. Not that it was really necessary; the people *knew* he was there, for he had broadcast to them that he was still at his post. That had been imperative because the enemy had broadcast from a captured radio station that he had decamped with the first salvo. He had to admit, if only to himself, that he found the visits extremely depressing; the city was gradually being reduced to rubble. Apart from the shelling the enemy was using captured airfields just across the Strait and were indulging in a wanton orgy of destruction with low-level bombing and straffing. They were also resorting more and more to using incendiaries and fragmentation bombs which created sheer havoc in the native quarters. In Chinatown, entire streets had disappeared, along with their occupants, and even in the white area hardly a street remained untouched; everywhere there were black gaps like extracted teeth in an otherwise healthy jaw, while the docks and the go-downs, packed with food and valuable materials, were being systematically destroyed. The railway station was also badly damaged, and even the squares of the cricket club had been churned up. That was unforgivable in his eyes; it had no strategic value whatsoever, and would never be as true and even again.

It was, he reflected, a pity that the army had not made a better job of destroying the Causeway, for what at first had seemed an impassable breach in the concrete had turned out to be a minor impediment; when the tide fell it was easily wadeable. As for the abandonment of the naval base, that had been beyond contempt; a cloak-and-dagger affair that did not reflect well on the navy, and the troops who had plundered it were quite right when they said it was like "robbing a still warm corpse". But he had not been consulted, he was presented with a *fait accompli*, so no blame could be attached to him.

Thankfully the troops were now digging in with a real sense of purpose and urgency and were ready to repel any boarders; it was an apt word, he thought, for in a broadcast to the people he had compared the island to a ship whose crew would never be abandoned. He recalled his own defiant words: "All we have to do is hang on grimly and inexorably, and for not very long; and the reward will be freedom, happiness and peace for every one of us", and later he had told the Legislative Council, "We stand by the ship, gentlemen. In any withdrawal or movement of population there will be no distinction of race. We stand by the people of this country with whom we live and work, in this ordeal."

True some people had detected a hollow ring to his words when a great number of European women and children started queueing to be evacuated to Ceylon, India and the UK, but that had not been his doing; had he not refused to issue an evacuation order? That, he had insisted, would be lowering to British prestige. And how right he had been. One had to witness the disgraceful scenes at the P & O Agency House set up at Cluny to realise that. Understandably, therefore, some of the native population suspected he was talking with his tongue in his cheek. It was, in their eyes, Penang all over again.

Apart from that, there was no great noticeable change in the way of life. With commendable stoicism people continued to queue for the cinemas, dance and dine and, to the best of their endeavours, carry on as usual. "Business as usual" had been his clarion call, and it had not gone unheeded. To dismiss it as resignation was a foul, despicable calumny.

Mercifully the Japanese army seemed to have run out of steam. They showed no sign of launching an assault across the narrow Strait, which was most encouraging, for every day it was delayed brought fresh hope as more and more reinforcements continued to arrive. Some of the reporters had unfortunately submitted stories that the island was now under siege, but the use of that particular word had been officially banned, and quite rightly so; such an emotive word only created alarm and despondency and was extremely bad for morale.

His reverie was interrupted by the Head Chef who submitted the dinner menu for his scrutiny, but he gave it only a cursory glance before expressing approval. What was the point? It was another cold joint; no strawberries and certainly no salmon, in fact choice was rather limited now that the vegetable gardens in Johore had been lost and few people were fishing. And at a time like this, Australia could not be expected to fly out luxuries. But apart from the rather monotonous fare, there was nothing to worry about, the island had enough food for six months.

His thoughts turned anxiously to his wife who was extremely ill with dysentery, and who now slept under the banqueting table buttressed from bomb and shell splinters by a barricade of mattresses. She certainly had no interest in food. He was extremely proud of her; despite the discomfort and pain she stubbornly refused to leave. What more could they do to show they were at one with the people? Heavens above, although he was fully aware of the need to maintain appearances and standards, he had relaxed them considerably, in keeping with the gravity of the situation. Guests were no longer expected to dress formally for dinner, although he did insist on jackets and ties. He gazed up at the clear blue sky and was grateful that the weather was so fine and the monsoon had ended. The torrential rain did tend to dampen one's spirits. Then he felt a cloud of gloom descend as he accepted that despite his efforts he did not inspire the universal confidence and loyalty he deserved. He had even heard it expressed that his speeches were empty rhetoric and no substitute for the leadership that was needed. Well, he refuted that emphatically. He was in no doubt that this erosion of confidence was due in no small measure to the lack of support he received from London. That had come about through the machinations of Duff Cooper. The devious politician, he knew, had told Whitehall that there was a widespread lack of faith in the administration, and changes ought to be made. He had even gone so far as to press for *his* removal, but that had been rejected, quite properly, out of hand. But there had to be a scapegoat and poor old Stanley Jones, his Colonial Secretary, had been dismissed in disgrace. Now he wandered around like a fish out of water pleading to be given some job or other; anything was preferable to being shipped back home with his tail between his legs. He was also aware that Cooper's spiteful strictures had found a willing ear in Winston Churchill who told the House of blunders and a lack of foresight and incredible inertia when bold action was needed. That, in his eyes, was inexcusable buck-passing, and a clumsy effort to silence those critics who were demanding the PM's own dismissal. Cooper, thank God, had scuttled off to London and safety, volubly protesting, quite unconvincingly, that he wanted to remain. But *he* had remained at his post. Even so, he was not able to get the support of *The Straits Times* on which he thought he could depend. When he issued a circular to the Malaya Civil Service saying that the day of minutes was over and an obsession with files was to end, someone contributed the unhelpful comment that "it was two and a quarter years too late". And in the bars of some of the clubs they had even resurrected the old chestnut that he had preferred to stay on leave in the United Kingdom when the threat to Malaya became acute. Just imagine the effect it would have had on morale if he had not come hurrying back. Pressure had also been exerted to make Percival Military Governor, a move which to his credit the General had resisted. The criticisms seemed unending, for now they were blaming him for the troops having to unload their own equipment from ships; yet he had settled the question of rates of pay for coolies as quickly as conditions permitted – such things could not be hastened because of the long term implications – and it was not his fault that the coolies could not be tempted back to work, preferring safety to a fatter wage packet. It was all the more galling because his present critics were the ones who had stubbornly resisted any rise. In any case, what was so terribly wrong about soldiers doing a little labouring? Good heavens, the streets were filled with leaderless idle troops too often the worse for drink. At times it seemed to him that he had as many enemies on the island as there were on the mainland.

He retraced his footsteps towards the house thinking it was time to see how Lucy was faring; she was a great prop and had never faltered in her support, despite seeing his powers gradually whittled away. She still saw him as a force to be reckoned with.

The shriek of an approaching shell made him momentarily hurry, until he remembered that example was everything, and he deliberately slowed his pace, even pausing to admire a particularly beautiful bloom.

Jo Jardine stood on the brink of a huge hole some forty or fifty feet long and half as wide, supervising the laying out of the corpses in the six-foot-deep grave. This, she told herself, was what the old London plague pits I read about as a child must have looked like. Even though she wore a surgical mask, she could still smell the putrefying flesh. The soldiers who were tumbling the bodies into the hole were stripped to the waist and resembled grotesque insects, for they all wore respirators with big goggle eye-pieces and rubber breathing tubes which looked like proboscis, to counteract the stench. But every few minutes one was forced to leave his gruesome task to vomit behind a shrub or bush. On the perimeter of the mass grave, two armed sentries stood guard ready to shoot any of the hunger emboldened dogs which prowled, cringing low, a few yards away, prepared to defy the most brutal kicks in order to dart into the hole and tear off a piece of rotting flesh and devour it noisily while others tried to rip it from their jaws.

In the intense heat and humidity, burials had to be carried out with a minimum of delay, and only a short period was allowed for people to carry out a cursory examination of the laid-out corpses to identify next of kin, before they were tumbled into the grave. There was no time for religious observances, and the only concession was for Europeans to be at one end and Muslims, Bhuddists and Hindus at the other. It was the fourth such pit which had been dug on the waste ground outside the hospital, and Jo's stomach still heaved uncontrollably at the memory of some of the scenes she had been forced to witness. On one occasion a demented man who had arrived too late to identify his wife and child, jumped into the pit and began to turn over the dead. Eventually the bodies had to be removed in order that he could satisfy himself that they had died.

When the first mass grave was dug the bodies were doused

with kerosene and cremated, but now the number of corpses was increasing so fast that there was no time for that – it took an incredibly long time to burn a body – so now the holes had lorry loads of lime tipped into them before being filled in. At first the graves had been for people who had died in the hospital or been killed during a raid or artillery attack, but now their numbers were swelled by the dead who had been dug out of the debris or picked up by the corpse-collecting units. They were listed as DOA, a description which struck Jo as being needlessly callous.

She had not volunteered for the job, any more than the soldiers had; she had been detailed on the grounds that the more qualified nursing staff were better occupied treating the patients who were still alive. In fact, her presence was not really needed, but one of the senior doctors thought it indicated a measure of respect.

It amazed her that there had not been an outbreak of pestilence because the constant shelling and bombing had fractured many sewers and some parts of the city resembled open cess pits. Corpses were also floating in the reservoirs which meant people were drinking polluted water. Apart from that danger, water was also becoming scarce, so much was running to waste, and she now found that the daily ration she was issued had to serve several purposes. First she washed herself in the heavily disinfected water, then she washed her uniform, and kept it until next morning for a final bath.

As she watched the soldiers going about their gruesome task, she thought about the meeting she had attended the previous evening in the nurses' quarters when the auxilliaries demanded to know whether there was any foundation in the rumour that all the military sisters and nurses in Singapore were to be evacuated. The Medical Superintendent promised them he would seek an assurance from the highest possible level that this was not the case. It would be an act of unforgivable betrayal if they were to pull out and leave the relatively inexperienced volunteers to cope with the almost impossible situation. It was the duty of the professionals to remain in order to succour and treat the wounded soldiers and civilians. To everyone's immense relief, he was able to assure them that morning that it was purely malicious gossip without a grain of truth. They toasted the news with some neat gin,

257

for their relief was genuine. If the military medical and nursing staff had been evacuated, the consequences were too horrifying to contemplate.

Although she never voiced her fears aloud, she now seriously doubted if Singapore could hold out for long if the Japanese attacked across the Strait. She had no knowledge at all of military tactics and had to rely on what she was told by newly arrived wounded officers and men, and their opinion seemed to be that General Percival did not know "his arse from his elbow", while the Governor managed to confirm that he was the fool everyone thought he was every time he broadcast. Her nursing colleagues exercised the same discretion, but she could tell from their faces they shared her apprehension. Her doubts had further increased when her father arrived unexpectedly that morning and urged her to jump into the car and go home with him and pack her most precious belongings. "Now's the time to get out, before the real scramble starts," he said. "People are queueing to get aboard the convoy that brought in the last lot of troops. The buzz is that they'll be doing a sharp turnaround. I'm going up to Cluny to put our names down."

The temptation had been great, her father was no fool. Everything he possessed he owned to Singapore, and he was the last person to surrender if he thought there was still a remote hope of clinging on to it, but she had declined. He was so astonished and angry that she was forced to explain that she would not be able to look herself in the mirror if she walked out. It wasn't so long ago, she told him, that they had held a meeting to protest at stories that military nursing staff were quitting. Now he was asking her to do the same. He begged and pleaded with her to no avail, his voice droning on as persistent as one of the bluebottles that filled the wards, buzzing noisily over the foul dressings until she had closed her ears to it as easily as she did to the loathsome flies, although she vividly recalled his parting words:

"I'm not scuttling, Jo. I'd stay if I just had myself to think of, but there's your mother. She's no longer young. Anyway, I can be of much more use in Ceylon or India. This thing isn't going to last for ever and when it's over they'll need people with my experience and expertise to put the place back on its feet."

She had just wished that he would go, there was no need for him to protest so volubly and unconvincingly; there was no reason why he should remain. Half his warehouses had gone up in flames and there was no one to move the stocks from those that remained. He was what was currently being referred to as "a useless mouth", and the only thing that would justify his remaining was a sense of duty and loyalty, two things which had never figured prominently in his make up. The more he argued the more despicable he became in her eyes, and she did not want that. "You're quite right," she said, "Mother must be your first concern."

Then with an awkwardness that was not at all characteristic, he handed her a wallet bulging with $100 notes. "No matter what happens, money always talks", and she replied, "How many are there? Thirty?" But the irony had been lost on him and he replied, "Hell of a lot more than that, dear."

She watched his car drive out of the hospital while she waved in a desultory fashion, as if almost glad to see the back of him. She sincerely hoped that he and her mother would get away. Neither had the temperament or resilience to survive a period of long imprisonment should the worst happen.

She was brought back to the present by the sound of the last spadefuls of earth being thrown into the pit. The sergeant in charge of the burial party tugged her sleeve. "That's it then, Miss. I just hope we don't get lumbered with the next one. The lads want to get back to the Company. They want to be killing Japs, not burying our own kind." As he spoke he rattled the pile of brown identity discs which had been removed from dead soldiers from one hand to the other, like a gambler in a casino wondering where to place his chips.

She motioned towards an oil drum of disinfected water boiling on an improvised stove. "Get your men to have a good wash in that, Sergeant. No point in running unnecessary risks. Anyone with the slightest cut is open to infection."

As he turned to walk away he paused and said, "I've met some pretty brave people in my time, Miss, but none of them measures up to you nurses. Funny, when I first landed here I thought the memsahibs couldn't change their underclothes without a servant. I was wrong. Best of luck."

Jo smiled and said, "You know, Sergeant, I thought that

too once." She took out the wallet and handed him several notes, not even bothering to count them. "You and your men, please have a drink on me. I've nothing to spend it on."

As they marched away through the gates, she wondered how many of them would survive. They looked so young and eager to get to grips with the enemy which amazed her, for until they arrived Singapore had been no more than another red patch on a world map that was predominately pink. That made her think of Terence, and she wondered where he was. I suppose I do love him, and in normal circumstances would have liked to marry him. But if times had been normal I wouldn't have met him. All swings and roundabouts. But she realised there was little point in thinking of what might have been; it was a chapter of her life that was closed.

She heard a sister's voice calling stridently, "Nurse Jardine," and she turned and saw her ward sister beckoning her with a rigid finger. "There's no time for day dreaming, nurse. Three patients have just died and their beds need changing."

As she removed the soiled and grimy sheets and pillow slips and replaced them with clean ones in readiness for their new occupants, she wondered who, in their right mind, would seriously consider nursing as a noble vocation; it was anything but that. It was filth and dirt and suffering, with death as the outcome, and there was no dignity in that either. Until she had become a nurse her knowledge of death and war had been limited to what she had seen on the cinema screen when life departed after a few heroic words were uttered through gritted teeth, and a last cigarette was slipped from a close-up of stiffening fingers. But any sense of loss had been transitory, for the hero reappeared a few weeks later to die a similar death in a different location. But now she had witnessed the real thing, and there had been pain and screaming and a fearful reluctance to plunge into that abyss of darkness and oblivion even though it offered the much prayed for relief. In her mind's eye she saw again the pile of discs in the sergeant's hand, and felt like weeping aloud. God, how she envied her ward sister whose face never registered emotion and whose uniform was never soiled or rumpled, and who could move from the dead to the living as if one had simply fallen asleep and the other had just awakened.

Clive Jardine drove warily and slowly through Singapore, for the city now presented a spectacle of awesome devastation; the upturned shells of burnt-out cars and trams cluttered the streets, and tangles of overhead cables, brought down by shells and bombs, were an additional hazard to anyone who let their concentration wander for a second. On either side of the roads the stagnant monsoon ditches were filled with the floating, bloated corpses of humans, dogs, mules and oxen, and the stench was so overpowering he was forced to hold his breath until he felt his head and lungs would burst. Other bodies lay on the pavements, interesting only to the carrion crows and scavenging dogs.

He drove himself because he found it wiser to dispense with the syce whose presence behind the wheel attracted the attention of drunken soldiers who lolled on the steps of the public buildings and pelted the car with refuse and shouted abuse at what they considered a symbol of colonial incompetence and the reason for their present predicament. Many of them were deserters who had no interest in dying to preserve a way of life in which they had no role to play, and who were quite content to survive on what they could loot. Others were soldiers who had made a genuine effort to rejoin their units, only to give up because they could not get advice or guidance from anyone. There were gunners without guns, drivers without lorries, signallers without equipment, infantry without rifles, and because there was an acute shortage of official accommodation and tents, they were forced to sleep wherever there was room to stretch out. Even the YMCA was now one vast dormitory and part of the hallowed cricket club a hospital. There were even wounded in the cathedral.

Although he did not entirely blame them, they brought a flush of shame to his cheeks; where was the Dunkirk spirit? Why didn't they get off their backsides and help the emergency services? Couldn't they see that precious water was going to waste from broken mains because there was a manpower shortage, and that valuable rubber stocks were burning because the fire brigade couldn't handle all the fires? Every extra pair of hands would be welcome.

Penny-sized flakes of black soot floated from the sky forcing him to switch on his windscreen wipers, while the glow from some of the fires was so intense he had to shade his eyes with one hand. He viewed the scene with a mounting sense of dismay and disgust as he headed for home after his second abortive visit to the P & O Agency at Cluny where he had again tried to book a passage for himself and his wife aboard one of the departing troopers. On the first occasion he had not even got inside, having been told in the most uncourteous manner that there were far more urgent and needy cases, and to come back in two days' time but not expect too much. He had done so, but the pressure of people clamouring to leave had not diminished, and he had been subjected to a most humiliating ordeal from which he was still seething.

The road leading up to the spacious bungalow was lined with deserted cars, some of which perched precariously on the edge of ditches and were in imminent danger of toppling in. Nearly all of them were sieved with machine gun bullets from the low flying fighters which continuously straffed the road. The cars, many of which were laden with furniture and suitcases, had been abandoned when people found they could not drive any closer to the P & O Office which had been assigned the task of allocating all passages, and they were forced to get out and join the straggling queue of thousands which stretched out of sight and moved at a snail's pace up the steep hill to the wide driveway that led to the bungalow. Whenever an aircraft appeared people broke ranks and dived for cover, often into the ditches, seeking life among the dead, only to find when they emerged that they had lost their places. The chaos was indescribable as no instructions had been issued to refugees and there was a total absence of any organisation. Some people without money did not bother to try and get a passage, unaware that the Government would advance the fare; someone had forgotten to announce the concession publicly.

In spite of very nearly flattening his battery by persistent blasting of his horn, Jardine found that no one was prepared to let him jump the queue and he was forced to pocket his pride and join the serpentine column of women and bawling children which writhed at a yard an hour until, after what seemed an eternity, he entered the large room where officials sat behind desks marked Columbo, India and UK, laboriously writing in longhand in leather-bound ledgers the names of everyone entitled to leave. But even at a time of such distress and urgency red tape persisted and people who had no papers, having lost them up country, were turned away while others who did not possess a photograph were sent off to get one taken, but as the Japanese photographers had either decamped or been interned, it was a pointless instruction. He tagged on to the Columbo queue when he recognised the official as someone he knew, but was told in a very curt manner that he was still not eligible, priority was being given to women and children and the sick and elderly. The fact that many of the women and children were families of garrison troops whose presence in peacetime was considered an unfortunate necessity and who were now doing what so many residents had earnestly wished they would do, did not deter Jardine from kicking up a hell of a fuss and warning the official that he had not heard the end of things; he was not without influence and would bring it to the attention of those in a position to do something about it. His humiliation was added to when a policeman was summoned to escort him off the premises with jabs from his riot stick.

Those who were successful in obtaining boarding passes wasted no time in hastening to the docks; there were rumours that these could be the last ships to leave. It was, however, just the beginning of another long ordeal for the approaches to the docks were every bit as congested, and they were frequently accosted by people who offered them large sums of money for their berths. If anything, the congestion was even greater than at Cluny, and progress to the ships was slow because of the air raids and the log-jam of wrecked vehicles that blocked every access to the docks. Some ships sailed before their full quota of passengers had time to embark. Others were more fortunate; they found themselves allocated to ships which were still unloading troops and equipment. Many evacuees went aboard with no more than a knife and fork and some sandwiches. Incredibly the bars of some vessels were still open and doing a flourishing trade.

263

The quay was thronged with weeping men, waving goodbye to their loved ones and wondering if they would ever see them again. While in another section of the docks people who had been refused a passage were busy bargaining with junk and sampan owners to take them across the Malacca Strait to Sumatra.

Still seething with indignation, Jardine decided to drop in for a drink at Raffles and calm his nerves before he crashed the car. He still had a lot of good business contacts, he reminded himself, who, providing the price was right, would help him to charter a ship that would take him, his wife, and most of their possessions, to any destination that was beyond the reach of the enemy. Of course, England was out of the question, so was India, but Ceylon would do. It would not need a big vessel, a small tramp would do, and there were dozens of them around, skippered by drop-outs who would do anything for hard cash.

The bar was doing a bustling trade, but as he glanced around he could not see anyone who could be of immediate assistance, until he caught sight of Superintendent Nolan standing alone at the far end of the bar. Like many police-men, Nolan had many acquaintances but few friends; he was a useful man to keep on the right side of, but not one with whom you would establish an intimate relationship. He was what was known in the clubs as a "good fixer", a chap who would help you if you were in a jam with the police, one who used his position and influence under the "old pal's act"; even though there was always a bill to pick up at the end – a small gift to settle a racing debt, or a little something for his wife. No one ever suggested that he was corrupt, preferring to say he was a trifle greedy. Jardine considered himself to be halfway between a friend and an acquaintance; he found it rather distasteful to admit that, like so many others, he resorted to bribery to avoid appearing in court on some petty offence that would be harmful to his prestige. Nolan did favours. And being a recognised pillar of local society, Jardine salved his conscience by saying that was what friends were for.

When he joined Nolan, the policeman asked him what he would like to drink, only he used the word imbibe, and when he had ordered he surveyed Jardine with that inquisitorial look policemen acquire over the years which implied he was aware that he had been up to no good. Jardine had learned from experience that it did not presage any great perception but was simply a tool of his profession. "You look as if you've had a hectic time, Clive. Bit hot and flustered, not at all like you."

"I might say the same of you, but in your case I can *see* the reason. Been hammering it a bit? Line of duty, of course."

Nolan had something of a reputation for being a tippler, and he was aware of it, but he was always able to resort to the excuse that he had to consort with unsavoury types, and drink more than was good for him, if he was to keep his finger on the pulse of the criminal fraternity. "A copper who sits on his arse never caught anything but piles," was one of his favourite expressions.

Nolan lowered his voice as if fearing to be overheard. "Not exactly been drowning my sorrows, Clive, but lamenting the bloody incompetence of those who run this island. On the one hand Percival wants to know why the police aren't doing more to control the unruly bloody pongoes marauding through the streets, completely ignoring that it's a job for the military police, while His Excellency wants to know why more isn't being done to supervise the crowds at Cluny. He's the bloody man who won't issue an order for evacuation, and he gets all up tight if there's a shambles as a result. Enough to make any conscientious policeman throw his hand in and start thinking of himself for once. He rambles on about Singapore being a ship and how everyone should stand by his post. Well, I know for a fact that moves are already afoot to ship out all the military nursing personnel. No doubt HE will be the last to hear of that, and when he does he'll mount his high horse and bleat 'Why wasn't I told'. He's on the bridge all right, but he doesn't know what's happening in the engine room."

Jardine sensed that this was the opportunity he had been seeking, for Nolan was normally the most sycophantic of the Governor's admirers. Now he was clearly losing confidence.

"Don't talk to me about evacuation. I've just got back from Cluny where I've been treated like a bloody coolie.

I need to get out – not for myself, for my wife – and there's no chance. Priority is being given to a load of snotty-nosed kids and women who've contributed sod all to the prosperity of this place. They're in no danger. Who the hell wants to harm helpless women and children? Whereas people like me – the detested symbol of colonialism – are going to get very short shrift from the Japs. I'd be more than happy to remain if there was anything for me to do, but my businesses are grinding to a halt. I'm one of what Churchill calls *bouche inutile*, I'm just an extra mouth to feed. In Ceylon I could contribute something useful to the war effort." He heard his own voice, and although he did not believe a word he said, it rang with conviction.

"I'm in a similar position, Clive. My wife can't wait to get out, and I can fix that, but she won't budge without me. Now how on earth can a senior officer bugger off at the drop of a hat? Not that I want to, my job is here, but speaking frankly, my first loyalty is to her. Let's face it, law and order is falling apart at the seams, men are disappearing left right and centre; I can't go out and control crowds on my own." His voice dropped to a conspiratorial whisper. "I'm in the process of making arrangements to get out if the crunch comes. There's no hope of doing so through official channels. Sir Shenton has made it perfectly clear that he will remain whatever happens, he will not desert his people, and he insists that senior officials must adopt the same attitude. Well, they aren't *my* people. They loathe the sight of me. What's more, I've put too many behind bars to want to share the experience. Jail here is no ruddy holiday, especially Changi, and I'd be the first to go inside if the Japs overrun the place. I was responsible for rounding up the buggers, remember."

Jardine found his own voice fading to a whisper. "You mentioned arrangements. I wouldn't mind being in on them."

Nolan drew him aside, out of range of any possible eavesdroppers. "I've got no further than putting out feelers. It boils down to a question of hard cash. Remember Van Heyter, the Dutchman?"

Jardine had a vague recollection of an enormously fat and filthy man who would suddenly reappear in Singapore after being away for weeks on end to eat gargantuan meals, appease his equally phenomenal sexual appetite, and go on

266

a binge that lasted several days before vanishing again. He was the master of a rusting, battered coaster with no apparent regular customers, although he never seemed short of money. It was rumoured that he ran illicit cargoes to Sumatra, Java and Borneo, without asking too many questions, providing, of course, the money was there. Many suspected he was engaged in smuggling contraband. He remained such a shadowy figure because he was not accepted in any of the respectable clubs.

"I know of him. Not a very reputable character."

"Maybe, but he's got a boat he's happy to charter. He owes no allegiance to the Dutch, and he's got no great affection for the British, and he's no great wish to have his ship confiscated by the Japs. If he can find enough people to put up the cash he's prepared to take them wherever they ask. He's told me so. I told him he can count on having me and my wife, but he said I'd need to get a dozen more before he'd even consider it. I wouldn't pay for the fuel."

Jardine ordered more drinks before suggesting they retire to a nearby table where they could talk in confidence. He did not want a crush of people descending on them with offers to chip in.

When the drinks arrived Nolan resumed. "As you know, Clive, policemen don't make a fat living. Nothing put aside for a rainy day." He shrugged. "True, we get the occasional perk, but we have to maintain standards, and there's nothing left at the end of the month. Admittedly there's a nice pension waiting, but the Dutchman can't wait; he wants cash on the nail. So what I have to do is find some people of a similar frame of mine to my own. I'm in the process of sounding out reliable people, like you, who won't go shouting from the rooftops. Mind you, I'm not talking about tomorrow or the next day. I'm talking about the time when there are no other options open."

Jardine said, "I'm in a hurry. Wait too long and there'll be people fighting to get aboard anything that floats. Better to be among the first to leave than the last."

Nolan nodded. "I agree with every word, but the Dutchman won't budge until he sees the colour of their money. So far you're the only person I've approached. It'll take time to approach others."

"No need to look for any more. You tell him that I'll put up *all* the money, in cash or kind, whichever he prefers. There's no object in having a big group; there'll only be rows about where everyone wants to go, and they'll all want to take as much as possible. With just four of us all those problems will vanish. He'll also save on food which should make it that much more attractive."

Nolan was unable to suppress his relief. "I'll arrange to meet him tonight. He's an illusive bugger, but I think I can track him down. I think he's staying in a crummy brothel run by some White Russian madame. I'll ring as soon as I've made contact."

"Where's his ship?"

"No idea. Wouldn't tell me. All I know is that it's holed up some place where he can make a quick getaway if necessary. Like you, he's anxious to get out with his skin intact."

Jardine said, "Unlike you who's thinking solely of his wife."

Jardine drove home in a frenzy of suppressed excitement, ignoring his wife's greeting and going straight into his study to ring one of his few warehouses still functioning. He spoke to the foreman and told him to get the carpenters to knock up as many stout crates as they could in the shortest possible time, and see that they were brought to the house with a minimum of delay. He also told him to bring as many empty tea chests as he could lay his hands on. They at least were easily obtainable in Singapore. His sudden request might make the foreman a little suspicious, but there was nothing he could do about it. Anyway, a generous gift would ensure his co-operation; after all, being a Malay, he wouldn't want to leave himself and the cash would be welcome in the hard times to come.

When he had completed his instructions he went into the lounge where he embraced his wife with genuine affection and poured two generous stengahs.

"You look like the cat that has got the cream, Clive."

"We're leaving," he said.

"When?" she asked in genuine surprise.

"As soon as possible. I'm not hanging around until all the exits are barred and bolted."

"But what about Jo, and the house, and all the lovely

things we've collected over the years, darling?"

"I've pleaded with Jo until I'm blue in the face. Been down on my hands and knees, but she's determined to stay. I can't stop her being a ruddy martyr." He feared that his wife might think he had not pressed her hard enough and had given up too easily. "I tried everything. Said if she wouldn't come then we'd stay. She just wouldn't listen. Said she owed it to the patients and the other nurses. Absolute rubbish. I know for a fact that the army is going to evacuate its own nurses."

"Did you tell her that?"

"How could I? I didn't know it when I saw her. Anyway, what difference would it make? She'd only be more determined. There's a lot of me in her."

Mrs Jardine sat down, her hands clasped together in her lap. "Just think of all the plans we had for her and Terence," she said, before lapsing into a brooding silence, during which she thought of the home they had shared for so long and all they would be giving up.

"No good moping, darling. Her mind's made up, so is mine. We haven't got a lot of time, and there's a great deal to be done. First thing is to decide what we're taking and what we're leaving behind. We can, thank God, err on the generous side. What we can't pack we'll get the boys to crate up and bury in the garden. If we don't recover it the loss will not be too great."

"What about Cotswold Cottage?" she asked meekly. "We've been here so long."

"It'll still be here when we get back; if it isn't we can claim compensation for war damage. Now do start making up your mind about what we're taking."

"I don't think I want to go, Clive. I'd rather stay and take pot luck with the others. I can't desert Jo, she'd never forgive me," she said through the handkerchief that stifled her sobs.

He put his arms around her and said, "You know, I can't bear to see you cry. Jo would hate to think she's being a burden. After all, it's her choice and she quite accepts that *we* are entitled to one. It's a time for decisions and you must let me make them. Have I ever been wrong in the past?"

Any doubts or fears that may have assailed Mrs Jardine

quickly dissipated as she hurried through the house with a pad and pencil drawing up an inventory which had two separate headings – Take and Leave. In a short time she became totally absorbed in her task, pausing before every object to ponder which heading they should go under. The cutlery, silver and best glass would have to go. They were positive musts if they were to start a fresh life in an alien country. Clive would insist on taking his favourite pictures, and room had to be found for the photograph of Their Majesties. Clothes too were important. They couldn't turn up out of the blue looking like paupers. The same applied to her jewellery; not that that presented any real problem. All she possessed would fit into her jewellery box. And the big, framed picture of Jo in tennis gear, that would have to go; although it would be a constant reminder of her betrayal she could not bear to be without it. It would be like an unseen umbilical cord. That reminded her of Jo's christening robe; she could not leave that behind. She had worn it herself, as had her own mother and – who could say? – Jo might have children of her own one day. The collection of jade would also have to be packed; not that she liked it particularly, but it was the kind of thing to have in case of a rainy day.

Meanwhile, Mr Jardine had organised the gardeners who were digging several large holes in different parts of the grounds, while Chang was assembling all the steel chests in the house; fortunately, there were several of these as every home possessed a number of cabin trunks for home leave. As the holes grew deeper, Jardine reflected with some satisfaction that the trunks could remain burried for years if necessary without their contents deteriorating. There was always the risk, of course, that one of the boys would try and dig them up, but he proposed to let Chang live in the house and he would keep an eye on things. His devotion to his tuan besar was beyond question, and he could safely bank on him to be there when they returned, smiling and cheerful as if they had only been away for a long weekend. Naturally his loyalty would be suitably rewarded in advance. Fortunately, money was no problem. He had been withdrawing substantial sums for some time and transferring assets to the London Office. But even should Chang prove unreliable it did not matter all that much; everything was heavily insured.

It was well after midnight and they were still working when the telephone rang and Jardine answered it to find Nolan at the end of the line.

"The Dutchman is quite happy with the arrangements, provided it's cash on the line," said Nolan. "That's not exactly accurate; he'll take gold, silver, jade and precious stones – anything, just so long as the total works out all right."

"Tell him he has no worries on that score. Just say I want him here first thing in the morning."

"He's not an early riser, Clive," said Nolan hesitantly.

"He will be tomorrow. If necessary, go and pick him up. Once I've made a decision I act."

The policeman said, "Hang on Clive. We haven't even thought of what we're taking yet."

"If you've any sense you'll stay up all night as we're doing and get on with it."

He hung up and sat down heavily in his favourite chair, emitting an exaggerated sigh of relief. "Fancy a night cap, darling?"

She glanced around her and said wistfully, "I *really* shall miss this, Clive, as much as you'll miss your lovely Rolls Royce."

"That's coming with us. It can easily be hoisted aboard and lashed to the deck. Nothing like arriving in style."

She said gently, "Isn't that taking things a bit too far, darling? It's only a car. It owes us nothing."

"That's where you're wrong. It's more than that, it's a symbol, as I've said before. I'm not leaving it for some Jap general to ride around in. It's like a regiment abandoning its colours. Apart from that, I don't intend being idle in Ceylon, and the Rolls will help me get a foot in."

Chapter 14

The odour of impending defeat hung heavy in the air as Commander Paton threaded his way through the cratered streets towards Keppel Harbour where *Grey Seal* was still moored alongside. He had just been to a top-level meeting in the underground conference room at Fort Canning which was attended by the senior officers of the three services who were asked to express their candid opinion of the situation. The fleetless navy could add little in the way of an aggressive contribution, while the RAF with no aircraft was in a similar position. He was not at all sure why he was ordered to attend; he was not consulted on anything, neither did he receive any orders as to what he and his ship should be doing. In his opinion, it was a disastrous meeting and merely confirmed his earlier fears that any hope of holding the island had gone. In the stuffy overcrowded soundproof room, with its inadequate air-conditioning, the war seemed a long way off, although the fighting was only a few miles away. The voices droned on as monotonously as the slow turning ceiling fans, reluctant to state openly what was in everybody's mind for fear of being branded defeatist.

Three days had passed since the Japanese had launched their assault on the island which, despite its inevitability, caught its people unawares. Paton found it unbelievable because the assault had been heralded by an intensive softening-up process when Japanese aircraft and artillery pounded the defensive positions established on the northern side of the island. Those with long enough memories said it was as intensive as anything they had encountered on the Western Front in World War I. Then at 10.30 p.m. on 8 February, to the deafening accompaniment of guns, blue and red rockets cascaded high above the Strait, the signal for the first troops to start crossing. The army was taken by surprise, and in a short time nearly all the telephone lines were cut, virtually isolating men from their headquarters and adjoining units. From then on it had been a chronicle of disasters.

The Japanese had assembled an armada of a hundred large landing craft and two hundred collapsible boats with outboard engines which they had manhandled overland to avoid detection from the sea.

The Australian troops holding the vital areas on the north west coast and opposite the Causeway, quickly recovered from the initial surprise and caught the first wave of boats in a blistering hail of fire and almost decimated it, but for some unaccountable reason no one gave the signal for the searchlights to be switched on to illuminate the killing area for fear that they might be knocked out by marksmen, and no one gave the order for a retaliatory barrage to be laid down. At the Kranji River, numerous Japanese had literally been boiled in oil when the oil tanks were emptied into the water and set on fire. The Australians also inflicted heavy losses on the second wave, but they were literally fighting in the dark and during the night the enemy landed 13,000 troops and a further 10,000 the next day. Some of them waded across the gap in the damaged Causeway, while others swam across holding their weapons and ammunition above their heads. The fighting was ferocious with many hand-to-hand encounters, but the enemy adopted their favourite tactic of finding gaps in the line and encircling the defenders. The Australians began to retreat, and without maps or compasses soon lost all sense of direction and many were hopelessly lost in the mangrove swamps and jungle. Some managed to reach the city where they presented a pitiful spectacle; the flesh on their lacerated feet hung in ribbons and many had thrown away their arms. In a short time, the Australian 22nd Brigade ceased to exist as a cohesive fighting force, and the retreat degenerated into a disorderly rout. The enemy in their relentless thrust towards the city took few prisoners and committed the most appalling atrocities.

Despite the disaster, a sanguine Percival had announced, "Offensive action is being taken to mop up the enemy."

Although the people in the city – now almost treble its normal population – had little idea of how badly the fighting was going, it was depressingly audible. They were no longer in the dark about the gravity of the general situation. An irate ARP official broadcast an uncensored account over the Malay Broadcasting Corporation of the true state of affairs; furthermore, it had reached the ears of the outside world which now knew how the entire campaign had been bungled and mismanaged, and in Whitehall there was an acute awareness that the rot had to be stopped. On 10 February, General Wavell flew in haste from Java and was horrified at the speed of the withdrawal. He went over Percival's head and ordered an immediate counter attack to re-establish the vital Jurong Line which had been abandoned; if that fell, the road to the city was wide open. But it was too late to reverse the situation, and with no aircraft available it was repulsed with heavy losses. Percival, who had tasted the sharp edge of Wavell's tongue and was still smarting at the recollection of it, was subjected to an even more blistering dressing down. He was further humiliated by the knowledge that the attack had begun exactly where Wavell had predicted.

Wavell's mood was not improved by a caustic signal he had received from Sir Winston who wanted to know why Percival with 100,000 men had been routed by less than half that number of Japanese.

"There must at this stage be no thought of saving the troops or sparing the civilian population. The battle must be fought to the bitter end at all costs. Commanders and senior officers should die with their troops. The honour of the British Empire and of the British Army is at stake. With the Russians fighting as they are and the Americans so stubbornly at Luzon, the whole reputation of our country and our race is involved."

In a Special Order of the Day Wavell, like a ventriloquist's dummy, repeated the Prime Minister's strictures almost word for word.

The hapless and outmanoeuvred Percival added his own version which shifted all responsibility onto the shoulders of the fighting soldiers. "In some units," he said, "the troops have not shown the fighting spirit which is to be expected of men of the British Empire. It will be a lasting disgrace

275

if we are defeated by an army of clever gangsters, many times inferior in number to our own."

Paton thought it was hardly the clarion call the bewildered and bedraggled troops needed; they wanted inspired leadership, not wordy exhortations or unjustified criticism.

On the evening Wavell was to board his flying boat, he had slipped and fallen a considerable height, badly injuring his back which meant that he was unable to make a return visit to Singapore and could only direct things from Java. But the scene was changing so swiftly and the distance was so great he could have little influence.

To add to the army's confusion was the seemingly incompatible priorities which were being insisted upon; although they were being urged to fight to the last man and the last round, Churchill pronounced that a scorched-earth policy was to be embarked upon which would deprive the enemy of any equipment and materials which could assist them. It seemed to the battle-weary men that they were being asked to defend every inch of the island yet at the same time destroy everything.

Paton had since learned that the scorched-earth policy was only a half-hearted effort, for the Governor did not consider it fair or just to destroy modern equipment and machinery owned by Chinese; they after all, he reasoned, had to survive if the island was overrun. When objections were raised, he resorted to his favourite phrase, "Such a step would be bad for morale". And so equipment and plants which would be welcomed by the enemy were excused. This understandably led some Europeans, loathe to see a lifetime's work go up in smoke, to press the Governor to be exempted, and in some cases they were. But most of the fishing boats which would be priceless if evacuation was ordered, were destroyed along with harbour installations, repair yards, slipways and power plants.

All this went through Paton's mind as he walked through streets where the corpses had multiplied and the number of charred vehicles had increased to an incredible extent, and he decided on the spur of the moment to make a minor detour and go to Raffles and see if there was any news of Kate Hollis, for an order had just been promulgated that all Press and broadcasting personnel were to prepare themselves for immediate evacuation. There was, therefore, a remote possibility that she had returned to the hotel to collect what few belongings she would be allowed to take. It was another indication to him that despite the defiant words that were being uttered by the generals and the Prime Minister, there was little doubt that it was all over. The *Times* and *Tribune* had ceased to publish, although the Governor was printing a daily news sheet on the presses of the *Times*, but that was filled with official announcements which few believed. The number of people now clamouring to leave had increased enormously, and a considerable number of Europeans who had been told to remain deserted their posts and left. So quick was their departure that some Asians turned up at their place of work and found their employers had left taking with them all the available cash.

Paton entered the hotel through the Palm Court and was surprised to see some of the staff in the process of burying the silver roast trolley in a deep hole. He wondered why it was considered so important when so many things of military value had been reprieved. It was, he thought, typical of the cock-eyed sense of values which existed on the island.

He enquired at the reception desk if there was any news of Miss Hollis and was told that nothing had been heard of her since she left to go to the front. After a brief altercation with the receptionist, he managed to obtain the key to her room, and when he went upstairs he passed hastily evacuated rooms. Cupboards were open and the floors strewn with clothing and unwanted articles. He sat down at the desk and wrote a short letter wishing her luck and giving her his address in England. He toyed with the idea of packing some of her belongings and taking them back to the ship, but he realised it was far better to leave everything as it was in case she did return.

On his way out he was surprised to see a notice advertising a dinner dance that evening. He returned the key and gave instructions that on no account was anyone other than Miss Hollis to be allowed into the room. Looting was now rampant.

It took him an hour to reach the docks from the hotel as the approach roads to the harbour were jammed with people making a desperate attempt to get away before it was too late. It reminded him of the news reel film he had seen of French peasants fleeing from the German army, only this was on a much vaster scale. And their ordeal was made even worse by the constant bombing and straffing.

There was also another vast exodus moving out of the city. They were natives who had no hope of getting a passage and were heading for the remote parts of the east coast where they hoped to find relief from the bombs and shells. Many of them carried their pitiful belongings suspended in the middle of sagging bamboo poles, others had hand carts and prams. Children carried bundles of food on their heads, and wizened old men and women panted between the shafts of abandoned rickshaws laden with rice, bedding, and squawking chickens. Their slow progress was further impeded by creaking bullock carts piled high with looted furniture and incongruous articles such as pianos and cocktail cabinets.

When he eventually got aboard *Grey Seal* he sent for the first lieutenant only to be told that Carnac had gone with half a dozen hands to supervise the boarding of one ship soon to depart and which was having trouble with people not entitled to a passage.

Sub-Lieutenant Carnac stood at the bottom of the foreward gangway of a large troop ship which was embarking several hundred men, women and children, doing his utmost to try and instill some sense of discipline and order into the thrusting, jostling queue. "The more orderly everyone is the sooner you'll get aboard," he shouted. But his words were ignored and he felt like a man trying to counsel people in a burning cinema not to panic. Leading Seaman Morris and Able Seaman Miller were doing their best to assist him, while at the aft gangway three other ratings were fighting an equally uneven battle against another surging mass of people.

Carnac was amazed at some of the people who it had been decided should be given passage. There seemed no possible reason to include officials of the Harbour Board or senior men from the Public Works Department. There was still plenty for them to do. But his greatest shock was seeing the military nurses and sisters filing up the gangway. They were desperately needed as the hospitals were being singled out for attack. Many of them lowered their heads and averted their eyes, but one sister paused and said, "It's not our choosing. It's an order. Apparently General Percival didn't want a repetition of Hong Kong when the Japs raped and murdered the nurses."

There were similar queues all along the harbour and every ship capable of taking passengers had been brought into use.

Now and again people turned their eyes skywards for the dreaded sight of bombers, hardly able to appreciate their good fortune. Nearly two hours had elapsed since the last raid.

Suddenly there was a violent screeching of brakes and an army lorry slewed to a halt at the gangway where Carnac was standing and several armed soldiers leaped out and began to force women and children off the gangway at bayonet point. Some of the women stepped back docilely, while others clung to their children with one hand and grasped the guard rail with the other and refused to budge.

Carnac stepped forward and shouted, "You're a bloody disgrace to your uniform. Now clear off. No one is jumping the queue. It'll be over my dead body if they try."

A burly private with several days stubble on his chin and a breath that reeked of stale spirits, said, "Fuck off. You can be a ruddy hero if you want to. We're getting out."

Carnac stepped forward and said, "I'm placing you under arrest," whereupon the soldier swung his rifle and brought the butt down on Carnac's shoulder; at the same time he swung it upwards and caught him a glancing blow on the jaw. As Carnac fell to the ground, he felt a heavy boot thud into his ribs before he passed out.

Paton looked down at his first lieutenant stretched out on a bunk in the wardroom; he looked drained of life, but his pulse was reasonably steady. Morris said, "It all happened so quickly, Sir, we didn't have time to step in. Not that we could have done much, seeing as how they were armed and we weren't. We decided the best thing to do was get him back aboard."

"You did the right thing, Morris. I can't go back with an armed party. There'd be a blood bath which might spark off a ruddy mutiny. Now we've got to get him to hospital somehow or other. See if you can rustle up a taxi or a rickshaw, anything."

Carnac opened his eyes and smiled wanly, then coughed and grimaced with pain. "It's a real shambles out there, Sir. Can't understand why the police aren't there. But I don't really blame those pongoes when they see all those bloody officials going aboard. Talk about rats and the sinking ship."

"Don't talk too much. I'm no sawbones, but I think you've got some cracked ribs and a busted collar bone. You'll also need to have your head X-rayed."

"Examined, you mean. I was a fool to intervene."

"Most of us would have done the same thing. Now just relax till we arrange some transport."

Carnac said, "If it's all right with you, Sir, I wouldn't mind going to the hospital where Miss Jardine is. Haven't seen her for some time now. Apart from that, I might get a bit of preferential treatment."

"Good idea. At least you can tell Morris where it is."

The leading seaman appeared at the door and said, "Couldn't find a taxi or a rickshaw, Sir, so I took the liberty of borrowing one of the abandoned cars."

Paton took the key of the armoury off the rack in the wardroom and handed Morris one of the .45 Webley revolvers and Miller one of the Lanchesters. "If anyone tries to hi-jack the car, don't hesitate to use them."

Morris and Miller carried Carnac to the car and Paton said, "I'd like to come, Number One, but I daren't leave the ship. Some of those drink-crazed idiots might take it into their heads to try and seize it." To Morris he said, "Stay with him until you hear what the doctor has to say."

As Morris drove into the hospital, he said, "Jesus, you'd have been better off staying aboard, Sir."

One wing of the hospital was burning fiercely and the lawn was covered with stretcher cases who had been carried to safety. A doctor in a blood-smeared white coat stepped forward and said, "I can't take any more. We're bursting at the seams at it is. As you can see, the Japs are no respecters of the sick and wounded.'

Morris drew the revolver from its webbing holster and said, "He's coming in whether you like it or not. He got his injuries trying to stop some drunken soldiers turning women and children off a ship. All I'm asking you to do is look at him."

The doctor smiled thinly and said, "I wouldn't think of using that if I were you. A lot of people are dependent on me."

Morris holstered the pistol and said, "Sorry. I'm a bit worked up. So would you be if you'd seen some of the people who are running away. If you won't do it for me, at least do it for his girl friend who works here."

The doctor arched his eyebrows. "Really! What's her name?"

"Miss Jardine."

"Why on earth didn't you say so in the first place. She's done so much for others I'll be only too pleased to do something for her."

He shouted out for a stretcher and two orderlies quickly appeared wheeling one. "When you've got him into bed, tell Nurse Jardine she has a visitor."

Jo sat on the edge of his bed and said, "You'll survive, darling. A couple of cracked ribs and a broken collar bone. You must have a head like a steel helmet because there's nothing wrong but some rather bad bruising. But you're being kept in for observation. Just in case of delayed concussion. Shouldn't be too long."

Carnac reached out and grasped her hand. "Why didn't you leave with the other nurses? This is no place for you."

"First, it is the place for me, and second, we weren't given the opportunity. It only applied to the military nurses. Anyway, most of the nurses here are Asians." He detected the bitterness in her voice and said, "When the whole sordid story comes to be told, it'll cause a pubic scandal. The evacuation programme is a total shambles."

She leaned over and silenced him with a gentle kiss. "Not one of the volunteers has asked to leave. Would you walk out on all those poor souls? I must go. I've other patients to attend to, Terence. There's no favouritism here."

He watched her retreating back until she passed out of view. He heard Morris cough discreetly. "We'd better be getting back aboard, Sir. I'll tell the captain the good news."

"Tell him I don't want to be here a second longer than is absolutely necessary."

"I reckon he'll be thinking the same thing, Sir."

General Percival sat at his desk, an impotent Canute against the Japanese tide, wondering how it was all going to end. The army was now fighting on the golf course and race track. They had also captured the reservoirs, and the only water available was that being pumped from the Woodleigh Station, and most of that was going to waste. The water shortage was now so acute people were reduced to collecting it in buckets from the broken mains. Only that morning he had seen some soldiers washing their tattered uniforms under a broken pipe, and they had shouted, "It's all over bar the shouting". He had also been to St Andrew's for morning prayers and was shocked to see the plight of the wounded who lined the aisles for it was now being used as a hospital. The decision to evacuate the nurses he knew had been severely criticised, especially by the Governor, but events had justified it for the Japanese had stormed the Alexandra Hospital and massacred the medical staff and most of the patients. Some of the nurses had been forced to jump to their death from the top of a high tower. If one was honest, it was ridiculous to contemplate fighting on. What was there to fight for? Even Sir Shenton now accepted that the end was near.

He had vowed that he would never leave Government House, but he had been forced to and now had a room in the Singapore Club. From there he could probably see the Singapore River, parts of which were actually on fire. Yesterday, mused Percival, had been his daughter's twelfth birthday. Yet it had been the blackest day in his life. He forced his mind to think of the immediate situation. He hated to admit it, but the time had come to consider parleying with the enemy. He knew he had the support of Sir Shenton, who had given orders for the destruction of all alcohol fearing that drink-inflamed Japanese would go on the rampage as they had done in other places they had overrun. For hours Singapore had resounded to the sound of bottles being shattered against walls and gurgling down the drains. The bonded warehouses had been emptied and the stocks in the liquor shops seized, and millions of bottles of whisky, brandy, cognac, champagne and the finest French wines and liqueurs destroyed, along with tens of thousands of gallons of fiery Chinese spirit. Admittedly there had been some looting and a few people had hoarded the odd bottle, but generally everyone complied with the order.

Even now the city reeked of alcohol, like a drunkard's breath after an all-night binge, and one could get quite intoxicated just breathing the odour. Some of the clubs had indulged in a final wet night when four fingers of scotch and no water was poured in place of the normal measure, but there had been no stupid carousing and all drinks had been signed for. It was ironic, he mused, to think of that when people would have given anything for a glass of water. A conservative estimate suggested that there was only enough now for twenty-four hours. That had really been the deciding factor as far as the Governor was concerned. The phrase "money to burn" flitted through his mind, and he was glad to see he had not lost his sense of humour. Instructions had just been issued for all stocks of banknotes to be destroyed.

He pondered on the signal he had sent to Wavell remembering that he had wondered how it would affect his future prospects. "There must come a stage when in the interests of the troops and civilian population further bloodshed will serve no useful purpose. Would you consider giving me wider discretionary powers?" It was not the kind of signal a general was expected to send.

Archie, far away in Java and unable to see just how bad things were, replied in a manner that suggested he had read the signal with his glass eye. He must, he was told, fight on as long as his troops were capable of inflicting losses and damage to the enemy. Only then should he consider ending resistance.

It placed him in an impossible situation. Of course, the longer he ordered his men to fight the more casualties they would cause. But at what cost?

The Japanese seemed to appreciate the position better than Wavell, for leaflets were showering down on Singapore like confetti at a wedding, urging him in the most honourable language to end further resistance in what was now a hopelessly lost cause. But he suspected that Wavell was influenced by Churchill who also wanted him to fight on, although he had clearly abandoned hope of holding the island; reinforcements were being diverted to Burma which was now being given priority.

283

Fortunately, Sir Shenton had intervened and sent a cable to the Colonial Office which presented a harrowing picture: "General Officer Commanding informs me that Singapore City now closely invested. There are now one million people within radius of three miles. Water supplies very badly damaged and unlikely to last more than twenty-four hours. Many dead lying in the streets and burial impossible. We are faced with total deprivation of water which must result in pestilence. I have felt it my duty to bring this to the notice of the General Officer Commanding."

In face of that stark assessment, Churchill and Wavell had had no alternative but to give Percival a free hand.

But having sent off the signal, Sir Shenton had been adamant in his refusal to have anything to do with the surrender negotiations. That, thought Percival, was a bit unfair; it meant he had to do it himself. But one had to admire the Governor's courage; he refused to leave the island and he continued to tour the city to emphasise the fact, but it was like displaying a ship's figurehead when there was a gaping hole in the hull.

The same sense of duty had not been so strong with General Gordon Bennett commanding the Australian forces; he had slipped away on a privately commandeered ship on the specious excuse that he wanted to escape in order to continue the fight. Admiral Spooner and Air Vice-Marshal Pulford had also gone, but that had been under orders.

With a deep heartfelt sigh, he decided to seek terms of surrender, agreeing with Wavell that anyone wishing to escape in order to fight should be given the opportunity. He ordered the destruction of all codes and confidential papers, then in accordance with the Japanese instructions he issued orders for the Rising Sun to be flown from the flagstaff on the roof of the Cathay Building next day, indicating his willingness to parley.

Chapter 15

Isaac Morris sat on an ammunition locker near the twelve-pounder studying Jolson with an anxious expression on his face. For a couple of days now the dog had been off colour. He seemed dull and uneasy and kept looking for isolated spots in which to curl as if he preferred his own company to that of others. He was also doing some strange things like licking cold steel and chewing bits of wood, and when a stranger came aboard he no longer bothered to bark, a most unusual thing. Although he still responded to Morris's voice and was eating well, he was drinking a lot of water. Soon after "Hands to work" had been piped that morning, he had sought out Tiger Read and asked for permission to nip ashore and try and get some medicine. Tiger reminded him that for security reasons the captain had confined all hands to the ship and he could not make any exceptions. He pleaded and pointed out that the Labrador was not his personal property but the ship's, and everyone would be well and truly brassed off if he was allowed to suffer unnecessarily. In the end the coxswain relented and said, "If I look the other way and you slip off I won't notice, neither will I start looking for you, but if the captain sends for you that's your hard cheese."

After numerous fruitless enquiries, he was directed to a veterinary surgeon who was still practicing in a narrow alley not far from the harbour. A small queue had gathered outside the surgery, nearly all Europeans, cradling an odd assortment of dogs, cats, and monkeys. He had to wait nearly half an hour before it was his turn, and during that time his concern mounted for when anyone came out they no longer had their

285

pets with them.

The surgery was one of the grimiest places he had ever seen, cluttered with sterilising units, ancient surgical instruments, syringes and an operating table that looked as if it had seen service in a Crimea field hospital. There were two chairs with stuffing oozing from the seats, and pinned to one wall was a coloured poster with minature illustrations of the various breeds of dogs. The Anglo-Indian vet wore a grubby white coat in keeping with his surroundings, and incongruously continued to wear a sweat-stained khaki topi, as proudly as if it was an ensign on a man of war. He was brusque to the point of rudeness when Morris said, "I wonder if you'd give me something for my dog?"

"I am not buying animals, especially at a time like this."

Morris thought he was trying to be amusing until he realised the vet had misunderstood him. "I meant medicine."

The vet who had a sing-song voice had trouble pronouncing his r's and l's so that he sounded like a music hall caricature of an Indian trying to be very pukka. "I am no longer in the business of curative medicine, old boy. People are coming to consult me only to have their pets put down. In normal times, few Europeans sought my services considering quite untruthfully that I was not up to par. Now everyone else has flown the coop I am in great demand." He shrugged indifferently. "Animals lovers are strange creatures. Before when I presented bills for animals I had made well they invariably protested at the cost. Now they offer me anything to put them to sleep. That is a euphemism for asking me to pop them off."

"Look, I won't gripe at the ruddy bill. Just give me *something*."

"How can I possibly comply with that without seeing the animal, old chum? That would be most unprofessional. In any case, I do not possess magical qualities that enable me to carry out a diagnosis at a long distance. Anyway, why not destroy it? All sensible people know that shortly they will be interned, so they bring their pets to me."

"I'm not hanging around till that happens. I'll be off soon."

The vet sighed in an exaggerated manner. "What are these symptoms?"

Morris described them as accurately and in as much detail

as he could and the man said triumphantly, "Hydrophobia. Shoot it."

"What the hell's that?"

"Rabies, my dear fellow."

Morris had only heard of it as a terrible disease which could be transmitted to humans if they were bitten and who subsequently died in a most horrifying manner.

"Are you sure?"

"Of course not. But it could be the early stages."

"It might not be, on the other hand," he had persisted.

"Quite correct," and the vet went to a bookshelf lined with tattered books, took one down and thumbed through it. "Here there are pages and pages on it. I just do not have the time, or the inclination to go through them all. But let me explain briefly. It is malady that takes about a week to run its whole course. The dog goes off his food, then begins to secrete a viscid saliva which it tries to rub off with its paws. Sometimes the jaw drops and the dog cannot close its mouth. Its bark becomes very strident and it can become snappy. Some have been known to become so ferocious they break their teeth. Eventually paralysis sets in and it slips into a coma and dies." He snapped the book closed as if bored with the whole thing. "Do not bring it here. Shoot it. It isn't worth the risk."

Morris put a handful of notes on the operating table and nodded dumbly, too upset to talk. The vet pocketed the money without bothering to count it. "I do not like to take it for giving you bad news, but soon I fear I shall have to take down my shingle."

Now as he looked at the dog he knew he had to inform the captain of his illicit trip ashore and the vet's diagnosis.

He rose and made his way aft to Paton's cabin and knocked on the door. When Paton called out to him to come in he could not wait to unburden himself. "I went ashore without permission this morning, Sir."

"Most unlike you Morris. You must have had a very good reason for disobeying orders. Like to tell me?"

"I went to see a vet about Jolson, Sir." Whereupon he recounted all that had happened.

"I'll forget the trip ashore; if you'd asked I'd probably have agreed anyway. The thing is, what do we do?"

The tears rolled freely down the seaman's cheeks and he made no attempt to conceal them or brush them away, making him look extremely young and vulnerable, and reminding Paton that that was exactly what he was. "I thought you'd know, Sir. The vet bloke wasn't at all certain."

"Some time today, Morris, we shall be taking aboard as many women and children as we possibly can. I can tell you now that General Percival is going to surrender soon. That's why everyone was confined to the ship. Didn't want it spread around that we're leaving. We've a reasonably long trip ahead, and I just daren't risk taking a chance. What if the vet was right and he bit someone? He'll have to be shot."

Morris said, "Crikey, he means more to me that almost anything. He's been aboard since the beginning. I was the one who bought him in the Pompey pub, Sir."

"He means a lot to all of us. But there's no alternative. Would you rather I did it, or would you prefer to yourself?" Paton made his voice sound particularly harsh.

"I'll do it, Sir. I couldn't ask anyone else. It wouldn't be fair."

Paton patted him gently on the shoulder. "It'll be quick, and perhaps a merciful release. We'll just have to think so."

He withdrew one of the revolvers from the armoury and handed it to the leading seaman. "Don't think about it. Just do it."

He watched Morris leading the dog over the gangway, the revolver dangling down the side of one leg. It seemed as if the animal sensed that something was wrong and he must convince everyone that he was perfectly all right. He looked up appealingly at Morris and wagged his tail, even his step seemed jaunty. Morris led him to the rear of one of the deserted sheds and the dog squatted obediently when he ordered him to "Sit". He raised the pistol and realised his hand was shaking uncontrollably and he would have to press the muzzle against the dog's head to be certain of not missing. He took a fresh grip with two hands, and as he leaned forward Jolson bolted off and halted some twenty yards away, his eyes peering over the top of his outstretched paws as if they were enjoying a new game. And every time Morris went forward the dog retreated to a safe distance and lay down again.

"All right, you crafty old bugger. Go off and find some Japs to bite." He raised the Webley and fired, and the bullet kicked up a cloud of dust several feet away from the dog. Jolson jumped up and ran off only to halt again and resume his stalking position. Morris fired three more shots, and only when the last one had been perilously close did Jolson scamper off. Morris shouted after him, "If you've got any sense, don't come back. The next time I'll have a Lee-Enfield."

Paton was waiting in the waist of the ship, and when Morris returned he said angrily, "What the hell were you doing? Sounded like a pitched battle."

"He ran off, Sir, and I just couldn't hit him."

"You mean you let him go?"

"No, Sir, God's honour. He thought it was some kind of game."

"I'm not sending a ruddy hunting party ashore. I don't suppose he's the only menace. If he's caught rabies he got it from somewhere. Who knows, he may survive. Miracles do happen."

"I'll pray for one, Sir," said Morris earnestly.

By mid-afternoon nearly one hundred women and children had embarked on *Grey Seal*. The mess decks were crammed to overflowing and every inch of deck space was occupied. Most of them were wearing little more than rags and carried hardly any personal possessions. Paton summoned Read to his cabin and said, "Post a couple of extra hands to the galley, Coxs'n, and see they get something hot to drink and eat. Some of them look as if they haven't eaten for days."

Paton decided to sail as soon as it became dark, and head for Ceylon. Sumatra and Java were much closer, but he was convinced that the Dutch East Indies would soon capitulate. Apart from that, he wanted to avoid the fate of the last big convoy which had sailed and headed there. The Japanese navy had been lying in wait and blown most of them out of the water, and Tokyo radio announced the massacre with a certain amount of pride saying the British had not been allowed to get away with another Dunkirk. No one yet knew how many survivors, if any, there were.

Paton reasoned that a solitary ship stood a better chance of remaining undetected, and if he could slip through the

Malacca Strait, which was the most hazardous part, he could sail almost due west for Trincomalee some 1,600 miles away. An added advantage was that so few knew of his imminent departure.

He went into the mess decks and told everyone of the risks entailed and if anyone had a change of heart and wanted to remain they could do so. He repeated the same message to those on the upper deck. Without hesitation they all said they preferred to take a chance.

Read reported to the captain that the ship was secured and ready for sea, and an oil and soot grimed Reynolds said the same for the engine room. Paton expressed his satisfaction and promptly sent for Morris. "Just one last thing to do before we sail. Get Mister Carnac back aboard. Have you still got that car?"

The killick grinned. "Thought we might need it again, Sir. Didn't think we'd go without him when the time came. I hid it in one of those empty wharves and put a padlock and length of chain round the steering wheel and clutch pedal to stop anyone boning it."

"Good. Take Miller and a couple more hands, collect some arms and be on your way."

The sub-lieutenant was fully dressed and sitting on the edge of his bed reading when they arrived, and apart from a sling he looked perfectly fit. "I've been keeping a weather eye open through the window in case the Japs appeared. Thank heavens they don't seem interested. How about you? Seen any?"

"The whole place seems deserted, Sir. Didn't pass anything on the road. You ready, Sir? We don't have a lot of time."

"I had a feeling Commander Paton couldn't do without me. I've been waiting for hours. The buzz had already reached this place that it'll soon be all over. Couple of cars filled with officers went up the Bukit Timah Road some time ago flying a white flag. Probably an advance party setting off to find out exactly what is expected of General Percival."

"That means we could be cutting it pretty fine, Sir. There's a whole lot of women and kids aboard who can't wait to see the back of this place."

Carnac said, "Give me three minutes. I'm going to make a last effort to get Miss Jardine to come with me."

He found her in one of the wards replacing a soiled dressing on a wounded soldier, and when he asked her to step outside for a minute she said casually, "As soon as I've finished this."

He waited anxiously glancing at his watch, although the gesture indicated nothing more than his mounting impatience. When Jo appeared he said, "*Grey Seal* is leaving soon. There's a berth for you if you want it."

"It's no good going over the same old ground, Terence. You know how I feel, I've told you often enough. I'm sorry, but I couldn't live with myself if I walked out now."

"One barely trained nurse isn't going to make all that difference," he said aggressively.

"If everyone who knew as little as I do adopted that attitude, Terence, the place would be half empty. I'll keep in touch, I promise, and you can write to me care of the Red Cross. This thing isn't going to last for ever. If you haven't changed your mind by then I'll be happy to take up where we left off. You'd better not keep your men waiting." She drew him towards her and kissed him fiercely, clinging to him possessively for several seconds before she let go. "Don't worry, Terence. We've been told that the Japanese have given an assurance that once the surrender is signed hostilities will cease immediately. Come to that, they seem to have stopped already. No one will be harmed, and we'll all be treated according to the Geneva Convention."

He heard Morris cough over-loudly somewhere in the distance. "I'd better go. If I had any choice I'd stay, but I'm under orders. Is there anything I can do?"

"I can't think of anything," she said lightly. "Unless you can convince the Japs to clear off and leave us in peace." She became serious for a moment. "If you should happen to hear anything of my parents, do get in touch and tell them I'm perfectly happy."

He embraced her briefly, unstrapped his watch and said, "It's the only thing I have with me", then turned and hurried to the waiting car, praying that the Japanese would honour their pledge not to harm any civilians or prisoners of war. It wasn't too much to hope for; they seemed to attach a lot of importance to their code of chivalry.

Morris drove like a rally driver with a trophy within his

grasp, calling out cheerfully as they careered down the road throwing up vast clouds of dust. "It doesn't matter a monkey's if we write if off, Sir. We won't be needing it again."

When they drew up alongside the ship, Tiger Read was already at the wheel and Paton had singled up to a stern spring in readiness for a swift departure. As soon as everyone was aboard he gave orders for the gangway to be hauled inboard. As Morris bent low to untie the lashings, he heard a voice call urgently, "Isaac, Isaac, I have an important message for tuan Paton."

He looked towards the quay, and to his astonishment saw Amy excitedly waving an envelope. "Better nip aboard, in that case."

A rating standing nearby said, "Don't fall for that cod's wallop. It's only a chi-chi trying to bum a lift."

Morris raised a menacing closed fist. "That lady happens to be my fiancée, and if you refer to her again like that you'll be spitting teeth all over the deck."

As Morris helped her aboard, the rating made a discreet withdrawal aft. As he led her to the wardroom he asked, "How did you get here, Amy?" and she said, "I simply borrowed a cycle and pedalled here."

In the wardroom he said, "This is my young lady I told you about, Sir. She has some kind of message."

Paton gestured to her to take a chair and motioned with his head for Morris to leave them alone. He ripped open the envelope and began to read the enclosed letter from Kate. It was short and simply said that she wanted to wish him good luck just in case she did not manage to get back to Singapore. Apart from a bad bout of malaria which she couldn't seem to shake off, she was as well as could be expected, although she would give a month's salary for some medicine. Being in a rather remote fishing kampong she was understandably out of touch with things, but the headman did have a radio that worked so she had been able to listen to the BBC. She gathered that things weren't going particularly well. A couple of the fishermen had managed to sail down to Singapore and pick up odd items of news which suggested it would soon be over. "I've thought of you continuously and I've prayed that you and your men come to no harm. It looks like being a long and bitter war, not the short sharp one we hoped for. But I'm consoled by the knowledge that although the Limeys lose battles, they always win wars. It was wonderful knowing you, Crispin, and I'll treasure our friendship. If you ever get to the States, look me up and we'll relive old times. Providing, of course, that I make it back. I haven't really given a lot of thought to the immediate present. Frankly I need to get well first. All my love, Kate."

Paton folded it and replaced it in the envelope. "If I showed you a chart, Amy, which is really just a map, could you point out the village?"

"Of course," she said indignantly. "I know the island like my own face. It is not very enormous."

Paton sent for the chart to be brought down from the bridge, and as he spread it out on the table he pointed out where they were and various other landmarks that would enable her to get a general picture.

She traced a finger along a stretch of coastline to a spot not far from the most south easterly tip of the island. "That is it."

"Are there any enemy troops or ships there?"

"We have not seen *any* Japanese. There has been no fighting in that part."

Paton measured off the distance with a pair of dividers. It would take less than two hours steaming to reach it and would hardly take him out of his way. If necessary, he could camouflage the ship and remain there till it was dark again, although that would not be needed if everything went without a hitch.

"We'll go down and pay Miss Hollis a visit, Amy. I think she'd welcome it."

There was a discreet knock on the door, and when Paton called out, "Come in," Morris entered and said, "Hope I'm not barging in, Sir, but I have a personal favour to ask." Paton suspected he had been listening from outside. The seaman stood awkwardly shuffling his feet until Paton said impatiently, "Well, I can't answer until I know what it is, so you'd better get it off your chest."

"I was wondering whether you'd allow the young lady to remain aboard with the others. We were going to get married some time. We still could if she came with us, Sir."

"I don't suppose one more will make any great difference,

293

but it really is up to the young lady. I'll leave you to talk it over between yourselves."

As soon as Paton had left the wardroom, Isaac said, "It's the last chance you'll ever have, Amy. Any moment now the curtain'll come down and no one will be able to get away."

"It is good of you to ask, Isaac, but I do not want to leave. This is my home. My family is here. What would I do in a strange land?"

"What the hell can you do here?"

"Carry on as we have always done. The Japanese are only at war with you."

"I thought you once told me that you were more British than anything else."

"I am, Isaac. I will only pretend to be more Malayan. You may have stopped fighting, but there are still many who will not do so. Already what you call resistance groups are in being in the jungle. I wish to join them. Some have British leaders."

"And what do you think a bunch of guerrillas can do against a whole ruddy army? Tell me that."

"One day the British will return. Just as you say you will to France. Perhaps you will be with them. Now I must leave."

"I thought you were coming to this village?"

"I never said so. There is nothing to do there. I have to go across the Causeway."

He saw her to the side of the ship where he stood for several minutes pleading with her to change her mind.

"I cannot for yet one more very good reason. I have your Jolson to look after."

"You've what?" he said in amazement.

"He ran after me as I cycled through the docks. He knew me instantly. Why have you turned him away?"

"I didn't. He ran off. I was going to shoot him. You can't keep him, Amy. He's sick, very sick. He's got rabies."

"I do not think so, Isaac. He chased me hard. I have seen this rabies."

Morris said, "Look, I went to see a vet," and he recounted what he was told. "You've got to turn him loose. Someone will shoot him sooner or later. If he bites you, you'll have had it."

"He is not like you say at all, Isaac. Anyway, why should

I turn him loose when he is not tied up? He is sitting by my cycle, just as if we were on the beach again. He is not sick."

"For God's sake, listen to me. He is. He can't have got over it. Now promise me one thing. If he gets sick again, you will get someone to shoot him. A bloody Nip if necessary."

"Where I am going, there are many empty houses. I will put him in one and give him food and water every day. I will know soon if what you tell me is true. Then he can be killed. Not otherwise."

The sailor said, "I can't keep arguing with you, Amy. We'll be casting off soon. All I can hope is that prayers do get answered, though it'll be the first time in my case. What you said about coming back is true, Amy. Maybe it won't be for a long time, but I will. Take my word for it." He kissed her lingeringly, loathe to let her go. "Look after yourself. And write sometimes. You can always reach me if you send a letter to HMS *Grey Seal* care of the Admiralty, London. That's about the only thing the Andrew doesn't mess up."

"Do not worry about time, Isaac. It is nothing. In Singapore the Chinese keep an egg for many years. It is at its best then." She reached inside her blouse and produced a photograph taken in one of the booths at The Happy World. "I meant you to have it before I went away. I do not want you to remember me as I am looking now."

He watched her walk towards the dock gates until she vanished in the deepening shadows. You'd better get on your knees again tonight, Morris, he told himself. Just in case the first one wasn't answered. He felt a flush of shame as he realised the Labrador was still uppermost in his mind. But Amy had had a choice which was more than Jolson could claim; he had been turned away by the one person whose support and affection he was entitled to count upon. Jesus, war did funny things to people, and no mistake. Some people, like those pongoes, would kill women and children if necessary to get away from this place, while others like Amy, and Sub-Lieutenant Carnac's girl whose old man was rolling in it, wanted to be ruddy heroes.

Paton, who was now on the bridge, gave an engine order which tightened the spring and swung *Grey Seal's* bow away from the quay. "Let go the spring," he called to Carnac, and as it was hauled inboard he increased the engine revolutions and set a course for the kampong.

An unearthly silence seemed to have settled over the island, and although fires were still burning sporadically, for the first time since the mainland was abandoned, there was no sound of gunfire or the menacing throb of aircraft engines.

Grey Seal moved like a phantom galleon over the star-flecked water, her deadlights secured, her wake barely visible. It took less than two hours to reach the village where Paton anchored offshore while an armed party with Morris in charge went ashore in one of the whalers which they tied up at a ricketty wooden jetty. Several fishing boats had been hauled up the beach and concealed under foliage, and a row of nets were hanging out to dry. They held their weapons at the ready as they moved as silently as possible along the creaking planks. The place seemed to be deserted as they walked between the rows of native huts, the only noise coming from the insects and disturbed birds. Morris whispered, "Cover me while I go in one of the huts."

He pushed his way through a beaded screen and called out, "Anyone around?" and to his surprise a voice replied anxiously in English, "Who are you?"

Morris moved towards the sound and said, "British sailors. "We've come to collect you, Miss Hollis."

The voice replied cautiously, "I'm Vera Brooks. Kate is resting, she isn't at all well. You'd better come through."

He followed the voice into a room where a feeble oil lamp flickered in a slight draught. When his eyes became accustomed to the semi-darkness he saw the American lying on a charpoy. Although tossing restlessly and murmuring unintelligible things she was fast asleep and he shook her gently until she was awake. "It's all right, Miss. We've come to take you back with us. Tell me what you want to pack and I'll help. We haven't got a lot of time. Commander Paton wants to leave while it's still dark."

Kate slid her feet onto the floor and rose unsteadily, and Morris stepped forward to support her. "I never dreamed he'd be crazy enough to bring his ship down here. But I'm not complaining, no sir. I've nothing to pack except my portable," she said.

Mrs Brooks said hesitantly, "Do I come too?"

"The captain didn't know there was another white lady here, but he'd skin me alive if I left you behind. Are you the only people here?"

"No," said Mrs Brooks, "there're a number of villagers, not to mention the people we came here with. They probably scuttled off thinking you might be Japs."

"Can they be trusted?"

"One hundred per cent," she replied indignantly. "They've looked after us as if we were their own kind. Especially Amy who is a real darling. We haven't been out at all, but they've told us there are no enemy troops around."

"Even so," said Morris, "we'll creep out of here like Roger the lodger."

Ten minutes later the women were being urged into the whaler and cautioned to remain very still. "Going to be a bit cramped, but we don't want to make a second trip," said Morris.

A small group of villagers emerged from hiding to assemble on the jetty and wave them off, and Kate handed her remaining money to the headman. "Thanks a million," she whispered.

As soon as they were aboard and the whaler secured in its davit, Paton weighed anchor and headed for the open sea. He reckoned they still had several hours of darkness remaining during which time they could cover a lot of water.

Soon afterwards, Carnac relieved him on the bridge while he went into his cabin which he had placed at Kate's disposal. He wouldn't he told her, be needing the bunk as he would be required on the bridge most of the time; he couldn't expect Carnac to take on too much as he was still in considerable pain from his injuries.

Kate was lying on the bunk looking very thin and wasted, her eyes dark sunken hollows. He took her temperature; it was 103 degrees, and she was very feverish and her teeth were chattering noisily. He looked at her nails and noticed they were a bluish colour. He had a shrewd idea what it was, but thought it wise to check with the handbook in the medicine chest. His suspicions were confirmed when he read through the notes on malaria. "You've got a really nasty bout. I'll give you some quinine. How long have you been like this?"

Her voice was flat and toneless. "Some days. I can't say for sure. Vera says I was delirious at times. I know I slept a lot and there were times when I thought I was freezing and others when I thought I was roasting. Then I'd have a good spell, only to be laid flat again. If it hadn't been for Vera I wouldn't be here. She's seen a lot of it in her time."

Paton rang for Hall and said, "I want you to look after Miss Hollis. Keep bathing her with cold water and keep taking her temperature. The quinine's on the table." He squeezed her hand. "We'll soon get you to a doctor. Meantime, just rest. There's nothing for you to do."

He went into the wardroom where Mrs Brooks had been given Phelp's bunk. "She really is in a poor way."

"We did our best for her, but the place was alive with mossies and we had no nets. I just hope and pray it isn't one of those particularly virulent forms, like cerebral malaria. That can be really dangerous."

"How can one tell?"

Vera Brooks shook her head, "I don't know. I've heard about it but never actually encountered it. I know people up country died of it, but it was very rare."

"I'd be most grateful, Mrs Brooks, if you popped in from time to time. Nothing like another woman to cheer her up. I'll be on the bridge if you need me. But before you go, is there anything you want?"

Mrs Brooks smiled shyly, "I'd love a nice long gin with lots and lots of ice cold water and some lime. But that's a pretty tall order."

"You happen to have picked on the three things we aren't short of. I'll tell Hall to see to it."

"It's a funny thing, but I never dreamed there'd come a day when I'd be craving for a drink of water. When I think how we used to waste it, it makes me quite ashamed of myself."

Paton returned to the bridge where he sat hunched in his chair for hour after hour feeling as if the ship was steaming down a long dark alley. Below him on the deck he could barely make out the muffled and blanketed forms of the evacuees who preferred the open air to the stifling heat of the mess decks.

When dawn came he was delighted to find the sea shrouded in a thick mantle of impenetrable mist. He knew that Malaya lay to starboard and Sumatra to port, but neither was visible. He moved across to the chart table and poked his head and shoulders through the canvas curtain, making sure no light would be showing when he switched the small light on. Soon, he estimated, they would be approaching Banda Atjeh, the most northerly tip of Sumatra. Shortly afterwards he would alter course westwards leaving the Nicobars on his starboard side. Then it would be a straight run to Trincomalee.

The mist persisted throughout the day and the clammy salty blanket gave way to darkness and a sky illuminated by millions of stars. Occasionally he nipped below to see how Kate was. She seemed a lot better, and when she wasn't sleeping Mrs Brooks was reading to her. "I think she's over the worst," she said.

Next morning the mist had gone as abruptly as it had appeared, and the horizon was clear as far as the human eye could see. Carnac clattered up the bridge ladder. "Let me take over for a while, Sir. I've had a good sleep."

"Fair enough. I could do with changing these clothes. The salt's caked hard on me. Still, I'd have put up with it if it had lasted all the way to Ceylon, Number One."

Carnac surveyed the horizon and then gazed skywards where nothing was visible but a few wispy strands of white. "A nice little gale wouldn't be unwelcome, Sir. Just enough to keep aircraft grounded and subs below the surface."

"We've had more than our fair slice of luck already, but who knows? The good Lord may yet provide."

He showered in the PO's mess and changed into clean shirt and shorts in the wheelhouse. Then he toured the upper deck where some seamen were serving a breakfast of corned beef hash and scalding tea and asking everyone how they were getting on. He did the same in the messdecks, then went to see Kate. She was sitting up in the bunk making notes on sheets of paper. Although she still looked tired and gaunt, she was quite cheerful. "Vera says my temperature is a lot lower. I must admit I feel a hundred per cent better."

"What'll you do when we reach Ceylon?"

"I haven't given it much thought. I'll file what I must to the office. There's a lot I need to say. Then I'll take a breather. I suppose there'll be an American Embassy or Consul there where I can borrow some money till the office sends some."

"We might be able to take up where we left off, instead of waiting till it's all over," he said jokingly.

"I'll take you up on that Crispin, but let me get my looks back first. I feel like that hag of a witch in Snow White."

The windscoops had been inserted into the ports, and Paton felt a sudden and unexpected cooling draught which suggested the wind was getting up. Then *Grey Seal* began to roll and pitch, the bows coming down with a crash that sent a judder throughout the ship.

"I'd lie down if I were you, Kate, or you'll find yourself being bounced around like a pea on a drum. A storm's on the way. Thank God."

He hastened to the bridge where Carnac's face was wreathed in a boyish smile. The white horses were riding furiously across the water and pounding like cavalry against the hull. Within half an hour a force nine gale had developed, and Paton was grateful that *Grey Seal* had been built to withstand the harshest seas in the world. The bow rose high, then crashed down to be buried beneath hundreds of tons of foaming water, then as it rose like a spouting whale, water cascaded onto the bridge until their ankles were covered.

"Get the hands to secure everything topsides, Number One. We're in for a rough time," he said gleefully.

Below on the deck the seamen began to lash and secure things to prevent them being swept over the side, while others were doing their utmost to get some of the women below decks, but many were so sea sick they could not be budged and they just lay there awash with water and their own vomit. They may be suffering agonies, thought Paton, but that's infinitely better than being bombed or shelled.

The ship rode the storm like a bucking bronco and by dusk it had blown itself out into what was no more than a lively squall. When he went down to his cabin he was angered to see Kate sitting at her typewriter, a wet towel draped around her head, furiously hammering out a long article on a rapidly mounting pile of cable forms. He bellowed for Hall who appeared immediately. "You're supposed to be looking after her. She's in no fit state to be doing this."

"I couldn't stop her, Sir. Short of tying her up, that is," he said plaintively.

"Well, you should have ruddy well done that. Where's Mrs Brooks?"

"Sea sick."

Kate said wearily, "Do leave him alone, please. This is something I *must* do. I'm not a member of your crew."

"You are under *my* orders, the same as anyone else who sails aboard my ship." He motioned for Hall to leave, and when he had gone he sat down and said in a voice edged with fatigue. "I've enough on my hands, Kate, not to have to cope with a bloody mutinous woman. Now, please, just get back into bed."

She fixed him with defiant eyes. "If you really want to do something useful, pour me a really hefty scotch. Vera says some of the old hands killed the malaria bugs with it."

He poured a large drink into a tumbler and topped it up with water. "Mind if I join you?" he said with a hint of sarcasm.

"It's your booze, darling,"she said with exaggerated sweetness.

"When you've had that, will you do as I ask?"

"No. This is one story I have to write. I want everyone back home to know what really happened. Not some bloody account issued from official quarters, laden with half truths and evasions. I've got a nasty feeling that the whole sordid affair will be whitewashed over. That's if anyone in London even bothers to say anything. Churchill just can't afford to admit to another humiliating disaster. More than likely it'll be presented as a modern charge of the light brigade. A balls-up made to look like an epic."

"Will you accomplish anything, Kate?"

"We had a similar argument when first we met, Crispin. That shambles we've just left could have been avoided, and you damn well know it. You may feel honour bound to maintain a dignified silence. My only allegiance is to the truth. We're going to Ceylon, you say; well the same bloody thing could happen there if the bells aren't rung. Anyway, I've nearly finished. Then I'll go to bed like a good little girl."

He realised it was a waste of time to argue further. "Help yourself to another drink if you want one, and don't hesitate to call Hall."

"Thank you kind sir," she said, and he could not help smiling at her flippancy.

"I'd better see how Mrs Brooks is getting on. You could take a lesson from her. I don't even know she's aboard."

He found her sitting at the table, her chin propped on her hands, looking very greenish and trying to peck at a sandwich. "Thank the Lord it's calmed down. I was ready to die, I really mean that. I just wished the ship would turn over and take me with it. But you wouldn't understand, would you, being a sailor?"

"As a matter of fact I do, Mrs Brooks. When I first went to sea I thought I'd have to give it up. But I got over it. Some never do. Nelson was always ill."

"I wouldn't mind a gin," she asked hesitantly. "My husband always swore that it was the finest thing for settling a queasy stomach."

As he poured the drink he asked, "What happened to your husband?"

"No idea. I think he volunterred for one of those special groups. I hope I'll find out when we reach Ceylon."

Paton wondered just how many of the women aboard were in a similar situation.

Just then a bridge messenger knocked on the door and said, "Number One would like you on the bridge, Sir."

When he arrived, Carnac was pointing excitedly ahead, "There he is, Sir. Bang on target." Through his binoculars, Paton could clearly see the coastline of the pear-shaped island, and just visible the high peaks of inland mountains. He sent Carnac to the wireless room with instructions for the telegraphist to break radio silence and inform naval headquarters at Trincomalee of their imminent arrival, and to request a destroyer escort to see them in. He further requested medical assistance to be available as soon as they docked.

He craned over the bridge and saw the sides were lined with waving evacuees indifferent to the fact that their joy was invisible from the land. Some of the children were jumping up and down and clapping their hands. But their jubilation was shortlived, brought to an abrupt halt by the voice of a lookout. "Unidentified aircraft approaching. Dead Ahead." Paton seized his megaphone and ordered everyone below deck, at the same time sounding the alarm bells, and there was a frantic scurry on the deck as sailors running to their action stations collided with women and children trying to get below.

A lookout shouted, "It's another of those bastard Bettys."

Paton focussed his glasses on the approaching bomber. Having been fortuned with so much good luck, it seemed a betrayal to face disaster at this stage. He reached for the megaphone, "Open fire as soon as she's in range."

The Mitsubishi went into a shallow dive, like a gannet that had sighted a shoal of surface fish. The twelve-pounder boomed and the acrid smell of cordite drifted up onto the bridge. The bomber swept low seeming to brush the mast, but it did not open fire and Paton looked astern and saw it soar up like a gull. It swung on sharply tilted wings and began a fresh run in. This time the Oerlikons joined the fo'c's'le gun. The bomber veered to starboard and fired a burst of machine gun fire which passed harmlessly over the bridge. The noise of the engines being given full throttle filled the air as the bomber groaned and strained to gain height in a hurry. A lookout bellowed, "Aircraft approaching. Port bow. Twelve o'clock high."

Carnac appeared beside him and he followed his pointing finger to some black dots emerging from the sunlight. They were flying fast and began to peel off and dive towards the Japanese aircraft. "Ours for a change, Sir. Hurricanes," shouted Carnac.

The fighters pursued the bomber until they were all out of sight, but fifteen minutes later the Hurricanes passed overhead and one gave a victory roll.

In the distance, two massive plumes of foam were being tossed up by the bows of the requested destroyer, and Paton slapped Carnac on the shoulder. "We made it, Number One. Bloody close, but we. made it. Send them a signal saying they're as welcome as a sunny day in Manchester."

He picked up the megaphone and announced, "We should be alongside in a couple of hours or so. Now's your last chance to powder your noses." He turned to the first lieute-

303

nant, "I'm going down to have a drink with Miss Hollis. I've earned one."

She was fast asleep when he entered, and despite his excitement he refrained from waking her. He poured a drink, and as he sat down his eyes fell upon her pile of cable forms. He guiltily picked up the top sheet and began to read, and once he had started he was unable to stop. It was a personalised account of her time in Singapore from the time she arrived until she left in *Grey Seal*. The bitterness and resentment burned through the words as they recounted the military incompetence, the Government's complacency, and the ostrich-like attitude of a European community which could not advance with the times. It was the most bitter indictment he had ever read. It was not the defeat which had hurt, she wrote, but the shame and disgrace, because it had all been avoidable. And she cited example after example to justify her condemnation. He realised it would arouse bitter controversy and criticism in America which had lost battles too, but not in such a humiliating and dishonourable manner. He hated to think what would happen if it was relayed back to London. Someone might have the courage to print it. But on reflection, he thought, that was unlikely. Whitehall would probably suppress it on the grounds that it would be bad for morale.

He felt an urge to wake her and tell her how right she was, and he crossed to the bunk and felt her forehead, it was icy cold. He drew back the sheet and blanket and pressed an ear to her chest, but he could not detect even the faintest of heart beats. He felt for the pulse in her wrist and then her neck, there was not the slightest murmur. He held his shaving mirror to her bluish lips, it remained unmisted.

He could not bring himself to accept the harsh truth; it seemed such an unsatisfactory way to die. After all she had been through and endured she deserved a more heroic departure than to be killed by an insignificant gnat.

And he found himself reliving a similar occasion when he was a cadet at Dartmouth. Rupert Brooke had been his boyhood idol; a poet of genius, but also a splendid cricketer and footballer. The perfect Englishman – a scholar and a man of action. "The Soldier" had been capable of moving him to tears for the chivalrous ardour of the words summed up his own feelings should he be unfortunate enough to die in action. Brooke *had* died while serving with the Royal Navy in the Dardanelles. His poem had been almost prophetic. Then he had been shocked to discover that his hero had died of blood poisoning after being bitten by an insect. He had never read the poem again. Brooke had somehow been demeaned.

He leaned over her and gently kissed the closed eyes, then went in to see Mrs Brooks. "I'm afraid Kate has passed away," he said softly. "Would it be asking too much of you to wash her?"

"I'm sorry," she said. "I'll be only too pleased."

It was an odd way of saying things, but he knew exactly what she meant.

The two destroyers resembled greyhounds as they whooped their sirens and took up station on either beam of the trawler, and an Aldis flickered from one of the bridges, "Ambulances and medical staff waiting."

As they steamed into the massive natural harbour of Trincomalee, Paton was reminded of Singapore. Coconut palms stretched down to the water's edge and everything seemed green and lush. Bum boats filled with trinkets and souvenirs were already approaching, the voices of the vendors calling out what bargains were available. Fishing catamarans with bright red sails scuttered across the water of the placid harbour. The smell of spices was wafted on the offshore breeze.

Paton knew little about the island except that it had had its Raffles in the form of an unscrupulous Scot named Hugh Cleghorn who had intrigued until Ceylon became a part of the British Empire, and for which he was paid £5,000. He knew too that its history was steeped in violence and bloodshed, and, now there was a war, it was under the supreme control of a British admiral.

The harbour was a forest of masts as *Grey Seal* tied up alongside and the hiss and clank of winches and derricks mingled with the cries of the chanting coolies. The local WVS was already in position behind tables sagging with scones and sandwiches and bubbling urns of tea – the British curative for everything. Stretched along the quay was an impressive line of immaculate ambulances.

As soon as the gangway was in place, a reception committee began shepherding the women and children to the tables, then into waiting coaches, first checking on whether or not anyone required on-the-spot medical attention. Two medical orderlies in spotless khaki with knife-edge creases carried the sheet covered body of Kate ashore to a waiting ambulance with the deference of professional undertakers.

Paton watched from the bridge until everyone was ashore before turning to Carnac and saying, "I'd better put on my best bib and tucker and report to headquarters. Keep an eye on things."

He went to his cabin and changed into his best whites, then picked up the pile of cable forms and Kate's press collect card. After making his report he would go to the cable office and file her story to America. That would be the finest possible epitaph as far as she was concerned. He stepped ashore and went to a rank of battered taxis and instructed the driver to take him to naval headquarters.

He passed short-tusked elephants with whitish trunks and tar black bodies laboriously shifting huge bulks of timber, and countless posters carrying stylised reproductions of the famous frescoes at Sigiriya depicting bare-breasted women bathing below a slogan which proclaimed Yesterday's Leaf Today's Cup of Tea. Others carried less exotic messages for Lipton's – Direct From Tea Garden to Tea Pot. Saffron robed priests with shaven heads wended their way through the crowded pavements, their bowls extended, not begging but demanding recognition of their holiness. His driver hooted at the sweat-streaked rickshaw wallahs hauling Europeans in white suits and matching topis lolling in the back. Some of the buildings were splendid and glistened in the sunlight like bleached bones, others were no more than hovels of corrugated iron and wood from discarded crates. There were roadside paan stalls, and men spitting beetle nut.

A furious incessant hooting forced his driver off the road, and a magnificent open Rolls swept past in powdery cloud of choking dust. Cyclists hastily dismounted to avoid being knocked off their machines, while beggars in the kerb displayed an unexpected agility in their deformed limbs as they scuttled crabwise to safety. Paton thought it looked familiar, but he had no time to identify the two men and the solitary woman in the back.

It reminded him so much of Singapore. The French had a phrase for such a feeling. What was it? *Déjà vu*? He leaned forward and called to the driver, "Cable office first".

It seemed to him that that part of his journey was more important.

Bibliography

Noel Barber, *Sinister Twilight*, Collins

Winston S. Churchill, *The Second World War – Vol IV*, Cassell

O. D. Gallagher, *Retreat in the East*, Harrap

Richard Hough, *The Hunting of Force-Z*, Collins

James Leasor, *Singapore*, Stoughton

Major-General S. Woodburn Kirkby, *The War Against Japan – Vol I*, HMSO

Martin Middlebrook and Patrick Mahoney, *Battleship*, Allen Lane